ESCAPE VELOCITY

The Quantum War: Book One

Jonathan Paul Isaacs

This is a work of fiction. All of the characters, organizations, and events portrayed in this novel are either products of the author's imagination or are used fictitiously.

ESCAPE VELOCITY

Copyright © 2017 by Jonathan Paul Isaacs

All rights reserved.
ISBN-13: 978-1983945045

To Garrett, Karys, and Hudson:
May you always dream

ESCAPE VELOCITY

1

Exfiltration Route
Tiamat, Proxima Centauri
18 July 2271

"We're losing number two," the pilot said over the comm.

RESIT First Lieutenant Wyatt Wills sat on his command chair next to the flight deck hatch, facing aft toward the trooper bay. He saw Laramie looking back at him. His squad sergeant's blonde hair lay matted against her face, sweaty and damp. A severe expression conveyed this wasn't the way she'd hoped the mission would end.

Their Javelin had been shot, and one of its four engines had already failed. It wouldn't fly if they lost another.

"Helmets on!" Wyatt ordered.

Laramie's eyes disappeared behind an opaque faceplate.

Everything took on an unreal quality as the squad prepared for a hard landing. Wyatt tightened his safety harness while the interior lights flashed the blue-red warning of an unbreathable atmosphere outside. Troopers cradled their weapons tightly with both arms. Somewhere in his peripheral vision, Wyatt caught a glimpse of the telemetry readings on his tactical display by his chair. The altitude and airspeed readings were both getting smaller.

"Number two is out," the pilot confirmed. A finality entered his voice. "This is Fury Two, we are going down, I repeat, we are going down."

"Brace for impact!" the copilot yelled down the troop compartment.

Wyatt wished he had a window. As far as planets went, Tiamat was bleak and harsh, but watching the rocky landscape rush up at them would have been better than staring at a motionless interior.

The crew chief across the aisle waved to get Wyatt's attention. "Lieutenant!" He made a yanking motion near his chin.

Wyatt realized with a start that he still hadn't donned his own CORE helmet, the combat rebreather that RESIT relied on in so many situations. He dipped forward and pushed his head into the sweaty padding. His vision went momentarily dark as the built-in cameras recalibrated.

A shrill whistle invaded the interior. The remaining engines struggled to keep the Javelin airborne in a losing battle of breaking seals and over-pressured lines . . .

Floating.

***

A profound silence engulfed Wyatt. His body swirled. He felt disoriented, like a swimmer who had just plunged into deep water and lost track of which way was up. A random summer entered his mind and he was daring his fiancé Sara to jump with him from the top of a tall cliff into the lake below. It had taken them an hour to hike up to the top. She pleaded with him not to be so reckless. But Wyatt couldn't resist, and ended up doing a backflip off the edge for good measure. The chilly water thundered around his body with a muffled *whump*.

Now he gradually became aware of a faint tickling from the surface, a distant noise at the edge of his hearing. He searched for it, looking up, scanning the darkness, hunting down the location of something barely discernable. He couldn't find it, yet it was somehow becoming closer, louder, more urgent. His heart beat in alarm as he tried kicking toward the surface. He was too deep and his lungs hurt. An inadvertent attempt to inhale raked his insides with an acrid sting, making him convulse. Sparks stabbed at him from the darkness. Alarm. Alarm, alarm, *the alarm* . . .

The master alarm blared in angry tones. They had crashed.

Wyatt lay flat on his stomach. He turned his head and could just make out portions of a mangled body inside what used to be the flight deck. He tried to rise, but as soon as he drew a breath, his lungs screamed in pain as if he had just snorted a beaker of acid. He realized his helmet was gone. It must have flown off in the impact.

Wyatt's training took over and he forced himself to remain calm. Oxygen was the elixir of life, but at the concentrations found in Tiamat's atmosphere, it became a corrosive poison that would eat him from the inside out. He pushed up on his elbows and cupped his hands in front of his mouth. Multiple quick exhalations helped build a small buffer of carbon dioxide to dilute the next breath. A few repetitions helped him feel clear-headed enough to move.

But that too proved to be a mistake. He shifted his weight and a wave of pain crushed the breath out of him.

Wyatt turned to see a bulkhead had torn from the fuselage and now lay crumpled across his lower body. Blood soaked his pant leg with the vibrant red of superoxygenation.

He wondered how he could have been thrown from his seat down to the deck, especially with his safety harness so tight. But now was not the time. He tried to free himself from the metal but couldn't even twist around enough to reach it.

"Lieutenant," said a woman's voice. "LT."

Wyatt let his forehead drop back against the deck and he breathed a few more handfuls of cupped air. His lip twitched, indicating the first signs of oxygen poisoning. He fought to stay calm. The dizziness started to return, but a moment later Wyatt realized that maybe it was just his head tilting back as gloved hands slid an emergency mask over his face.

"LT," the voice said again.

"Laramie?" His breath fogged up the mask, blinding him.

"Yes. How badly are you hurt?"

He could barely make out the silhouette of a figure squatting down next to him. "I'm pinned," he managed.

Laramie patted down his body until her hands were at his knee. One pull was all it took to make Wyatt spit up in pain.

"Clean out your mask. Here—" She lifted up the bottom edge and wiped out the vomit.

"What's the squad status?" Wyatt grunted.

She hesitated. "Five dead. We crashed hard, port side first. Everyone sitting on that side is gone. Except you."

My God.

Wyatt closed his eyes. He'd already glimpsed the carnage on the flight deck and was hoping he just had a bad angle. But deep inside he knew that Laramie was right.

A little voice whispered in his ear. *You're the one who designed the mission. This is all on you.*

"Who's still . . . ?"

"Hal, Carlos, Gavin, you, and me. The crew chief's alive, but he ain't walking anywhere."

"Staff Sergeant!" someone called from further away. "You on the comm? Fury One says hostiles inbound on foot."

Laramie turned her head. "How many and where?"

"Twenty-plus. The south ridge, one klick out. I think they want payback for their generators."

"We need to get out of here, LT."

"No. We need to . . . the . . ." His lungs caught fire and he couldn't get the words out. They would defend the wreckage, use it as cover. Some of it might be salvageable. Some of his troopers might still be alive.

Laramie apparently knew where he was going. "Wyatt, the Oscars took us down with anti-air. They'll have more. We can't stay in the Javelin. They'll blow it to pieces and roast us inside."

"No . . ." Wyatt broke down into more coughing.

"Gavin, Hal, get over here!" Laramie barked.

Two hulking shapes appeared. Wyatt watched through the haze as the troopers tried to shift the collapsed bulkhead. It didn't move, but judging from the pain he felt, they might as well have sharpened the edges and jumped up and down on it.

"Come on—again!"

The troopers squatted on either side and found new handholds. Gavin was two meters tall, and his hulking bare arms flexed under the tension. Hal wedged in across from him. Laramie grew up in the heavy gravity of Juliet and had plenty of muscle too, even if she wasn't as big as the men. They heaved again, and Wyatt joined them in grunting as his backside exploded in agony.

"Staff Sergeant," Carlos called. "Oscars half a klick away."

Wyatt clutched Laramie's arm and focused on getting his words right. "Take the others. Leave me here. I'll . . . scuttle . . ."

Laramie grabbed what was left of his tattered safety harness hanging from the hull. She drew her Ka-Bar and began to cut a length of orange strap free. "Gavin, get the chief. You're carrying him. Carlos, you're point."

"Got it."

She looped the strap around Wyatt's pinned leg. Wyatt grunted as Laramie cinched it tight, just above the knee.

"I gave you . . . an order, Laramie."

"I have the chief," Gavin said.

"Ready to move, Staff Sergeant," Carlos said.

"Ready," Hal repeated.

Laramie stood with the harness strap taut in her hand. She was distracted, fumbling around with something. Wyatt waved his hand to get her attention. If three troopers in top-notch condition couldn't deadlift the wreckage free, he didn't see how winching his leg out with a strap was going to work.

"Save yourselves," he said. "Leave me behind."

"Two fifty meters," Carlos said.

"Laramie . . . go," Wyatt said.

She turned around and leveled her L-4 Vector rifle at him. "I'd rather have some of you than none of you."

"What are you—"

And that's when Staff Sergeant Laramie McCoy blew his leg off.

2

"I didn't think you knew those words, LT." Laramie's ears still rung from Wyatt's tirade as she pulled him through the hatch. Now the midday haze of Proxima Centauri bathed them in its eerie warmth from above.

"I can't . . . believe . . . *you did that*," he croaked. "Court-martial me later."

She hauled him into a fireman's carry and trudged toward the edge of the impact crater. Wyatt still weighed plenty, even without a lower leg. But Laramie always prided herself on being tougher than the men. Patrolling the vast, unforgiving space between Earth's precious colonies was dangerous work, and entry into RESIT—the Remote Environment Search and Interdiction Teams—proved difficult even for the hardest applicants. The ranks were overwhelmingly male. So, when the vets saw Laramie step off the shuttle her first day at Providence Station, it didn't take long for the testing to start. *Testing* in this case meant hand-to-hand combat in dark corridors after mess. Nothing lethal, of course. But Laramie understood. RESIT troops weren't about to risk their lives in a zero-tolerance environment because of some bad assignment that stuck a *chica* in their squad.

Several troopers learned two things that day: First, anyone born in the heavy gravity of Juliet grew up strong. Second, Laramie fought dirty.

Now she was carrying Wyatt across her shoulders. She stole alternating glimpses between where they were going and the marshy ground beneath her feet, red rock covered in the black algae slime of the planet's stunted ecosystem. In the distance, lightning flashes ended in an occasional fireball as they ignited pockets of super-concentrated oxygen. The deep purple of the sky gave everything a surreal color palette.

Carlos called them over to a low ridge ahead. "Over here—come on, get to cover!"

Laramie stumbled over the ridge and sent both of them tumbling into a puddle of goop.

While Wyatt busied himself with flopping around, Laramie remained on her belly and elbowed her way back to the ridge. She saw the wedge-shaped airframe of the Javelin about fifty meters away. A crease from the forced landing stretched the length of the fuselage, with one of the wings twisted vertically like the limb of a dead animal. A ragged hole was all that remained of one of the engine housings.

Gavin was still trudging up the ridge with the crew chief on his back.

"Put it in gear, Gav!" Laramie yelled.

She saw the flash. A laser blast hit Gavin on the back and vaporized the ablative resin from his vest. The burly trooper stumbled and went down, the chief landing on top of him.

Laramie flew over the ridge in an instant.

Gavin managed to get up to his hands and knees. He was a tough trooper, quiet and professional, and wobbled his way forward like an infant unsure of how to crawl. Laramie took two fistfuls of his collar and heaved him toward the ridge. The crew chief still lay in a heap. She grabbed him by the arms next. Her legs pumped in the Tiamat mud as she dragged him, each step threatening to slide down the face of the hill and leave them in full view of their pursuers.

Carlos and Hal both had their Vectors up, filling the air with the *snap-snap-snap* from the chemical reactions that drove each laser blast. Even Wyatt had pulled himself into a sitting position and shouldered his own Vector. Without a CORE helmet, he squinted through the reflex scope mounted to the rifle frame.

Gavin tumbled ungracefully to the ground on the other side of the ridge. Laramie tossed the chief next to him before she dove over herself. She rolled and came instantly back up, taking aim from a kneeling position.

"To the left!" Carlos called out.

Laramie tracked left and saw three silhouettes laying on the dirt. The targeting system in her helmet marked each one with an orange triangle. She evened her breathing and took aim at the middle one.

Snap.

The shot hit the figure's head and it jerked back in a puff of smoke. Carlos shot the one on the left before the remaining enemy rolled out of view.

"Carlos, blow the charges!" she ordered.

A harsh flash filled the interior of the Javelin as an explosive detonation fried the sensitive equipment left behind. Moments later, Laramie felt the heat wave roll over the ridge. Her throat tightened as she thought of their squad mates' remains left inside.

She glanced to her left and saw that Wyatt had crawled over to Gavin. A wide divot had blossomed on the back shoulder of Gavin's ablative vest. The resin had already dissipated the energy of the laser blast but left indications of the hit behind—blackened edges, paint puckering away from the impact site. Ironic that the punch that knocked him down came from the vest itself, not the laser. The laser would have just melted a hole through him.

"Gav, you okay?" Wyatt asked. He patted his shoulder, checking for more holes.

"Aye, aye, Lieutenant." He brushed the air aside in an unconvincing wave. "Oscars can't kill me."

"Figures the biggest dude would be the one to get hit."

"Not any worse than being kicked by a horse."

Gavin seemed all right, but Laramie knew the trooper was incredibly lucky. The vest had taken a direct hit.

Movement caught her attention. "On the right," she said, and both she and Hal started shooting.

The ridge they were using for cover was shaped like a horseshoe facing away from them. Shadowy silhouettes moving low and fast bobbed around the edges. Laramie realized that while the ridge provided them cover, it also obscured their advancing enemy. The Oscars were undoubtedly pissed the RESIT team had just torched their contraband in the belly of the Javelin. They would be out for blood. And they were doing a pretty good job of flanking them.

Wyatt saw them too and turned to her. "Laramie, we need to displace."

"I know!" She aimed at the head of an Oscar, but he dipped behind cover before she could squeeze the trigger.

"I don't have a comm," Wyatt said. He jerked his thumb at his emergency mask. "You need to—"

The threat indicator in Laramie's helmet barely had time to tag the hostile before the shot hit Wyatt's chest.

***

Floating.

Disoriented, Wyatt gradually realized he was staring at the sky. The intense red disk of Proxima hung above him, never moving, never blinking. He noticed his shallow breathing didn't match the rapid heartbeat in his chest. The staccato snapping of frantic laser fire surrounding him seemed a muffled, distant dream.

A woman was talking to someone, but Wyatt couldn't quite follow the conversation. ". . . affirmative, I read you, Fury One. We have six total, three are wounded. Negative. Negative." A long pause. "Say again, Fury?"

"Hal's down!" someone shouted.

Curse words and more gunshots.

"Displace!"

"Move—no, contact left, contact left—"

Snap-snap-snap.

A dull thud of boots reverberated through the ground nearby. Something hauled Wyatt upright and out of the dirt.

He was moving again. His brain struggled to catch up. The terrain below them bounced by, brown and broken, a stark contrast to the violet of the sky.

"Wh-What happened?"

Laramie didn't reply. He could hear her breathing hard. The ground was changing, the black algae slime now giving way to dark, stalk-like plant shoots that meant higher ground.

The crisp smell of ozone signaled a laser blast. Near miss.

"Laramie—"

"Can you shoot?" she asked abruptly.

His disorientation was such that he had to think for a moment. "I can shoot."

The little voice whispered in his ear again. *You're the one who designed the mission. This is all on you.*

Wyatt shook it away. His eyes swept across his leg. Funny, he had all but forgotten about the injury. The orange harness strap was still acting as a tourniquet, but just below it was . . . nothing. He didn't feel any pain, and he didn't feel like anything was wrong. He might as well have been looking at someone else.

Laramie stumbled another few steps and dumped him on the ground. Wyatt felt his training take over. Without conscious direction, he had his Vector up and trained on the moving shapes that followed. The Oscars were chasing them, seeking revenge. One of them raised a weapon.

Wyatt gave an autonomous squeeze of the trigger. *Snap-snap-snap*.

How easy it was to end a life with a plastic ray gun. The shape fell. At least, Wyatt thought it did. The world was spinning and it was getting harder to focus.

Laramie stopped firing and grabbed him by the collar. "Come on."

"Where are we going?"

"Over the hill. Fury One won't wait."

Wyatt tried to stand and fell to the side. His head spun as he looked at his legs. One of them seemed to be missing. He laughed. Where was his leg?

Laramie hoisted him over her shoulders and let out a grunt.

"Jesus. What do you eat, cement?"

"I can walk," Wyatt insisted.

"It's okay, LT. I got you."

"My chest hurts."

"You got shot, LT." They were moving again. "Your vest only got part of it."

"Bad in-vest-ment." Wyatt snickered, but it was harder this time, and he couldn't tell if his eyes were open.

"Stay with me, we're almost there."

"I didn't get shot. I shot them."

"Yes, you did," Laramie panted. They were climbing higher, toward a familiar, high-pitched noise.

"Staff Sergeant!" called a distant voice. "Over here!"

"A little help, Carlos!" Laramie shouted back.

"I can help," Wyatt offered. He wanted to be helpful. His head was swimming, with funny little black spots dancing in front of him. "I can walk."

"Hang in there, LT."

The pain had gone. The high-pitched whine was closer now, and the dirt was swirling around them like rain in a hurricane. But Wyatt didn't care. People shouted words that he should have recognized but had trouble following and couldn't be bothered to try. More hands grabbed him. He was moving sideways.

"Hang in there, Wyatt," said the woman's voice.

You're the one who designed the mission. This is all on you.

A harsh shout. "Corpsman! Get over here *now*!" Then softer. "Wyatt, stay with me. Can you hear me?"

He felt so tired.

"Wyatt?"

Maybe he would just sleep for a little bit.

"Please stay with me."

Floating.

3

USIC *Cromwell*
Tiamat Orbit, Proxima Centauri
6 February 2272
7 Months Later

A hand tapped Wyatt gently on the shoulder. "Sir, wake up. We're on final approach to *Cromwell*. We'll be docking in four minutes."

Wyatt blinked a couple of times before he realized where he was. He hadn't meant to fall asleep. Shuttle rides could have that effect, floating in the relaxation of weightlessness while the oxygen vents hissed a cocoon of white noise. It had knocked him out cold.

Four minutes. Four minutes left in a seven-month journey back to active duty.

Wyatt sniffed and shook his head. Despite all the preparation he had done for this moment, he still found himself queasy. He hadn't been able to talk to his platoon at all during recovery. Mail packets between Sol and Proxima were hard to come by these days, and his one successful attempt didn't seem to make it all the way downrange. At least, even if it had, he didn't get a reply. A tiny fear welled up that maybe Laramie didn't care to respond.

No, he thought. *That's not Laramie.*

Wyatt opened a pocket on his utilities and pulled out a handful of papers. Well-worn creases

ESCAPE VELOCITY

divided the two hard copy reports into neat little rectangles. He unfolded them so that he could read them for the hundredth time.

AFTER ACTION REVIEW
OPERATION ICY NIGHT, 2271-07-18

Background: Fitzmaurice-Ellis Nitrogen Reclamation Industries (FENRIS) nitrogen mining facility captured by Oxygen Shock Cartel (OSCAR)

Objective: Eliminate OSCAR's ability to manufacture breathable air for their use in terrorist operations on Tiamat

Summary: Platoon deployed into two squads FURY ONE and FURY TWO. Squads successfully inserted undetected into enemy-held territory via Javelin. FURY ONE implemented a diversion on east side of the facility. FURY TWO entered power plant from the south and successfully destroyed all four generator units. Squads extracted via Javelin and took incoming fire causing FURY TWO to crash. Pilot, copilot, and three troopers were KIA upon impact. SSGT MCCOY took command of FURY TWO based on injury to 1LT WILLS. While under heavy fire, SSGT MCCOY scuttled Javelin and displaced to superior defensible location. Further enemy contact resulted in additional 1 KIA and 2 wounded. Squad rendezvoused with FURY ONE and extracted back to friendly territory.

KIA
1LT James PRUETT
CW2 Eliza CANNON
SGT Francois BERNARD
SGT Adi DAFALLAH
SGT Harold SIMPSON
LCPL Michelle MICHELOTTI

<u>WIA</u>
1LT Wyatt WILLS
SSGT Gavin FOWLER
SSGT Martin HAUER

Wyatt's eyes lingered over the list of names. Somewhere deep inside him, an empty hole ached for the departed. He knew it was there. But he couldn't let himself feel it right now. He had to keep it packed away in its little partition, because he had a job to do aboard *Cromwell*.

Shuffling the papers, Wyatt moved on to the second report. The lines of his Discharge Summary were long committed to memory. Oxygen poisoning from Tiamat's oppressive atmosphere. Third degree burns, courtesy of a laser blast vaporizing his ablative resin carrier, his ARC vest. Broken ribs. A concussion. A lost leg due to friendly fire.

The road to recovery went on and covered multiple operations, agonizing therapy, an artificial limb. Then there was the behavioral health section of his discharge instructions. Wyatt tried to force the words into his brain to satisfy his cravings for legitimacy.

<u>FINAL EXAM, MENTAL STATUS</u>
Wyatt is calm, friendly, attentive, and relaxed. He exhibits speech that is normal in rate, volume, and articulation. Language skills are intact. Mood is normal, with no further signs of depression or mood elevation. Social judgment is intact. There are no signs of anxiety. There are no signs of hyperactive or attentional difficulties.

ESCAPE VELOCITY

    Type of Discharge: Regular
    Condition of Discharge: Greatly improved
    Prognosis: Excellent
    Medication Instructions: Patient should continue with current medications and follow up with forward medical staff as needed
    Physical Activity: No limitations on physical activity
    Dietary Instructions: Regular diet

    <u>CLEARED TO RETURN TO ACTIVE DUTY</u>

Cleared. Now he just had to get to it.

A dull thud reverberated through the hull of the shuttle. Wyatt heard the hiss of a docking ring as it equalized pressure between spacecraft temporarily joined as one.

The crew chief helped him out of the shoulder restraints and pulled his duffel from the cargo net. The pilots were distracted by the post-docking protocol with Flight Ops, so Wyatt just banged the side of the cockpit hatch to signal a farewell. A gentle push sent his duffel through the hatch, and he quickly followed. After seven months, he once again found himself on the threshold of a ship built for fighting.

A small ensign with the insignia of the *Cromwell* hung at the far end of the docking boom. Wyatt gave the pennant a salute before he faced the officer of the deck and saluted again. The officer had both feet looped into a deck strap to give the illusion of standing.

"Sir, Lieutenant Wills requesting permission to come aboard."

"Permission granted. Please wait and I'll retrieve your orders."

The OOD stared into nothing as his fingers scrolled across a small personal tablet. Wyatt noted the adhesive patch of a neural stub next to his eye socket, transmitting the tablet's output directly to his optical nerve. The officer's pupil vibrated in protest at the bypass.

"Sir, you are to report to Major Beck in B-ring immediately upon your arrival."

Wyatt blinked in surprise. "Beck? He's not onboard *Vigorous*?"

"No, sir. Do you need an escort?"

"That won't be necessary. What berth?"

"K-one-oh-one."

"Thank you," Wyatt said, and pushed himself through the airlock.

This was beyond peculiar. Major Beck commanded Havoc Company, one of the three RESIT units that made up Caustic Team stationed around Proxima. He was Wyatt's boss's boss. Why would he be here on the *Cromwell* instead of his own troop carrier? And why did he want to see Wyatt instead of having him just report to Captain Chappelle? Wyatt couldn't be in trouble already. Could he?

A step through the docking collar put Wyatt in the middle of a crowded command ship. He kept his duffel strapped to his back and pulled himself along the yellow hand bar mounted to the corridor wall. Different colors led to different places, and yellow went to the spinning artificial grav rings amidships. Unlike the troop carriers, where gravity came from the constant acceleration of patrolling their routes, *Cromwell* had a centrifugal force-based system to complement long periods of resting in orbit.

Crew members floated past him as he made his way through corridors that were constricted by cargo nets and storage lockers. Occasionally one of the crew would notice his rank insignia and give him a "sir" and a nod. But most were focused on other things, and since Wyatt belonged to a direct-action team, the crew usually ignored him.

He floated past A-ring and skipped the elevator in favor of the narrow ship's ladder that stretched down the spoke. It wasn't until about halfway down that he felt heavy again.

At the bottom, his weight reminded him he had a prosthetic leg.

A pang of self-consciousness hit him. His medical clearance was only a few weeks old. He suddenly felt very fragile. He had returned to a military vessel, headed back into harm's way. At least, most of him had.

Wyatt had gotten off easy.

Half his squad had died. His Javelin, destroyed. Who would follow him as a combat leader now? Who would allow him to design his next mission? Spaceborne assets were incredibly expensive to replace. Who could possibly place their confidence in him again?

A young trooper in brown-black fatigues walked by and saluted him.

Wyatt took a deep breath. His heart was trying to beat out of his chest.

Was he really ready to come back to active duty? Had he really prepared for this?

Why was he here?

K-berth was where the officers lived. The adjutant let him into the small office attached to Colonel Acevedo's quarters and explained the major would be there shortly. Alone for a moment, Wyatt studied the cramped compartment. A peninsula desk extended from the wall with a lone tablet keyboard resting against the wall. A translucent locker embedded in the bulkhead contained a number of books—actual paper books—in a smart display of historic knowledge. Behind the desk a small, oblong porthole revealed the inky blackness of space.

Wyatt wandered over to the porthole. If they had been in deep space, a star field would have whirled by in a slow, counterclockwise circle. But in orbit around Tiamat there was only room for the angry red light of Proxima Centauri.

"What do you see when you look out there, Lieutenant?"

"Sir." Wyatt jumped and snapped a salute. He hadn't heard the hatch open.

Beck dismissed the formality with a wave. "No need of that here." His eyes flicked at the window. "What do you see?"

Wyatt turned back to the porthole. Tiamat dominated the view, a waxing sphere tinged with the light of the nearby red dwarf. The surface was dirty gray except for the substellar point beneath Proxima, where tidal locking caused the ice to melt into a round ocean surrounded by brown, murky swampland. Wisps of rose-colored water vapor swirled around a thin film of atmosphere, clinging desperately against the vacuum. The entire effect was that of an unblinking, bloodshot eye, doomed forever to stare at the sun.

Somewhere down there, the remains of his friends were oxidizing into nothing.

"What do you see?"

"A cesspool. I hope my leg is rotting in it."

Beck sniffed a laugh. "I can appreciate that." He walked up and peered out the window himself. "I see a wealth of oxygen and water ice. Extremely valuable. I want to take my vacations there."

"Sir," Wyatt said, feeling the admonishment.

"But maybe I'll avoid drinking from the pool with your leg in it. Please, Lieutenant. Have a seat."

Major Gustav Beck lowered himself into the chair behind the peninsula desk. Mid-forties, gray hair in a high and tight, big forearms from a lifetime of grabbing things in zero gee. Beck was known and respected as an intelligent and practical leader. Now he commanded the troop cruiser *Vigorous*, currently assigned to clean up the pirate activity in the Proxima system.

"I'm surprised to see you here, sir. Why are you aboard the *Cromwell*?"

"Meeting with the colonel, along with Majors Beckham and Chang. We wrapped up this morning. The others already left. I heard you were inbound, so I decided to hang back."

So, Wyatt wasn't necessarily some special snowflake that required attention. Beck was just seeing him as a courtesy. Wyatt began to relax. "I'm flattered, sir."

Beck smiled, but it didn't touch his eyes. Wyatt started to sense that maybe the meeting wasn't just a nicety.

"Where did you get your medical treatment?" the major asked. "Back on Earth?"

"Providence Station, sir. Earth would have been nice. But for just an artificial prosthetic, they decided that wasn't necessary."

"Interesting choice. An artificial replacement over organic?"

Wyatt felt the cool flush of adrenaline course through his skin. Rehab with cloned limbs took years. It would have meant a medical discharge.

He thought of the vidcall arguments with his parents, their fear, their anger. His father demanded he leave the teams. His mom begged him to not go away again. His sister, sobbing, tried to convince him to visit Sara and repair the relationship that almost was.

Why was he here?

He couldn't just turn his back on his squad. His unit needed him back. *He* needed to come back. If he took the easy way out, accepted a discharge, moved back to Earth, what would the team think of him? *When the going got tough, Wyatt packed it in. He's learning to use his new leg while he left our buddies downrange, dead and rotting. It's obvious where we stand in his priorities.*

He had designed that mission. Its failure was on him. There wasn't any other choice. He needed to prove . . . something.

"Sir. An artificial leg was the only way I could get back to duty."

"Are you sure that's what you want?"

"Of course, sir. The team is my family. I would do anything to get back here."

"What if more of them die?"

An uncomfortable silence fell over the compartment. Wyatt locked eyes with the major. It was the only thing he could think of to not go out of his mind.

Mercifully, Beck leaned back in his chair and the mood relaxed—a little. "Look, Wyatt. I've read the medical and psych reports. I can tell from the way you're acting that they're accurate. You can't blame yourself for what happened. That was a tough mission. This is a dangerous business."

"I've had people die under my command before, sir. I'm accountable for each one."

"Of course you are. I need accountable leaders. But I don't need them to drag a bucket of guilt around with them. Guilt makes you second-guess, make bad decisions." He sighed. "Guilt gets more people killed."

"It won't be a problem, sir."

"Easy to say. I can't say the choice you made about the leg gives me optimism about your present judgement." Beck squinted in thought. "Do you know how many troopers I have in my command with a mechanical prosthetic?"

"No, sir."

"Two. Gunnery Sergeant Santos lost his left arm and refused an organic because of religious reasons. And you. But the Gunny rides a desk. He isn't asking to lead a direct-action squad."

Wyatt glanced out the window. Tiamat basked in a wide band of sunlight now. How he hated that place. Barely habitable, full of roughnecks and lawlessness and pain. The Oscars, the Oxygen Shock Cartel, weren't the first crime syndicate to steal and extort. They certainly wouldn't be the last.

Could he really come back? If he got a new squad, it would be full of replacements. Wyatt wouldn't know most of them anyway. A brand-new squad leader from the academy would command just as much loyalty. A new lieutenant to slog through the oxygenated mush, while Wyatt got a new life on Earth.

Of course Beck was questioning his decision. He didn't think it made any sense. Just like Wyatt's mom and dad.

"Sir, may I speak candidly?"

"Go ahead."

Wyatt fought to make his voice sound natural. "I know my choice is atypical. All the things you've said are fair. I am taking it hard about my old squad. I think about them every night. Hal, Francois, James, Elgin. Heath and Berk, my pilots. I drew up and pushed for the mission that killed them. And you're right, there's guilt. I'll live with their deaths for the rest of my life.

"But at the same time, sir, we went into it together, doing something important. I can't think of a better way to honor them than to come back and keep pushing. Feeling for their loss doesn't make me a weak leader. It just makes me human.

"I absolutely believe this is what's meant for me, and that my time with RESIT isn't done. All I can do is pray for the strength to see it through. And I will. Sir."

Beck watched him impassively. "I'm impressed, Wyatt. That didn't sound rehearsed at all."

Wyatt resisted the urge to shift in his seat again.

The major didn't look convinced. Wyatt wasn't sure he was convinced himself. Sweat dripped down his back, tickling his skin.

"Well," Beck said finally. He stroked his chin under a hard gaze. "I guess it's your lucky day, Wyatt, because I've got a bit of a manpower shortage. I have just the assignment for you. Since you're here to see it through."

4

Lost in thought, Wyatt moved through the corridor toward Rec Room A. Beck's assignment wasn't at all what he hoped for. He wanted to get back into the action, take the fight to the Oscars. He wanted to rejoin Havoc. Most of all, he wanted to erase the stain of an aggressive mission where the odds were more than happy to catch up. He'd screwed up, and he needed to make it right.

Now he wouldn't get that chance.

Wyatt thought about what he was leaving behind to stay in RESIT. Parents who wanted him home. A sister who just had a baby. Sara, turning him down and with ring in hand, flatly stating she couldn't handle having a husband she'd never see. Alone in a spacecraft corridor, it all seemed a poor trade.

Maybe this was all a big mistake.

He stopped in front of the rec room hatch and took a deep breath before pushing it open.

"Lieutenant!"

Carlos saw him immediately. He led the charge of troopers who surrounded Wyatt, hugging and slapping and pounding shoulders. Everyone voiced their excitement that he was back to active duty. Everyone argued over who got to see his prosthetic first. Wyatt found himself grinning in the surge of camaraderie and pulled up his pant leg. He propped his foot up on a supply crate to appease the rabble.

Growing up in the streets of Mexico City, where keeping obsolete equipment running was a life skill, Carlos loved machines. He had a knack for fixing things no matter how bad off they seemed. Now his fingers were all over the prosthetic with a borderline indecency. "What did they give you?"

"Titanium frame. Those synthetic fibers around it? They contract under current, just like a muscle. All I need to do is think what I want it to do." Wyatt patted the wireless implant at the back of his skull.

"You gotta charge it up?"

"Nope. Kinetic battery. As long as I don't sleep for a week, it'll recharge itself a little every time I move."

"That is bad*ass*," Carlos said. He crouched on one knee and groped the ankle joint with his fingers. "You're Maximilian, all the way."

More curious looks and probing fingers. Wyatt removed the protective cowling from the calf to assist in the display. Hardened veterans voiced an *ooooh* of collective wonder.

"Titanium linkage, nice."

"Is that fused right to the bone?"

"See how the fibers contract when he points his toes? Do that again, Lieutenant!"

"What's that thing there do?"

It took ten minutes for the reunion to wind down. Wyatt received the congratulatory welcome backs with genuine delight. As he reassembled his new permanent toy and rolled down his pant leg, he became aware of one last set of eyes staring at him from the adjacent bulkhead.

***

Laramie straightened up as Wyatt walked toward her. She thought she had prepared for this moment. Countless mental run-throughs of what to say, how to act, how to *re*act. Now her mind seemed sluggish and inflexible, rebelling like her muscles did when exercising in the cold.

Keeping her arms folded across her chest felt like poor protection. Laramie peeled them apart and carefully lowered them to her sides.

"Hi, Laramie."

"LT." Her voice sounded stiff even to her own ears.

"Looks like I'm back on duty."

"Yes, sir."

Wyatt blinked, a wrinkle forming at the bridge of his nose. It took a moment before Laramie understood why. She never called him *sir*.

A flood of insecurity caught her like a sudden rainstorm. Wyatt was a good man. He had come to their squad at a time when they'd been in desperate need of leadership. They'd worked together now for four years, through countless life-or-death situations. They were practically brother and sister.

The last time she had seen him, Laramie had pulled him from the wreckage of their Javelin, under fire.

The last time she had seen him, she'd made him a cripple.

It felt like such a betrayal. Laramie tried so hard to take care of their squad. Wyatt was part of it. Yet she had hurt him terribly. How did one react to what she did? Stoicism? Avoidance? Did she believe Wyatt could just forgive her for possibly ruining his life?

The silence seemed to stretch for miles between them. Laramie wished he would just start yelling before her false bravery crumbled around her.

Wyatt held out his hand.

She stared at it for a moment, unsure of what to do. Then she extended her own, warily, as if reaching for the tail of a poisonous snake. They gripped palms. Then forearms. Then each other. She could feel the tension drain from her body as he hugged her.

"You saved my life," Wyatt whispered into her ear. "Thank you."

"I—" she managed.

They held together for a moment before finally separating. Laramie saw the dampness in his eyes. She could feel the sting in her own. A quick sniff failed to keep her nose from running more than necessary.

"It's good to be back," he said.

"Good to have you back. We missed you." Laramie sniffed again. "I have to say, though, the captain did a decent job running things without you."

"Chappelle must have been disgusted with you apes."

"We're still *his* apes. Just one level down." They began to walk along the berth wall until they found relative privacy next to some overstuffed cargo netting. Laramie glanced at her new troopers cleaning their weapons on the other side of the compartment. "He did get us some decent replacements. Green, but decent. You'll like them."

Wyatt's lip turned sour.

Laramie realized she had made a mistake. She held up a hand. "I know. The guys we lost—it's taken a toll on everyone."

"Yeah."

A stillness blanketed the conversation again.

Wyatt cleared his throat. Laramie could tell he was about to do what good soldiers did when emotion peeked over the wall. He was changing the subject.

"Beck's got a mission for us," Wyatt said.

She forced a smile, grateful to move on. "The *major's* giving you your assignments now? You must be special."

"Special in the wrong way, maybe. It's a recon patrol. Out of system."

"Out of—are you kidding? We're not rejoining Havoc?" They were up to their eyeballs mopping up Oscars. How could Beck send them away?

"No. Guess where we're going."

Laramie stared at him, waiting for the punchline.

"Juliet."

The words seemed nonsensical. Laramie closed her eyes, subconsciously trying to reduce the stimulation around her and make sense of it all.

"We're being sent to do a recon on Juliet," she repeated.

"Yeah."

"The *colony* of Juliet. My home."

"Yes."

"With twenty million people who live there."

"I know. It sounds crazy."

"Like trying to explain water is wet." Laramie's hands went to her hips. She felt like she was having some silly playtime conversation with one of her nieces. "LT, if Beck wants intel, I'll just ask my parents. My dad has the run on *everything*."

"When's the last time you heard from them?"

"I sent them a vid packet... When was it? Three weeks ago? Whenever the last quantum gate window was. I wrote up a deal on our new guys. The Irish kid is a really good shot. My folks are country people—they like to hear about that sort of thing."

"But did you hear back?"

Laramie frowned. "No, but . . . I mean, it's harvest time, they were probably just really busy."

"What about anyone else? Brothers? Your sister?"

It *was* unusual not to hear from Jessamy. No stories. No pics of her boys.

Wyatt searched her face. "*Nobody's* responding, Laramie."

"Nobody?"

Wyatt shook his head. "Nothing through the quantum gate. No freighters. No message buoys. Not even RESIT Team Dagger. Beck wants us to check it out."

"How long have we been out of contact?"

"Eighty days."

"That's not right." She shook her head, still unbelieving. "We're doing a recon on Juliet. Who else is going?"

"No one. Just A-Squad."

"What?"

"Beck said he can't spare the manpower."

"He's not even sending our whole platoon?"

"No."

"Unbelievable." Laramie dropped her hands and let out a huff.

Wyatt shrugged. "A meteorite could have taken out the gate's nav transmitter for all we know. Hopefully it's nothing. Maybe you'll get some unofficial leave."

"Yeah. One squad. They obviously think it's an important mission." Her voice dripped the sarcasm she felt.

Wyatt's cheeks turned a pale shade of red. Instantly Laramie felt like an ass. It wasn't an important mission. It was a crap mission. And here was her squad leader, making all kinds of sacrifices, doing everything he could to get back in the fight. Major Beck had basically stowed him in the corner. She couldn't think of anything worse than volunteering in front of everyone and being told you were not allowed to help.

Time to change the subject again.

"I'll get everyone together for the ops briefing," she said. She gave him a tight-lipped smile before ambling off.

5

"Knock off the noise," Laramie yelled. The ready room grew quiet as her troopers clicked into business mode.

She scanned the room. RESIT wasn't much on formality between ranks—the teams were relatively small, with men and women crammed into insanely close quarters for extended periods of time. But every operation could be exceptionally dangerous. Search-and-Rescue or Interdiction missions in an unforgiving environment meant no room for error, and troopers had to trust each other with their lives.

Yet here sat some new faces who had never worked directly with each other before.

Sergeant Maya Wahine had just been reassigned from RESIT Team Anvil covering Sol. Four years of active duty. Not much direct-action experience. She was short and had the dark complexion of her Polynesian heritage, with her hair hanging to her jawline in the same trooper-cut style Laramie wore. She didn't talk much. Not really surprising considering she was assigned as their tech expert, a specialization that attracted the thinkers.

Corporal Rahsaan Moore was newly rotated out of Advanced Hard Vacuum Infantry Operations School. AHVIOS was hard to get into. Supposedly that made him top-notch, but he was still green, having been with RESIT for only twenty-three months. Rahsaan was tall, lean, nearly black skin and hair. Sniper- and zero-gee-combat qualified. Spent a lot of time cleaning his Vector. A tattoo of the AHVIOS program's crossed lances graced his forearm in orange ink.

Lance Corporal Kenny O'Leary was twenty years old and fresh out of RESIT boot camp. He had the red hair and easy manner of his Irish ancestry, not to mention the highest scores for unaided marksmanship out of the whole team. He had sharp eyes that watched everything and everybody.

Corpsman Second Class Isi Watanabe, quickly dubbed "Izzy," came from Japan and had pale skin and dark eyes. He also was green when it came to space, but Command was so desperate for medical specialists that they had fast-tracked him to Caustic Team. Izzy seemed obsessed with inspecting those around him for ailments and didn't like to smile.

Thankfully, anchoring the squad were the two veterans, Gavin and Carlos. Gavin was big and tall, born in Texas, with a thick beard that he kept trimmed close enough to not foul his CORE helmet's respirator. He had a stoic personality, didn't say much, but was absolutely reliable. Carlos, on the other hand, talked enough for both of them. He was also the squad's cutup, and Laramie had to rein him in from time to time whenever they were in barracks. Luckily, he was the consummate professional when it came time to work downrange.

Laramie turned her attention back to Wyatt. He was studying each member of A-Squad/1st Platoon,

Havoc Company, RESIT Team Caustic. A rebuilt team full of replacements who had never worked together. She wondered what he must be thinking.

Whatever it was, it lay hidden behind the mask of a professional squad leader.

"Team," he began, "we are performing a reconnaissance mission. Unlike our normal patrol routes, this one will take us out of the Proxima system. This is not a typical assignment we would draw. But Caustic Command feels it's important, and we go where they tell us."

Laramie scanned the room and saw everyone listening intently as Wyatt took on a lecturing tone.

"Background is as follows. Interstellar shipping between Proxima and Alpha Centauri A is supposed to run on a repeating, twenty-five-day transit schedule. Lance Corporal O'Leary, why is it twenty-five days?"

"Sir, it takes that long for the quantum gates to reset."

"Very good. I guess you actually listened in class." He looked at the other newbies. "Quantum gates come in pairs. Each gate is entangled with the other in ways I will not describe and you will not understand. However, when they fire, a pair of gates allows instantaneous travel from one end to the other. A freighter from Proxima can traverse 13,000 AUs to Alpha A in the blink of an eye. Without the gates, interstellar travel would be impossible. This is what allows the wheels of spaceborne commerce to turn—and for you and me to have a job."

Carlos chuckled. Laramie gave him the eye.

Wyatt didn't miss a beat. "That, as you can imagine, takes a lot of beef, Carlos. A transit window can only stay open about ten hours. Then it takes almost a month for the quantum gate to discharge radiation, re-index mapping matrices, certify the reactor for the next go.

"It shouldn't be a surprise that scheduling a transit window is expensive. Freight carriers fight tooth and nail to get a slot, months in advance. And for the past eighty-odd days, there have been exactly zero spacecraft traveling outbound from Juliet to Proxima. This is unusual."

Laramie felt her stomach turn a little. She thought of all the little beats of life she had left behind for a career in space. Her mom and dad arguing over how Constable Miller got elected. Four older brothers who had more bravery than sense. Her big sister living on a ranch, chasing a bunch of loud, ten-year-old boys who were even more foolhardy than their uncles. She hadn't heard from any of them. But she was sure they were fine—probably just a busted transmitter, like Wyatt said.

Wyatt stopped pacing and crossed his arms. Everyone else was listening intently.

"On order, A-Squad will travel via quantum gate to Alpha A to conduct a zone reconnaissance of the planet Juliet and surrounding vicinity. We are to assess gate functionality, identify the location of any missing commercial spacecraft, and establish communication with Dagger Command. We are the main effort."

Carlos, never a stickler for protocol, blurted out the question on everyone's minds. "Just us, Lieutenant? One squad for a deep-space recon?"

"We're it," Wyatt confirmed. "*Vigorous* is staying on station in Proxima. For us, that means insertion via Javelin, with a deep-space booster for extended operations. We'll attach to the freighter *William Tell* on the outbound leg to Lagrange Point Four. Their EM field will provide better protection from cosmic rays than the booster can. After that, we separate and get to work."

Carlos dropped his head, despondent. A moment later he kicked Gavin's boot. "Bring your deodorant, *muchacho*. You'll need to police that body odor."

"I don't think I can stand you on a month-long BOREX," the Texan replied. "You might not survive."

"*Ya basta*, Carlos," Laramie said. Knock it off.

"Yes, Staff Sergeant."

Laramie stifled a sigh. Even their team knew a boring, repetitive exercise when they heard one. She tried to put it out of her mind.

They spent the next two hours going through logistical details. As versatile as a Javelin was for troop delivery and air support, using it for an extended period in hard vacuum would push its operating envelope. The deep-space booster would provide the extra consumables and equipment necessary for closed-loop life support. But even with the additional resources, they still needed to cover specific responsibilities and procedures. Space tended to be unforgiving.

Wyatt finally looked at his watch. He had covered the key aspects of the mission and the energy level in the room was ebbing. Time to wrap up. "The next transit window is in six days. We have a lot to do between now and then. Any questions?"

The team remained silent.

"Then let's get to work."

***

Wyatt strolled through *Cromwell's* A-ring until he arrived at the carrier's nondenominational chapel. Poking his head through the hatch found the berth deserted except for Father Bradley, who was wiping down the tiny altar with a rag and a bottle of cleaning fluid.

"Father?"

Bradley unbent himself with obvious effort. "Wyatt. Good God, you're back to duty."

"Yes I am. With a few new parts," he said, tapping his leg.

Bradley shuffled over with the gait of someone who had spent too much time in microgravity. At first Wyatt thought he meant to shake his hand, but the priest quickly put his arm around him and clasped him tightly. "So good to see you, Lieutenant, new parts and all. How's your family?"

Wyatt stiffened.

Bradley took a step back and appraised him. "Didn't approve?"

"It's been . . . difficult."

"I'm sure it has." Bradley shuffled over to one of the tiny benches and motioned for Wyatt to sit. "I don't suppose you want to talk about it."

"Not really. I did my part trying to explain coming back. I can't make them understand it."

The priest bobbed his head up and down, nodding. "RESIT is a calling, Wyatt. A lifetime in space, traveling distances that boggle the mind. It takes great discipline and sacrifice. Rare to have a spouse, children, grow roots. At least, while you're in. That's difficult for many to accept." He tugged his vestments. "Believe me, I know about this."

Wyatt chuckled. "I think you got hit twice, Father. RESIT *and* the priesthood."

Bradley winked at him. "So what else is on your mind? Or did you come down here just to say hello?"

"No. Well—partially," he corrected. Wyatt sat in silence for a moment. "I did want to come see you. But I was hoping to get your take on something."

"Go ahead."

"The major isn't assigning us back to *Vigorous*. He gave us a recon patrol. My first mission back and I get a bunch of leftover table scraps."

"And why do you think that?"

"I think he's questioning whether I'm ready. Whether I have my head together." He stared at the deck. "Half my squad got killed on my last mission, Father. Plus the flight crew."

"Your other family," Bradley offered.

"Exactly."

"Do you mind me asking if *you* think you're ready?"

Wyatt stared at the small altar at the front of the berth as a reminder of where he was. He could talk freely here. It was why he came.

"I thought I was, Father. I mean, something bad happens, you dust yourself off, right? I've never had a problem before. But for whatever reason, I'm struggling right now. It was my call to launch that raid. It was aggressive. I planned it. We had a chance to give the Oscars a bloody nose." He shook his head. "I cost us six lives. For what? For a million kilos of liquid nitrogen?"

The old priest studied him.

"Wyatt. I'm glad you're a person of faith. It makes what I'm about to say just a little easier."

"What's that?"

"Suck it up."

Wyatt raised his eyebrows in surprise. "That doesn't sound very priestly."

"Maybe it's not. The point is, things will work out. God forgives. You need to forgive yourself."

Wyatt stared some more at the altar. Even though it was against regulations for nondenominational affiliation, Father Bradley had hung a small figurine of a crucified Jesus Christ on the front.

"You're not convinced you're worthy of forgiveness, Wyatt?"

"I don't know."

"Wyatt." Bradley's voice was heavy with disapproval. "Come with me."

The priest led him past the red curtain behind the altar to a small porthole. "I want you to look out there and tell me what you see."

Wyatt sniffed a laugh. "Major Beck already pulled this one on me, Father."

"Indulge me. What do you see?"

"I see a strange place for a window."

"Really? Almost every cathedral on Earth has stained glass windows that depict some manner of God's creation. Usually that means something biblical, to show off the wonder of the divine." He paused. "Isn't this the same?"

The curtain behind them helped cut out the compartment lighting. This porthole faced away from Tiamat and into the darkness of space. Wyatt saw the luminescent haze of the Milky Way in a broad stripe that cut from top to bottom.

Bradley put his hand on Wyatt's shoulder and spoke in a whisper. "Look at this great, vast universe of ours. Fourteen billion years old. We live eighty, ninety years if we're lucky. What do we know? We human beings are tiny and insignificant, Wyatt. We're ignorant and foolish. We place our faith in ancient texts we believe to be divinely inspired. And why? Because God is so beyond our understanding that he had to dumb it down for us.

"But if you look closely, you can see God's fingerprints everywhere. Galaxies out of the emptiness. Light out of darkness. Energy from matter. There's an elegance that displaces the entropy of the void."

A field of a thousand stars drifted in a lazy, counterclockwise spiral. Wyatt's reflection stared back at him from the glass.

"God is there, Wyatt. A God who loves and forgives. All you have to do is believe in him and accept him."

"I do believe, Father."

"Good!" Bradley exclaimed. He swatted Wyatt on the back. "Because the atheists think all this happens randomly. And if that's the case, well, I'll be taking that Mercedes that's going to spontaneously assemble itself in my driveway any day now."

Wyatt turned from the porthole and laughed. "Thanks, Father."

The old priest clasped his arms. "You can honor the dead, Wyatt. But God didn't create you from the chaos to have a pity party. Have faith in him.

Have faith in Beck. Most of all, have faith in yourself."

Wyatt rubbed his eyes with his fingertips.

"I want is just a chance to make it right."

"God doesn't provide what's wanted. He provides what's needed."

6

Gibraltar Gate
Proxima Centauri
13 February 2272

The cramped interior of the Javelin already felt claustrophobic.

Cargo boxes secured to the deck conspired with overstuffed cargo nets to steal the precious space belonging to the troopers. Between his eight-person squad, two pilots, and crew chief, Wyatt wondered how long it would take for the short tempers to appear. He could see several of them taking advantage of the microgravity to tuck themselves into odd corners away from the others. They were a U-Boat crew of the future, sweating and stifling inside a tin can, patrolling a sea of never-ending black.

"Lieutenant, we're lining up for our approach," Chief Warrant Officer Teo Parata called from the flight deck.

Wyatt had never worked with Teo before, but the pilot spoke with an easy confidence that helped him relax. Wyatt unbuckled himself and floated through the cockpit hatch. The flight deck felt focused and businesslike, with the pilot and copilot's chairs placed side by side in front of a panel full of discrete controls.

Teo was busy cycling through the telemetry displayed on the control panel's holo monitor. In a testament to personalization, he had placed a tiny cactus on the top of the panel inside a zero-gee bulb full of water and dirt.

"You don't use a neural stub?" Wyatt asked.

"No, they give me a headache. I like being able to see out of both eyes, not have one of them turned into a computer display."

"Fair enough."

"Plus, our friend here is doing all the flying," Teo said, pointing through the cockpit glass at the *William Tell*. The freighter stretched alongside them a hundred meters in either direction, connected by a docking boom at the Javelin's top hatch. Floodlights illuminated the vessel and burned away the night. In the distance, Wyatt saw two more freighters that gleamed like lonely silver specks.

"How long until we go through?"

"Thirty minutes. Really light on the schedule this time. We're third out of four, assuming our ride here doesn't get cold feet."

"He won't. Captain Holland might be pissed about dropping a cargo capsule to make room for us, but he'll do his job."

"Aye, sir."

Wyatt ducked back out and updated Laramie on the timeline. A minute later he heard her shouting orders at the team. "T-minus thirty, people. I want everybody in pressure sleeves, with CORE helmets ready, so hit the head now. Comm check in five.

Carlos, quit your moaning, you sound like a little girl."

Card games and dozing gave way to gearing up and buckling in. Wyatt peeled off his utilities so that he could wriggle into his own pressure sleeve. The snug bodysuit would keep his insides from squeezing out if the cabin became exposed to vacuum. Once he had it on, a flip of an actuator switch constricted hundreds of shape-memory coils like a multithreaded tourniquet woven into the fabric. The compression bordered on discomfort. But as Wyatt loosened his arms in wide circles, he was thankful he didn't need to don the hardsuits necessary for EVAs.

The interior light switched to red as a reminder that they were headed into an operational area. Wyatt pulled on his CORE helmet and took a moment to test the tactical HUD. Pressed against his eye socket, the neural stub hijacked his vision and mapped seven green chevrons lined up neatly behind his position.

"Laramie."

"What is it, LT?"

"Why are you and Corpsman Watanabe sitting backward?"

"Because they don't make 'em like they used to, LT."

Wyatt broke the seal and flipped up his rebreather. He saw Laramie and Isi using their combat knives to pry away some sort of obstruction that kept the seat from flipping down. He suddenly realized Laramie had been talking about the Javelin, not his new trooper.

"Gibraltar's powering up," Teo said. "Want to watch?"

Now that was something you didn't get to see every day, Wyatt thought. He unbuckled himself and poked back onto the flight deck. Ahead of them, a distant white ring flashed station-keeping lights.

"That's the gate?"

"Yes, sir."

"Looks small."

"It's far away." Teo turned to the copilot. "Dave, what is it, forty meters in diameter?"

"Sounds right."

"See? Big. Though it'll still be tight—that docking boom from the *Tell* has us sticking out like a broken finger. Might scratch the paint."

"Like I said. Small."

Teo threw him a distasteful glance. "No more windows for you."

The quantum gate grew in size as they approached. One of the other freighters began to cross the threshold and glided silently through without so much as a shimmy. Wyatt laughed to himself at the anticlimactic nature of it all—no fire, no lightning, no cymbals crashing. A circus seal jumping through a hoop received more fanfare.

Then the freighter ahead of them turned to port, and it began to disappear past the edge of the ring.

The realization of what he'd just witnessed hit Wyatt. This wasn't a circus hoop. This was a hole in space-time, a grommet through the fabric of the universe.

"Whoa, that's really freaky."

"I was thinking the same thing," Teo said. "Holographic universe, exposed."

"Holographic what?" a voice asked.

Wyatt turned and saw the crew chief peeking through the hatch. "This new to you?"

"Yes, sir."

Wyatt frowned. How to explain months of astrodynamics training in as few words as possible? "You know what quantum entanglement is?"

"I've heard of it, sir."

"You take a pair of quanta and separate them. What you find is that they still influence each other—whatever state one is in, the other is in an opposite state. This happens no matter how far apart they are. It can be light-years. Anything about that bother you, Chief?"

The crew chief shook his head.

"They shouldn't be able to talk to each other that fast. General relativity says the speed limit of the universe is the speed of light. Yet these particles—entangled particles—can somehow influence each other instantaneously. 'Spooky action at a distance', according to Einstein."

"Okay."

"Turns out, those two particles aren't really light-years apart. We think of the universe as three-dimensional. But even though we describe gravitational mechanics in three dimensions, quantum mechanics can be calculated with just two. Those 2-D models still map exactly over the other models. In other words, you have all the information you need to make the universe run with just a set of 2-D calculations. This is the same way a holo monitor works—the projection is really 2-D, but there's extra encoding in there that makes it look 3-D to our eyes. With me?"

"Sounds really weird." The crew chief showed an obvious struggle in keeping up.

"It is. I'm basically telling you that we live inside a hologram. Spatial distance is a derived property. So, if we want to travel light years from one star system to another, all we need to do is skip the 'spatial' part. That's what a quantum gate does. It turns our particles inside out. We blink out of existence here and blink back at the other end."

The chief glanced evasively at the deck, discomfort on his face.

"You know what the rub is, though?" Wyatt was having fun now. "The gates only come in pairs because they have to be entangled. You know how you get one of the gates to the far end of where you're going, right?"

"How?"

"You haul it there the hard way. It took Project Longshot sixty years to reach Proxima."

"Oh." The chief frowned. "I'll stick to fixing Javelins, then."

"That's right, brother!" Carlos shouted from the cargo bay. "We're just gun monkeys and vacuum junkies! Leave all that other crap to someone else."

Outside the Javelin, the next freighter began to pass through the quantum gate. Wyatt watched again as the spacecraft transitioned to the other side, still sitting in plain view despite existing nearly a fifth of a light-year away. It soon disappeared altogether as it moved past the edge of the ring.

"Our turn coming up," Teo said.

The *William Tell* approached at a brisk clip, its navigation systems synched with those of Gibraltar Gate. Wyatt began to feel uncomfortable as the ring grew in size. He had traveled through quantum gates before. But Sean's questions gnawed at him, striking a chord with the alien way of thinking one had to adopt to understand how the gates worked. Could everything he saw, touched, or tasted really be just some kind of veneer over the true nature of existence? The air he breathed. The jump seat against his back. All of them, an assembly of strange subatomic particles held together in even stranger energy fields. These glimpses into the mathematical substrate of space-time—were they really the fingerprints of God, as Father Bradley suggested?

"Ten. Nine. Eight . . ."

The station lights on the ring housing blinked at them.

"Three. Two. One. Transitioning now."

The bow of the *William Tell* crossed the threshold. Wyatt held his breath as the ring passed overhead. Then it was over.

"Congratulations, Lieutenant," Teo said. "You're now officially in Alpha Centauri A."

"Remind me to get my passport stamped," Wyatt said. "Give me a sitrep. What do you see?"

Teo studied the telemetry from the Javelin's observation gear. "Three freighters so far, all ours. No return shipping. No station patrol craft."

"Any radio contact from the gate crew?"

"Some scattered noise from Gibraltar, back in Proxima. Nothing from Thermopylae on this side. Everything's dark."

Wyatt scowled. Very strange.

"Fourth freighter's through."

"Put me through to Captain Holland," Wyatt said.

Teo tapped his way through some controls until he had the bridge of the *William Tell* on the line. "Over to you."

"Captain," Wyatt began. "What do you make of our arrival?"

"*This isn't going according to protocol, Lieutenant.*" Holland's voice telegraphed his anxiety. "*Thermopylae Control should contact us and assign a transition vector. We haven't received anything. We're sitting here making a big traffic jam right in front of the gate.*"

Teo's holo monitor showed a tactical display of the nearby vicinity, with multiple blue chevrons indicating the different positions of spacecraft. One of the freighters, *Mozambique*, was continuing to turn in a wide arc and had almost completed a circle.

"What is the *William Tell* doing?"

"I'm on a heading at forty by minus-ten, which takes us to Juliet orbit."

"Okay. Stand by." Wyatt switched to his command channel. "Laramie, get up here."

"You got it, LT."

Twenty seconds later, Laramie crowded into the flight deck hatch. Thermopylae Gate had receded to the size of a thumbnail in the holo monitor. Wyatt briefed her on the situation.

"What's next, boss?" Laramie asked.

"There's supposed to be a crew directing traffic from onboard that quantum gate, but they're not doing it. I want to know what's going on. Get the team ready for a boarding action. We'll detach from *William Tell* and take the Javelin back to Thermopylae."

"Hardsuits?"

"No, I don't think that's necessary. Thermopylae should have a docking boom. Pressure sleeves, ARC vests, CORE helmets."

"Lieutenant," Teo said.

"What?"

"That first freighter that came through? Looks like she's chickening out. She's accelerating back toward Thermopylae."

Wyatt watched the tactical. *Mozambique* now followed a trajectory to return to Proxima Centauri.

"Get me Holland."

A moment later, *William Tell* was on the comm. Wyatt cleared his throat. "You see what's happening, Captain?"

"*Yes. They're spooked.*" A moment later, he added, "*I don't blame them. So am I.*"

"I understand, Captain. That's why we're here. Be advised, we're going to detach our Javelin and board Thermopylae. We'll see if we can start to unravel the lack of traffic management here. I appreciate the ride."

"*Good luck, Lieutenant. I'll speak for my whole crew in saying that we'd really like to go home after we deliver our cargo—*"

A different, harsher voice broke over the comm and interrupted their discussion.

"*All vessels, you have entered a controlled area. Power down all reactionless drives and await further instructions. Freighter* Mozambique, *change your vector to one-one-three by forty-seven immediately or you will be fired upon.*"

7

Thermopylae Gate
Alpha Centauri A
13 February 2272

Wyatt turned to Laramie. "Get buckled in."

"Aye, aye," she said. She threw him a strange look as she headed aft. Wyatt wondered if she was concerned more about the hostile threat, or the decisions he was about to make.

Teo scanned the telemetry on the holo monitor. "There, six o'clock high. She was hiding past line of sight."

"Who's hiding?"

He switched the monitor to the optical feed. The computer adjusted the zoom until they saw the unmistakable profile of a RESIT Fast Attack ship. Normally these spacecraft performed high-velocity interdiction of smuggler and pirate vessels. Why would one be guarding the quantum gate?

The deadly vessel slid through the void like a shark circling its prey.

"Do you have an ID on them?" Wyatt asked.

The copilot was already directing the onboard computer to profile the spacecraft. "DEFCOM says it's FA-476 *Razor*," the copilot said. "Part of Dagger team. Assigned to Jackal Company, on the *Crusader*."

"And any sign of that troop carrier?"

"No."

Wyatt wasn't sure what to think of that. Fast Attack didn't typically go into deep space without their accompanying cruiser.

"Is *Mozambique* changing course?"

"No. They're still accelerating," Teo said. He shook his head in disbelief. "Jesus. There's no nav signal from Thermopylae. She doesn't have anything to lock in his vector. *Mozambique's* just eyeballing it."

Wyatt felt the blood drain from his face. Maneuvering a freighter hundreds of meters long through an incomprehensibly expensive quantum gate was best left to computers. If the *Mozambique's* captain misjudged the angles, there wouldn't be another transit window for a long, long time.

"She'll be at the gate in six minutes," Teo said.

The words had barely left his lips when a red warning light strobed on the control panel.

"Weapons launch," the copilot said. "Anti-ship. Looks like a drone package."

The optical sensors tracked an oblong capsule rapidly closing the distance between *Razor* and *Mozambique*. A few seconds later, the capsule crashed into the hull.

"Hit. Right near the bridge, I think."

Wyatt closed his eyes and said a silent prayer.

"Lieutenant, do you want to talk to Holland? He's going bonkers on the other channel."

"Okay. Open it back up."

"—hell is going on, guys? Did your boys just shoot up that other ship? Are you listening to me in that little tin can of yours?"

"Captain," Wyatt said. "I hear you. Take a breath."

"What just happened over there? We picked up some kind of projectile launch."

"What happened is that Fast Attack shot a boarding drone into that freighter, and it probably just finished killing the bridge crew. Now it's going to plug in and take over navigation."

The comm fell momentarily silent.

Teo changed the holo monitor back to tactical. Sure enough, the *Mozambique* began to change course away from Thermopylae and moved toward the vector assigned by Razor.

"Jesus Christ," Holland said. *"What should we do?"*

Teo turned around and looked at Wyatt, obviously wondering the same thing.

Wyatt shrugged. "You should shut down your drive system like they said."

***

Over the next ninety minutes, *Razor* herded the freighters onto a course that would take them further into the system. The *Mozambique*, now under remote guidance, remained behind for what Wyatt presumed would be a boarding and cleanup exercise. Wyatt had only been party to one drone launch in his entire career, and it had been a last-ditch response to a hostage situation. The way the *Razor* had so quickly used the weapon sent chills down his spine.

He decided to brief Laramie on what she'd missed.

"So they blew away the crew?" she asked.

"Yeah. *Razor* gave one warning. Then, whack."

"They shouldn't have made for Thermopylae without nav guidance."

Wyatt squinted. "Laramie, they murdered an entire flight crew."

"I get that, LT," Laramie said. "But hear me out. If the freighter was even a fraction of a degree off, they could have taken out the whole gate. Firing energy weapons wouldn't change the trajectory. What if the captain of the *Razor* thought he didn't have any other choice?"

Wyatt tried to visualize the people he knew, acting under similar circumstances. "I don't think that's what's going on here, Laramie."

"How so?"

"*Razor* set up a surprise ambush. These freighters aren't pirates, they're legitimate, legal shipping vessels. This isn't what RESIT does. Something's not right."

"Okay. Then what's next?" She floated near a cargo net full of rations boxes, a reminder that they could be looking at an extended length of time in space.

Wyatt poked his head back into the flight deck hatch. "Teo, if we detached, how long could we remain undetected?"

"This close to a RESIT vessel? Probably not long. We've got stealth paneling, but their sensors will be good enough to find us. And if they didn't, they'd see us when we did an engine burn—which we'd have to do unless you just want to end up wherever the freighters are going."

Wyatt folded his arms and thought.

"Lieutenant," Teo continued, "I'm not necessarily advocating for this, but any thoughts on declaring ourselves to *Razor*? Normal protocol would be to establish communication with another RESIT team."

"Protocol doesn't include murdering the crew of that freighter. No. I'm not ready to show our cards yet."

Laramie nodded in agreement. "Thank God for common sense, LT."

"Funny. I'm not sure you've accused me of that before."

"Why would I? You're an officer."

Wyatt thought some more. "Okay. We'll stay attached to *William Tell* for now. That means we're headed to Juliet. How long before we make orbit?"

Teo did some quick calculations. "At current acceleration, assuming a midpoint turn and burn, about six days."

"Okay. Keep us dark and let me know if anything pops up." Wyatt stowed his CORE helmet. "Laramie, tell the guys to settle in, it's going to be a while."

"You got it, boss. Where are you going?"

"Aboard the *Tell*, to tell Holland what's going on and keep him from wigging out."

William Tell maintained a constant acceleration that provided artificial gravity for the transit over the next several days. Most of the troopers remained on the Javelin and cleaned weapons, maintained personal equipment, or worked out with elastic bands attached to the fuselage. Wyatt moved back and forth between the ships and kept them briefed with what little information they picked up from the sensors. He had less luck controlling gossip about Juliet, particularly with Carlos.

"Laramie, you're from Piper's World—what are we in for?" Carlos asked.

"Don't call it that."

"Call it what?"

"That word. It's Juliet."

"What's the big deal?"

The fire in the staff sergeant's eyes should have been a warning. "The big deal is it's Juliet. Get it straight."

"But isn't Piper the one in the surveyor logs?"

"That man," Laramie said, "may have technically been involved. But it's *Juliet*. Don't let anyone from Juliet hear you say the other. Including me."

"Okay, already," Carlos said. He held up his hands in capitulation and backed away.

The crew chief leaned forward from his chair outside the flight deck and whispered to Wyatt, "Lieutenant. What was that all about?"

Wyatt looked at him, again surprised by the chief's greenness. "Do you know who Duncan Piper was?"

"Sure. You learn about him in school. He was the Longshot captain for Alpha A."

"Did you know he went crazy and slaughtered his crew once they got here?"

"Oh." The crew chief blinked. "I don't remember that part."

"Yeah. Piper was, what, twenty-eight years old when Longshot left? With three other crew that were probably even younger. The original idea of Longshot was to get the quantum gate to its destination, then once it was installed, use it to get back to Earth. Only that never happened. It took NASA a decade of tinkering to finally activate the gate remotely." Wyatt reflected on how tempers already seemed a bit short inside the Javelin. "I suppose sixty years in a tin can push anyone over the edge."

"But why is Staff Sergeant McCoy angry?"

"Julietans get touchy around the idea of their founder turning into a murderer. The reference Carlos made, calling Juliet 'Piper's World,' would be taken as an insult. A bad one."

The chief peered down the fuselage at Laramie, who was now cleaning her Vector with unnecessary emphasis. He nodded to himself. "Juliet it is."

The days clicked by. Wyatt periodically watched the cockpit window as their destination grew from a tiny dot to something much more recognizable. At first glance, Juliet looked a lot like Earth—green and blue, white clouds swirling through the atmosphere, rendered by Alpha Centauri A in a color palette like that of Sol. Gradually, the differences emerged. Oceans covered significantly less of the surface and allowed the continents to dominate with their browns and greens. The massive ice caps extended further from the poles, a testimony to the cooler climate. And once a day, the shadow of the moon Romeo crept across the surface with a significantly smaller footprint than that of Luna.

The sixth day had the *William Tell* commit to a final deceleration burst that inserted them into orbit around Juliet. Wyatt climbed through the flight deck hatch once again to review options.

"We're on approach to Gateway Station," Teo said. "I bet *Razor* means for us to dock."

Wyatt thought this might be coming, and he already knew what his response would be. "They'll send a boarding party. I don't think that moves our mission forward, do you, Teo?"

"No, sir, the brig does not move our mission forward."

"All right. Let's go groundside. We'll see what intel we can gather down there. Prep for atmospheric entry."

"Roger." Teo started to cinch the safety harness of his pilot chair. "We'll need *William Tell* to roll so we have some visual cover. I'll coordinate with Holland."

As the comm chatter went back and forth, Wyatt strapped into his own seat and switched on the tactical display on his holo monitor. They needed to make this as subtle as possible. *Razor* lurked behind them, a predator ready to pounce on the first animal to stumble.

"*Docking ring is unlocked,*" Captain Holland said from the freighter's bridge. "*You can separate at any time. Good luck, guys. Don't forget about us.*"

"Roger, *Tell*. We won't. Godspeed," Wyatt said into his microphone.

Teo's hands wrapped around the Javelin controls. "This is Savage Echo One, begin roll in three, two, one, mark."

Wyatt's stomach resisted the new momentum as the freighter rotated along the long axis. Then the fuselage shuddered, and the Javelin's thrusters pushed them gently away.

"Docking boom is clear," Teo said. "Fifty meters apart."

Wyatt's eyes burned a hole into the holo monitor. *Razor* couldn't see them at the moment, but neither could Wyatt see *Razor*. The measure of their success would be purely from inductive reasoning.

Teo spoke again on the comm. "Two hundred meters. Anyone notice us yet?"

"Not yet," Dave said from the copilot seat. "Keep your wingtip to him."

"Copy that."

The clock ticked on. At twenty klicks, Teo changed their vector to track toward a landing zone outside Juliet's capital city, Venice.

Wyatt saw a chevron for *Razor* appear on the tactical as the angles and distances played out.

"How long until atmosphere?" Wyatt asked.

"Ten minutes," Teo said. "Deceleration in two."

Wyatt forced himself to take steady breaths. Not that *Razor* was necessarily looking, but the odds of detection grew higher the longer the Javelin flew on its own. He prayed they could get down to the surface of Juliet and hopefully figure out what was going on up in the space around it.

"Time to hit the brakes," Teo said. "Three, two, one, mark."

Rocket nozzles fired and the Javelin jerked aft with a deceleration far more jarring than the reactionless drives of interplanetary spacecraft. Wyatt's stomach did a strange little twist. For a moment, he thought he might need a sickness bag.

The chevron indicating *Razor's* position suddenly turned orange.

"Uh-oh," the copilot said.

Wyatt watched the screen with utmost intensity. "Did he see us?"

A pause. "Stand by. I might have to—"

BOOM.

The Javelin lurched forward into an uncontrolled tumble. Warning indicators blared furiously from the flight deck.

"Energy weapon hit, aft," the copilot said, his voice perversely calm. "They hit the deep-space booster. Power loss in main lines. Venting gas."

Teo had both hands struggling with their joysticks. "I'm losing control. Wyatt, we need to eject the booster or we're done—"

"Eject it."

"Dave, eject booster on my mark." He waited a moment as their orientation spun closer toward the rotation he wanted. "And . . . mark."

Noises reverberated through the fuselage as the deep-space booster detached. The tumbling slowly stopped. But without the booster, Wyatt knew they were looking at a one-way ticket to the planet surface. The Javelin wouldn't have the fuel necessary to climb back into orbit.

Once again, he was making calls that committed their fate. He thought of Father Bradley and said a silent prayer to God. *Please give me the strength to handle what is needed.*

Laramie shouted at him and he looked down the fuselage. She made a yanking motion toward her chin to don his CORE helmet.

"Time from last shot?" Teo asked.

The copilot swiped through the telemetry. "Twenty-one seconds."

"Got it." The Javelin lunged forward.

"Teo?" Wyatt said, his voice constricted by the sudden acceleration.

"Running for atmo, Lieutenant." His tone was so cool, he could have been talking about tying shoelaces. "We have to do a ballistic entry. There are thirty seconds before he can fire again, and I'm not waiting."

At least God hadn't forgotten that capacitors needed time to recharge.

Wyatt pulled on his helmet. The blanket of atmosphere would diffuse the accuracy—and lethality—of a second laser blast from the Fast Attack. But re-entry the way Teo intended meant a steep descent angle with a damaged vehicle. They very well could end their lives without the help of *Razor*.

8

Juliet Orbit
Alpha Centauri A
20 February 2272

It started with wisps of color outside the cockpit glass. Intermittent flashes of light became increasingly steady as friction turned atmosphere into plasma. The momentary weightlessness from orbit gave way to a gradual heaviness that complemented the blast furnace outside the hull, barely a meter away from Wyatt's head.

"We're too steep," the copilot warned.

"Roger. Just watch the temp."

Oppressive silence blanketed the cabin as the glow in front of the canopy became a steady orange. The smooth ride belied the danger. One mistake here and they'd be burned to a cinder before any of them had a chance to realize they were dead.

"It's getting warm back here," a voice called from the trooper bay.

The copilot checked the holo monitor. "Aft belly panel is reading fourteen hundred C."

"The laser blast must have gotten part of it," Teo said. "I'll try to shield it."

Wyatt blinked. He felt the sweat sting his eye sockets even though the neural stubs in his helmet bypassed his natural sight.

Indeterminable minutes passed. Teo pitched and banked as they descended at twenty times the speed of sound.

"Aft belly panel holding steady. Eighteen-three-forty."

"Copy."

Tension switched to terror when they broke the sound barrier.

The sound of shrieking wind enveloped the cabin as the flight computer fought to maintain control. The Javelin bucked like an angry animal trying to throw its rider. Four engines quickly added their howl to the symphony with a teeth-grinding buzz.

"Engine start is good," the copilot said.

Teo's voice vibrated as he spoke. "Control surfaces aren't responding. Hang on, it's going to get bumpy."

Going to get? Wyatt thought.

The Javelin pitched all over the place. The cabin dropped away suddenly and put them back in freefall. Then it came back up and threatened to squash everyone's insides into jelly. Four minutes of pure fright went by before Teo put them into a somewhat level approach to land in the middle of nowhere. By the time they set down, Wyatt's hands ached so badly that he wondered if he'd embedded his fingerprints in the grab handles.

Soon, Wyatt and the rest of the squad were circling the vehicle, inspecting for damage from hostile fire and an overly aggressive atmospheric entry.

"I'm not riding in Javelins with you anymore," Laramie told him.

Wyatt patted a nearby landing strut, wondering how pale he must still look. "We got here, didn't we?"

Laramie shook her head and went back to inspecting her zone.

The sun hung low in the early dawn, shining its cold light over the field where Teo had set them down. *No, not the sun*, Wyatt thought. Alpha A. Bigger than Sol, releasing more energy, further away than from Earth. It felt different. Wyatt thought back to growing up in Michigan, how strange Florida seemed the first time he went there on vacation. Flat. Palm trees. The air, heavy and humid. He felt a similar oddity now. The blue of the sky was the wrong shade, like the waters of the Caribbean compared to open ocean. He saw no trees. Dark, meter-high grasses covered the rolling hills in all directions.

Then there was the gravity.

Anyone who spent time in zero gee felt sluggish or worse when first making landfall. But here, Wyatt felt *heavy*. Juliet was big and dense. And the extra ten kilos Wyatt now carried seemed to push directly down on his prosthetic. Nerves he no longer had screamed from the beyond, channeling their protest into metal fused with bone.

He hadn't felt this in space, even in the artificial gravity of Providence Station. A flicker of doubt crept into Wyatt's mind as he thought back to his interview with Beck.

It didn't matter if he was ready. He was committed now. He'd have to deal.

Teo and the crew chief approached him from the other side of the aft ramp, passing a red towel back and forth to wipe grease off their hands. Wyatt looked up from his introspection.

"We got lucky, Lieutenant," Teo said. "Two meters over and that laser blast would have vaporized the cargo bay. But it didn't. The brunt of it got taken by the booster."

Wyatt raised an eyebrow. "You're saying we don't have damage? My insides are beyond bruised."

"Oh, we've got damage. The booster practically exploded. My bird has shrapnel holes all over the place. Lost fuel, too, before the starboard tank sealed itself."

"What's that mean for our range?"

"If I had to guess? Five hundred klicks."

"I'm not sure that gets the job done."

"Depends where you want to go."

Wyatt nodded with a sigh. It could have been far worse. "Okay, let's figure out what's next."

Five minutes later, Wyatt, Laramie, and Teo clustered around the holo monitor on the flight deck. Teo brought up digital charts of the surrounding area. They had landed literally in the middle of nowhere, in a broad grassland a hundred kilometers from the nearest settlement.

"Here," Wyatt said, pointing to a large city marker. "This is Venice, by the coast? The capital?"

"That's right," Laramie said.

"This is your neck of the woods, Staff Sergeant. What can you tell us about it?"

"Venice?" She thought for a moment. "Population of two million, maybe. A lot of the white-collar stuff is there—business, finance, tech. Government, obviously. But it's big on trade, too, since so much of the rest of Juliet is rural. There's a port facility on the water that handles shipping to other cities along the coast."

"What about inland, where we are?"

"Once you get into the grasslands, you're going to either find ranching or farming. Go past that and you hit the mountains and the mining towns. But I don't think anyone out that way will know about disruptions to interplanetary shipping."

"Okay." Wyatt felt a headache coming on and rubbed his forehead. Maybe it was from the gravity. "What sort of communications are we picking up? We just got shot down. Are we hearing anything that might explain that?"

Teo shook his head. "There's some satellite broadcasts, mostly entertainment. Haven't seen any news reports yet. No radio chatter or anything, but then again, we're in a pretty isolated area."

Laramie looked up from the holo monitor. "We need to infiltrate into the capital, LT. That's where the spaceport is. That's where we might find some intel."

"Agreed," Teo said.

"Thoughts on how to insert covertly? I'm not going to have a wounded Javelin blunder its way in."

Laramie studied the chart some more. "We could hitch a ride on a train."

"How do you mean?"

She pointed to a bold line that ran inland from the capital. "These lines are maglev rails. They run between Venice and the Carrell Mountains over here. That's where the aluminum mines are. Miners extract the ore, smelt it into ingots, and ship it on the maglev back to the industrial district, here. The trains are run by computer. Why don't we hop on one of them as it's headed in?"

"Can we do it? Teo?"

The pilot pointed at one of the mining-town dots. "You want to fly all the way to the mountains? That'll be a one-way trip. We don't have the fuel to go there and back."

"No," Laramie said. "What I meant was, why don't we hop on a train as it passes by us?"

"Moving?"

"Yes."

"How fast do they go?"

She shrugged. "Pretty fast?"

Teo shook his head. "If they're anything like the trains on Tiamat, we're talking about hundreds of knots. Is it your life's ambition to climb inside a leaf vacuum? There's no way you could move from one vehicle to the other."

"What's a leaf vacuum?" Laramie asked.

"A machine to clean up leaves when they drop off trees."

"Never seen a leaf."

"What?"

"Juliet doesn't have trees."

"Really?"

"Enough," Wyatt said. He pointed at the monitor. "What about here, at this curve? Most maglevs slow down so they don't jump the track. We could come up alongside and zipline aboard."

Teo took a deep breath. "If it slows down to forty or fifty knots. Still going to be a heck of a wind blast."

"Do you have a better idea?"

The three of them stared at the chart.

"So, a modern-day stagecoach robbery," Teo said.

"Something like that." Wyatt glanced at Laramie. "It's just a forced boarding exercise. We did them on Tiamat."

His staff sergeant straightened her posture. "We can do it."

Wyatt folded his arms, steeling himself. With a damaged Javelin, no refueling capability, and no booster to make it back to orbit, his alternatives were proving scarce.

"Okay. Let's draw up the op."

***

The Javelin skimmed along the ground at three hundred knots, slowly reeling in the distance between their initial landing point and the maglev rail. Wyatt stood near the flight deck hatch and peered out the armored canopy. Grassy hills extended in all directions. Occasional bird-like animals flew in the distance, though Laramie explained that the Julietan version of a bird was more like a bat. The off-blue sky held back any hint of clouds. The panorama drew out boyhood memories of the American Midwest that Wyatt had long since forgotten from his time in space.

"A lot prettier than Tiamat," he said.

Teo snorted. "That's not hard."

Wyatt ducked back into the hold and sat with the troopers to review their boarding tactics again. The plan was simple. The train was propelled by the maglev rail and would have upward of twenty cargo cars connected together. As the train took the curve, Teo would fly alongside it with the cargo ramp open. Carlos would fire the grappling hook out the back. Then Wyatt and his squad would zipline to the train, the Javelin would detach and go to ground, and the team would ride into the capital to gather intel until they ultimately arranged for extraction.

An hour from reaching the rail, Teo called Wyatt to come back to the flight deck.

"We have a visual on some kind of town coming up ahead." He pointed out the canopy at one o'clock. "It's not in the chart pack loaded into the computer. I can go around, but thought you might see it as a recon opportunity."

Wyatt turned to Laramie. "Any idea where this is?"

"No."

"None?"

"Do you know the name of every Podunk town on Earth?"

"Fair point."

Wyatt thought about the remoteness of their location. "We're really out here. Think we could pop in and ask some questions without drawing attention?"

Laramie peered out across the grasslands. "Just a little ranching town? Sure. They're not going to care about us as long as we don't hork up their stuff."

Another decision to make. Wyatt wanted to get it right. Avoiding contact would keep them from being compromised. But they had an entire planet spread out before them, and didn't really have any sense of what might be going on. Popping into a rural village for some local news might save them from finding out things the hard way later.

"All right, let's do it. Teo, set the Javelin down out of sight. We'll take a small team in and ask around. Me, Laramie, Carlos, and—"

"And Maya," Laramie said. "She and I can go in. You guys hang back."

"Why?"

"You want info? A pair of *chicas* will get it for you." Her green eyes smiled at him. "Trust me, this is my turf, Wyatt. Let a country girl do her thing."

***

Teo set down behind a hill a good klick away from the town. Javelins weren't quiet, and Wyatt suspected that every resident knew some kind of vehicle had flown in. He took his small team out on foot and found a small rise a hundred meters from the edge of the town. The women shed their ARC vests and RESIT patches until they better resembled a pair of field hands. Each kept their side arms in case of trouble. Wyatt and Carlos were relegated to backup.

As Wyatt started to lie down, Laramie grabbed his arm. "No."

"What?"

"Lie over here. Avoid the dark green grass."

"Why?"

"This is all harpoon brush." She pointed at the grasses around them. "The tips have a silicate barb. You don't want that stuff getting into your clothes. Stay over to the light green, where it's not mature yet."

"Harpoon brush," he repeated. Wyatt eyed where he had been about to go. "Anything else?"

She shrugged. "Not really. Watch out for hoppers, I guess."

"What's a hopper?"

"What do you call those green things on Earth that live in swamps?" Laramie scrunched up her face. "Cracko-dillies?"

"Crocodiles?"

"Yeah. That. Juliet's version of that."

"You're saying something called a hopper, which is like a Juliet heavy-gravity crocodile, might come up and eat us while we lay in sharp grass that will slice us to bits." He raised his eyebrow. "That about right?"

She gave him a dismissive wave. "Nah. They won't come this close to a town. You'll be fine."

"Okay. We'll try not to die while we lie completely still."

He heard Maya chuckle as they set off. Wyatt and Carlos traded incredulous stares.

"They always said Julietans were tough," Carlos said.

"Yeah. Can't wait for the next surprise."

The next one came fifteen minutes later.

"Acid One, Acid Two, do you copy?" Laramie whispered on the comm.

"Copy you, Two."

"Town appears deserted. There was a major fight here. Rubble, lots of small arms fire. Requesting support."

"Where are you?" Wyatt asked.

"Red two-story building. First floor. Southwest corner."

Wyatt pushed himself off the ground. "On our way. We'll be coming the same route you took."

"Roger."

Wyatt switched channels. "Acid Three, did you copy that?"

"Affirmative, Lieutenant." Gavin and the others had remained back at the Javelin. His drawl sounded almost sedated.

"Stand by for dust off and air support. Get the others geared up."

"Got it."

Wyatt and Carlos set a hurried pace. Buildings made of stacked cargo containers loomed over deserted streets. They approached the reddish-brown stack Laramie had referenced, the words *Harley's Hall* stenciled just underneath windows cut out of the upper container.

"Friendlies," Wyatt called. They pressed against the wall, their L-4 Vectors ready.

"In here."

He ducked around the corner and into the container. The interior had been fashioned into a sort of pub, with a large bar against one wall and a bank of gaming consoles in the corner. The bar was covered in broken glass. Smashed furniture filled the rest of the room.

Laramie and Maya hunched down against one of the first-floor windows. They quickly holstered their pistols in favor of the rifles Carlos handed them.

"Any signs of life?" Wyatt asked.

"Not yet," Laramie said. "The weapon damage looks old. No smell, either."

She was right. The burned aroma of charred flesh from laser impacts had long faded. "This fight took place a while ago. Let's have a look. Fan out."

Laramie nodded, but Wyatt could tell she was bothered. Juliet was her home. If a civilian town in the middle of nowhere showed signs of a firefight, what else might be waiting for them?

The troopers formed a skirmish line and walked slowly up what could only be called the main street. Most building windows were shattered and open. The charred hulk of a utility ATV sat half-crashed in a nearby doorway. Scorch marks from some homemade fire bomb shrouded the entry to another.

"See any bodies?" Wyatt asked.

"Negative."

By the time they got to the town center, everyone had lowered their Vectors. They had clearly missed whatever had gone down. Wyatt radioed Gavin and told him to bring up the rest of the squad.

Laramie pointed at a tall structure composed of cargo containers three wide and three tall. "That building there will be the Town Hall. We should find legal documents, security records inside."

Looking for anything that potentially chronicled what happened made sense to Wyatt. "Maya. Check the entrance."

"Yes, sir."

A gust of wind blew dust down the street in front of them. Maya stalked to the side of the main entrance and pushed on the door. It wouldn't budge. She peeked into a window full of some sort of obstruction. "Looks like it's been barricaded."

"Barricaded? Sweep the outside for other entry points."

A few minutes of searching found no other access. The building had been made into a bunker.

"Acid Three," Wyatt said into the comm. "Send the rest of the squad to my position. Bring a breach charge. We're going to have to force entry on a structure."

"Roger."

Wyatt and Laramie watched the perimeter as they waited. It didn't take long for the others to appear, led by Gavin's hulking frame at the front. He carried an L-6 Viper, a powerful rifle that had considerably more accuracy at range than a Vector.

Gavin frowned as his eyes took in the deserted street. "What happened here?"

"A bigtime rumble, some time ago," Wyatt said. He pointed at the Town Hall entrance. "Maybe we'll find some clues in there, but I need you to blast that door open."

"On it."

Every RESIT trooper was trained on breaching hatches and airlocks. The only difference here was that they'd be boarding a cargo container instead of a spacecraft. Gavin trotted up to the door and unfolded a satchel into a one-meter-wide oval pad. He made a quick study of the construction, the hinges, the framing. Then he pressed the adhesive side of the pad onto the door.

"Maya, Carlos—stack up on me," Laramie ordered, moving to the side of the entrance.

"Ready."

Gavin took cover a couple meters away. "Fire in the hole!"

Crack. A brilliant flash quickly disappeared into a cloud of rolling smoke.

Laramie held her Vector up and swept inside. Maya and Carlos immediately followed. A few moments later her voice crackled on the comm. "First floor's clear. Maya, Carlos—take second."

"On it."

Wyatt pushed aside the fragments of the barricade and saw a desk now overturned by the entrance. He was surprised by the modern appearance of the interior—except now, furniture and administrative stations were strewn about in various states of disarray, intermixed with sleeping pallets and trash against the wall.

Someone had holed up here for a while. *Why?*

He switched on his weapon's tactical light. The beam revealed foil wrappers and emergency rations on the floor.

Laramie swept the opposite side of the room until her light crossed his. Their eyes met and Laramie wrinkled her nose. Wyatt smelled it, too—the faint, sickly-sweet odor of decay, drifting through the air.

The comm crackled with Maya's voice. "Lieutenant. Second floor is clear, but you need to see this."

"On my way." He looked at Laramie and she nodded. She would come too.

They marched up a set of stairs through a tidy opening in the ceiling. The stench of death grew stronger. When they emerged onto the second story, Wyatt immediately saw why. Half a dozen bodies lay strewn across the floor, contorted and desperate.

"Jesus," Wyatt said. He covered his nose with a gloved hand. "What happened here?"

He pushed the lifeless form of a woman nearest the stairs with his foot. Her clothes appeared to be some kind of civil uniform. She had been dead a long time, weeks perhaps, her skin dry and gaunt against her cheeks. Part of her skull was missing. Wyatt kneeled down next to her and examined the hole. The charred edges betrayed the impact of an energy weapon.

"This woman was shot."

"This guy did it," Maya said. She kicked away a pistol from the hand of a male corpse. She had pulled on her CORE helmet, presumably to block the smell.

Wyatt went over to the body and saw an older man with thinning blond hair and a goatee. He wore a similar uniform to the woman and had a blast wound through his left kidney. Wyatt traced the line of fire to another male, maybe early twenties, slumped against a barricaded window.

"Some kind of firefight went down," Maya said.

"That's for sure," Wyatt said. "Everyone shooting at everyone. Total chaos."

"I wonder why?"

The afternoon sun streamed through the few windows not covered by furniture. Wyatt squinted into the light. "That body against that opening looks different."

"That's because he died the same way as this *chica*," Laramie said. She stood up from a small, frail-looking woman clothed in canvas utilities. "See? Less decomposition. These two didn't croak until after the others. Everyone else has a blast injury and looks like trash."

Sure enough, two of the seven bodies didn't have gunshot wounds and had apparently expired more recently. Their skin had a blue-green tint indicative of active bacterial decay. Wyatt squatted next to the last woman and poked her with his Vector. She fell over with a wet *thud*.

"I think they starved to death," Wyatt said. "Tough way to go."

Carlos muttered a prayer in Spanish.

Wyatt stood back and surveyed the room. Furniture and scrap metal blocked most of the windows. He saw ammo boxes stacked against the walls. Unopened ration canisters formed a pile in the far corner.

"These people were planning to be here for a while," he said finally. "Something must have been going on outside. They holed up in here and barricaded the door. Then . . . well, at some point, they turned on each other. Why? And why would the two remaining survivors let themselves starve? There's still food here."

"Suppose something else killed them."

"Something else, Laramie?" Wyatt mused. "Like what?"

"Like whatever they were hiding from."

He started to take a deep, contemplative breath, but a whiff of death made him think better of it. "Let's get back downstairs."

9

Wyatt broke his squad into four pairs to secure the area around them. A search found more corpses and evidence of gun battles. One set of bodies in the street had been hacked apart by farming tools. Another group had barricaded themselves in a small warehouse, but the barricade hadn't held. Wyatt got the overwhelming impression that the violence came from some sort of riot. But over what was anyone's guess.

Maya went to work bypassing the Town Hall computer system. As their electronics technician, she had specialized training in how to hack or circumvent practically any modern security shield. Usually, that meant opening a locked hatch or gaining navigation control of a spacecraft. In this case, she used her skills to get access to police records.

It didn't take long.

"Lieutenant? I'm in."

With the barricades still in place, the windows didn't permit enough light to dispel the eerie cast inside the Town Hall building. The bluish glow from the holo monitor now set strange shadows dancing in the corners. Wyatt walked up and looked over Maya's shoulder. "You're kidding. What was that, sixty seconds?"

"This was nothing." She closed her portable codebreaker tablet and stowed it in her gear. "The stuff in Sol is much tougher."

"Why is that?"

"You have to be sneaky if you want to smuggle stuff around Earth transit routes. Anvil Team has eyes everywhere. Crooks get real good at hiding things."

"Sounds like lots of practice."

"Yes, sir. It was great."

"Why'd you apply for a transfer out here, then?"

Maya straightened up. "Sir, I kept stalling on the promotion ladder. Command said I needed more direct-action experience. But there just aren't that many assignments available in Sol."

Wyatt wanted to be running those sorts of missions, too. He stifled a frown. "Well. Let's get through this recon together, and we'll see what assignment we can draw next."

"Yes, sir."

"In the meantime, great work. I don't think I could have logged in to my own system that fast."

"Well . . . no comment, Lieutenant."

Wyatt arched an eyebrow. "Huh. You'll fit right in."

Maya chuckled and left him at the console.

Wyatt spent several hours looking through records and attempting to piece together recent events. He didn't find much. Crop surveys, shipping manifests, and occasional arrests for public intoxication dominated the filing system. The town of Parrell was indeed a sleepy frontier community. Whatever had led to ransacked streets and defensive barricades had occurred too quickly for government documentation.

As afternoon approached, Wyatt shelved his frustration and ordered the platoon to make camp. Teo moved the Javelin to within a hundred meters of the town perimeter. Izzy and Maya drew the first security rotation. When the sun went down, the squad would hole up in the Javelin, clear of the town and in a defensible vehicle. No one wanted to sleep in buildings with dead bodies in them.

The horizon turned faint orange. Wyatt sat outside on the wheel well of a wrecked trailer and watched Alpha A slide toward the grassy hills. His prosthetic leg was killing him. He'd expected some aching once he got back in full gravity. But the stress of the past two days had somehow jacked up every nerve where bone ended and titanium began.

You chose to come back, he reminded himself. *You chose this.*

True, but did it have to hurt like hell?

Laramie wandered toward him, digging a spoon in a plastic meal pouch. She sat down next to him without a word.

"No witty banter tonight, Staff Sergeant?"

"No."

Wyatt turned toward her. Her dirty-blonde hair hung to her jawline, framing a face that would have been pretty with a little bit of attention. But all Wyatt could see was a woman in troubled thought.

"Something on your mind? Spill it."

Laramie stared at the ground, a frown wrinkling her forehead. She poked through the meal pouch again. Wyatt noticed she wasn't eating any of it.

"It's been forever since I've been back home. Not exactly the homecoming I expected."

"Yeah. I wonder if Beck suspected something."

"I mean, an interdiction by a RESIT attack ship? Towns full of dead bodies? What happened here, Wyatt?"

"I guess that's our mission to find out, isn't it?"

Laramie didn't answer. She took a tentative bite from her spoon.

Wyatt watched her not eat. "Where down here are you from again?"

"West Hadensville. Farm community on the other side of Venice. Like this place, only bigger."

A light breeze blew a torn magazine cover by with a crinkling sound, mixing with the music of unfamiliar insects.

"I mean . . . what if . . ." Her voice trailed off.

"Hey." Wyatt swatted her arm. "Don't do that."

"Do what?"

"Worry. About family, friends, whatever. You don't know what's happened. Don't let your head get ahead of itself."

"How can I not? I mean, look at this place. There are corpses everywhere, huddled inside buildings like they're hiding from the freaking bogeyman. What if it's not just here?"

Wyatt shook his head. "You don't control that. Your job is to make this squad function so we can complete our mission."

Laramie let the meal pouch sink to her lap and stared at the ground. For an ultra-athletic girl who never missed a meal, it was an obvious sign of her distress.

"Look," Wyatt said. "I know Juliet is your home. But you've got to put that aside. We don't know what happened. We don't know if other settlements look like this. So don't go there."

"I know. I'm sorry. I'm sitting here bleating like a sheep. Not very professional of me."

Wyatt blinked. "Juliet has sheep?"

A tiny smirk appeared on Laramie's face. Then her eyes darted past Wyatt's shoulder and her face turned all business. "What is it, Maya?"

Two troopers approached with soft bootsteps crunching against the street. "Staff Sergeant, Corpsman Isi and I were walking the perimeter, and—well, we saw this big flock of birds circling over the west edge of town. They looked like vultures or something. We thought it might mean fresh dead."

Wyatt cleared his throat and looked at Laramie. "Juliet has vultures?"

"Not . . . birds," she said simply.

"Then what did they see?"

"Probably karks. Big flying snakes. Carrion feeders."

"Flying snakes."

She gave him a shrug. "Basically. But we can call them vultures if it makes you feel better."

Wyatt arched an eyebrow. It was one thing to joke about the differences between Earth and Juliet. It was another thing to see it.

Laramie shielded her eyes against the sun. "We've got a good hour of daylight left. Let's go check it out."

"Yeah, let's." Wyatt stood up and hit his comm. "Gavin, this is Wyatt, over."

"Copy, Lieutenant."

"Laramie and I are heading with the perimeter team to scout out a bunch of . . . vultures circling. You're holding the fort down till we get back."

"Roger that."

Wyatt and Laramie grabbed their Vectors. After several blocks, Wyatt heard strange croaking sounds echoing off the walls of the container buildings. Black shapes with outstretched wings floated overhead, circling lazily over something a hundred meters away.

He pointed. "There."

"Yep," Laramie said. "Karks. Let's keep going."

They proceeded down the street in silence, hemmed in on either side by the abandoned hulks of more containers. Wyatt scanned dark entrances and empty windows as he tried to put aside the alien vibe of Juliet. Laramie patrolled to his right. They had been friends for years, but the differences in their backgrounds felt suddenly very stark. Earth versus Juliet. City versus country. Vultures versus karks. Two human beings from completely different worlds—literally—forcing even a common vocabulary to take on new meaning.

Maya had point several meters ahead of them and kept track of the vultures' location as they moved. Each street ended with a T-intersection, forcing them to shift their path each time they completed a block. Wyatt began to feel disoriented after the fifth or sixth dogleg.

"Where did you all learn your city planning?" he asked. "There isn't a straight line in this whole town."

"It's on purpose, LT."

"Why?"

"This is a frontier town on a big, rolling plain. If you have unobstructed lines, you're going to get blown over by the wind. It's better to make the town act as its own windbreak."

"Huh." Wyatt supposed that made sense, but still, it just felt like being a rat in a maze.

"This place isn't much different from my hometown," Laramie added after a few moments. "We're in the residential areas now. All the business and government is behind us."

"You're a farm girl, Staff Sergeant?" Izzy asked.

"Farm girl, ranch girl. Country girl." Laramie's eyes didn't miss a beat as she scanned for threats. "There's a lot of that here on Juliet."

"Yes, Staff Sergeant. Probably not as deserted as this, though?"

A beat of silence. "No."

The street widened into a four-way intersection with a roundabout. A breeze kicked up dust from the street. Wyatt caught the sickly-sweet stench of flesh rotting.

A flock of karks milled about the clearing, chewing and hissing. Two coiled around a human corpse and croaked at each other over who got the eyeball.

"Fresh dead," Izzy said.

Laramie yelled at the scavengers, waving her arm in a big circle for them to leave. One of the lizards extended its wings and hissed in defiance. Laramie shot the ground near it with her Vector. Startled, the kark beat the air with a massive flap and took off.

"That reeks," Maya said. She pulled her CORE helmet over her face to avoid the smell.

"Izzy, check out that body," Wyatt said.

The corpsman knelt down by what appeared to be a teenage boy—at least, from what was identifiable. Most of the face and part of the hands had been eaten off in a horrible, gruesome feast. The clothing seemed untorn. The karks hadn't gotten very far.

Izzy wiggled the arm and watched it wobble back and forth. "Rigor hasn't set in. This is only a couple hours old."

"Maya, Laramie. Fan out. Look for any others." Wyatt loosened his Vector strap and knelt next to Izzy. "How did he die?"

"Hard to tell. Not exposure. There's no sunburn."

"Disease?"

Izzy frowned at the mangled hands and face. "I don't think so. The scavengers would stay away." He pulled out his utility knife and cut off the buttons of the boy's shirt. Translucent, splotchy skin stretched over gaunt ribs.

"Starved to death. These are all signs of malnutrition."

That was twice now. Starvation was something Wyatt saw all too often on deep-space rescue missions. But here? He thought back to the colonists holed up in Town Hall, the corpse of the woman who had starved surrounded by ration boxes. "This doesn't make sense. There's food in the other buildings."

A circle of karks let out angry croaks from above.

"LT, there's another one over here," Laramie said.

Wyatt walked to the other side of the roundabout. Laramie was examining the remains of a carcass slumped forward against a yield sign.

"Pecked real good by the beasties. Looks like she came from over there. See the blood trail?" She pointed at a thin, darkened stain that extended around the corner.

"That's fresh, too," Wyatt said. "Come on. Maybe there are survivors."

The four troopers followed the blood. The road here was mostly dirt, and the stain became difficult to follow in the failing light. A block later and Wyatt lost sight of it. He cursed at leaving his CORE helmet behind.

"Maya, can you pick up that blood trail with your optics?"

The sergeant scanned the street. She pointed at a large, one-story structure comprised of multiple cargo containers sandwiched together. Double doors mounted in one of the walls formed the entrance. "It goes off into that doorway over there."

Wyatt squinted at the unusual layout. Instead of being stacked, the containers were laid out side by side and seemed like they were newer models than those they had found around Town Hall. "Laramie, I thought you said we were in the burbs. What sort of building is that?"

"A big one."

"Didn't mean that."

"It's all I got, LT."

"Okay. Spread out and move up. Let's see if there are any survivors."

They arranged themselves into a skirmish line and approached the building. Wyatt noted the dark interior behind the wide-open entry and stopped to listen. He didn't hear anything, and wondered if they would find another massacre like the inside of the Town Hall.

He placed a foot inside the doorway and crossed the threshold. The air turned warm and humid, stiffening the hairs on the back of his neck.

10

A locker room. That's what it smelled like to Wyatt. Dank sweat, with a hint of body odor.

He switched on his Vector's tactical flashlight again. Izzy and Laramie did the same, leaving Maya to scan with infrared using her helmet. Tables and chairs sat empty in the room, their tops strewn with clothing and junk. Closed storage lockers lined the walls. The only exit was a doorway to an adjoining area that had been cut out of the original container wall, its hatch hanging half-closed on its hinges. The air hung heavily around them, with no ventilation of any kind to disturb the silence.

"Spread out. Find the blood trail."

Flashlight beams swept carefully over the furniture. Wyatt walked slowly around the corner of one table and noticed an old-fashioned tablet computer discarded on top. He tapped the screen only to find it had run out of power.

"Lieutenant, over here," Maya said.

He made his way over to the hatch and shined his light on the deck where Maya pointed.

"The trail goes into this other room."

"Laramie, Izzy, stack up on me," he said. "Maya, on my mark, pull the hatch open. Slowly."

"Aye, aye."

"Ready? Mark."

The hinges made no sound, which Wyatt found somehow more disturbing than if they had announced their presence. He wasn't claustrophobic—RESIT troopers couldn't be, or they wouldn't last past their first spacecraft boarding—but still a shiver went down his spine. The whole building felt like a tomb.

He entered the next room, which was really just the inside of an adjacent cargo container. A sweep of his flashlight revealed more storage lockers. Two parallel benches sat in the middle of the area. A bulkhead acted as a sort of partition that obscured the left side of the room, but Wyatt thought he saw a shower head mounted to the wall.

"I think this is some kind of rec center. Common area back there, now a locker room."

"That would explain the wonderful aroma," Laramie said.

He found the blood trail and saw that it wound its way around the bulkhead. He gestured to Izzy to move wide, then carefully stepped around the benches until he was next to the opening. He peeked around the corner. The beam from his flashlight illuminated a large shower room.

Wyatt didn't understand what he saw.

A dozen or so bodies knelt in a large circle, legs drawn up underneath them, foreheads touching the floor so that their heads were all near each other. Most had on athletic clothing. A few wore the heavy utilities of a Julietan farmer. One person was naked, his ribs and spine pressed against gaunt skin.

The blood trail led to a gap in the circle. It almost seemed like the person they had found outside had given up their space and left.

"What. The. Hell?" Laramie whispered.

The squad stood at the threshold, staring at the strange configuration of motionless people. Izzy glanced at Laramie as if this was yet another strange Juliet custom. The staff sergeant just shook her head.

"Are they dead?" Maya asked.

"The body outside walked out under his own power," Wyatt said. "Corpsman—check 'em out."

"Yes, sir," Izzy said.

He lowered his Vector and stepped carefully forward. Medic training was mostly about patching holes, but he had more clinical training than anyone else here. And because of that, what? He'd be better able to assess what was happening?

He chose a woman next to the open gap with the blood trail. His flashlight beam swept over a gray track suit with white stripes.

"Hey," Izzy said, his voice soft. "You okay?"

He knelt and put his gloved hand on her shoulder.

Instantly, the woman sat up and looked at him. Izzy jumped back with a start.

Despite having two tactical flashlight beams shining right on her face, the woman seemed oblivious to the others in the room. Her blond hair was pulled back in a frayed ponytail. Wyatt could see the splotches on her face from malnutrition.

She stared without expression at Izzy, who still crouched at eye level with her.

"Iz, ask if she's okay," Wyatt said.

The two of them continued a wordless gaze. After several moments, Wyatt cleared his throat to repeat himself.

Before he could get the words out, Izzy's body convulsed with a violent spasm. He grunted in pain.

"Iz!" Laramie yelled.

Wyatt's first thought was that his trooper was being electrocuted—a sudden seizure, a wet shower area, a potential short circuit that had darkened the lighting.

But the shower floor looked dry. And this disheveled, starving woman seemed unaffected, just sitting there in her kneeling position with her eyes locked on Izzy . . .

A hollow feeling hit him in the gut.

Wyatt raised his Vector and pointed it at the woman. "Get down on the ground! Get down on the ground *now* or I *will fire* on you!"

No reaction. The woman might as well have been stoned. She stared at Izzy with no emotion while every muscle in the corpsman's body clenched tightly.

Wyatt pulled the trigger.

The Vector punched a large hole through the woman's shoulder, vaporizing flesh with the sound of a bug zapper. Instantly she flopped to the floor.

Izzy slumped sideways next to her. Wyatt kept his weapon trained on the woman's body.

"Laramie, pull—"

The room spun. Wyatt couldn't tell if he was falling or floating. He put his hand out to steady himself and connected with something flat and hard, the floor maybe, and through sheer will forced himself to focus on the blur in front of him. His vision was strange, as if looking down a long tunnel surrounded by an angry swarm of golden insects.

Pain.

"My head!" someone said.

His mind ignited with a fire that burned its way into every nerve. Wyatt hit the ground in absolute agony. Through his tears, he could barely make out several human shapes watching him from the circle. Four or five of them now, turned toward him, sitting upright. Looking at him. The shining specks dove in at his eyes, ripping into his flesh.

"It hurts!" the voice cried out again. Maya.

A prone body caught his attention. Wyatt thought he recognized the clothing. It was a uniform of some kind, with a bulky vest and a short, stubby length of metal nearby.

Something told Wyatt it was important. He pushed off the floor with burning arms and moved toward the shape. His body screamed as his hand closed on the vest. He couldn't tell what he was doing. Every gasp of air hurt, every conscious thought writhed under the assault of the specks as they bit at his brain. Only the habits of endless training pushed him to keep his grip on the vest.

He pulled himself and Izzy back to the other side of the bulkhead.

A momentary lessening in the sea of fire. Wyatt drew a ragged breath and struggled to get to his feet.

He became vaguely aware of snapping noises. His mind cleared enough to see Maya firing a volley of laser blasts into the shower, her shots wild even though her helmet gave her assisted targeting. He turned to his right and saw Laramie with her arms wrapped around one of the benches. She was retching on the floor.

"Squad, fall back!" Wyatt shouted. "Out of the building, now!"

Maya stumbled backward into Laramie and almost took them to the ground, but Laramie's body weight won out. The two women locked arms and staggered toward the exit together. Wyatt lifted Izzy's limp body into a fireman's carry. The excessive pull of Juliet's gravity made him wobble, but the burning embers around his vision gave him all the motivation he needed to force his way outside.

A vibrant red on the horizon tinged the otherwise darkening sky overhead. Wyatt could barely see. There was no power, no streetlights to orient them or help them find their way back.

A few blinks of the eye and the embers drifted away.

Wyatt took another dozen steps and slid Izzy onto the ground. The corpsman's eyes were closed, his face slack. Wyatt ripped his gloves off and found a weak pulse in his neck.

"Izzy? Can you hear me?" Wyatt smacked him hard on the cheek. The trooper lay on the ground, unconscious and unresponsive.

"Isi Watanabe!"

Nothing.

He switched on his comm. "Acid Three, Acid One. We have wounded and need evac. Lock on my position and rendezvous, over."

Laramie was cursing like crazy and aiming her Vector at the door to the rec facility. "What *happened*?"

"I don't know." Wyatt flipped open his forearm tablet and poked at the interface. Why wasn't Gavin acknowledging his transmission?

"Acid Three, this is Acid One, do you copy?"

No reply.

"What the hell?" Laramie muttered again.

"Maya, you transmit. See if your helmet can boost."

"On it." Her chin dropped as she concentrated through her neural stub.

Laramie kept her Vector up as she took careful, uncertain steps backward. She edged closer to Wyatt. "How is he?"

"He's out. Weak pulse." Wyatt patted his cheeks again. "Izzy. Do you hear me, buddy? Wake up."

"Lieutenant?" Maya said.

"Yeah?"

"My comm isn't getting through. I have good . . . signal gain . . . *unnh*—"

Pain.

Everything started to go blurry. Maya's hands clutched her temples like they were trying to hold her skull together. Wyatt didn't need to ask—he saw the golden specks again, too. He looked at perimeter buildings and glimpsed dim silhouettes watching them from the windows. More filled the alleyways. Gaunt people, lots of them. Silent. Staring.

In the failing light, the brightness of the embers seemed even more terrifying.

"Maya, get us out of here!"

She stumbled away. Wyatt hauled Izzy back onto his shoulders and stumbled after her. He prayed her helmet navigation could get them back through the maze of buildings. His feet didn't want to go where he directed them, and it was everything he could do to keep his balance.

They reached the roundabout. The golden specks abated before suddenly flooding back with renewed intensity. A Vector snapped laser shots from behind.

"They're all around us, LT!" Laramie said from the rear.

"Keep moving!"

Maya was shooting too. A distant tickle of engagement protocol laughed at Wyatt from the back of his conscious self. *You're using lethal force against unarmed civilians. Have fun at the court martial.*

He let the thought fall aside and focused on putting one foot in front of the other, desperately trying to outrun the flood of searing pain that scratched and clawed at his mind.

"Left, here!" Maya called out.

They ducked left. Again, the embers lessened. Wyatt staggered between rows of container buildings, a warren of dropship housing for a ready-bake frontier town. His concentration cleared enough to try the comm again.

"Acid Three, we need emergency evac. Acid Three, do you read?"

Still no response. Deaf as well as blind. Wyatt could barely see Maya in front of him, his night vision struggling to stay ahead of the golden specs at the edges.

"Right!" she shouted.

Maya made the corner and gurgled out a scream. Wyatt felt it too as soon as he stepped past the edge. Angry specks burrowing with a heat so intense, he felt like his mind was on fire. His knees buckled and he tumbled to the ground.

Laramie shouted from behind. "Wyatt!"

"Get back!" he yelled. "Back from the corner!"

He managed to shrug Izzy off and pushed him to the side. His brain wailed in pain.

"Contact front!" Laramie yelled. *Snap-snap-snap.*

Wyatt felt the heat from the Vector exhaust. He turned his head and saw a dark human shape collapse in front of them. The agony of his mind diminished ever so slightly. But Maya had dropped to all fours and her own weapon lay on the ground next to her.

"Laramie, get her back!" he said, pointing. He fumbled with his Vector, trying to control his fingers through the haze.

The darting shape of his staff sergeant whooshed by and grabbed Maya by the collar. The return trip wasn't as quick. Wyatt could tell Laramie was struggling to move her feet. He searched the darkness for enemies and popped off shots at the shadows.

Laramie almost toppled over as she just barely got out of the intersection. She grabbed Maya's shoulder. "Where do we go?"

"We can . . . we can reroute that way . . ."

"Go!" Wyatt said. I've got Izzy, just go!"

Laramie gave Maya a shove to get her going. Wyatt let his Vector drop against its strap and lifted Izzy up a third time. His thighs screamed with a fury almost as great as the wisps of light in his eyes, but he forced them to move again, one foot in front of the other, desperate to keep up with his teammates. They were getting far ahead of him, nearly lost in the darkness.

"Turn right!" a voice yelled.

He thought he saw them dart around some kind of small tractor. Wyatt made to follow but he trailed by a good ten meters, and when he rounded the corner he didn't see either of them. He kept going on faith. The golden flecks seemed to recede. His head cleared enough to take stock of his body's exertion. Lungs burning, back under strain, his arms and legs leaden with fatigue. But at least his prosthetic felt great.

"I've lost sight of you, Maya. Where are you?"

The comm remained silent. Wyatt approached a T-intersection and slowed his pace. "Laramie, Maya, do you copy? Do I go left, or right?"

He stood still and waited for a reply. The chirps and whistles of nighttime insects spilled into the air, signaling the beginning of a new day for the lower orders of the ecosphere. But his comm was still dead, and no reply came back through the darkness.

"Laramie?"

Silence.

"Maya, where are you?"

A knot began to form in Wyatt's stomach. It wasn't fear, exactly. But as he stood in the intersection, he realized his mistake in dashing off to investigate the carrion birds. His team was in a town full of dead bodies. They didn't know what had caused it. And they shouldn't have done a recon without better preparation for whatever danger existed here.

Not they. *He.* Wyatt had given the order.

You're the one who designed the mission. This is all on you.

A distant, fiery roar scratched the back of his brain.

The embers were coming back. They were following him.

Left it was.

Wyatt trudged forward, hoping fate and God would give him a break. He went straight down a long road, then a left and a right around some buildings he didn't recognize. He thought he was heading in the right general direction. He just needed a bit of luck to not find himself trapped in a dead end.

Which was exactly what happened next.

The road ended in a sort of cove surrounded on three sides by cargo containers. Wyatt desperately searched for an alley or any sort of exit. The night proved too dark. Cursing, he let Izzy's weight slide off him to the ground and switched back on his Vector's tactical flashlight. A quick inspection revealed he was cut off no matter how hard he looked.

"Come on, Iz, back we go—"

Pain.

The embers turned hot. Wyatt fell to his knees and managed to squint past the golden flecks to see a dark shape stepping out of a doorway. The figure's eyes were impossible to see in the dark, yet they bored into his soul, the specks of light dancing in a vortex around his peripheral vision.

"Laramie, I'm in . . . trouble, do you . . . copy?"

The figure moved toward him. It was an older man, thin, frail, but walking with a power that seemed beyond the physical. Crippling agony ripped into Wyatt's head. He tried to lift his Vector but it seemed to weigh a thousand kilos. Instead, Wyatt crumpled as the flames rose around him.

"Acid Two . . . help . . ."

He had let down his squad on Tiamat. Six casualties in a reckless raid. Now he'd made another wrong decision. Izzy hurt. Maya. Laramie. Where was Laramie? His "little sister." Don't let her get hurt. Not Laramie.

Maybe it was right that he should die. Maybe it would be better for all.

God, the pain.

Wyatt tried to cry out but his lungs wouldn't let him.

A hot breeze swept through the air. Wyatt almost missed the spray of flesh that spurted out of the figure's chest. The man dropped in an ungraceful heap.

Two more singes of heat and the embers disappeared altogether.

The comm crackled to life again. "Targets are down. Get them out of there, guys."

Gavin.

Wyatt stared at the crumpled form of the old man. His mind struggled to make sense of what just happened. What he did know was that Gavin must have heard his transmission after all. And once he got line of sight to Wyatt's pursuers, the sergeant's L-6 rifle could take out the threat from a far greater range than a Vector.

Wyatt was safe. For the moment.

He glanced down the deserted street and fought back a wave of nausea. The lack of light gave the neighborhood an eerie, malevolent feel. There was nothing Wyatt wanted more than to get back to the Javelin.

11

Romeo. A lyrical name for Juliet's moon, orbiting its mistress in an eternal embrace. Wyatt sat on a rock and stared at it as it crept toward the horizon. Unfortunately, what he had experienced so far on Juliet was anything but poetry.

He was still having trouble processing the events from earlier. The burning specks. The worst headache of his life. Was there something toxic in that town? Hallucinogenic mold spores, poisonous paint on the buildings, anything that could be explained? All possible. But his gut came up with a different reason and he didn't want to accept it:

Shambling hulks who stared pain into people.

It had been foolish to just run off deeper into the town. Now they had casualties.

Wyatt decided to go check on them. He stood up, dusted off his pants, and walked toward the cargo ramp of the nearby Javelin. In the distance, the rooftops of Parrell reflected moonlight back into the sky.

Toward the rear of the cargo bay, the crew chief knelt next to a motionless Izzy. Several blankets folded to create multiple layers acted as a makeshift bed for their corpsman. The chief had just finished connecting an IV and was squeezing a saline bag.

"Any change?"

The chief turned his head. "Oh, it's you, sir. No, still in a coma."

"How are his vitals?"

"Weak, but stable. His body's functioning, so that's good."

"What about his head?"

"Well, MedSurg doesn't like his brain activity. Too low in the important places, too high in others. But it hasn't been able to figure out what to do about it."

That was bad. The Javelin's emergency medicine suite should have been able to give guidance on how to care for Izzy, even without their corpsman there to interpret it.

"All right. Well, keep him comfortable and maybe it'll figure it out soon."

The chief looked at Wyatt. "How are you doing, sir?"

"Fine."

"With respect, sir, that was not convincing. Want me to check you out?"

"No. I'm fine."

Wyatt knelt down at Izzy's side. His eyes were closed. He looked peaceful. But Wyatt remembered the convulsions that had tortured the corpsman inside the rec center. He said a silent prayer that Izzy would pull out of whatever it was that had happened to him.

When he finished, Wyatt opened his eyes and patted Izzy on the chest. Then he turned to the crew chief again. "How are our ladies doing?"

"Your trooper Maya seemed pretty shaken up. The staff sergeant spent a lot of time talking with her. Then she ate two meal pouches and went to sleep."

"Sounds about right for Laramie. Did Maya turn in, too?"

The chief shook his head, then jerked his chin toward the front of the cargo bay.

Wyatt peered down the fuselage and saw a lone figure sitting quietly on the deck, knees pulled up to her chin, staring at nothing. He walked over until he stood a meter away.

"This seat taken?" He pointed at the deck next to her.

Maya looked up at him with a start. "Oh. Yes? I-I mean, no, sir. Go ahead."

Wyatt sat down. She wouldn't meet his eyes. He took a deep breath and tried to focus. Even though he was still processing the encounter himself, he had to compartmentalize it and help his troopers do the same. Especially the new ones.

"How are you doing?"

"I'm okay, Lieutenant."

Maya's body language screamed she was anything buy okay. He needed to get her to talk. "What do you make of what happened earlier?"

"I don't know, sir."

"I thought we might be goners there. Lost, in the dark, hard to even think."

She didn't answer.

"What were *you* feeling as we ran?" Wyatt asked, pushing.

He could see her jaw clench, her face tighten. She turned away. Silence stretched out between them.

"Maya. We're in this together. It's okay."

She finally answered in a whisper. "I was so scared."

"I know. Me too."

"It hurt so much. Those specks." Maya blotted her eye with the back of her hand, trying to be discrete.

"Yeah."

More silence. A few moments passed before Maya seemed to regain her composure.

"When I came here," she said, "when I transferred to Caustic Team, I thought we'd be boarding spacecraft. Doing raids against Oscars. I was prepared for that. I worked on engagement protocol, marksmanship, close-quarters battle. It's just . . . I guess I wasn't ready for whatever happened in town over there."

Wyatt suddenly felt guilty that he was the reason they weren't doing those things. He suppressed a grimace. "Well, we'll be more prepared now going forward. It's a good lesson for us to be prepared. Even if we're doing a recon on our own colony."

"I'm sorry I didn't protect us better."

"What?"

"I shot at those people. I missed a bunch, even with my CORE helmet."

"Those specks seemed to disrupt our comms. Maybe they affected your targeting."

"And I didn't do a very good job navigating."

"Well—"

"And Corpsman Watanabe got hurt."

"None of us understood what was happening—"

"I was just *so scared*." Her voice cracked.

"Maya. Stop."

She stared hard at the deck.

"Look," he said, "we made it out. That's what counts. We're smarter now. Izzy's stable. You did fine."

"Yes, sir." She nodded, and blotted her eyes again.

"You did fine," he repeated.

"Aye, aye. Sorry for all this. I'll toughen up."

Maya took a deep breath and that seemed to level her. She managed a weak smile. He clasped her shoulder and pushed back up.

Wyatt didn't like this. He needed his troopers composed. As the squad leader, he had to apply encouragement and reinforcement in equal measure to keep everyone mentally squared away. Laramie helped the delivery a lot in that department. But with four new troopers on a remote deployment, he couldn't afford any of them losing their mental edge.

Then again, they were only human. Was helping Maya any different than what Father Bradley had done for him?

A clatter echoed off the cargo ramp. Wyatt turned to see Gavin and Rahsaan clomping inside. He realized their watch must be over.

"See anything out there?" he asked.

"A lot of empty." Gavin set his L-6 Viper against a bulkhead and tossed his helmet right after it, barely missing the SuperMag scope. "I shot some of those vulture-looking bastards. A couple kept coming after us, thinking we were food."

"Who's out there now?"

"Carlos and Kenny."

Wyatt nodded. His eyes fell back on Izzy, sleeping quietly on his pallet.

"Lieutenant," Gavin drawled.

"Yeah?"

He motioned toward their corpsman. "He'll be okay, Lieutenant. He's RESIT. He's tough."

He thought back to Maya. "I hope so."

For Gavin, who generally didn't talk much, the acknowledgment was solidarity accomplished. He started to walk away.

"I need to understand what happened to him," Wyatt said quietly, more to himself than anyone.

The bearded sergeant stopped and scratched his chin. "What you told me sure didn't make a lot of sense. A bunch of people in some kind of séance? Weird."

"We couldn't tell if they were hurt, dead, whatever." Wyatt replayed the encounter in his mind, searching for any new insight. "Izzy approached one of them. He started to talk to her. And then all that stuff started to go down."

"And you don't think it was anything in the air? A nerve agent?"

How did Wyatt explain that the pain seemed to emanate from the people themselves?

"I don't think so. When we shot the people, the pain went away. When you shot the guys moving toward me in the alley, same thing. I don't know how to describe what they were doing. It just sounds corny."

"Hostile telepathy," Gavin offered.

"Yeah. See? Worse than corny."

"At least we know hostile gunfire works." The sergeant turned to leave again. "I'm going to grab some chow."

"Hey—thanks for saving my ass."

"You're welcome. Remember—bourbon."

At least Gavin was completely unfazed. Wyatt managed a chuckle, then forced himself to climb into his command chair. He flopped down and pressed a neural stub to his temple, trying to ignore the unpleasant medicinal smell of the adhesive.

A computer interface appeared in his field of vision. He tapped through several icons to update his mission report. So far, he wasn't doing very well achieving his objectives.

His team had not secured Thermopylae Gate.

Their Javelin was damaged, their ascent booster lost.

One of his troopers lay in a coma.

He still had no useful intel around the shutdown in interplanetary shipping, the hostile posture of RESIT Team Dagger, or the situation with Juliet in general.

And with no troop carrier in orbit, he had no one to contact for backup. This was an Earth colony, but for all intents and purposes they might as well been operating covertly behind enemy lines. On their own.

Wyatt sighed. They *had* to get into Venice—the capital city, home to two million people, the seat of planetary government.

His squad already had a rough plan to insert covertly via the train system. If they set up an observation post, then maybe they could gather intel about what had happened in Parrell and whether it was connected to the blockade in place at Thermopylae.

It was a race against time to complete all this before the next transit window opened. Wyatt had to recover their mission with some sort of valuable intelligence, and avoid being marooned groundside.

Flashbacks of Major Beck crossed his mind. *Guilt makes you second-guess, make bad decisions.*

He felt so alone.

Wyatt closed his mission log and began to search the Javelin database for any information he could find on maglev trains.

12

Lo River
Juliet, Alpha Centauri A
22 February 2272

"I have contact," the copilot said. "Seven o'clock, one hundred eighty knots closure."

Laramie jumped to her feet and leaned past Wyatt into the flight deck just as the engines flared to life. The holo monitor displayed an orange carat representing the cargo train. Beyond the canopy, a landscape of rolling grasslands swayed in the wind beyond the idle Javelin.

Wyatt turned and jumped at Laramie's presence. "You ready?"

"Born ready, LT. Is that our maglev?"

Wyatt gave her a stilted nod. "Yep."

"How long?"

"Six minutes. Get the squad ready."

"Aye, aye."

He didn't make eye contact. Instead, he brusquely brushed past her to strap down in his command chair next to the hatch.

Laramie ordered her troopers to gear up and barely got back to her own seat before the Javelin tilted off the ground. She glanced again down the cargo bay at the lieutenant. Wyatt was usually cool under fire, decisive and confident. This distracted, angry edginess creeping into his behavior bothered her.

She needed whatever it was gone. She needed him solid, because the truth was she was having trouble keeping focused herself.

Parrell had shaken all of them, but no one more than Laramie.

Whatever happened in that sleepy frontier town, Laramie was scared to death of what might be happening elsewhere. Rubble and wreckage in the streets. Bodies rotting inside abandoned buildings. Residents turning on each other with lethal intent.

The terrifying ordeal at the rec center.

The memory of the incandescent embers still burned into her mind as if they were trying to melt her soul away and leave an empty shell. If it had happened at Parrell, could it have happened back home? Were Mom and Dad slumped against some street sign, being picked apart by karks? Jessamy? Her brothers?

A pang of guilt twisted her gut. She hadn't seen any of them in person in almost two years. RESIT was making her miss the regular cadence of her family.

You better make sure they're safe, then.

"Four minutes," Teo said.

She took a deep breath and forced herself to focus on the troopers in her charge. Her surrogate family.

Laramie did a visual check on the squad down the fuselage. Rahsaan and Maya wore CORE helmets. The rest had on goggles. Laramie had decided on the latter. CORE helmets were great for confined spaces and firefights, but climbing around on an open maintenance platform while a train moved at high speed? She'd rather keep her spatial awareness intact. The airflow just outside the aeroshell was too dangerous, and she didn't want to chance getting blown off into the grasslands.

At ninety seconds to intercept, the crew chief dropped the rear cargo door. Laramie's ears popped as the air pressure fled into the roar of the wind. Outside, the grasslands gave way to the rocky terrain of a shallow canyon. A narrow river snaked back and forth a hundred meters below with rapids that tossed water upward in great plumes. She could practically taste the humidity.

"Gavin, ready up!" she called.

Their third-in-command lumbered aft with their big projectile gun. He locked the weapon struts to the deck and loaded it with a harpoon projectile.

Teo's voice crackled through the comm. "Coming up on the track, port side."

The train came into view and approached the Javelin from behind, closing fast on an elevated monorail that hugged the riverbank. A dozen connected carriages, each shaped like an upside-down U, slid over the rail's modulated magnetic field at an excess of any sane velocity.

"It's moving too fast!" Laramie said.

"The bend is coming up," Teo replied. "It'll slow down to take the turn. Ten seconds."

Laramie watched as the train stormed toward them. She had never seen one up close like this. The sloped nose of the lead car paved the way for a series of cargo containers mounted on the maglev carriages themselves. A system of catwalks crisscrossed the containers behind the slipstream.

A glint of something shiny caught her eye.

She scanned the train cars to find it again, but everything was moving so fast that whatever it might have been, it was out of her vision now. The train looked like it might blast past them right underneath the Javelin. But true to Teo's prediction, the track banked into a gentle curve and the train began to slow.

"Line up the shot!" Wyatt told Gavin.

Gavin flipped off the safety. He aimed down the barrel of the projectile gun, pointing it at one of the cargo containers.

Laramie's stomach knotted up as she peeked past the edge of the ramp. The floor of the canyon slid by far below, treacherous and unforgiving. She wondered what hitting the bottom would feel like if she fell. Would it be over quick? Or would it be a crippling agony of broken bones and ruptured body parts?

She toed her way forward. As the senior enlisted officer, she got to go first. The things she did for her troopers.

"Weapons free!" Wyatt yelled.

A second later, Gavin pulled the trigger. A hollow *foomp* filled the fuselage as harpoon and towline streaked out the open door. A moment later it buried itself into the metal skin of one of the train's containers.

He locked the towline winch. "Line is secure!"

"Clip on!"

Eight troopers clipped carabiners to the line and sounded off in succession, starting with Laramie and ending with Wyatt.

Laramie's throat felt tight. She realized her hands were squeezing the zipline and forced herself to unclench. Space was so much better. There was no such thing as down.

"Go, go, go!"

Laramie leaped into the empty air. The sudden slide against the towline interrupted her freefall and she careened toward the train, landing a moment later on the expanded metal catwalk that wrapped around the maglev carriages.

She unclipped herself and moved forward to secure the landing area and make room for the others. Even though this part of the rail line was "slower," the ground still swept by to the wicked roar of rushing air. Laramie avoided looking down as she pressed forward toward the lead car.

Again, a glint caught her eye ahead of her.

Was it her nerves playing tricks on her? She squinted to find it again. The sudden rising pitch of the Javelin's engines pulled her attention away, and Laramie looked up to see Teo veering off, leaving seven other troopers lined up in single file behind her.

The ambient noise increased as the train began to accelerate out of its long turn.

On the catwalk, the air remained relatively still thanks to the train's aeroshell. Laramie vaguely recalled something in school about how the nose cone of a train ionized the air so that its electromagnetic field could push it aside. But the loud roar just a meter above her head served as an angry reminder of how fast they were moving—without any kind of safety equipment other than a simple hand railing.

Laramie returned to pushing out of the landing zone and suddenly froze.

Her gut told her something wasn't right. Aside from boarding, there shouldn't have been any danger on an automated train hauling chunks of metal.

But that glint . . .

She crouched on the catwalk and pulled her Vector off its chest harness.

"Talk to me, Laramie," Wyatt's voice crackled in her earpiece. "You see something?"

"Stand by."

Laramie leaned forward against the steady pull of the train's increasing speed. She spied a wider platform ahead, a sort of superficial scaffolding that crossed to the other side of the train between adjacent cargo containers. Maybe she could get a better view of the area from there.

"I keep thinking I'm seeing something, LT. Going to scout it out."

"Copy that." A pause. "These are automated cargo trains, right?"

"Ever since I've lived here."

"All right. We'll advance behind you."

The train was really going now. Wind howled past them at hundreds of knots as the monorail's maglev nodes propelled the carriages forward. Laramie reached the platform between the adjacent train carriages. Stairs climbed up to a wide grating that spanned the train's cross section. Another set of stairs led down to the other side. A distant thought crossed her mind around whether the train engineers normally left maintenance scaffolding on during operations. Maybe their removal slowed down the turnaround time?

The scaffoldings were near enough to each other to provide easy access between train carriages. Laramie started across the platform.

Then she saw what it was.

Her body reacted before her mind did. Laramie slammed to the deck just as a laser bolt hit the cargo container next to her. A spray of wet metal rained on her back and arms.

"Contact front!" She struggled to pull her Vector from underneath her.

She heard Wyatt bark terse orders to the others. Ahead of her, a head bobbed past the forward cargo container and shot again. Return fire flew overhead from her teammates. Laramie could smell the ozone of the ionized air from the exchange.

Then, silence. Laramie lifted her head and saw her teammates didn't have a good angle on the shooter. She also realized she was a sitting duck if she remained on the platform.

More laser fire suddenly burned the air over the platform. Laramie peeked to her left, saw how the catwalks on the side of the cargo container were lower than the cross platform, and instinctively rolled sideways to get to cover. An instant later she pushed herself down the stairs.

Several shots melted holes through the structure around her. Laramie shouldered her Vector but didn't dare expose herself to the incoming barrage.

"I need covering fire!" she shouted.

The comm came to life with the sound of an intense gunfight behind Wyatt's voice. "We're in contact on the other side. Multiple targets. Hang tight, trying to get to you."

She held her Vector above her head and squeezed the trigger. Her shots went high left. She tried again, this time punching random holes in the cargo container walls.

Laramie cursed the compact design of her weapon, great for boarding in the confined space of spacecraft but not when the target took cover at distance. She cursed her choice to not wear a CORE helmet like Maya and Rahsaan.

Most of all, she cursed that she was going to get a hole burned in her.

Laser shots snapped over her and she ducked back behind the stair hanger. Through the expanded metal grating she could see more enemy targets appearing, four in all. Two let loose a barrage that ravaged the structure around her. She jerked away as more hot particles of vaporized metal hit her cheeks.

The other pair would be advancing on her while she kept her head down. She had no choice but to engage, even if it got her shot. She'd be shot anyway.

She raised her Vector to fire back. Before she pulled the trigger, one of the enemy's heads exploded in a spray of pink mist.

Thank God. Wyatt.

Another blast came from behind her. She twisted her head to see several silhouettes advancing on her position. Her mind reeled as it tried to catch up. The tactical positions were all wrong . . .

"Wyatt, are you coming up behind me?" she asked.

A pause. "Negative. What's behind you?"

She looked again. The silhouettes were crouched down and moving toward her. The lead one raised a weapon and the crackle of an energy blast sizzled above her.

"Contact rear! Wyatt, I'm in trouble!"

"Copy."

More laser fire streaked past her, the snap of ionizing air causing the hair on her neck to stand on end. Laramie had a better angle on the enemies coming up behind her, so she pivoted in her crouch and took some shots. She missed, but two of them dropped to the catwalk. A third one now appeared to hug the side of the cargo container. A moment later he raised a weapon and fired.

More blasts burned the air. Laramie found herself in the worst possible place, caught in the crossfire between two enemy elements with limited cover. Steadying her breathing, Laramie aimed her Vector at the standing silhouette. She couldn't miss this next shot.

A loud hiss squealed nearby from a severed hydraulic line.

The catwalk shuddered and disrupted Laramie's aim. She suddenly realized that the cargo container next to her was sliding out of its mount. Horror filled her as another hydraulic line broke free and whipped around the air in a frenzied dance. With no remaining pressure to hold the mounting clamp shut, the cargo container lurched over the scaffolding and smashed into a support pole.

Crack.

The catwalk dropped a full meter. Laramie found herself momentarily airborne and grabbed at the stair handhold. But the walkway continued to bend away until the end poked out past the electromagnetic aeroshell.

The wind ripped off the remaining struts in a catastrophic snap. The catwalk turned sideways.

Laramie almost managed a scream before her hands slipped off the railing.

13

The catwalk twisted in a slow motion, surrounding Laramie in a vortex of screeching metal as she tumbled through the air. She saw the blue of the sky. The muddy river water far below. A cement pylon that held the maglev track, zooming by at high speed. Her mind raced to catch up with the fact that she was about to die.

A sudden jerk jarred her insides. Her hands reflexively clutched at the air around her and closed around something soft.

The strap on her Vector.

Somehow it had tangled around the stair hanger. She was dangling by the proverbial thread over a thirty-meter fall at high speed.

A terrible desperation seized her. Laramie couldn't tell if she was breathing or screaming as she tried to pull herself back onto the tilted catwalk. All she knew was the train's momentum was too much, that her feet were dangerously close to the edge of the aeroshell and she would soon be sucked away to oblivion.

Out of the corner of her eye she saw one of the enemy figures rushing up part of the remaining scaffold. The unmistakable shape of a Vector filled his hands.

They were coming to finish her off.

Wyatt, where are you?

It was too late. A ripping sound signaled her strap failing. Laramie felt herself slipping into the torrent of rushing air, her mind filled with the last panic of her life.

Something grabbed her wrist.

Laramie twisted in the vise grip, wondering why she wasn't falling into the vacuum rushing by at her feet.

Her eyes turned to the train. A figure wearing a CORE helmet hulked over her, one hand locked on a metal strut and the other on her arm. And he was trying to pull her aboard.

Survival instincts kicked in. Laramie grasped at the figure and managed to get her other hand wrapped around his sleeve. Together they strained to lever her up, her feet bicycling toward anything that might provide a chance foothold. Her mind noted pieces of the picture that didn't seem quite right: the jet-black helmet, the green tattoos on sunburned forearms. A thread of danger wove its way through her mind as it tried to find a way past the immediacy of a lethal fall.

Her toes caught the edge of a torn pipe. Pushing with all her ability, Laramie managed to haul herself closer to the scaffold until her chest flopped over the top. Her rescuer grabbed a fistful of her pant seat and dragged the rest of her up.

She gasped a quick breath before she rolled away and pushed up to her knees. Across from her was a man who was not one of her teammates. He wore a mishmash of gear, some familiar, some not. A pockmarked ARC vest covered his chest, and chem mags studded the ammo pockets around his abdomen.

Her Vector gone, Laramie's hand went immediately to her pistol. Her P-10 was a ballistic weapon and not an official RESIT issue. But she'd carried one ever since she was fifteen to protect herself from hoppers out in the fields. The projectiles were slow and large, and she was positive it would blow away a fat chunk of someone at this range.

The figure waved his forearm up and down in a cease-fire signal. "Friendly! Friendly!" he said, his voice muffled by the CORE helmet.

The electric sizzle of laser blasts made Laramie duck. The two other figures accompanying her rescuer were still shooting at the original targets further up the train.

A spray of slag rained down from the vaporized skin of a cargo container.

The man wearing the black helmet crouched low and turned toward the front. He seemed to be studying the tactical situation. Then he unclipped the L-4 from his harness and held it out to Laramie.

He gave her the hand signal for covering fire and pointed at the enemy.

This is crazy, Laramie thought. *I don't know who these people are.*

A vague voice shouted her name. With a start, Laramie realized her earpiece had fallen out during her trapeze act. She groped across her shoulder until her fingers touched the transmitter and slipped the clip back over her earlobe.

"—copy? Laramie, where the hell are you?"

"Wyatt! I'm okay. I fell, but—I'm okay."

"We can't get to you, Laramie. Trying to flank right, but hostiles are manning prepared positions."

She looked at the man who had pulled her back aboard the train. The eyeless glare of a black CORE helmet stared back at her.

Laramie made her choice.

"Wyatt, lay down suppressing fire. We might be able to flank from this side."

"Who's *we*?"

"Good question for later, LT."

She leaned forward into a firing position and began snapping the Vector at the shadowy figures behind what she could now see were reinforced gun nests. Her shots joined the barrage from her new companions. Combat rebreathers masked all of their faces. One of them was painted yellow, like the kind firefighters wore.

Who were these guys?

The man with the black helmet crouched low and crawled on the catwalk. Laramie kept her attention on the enemy contacts. When she exhausted the chem mag and stopped to reload, her rescuer had moved to within five meters of the nest. Laramie watched as he primed a grenade and tossed it.

A flash from inside the nest was followed a split second later by a sharp boom.

Several moments passed. No more return fire came their way.

Laramie stopped shooting. The man with the black helmet crawled to the edge of what looked like a low wall of cinderblocks and peeked over the top. He gave her the thumbs up and waved them forward.

Gunfire still crackled intermittently on the comm. Wyatt and the others were still engaged, and RESIT didn't have frag grenades. Laramie shifted into a crouch and hurried up to the man in the black helmet. Before she could reach him, he took off up the catwalk and disappeared around the far end of the next cargo container.

"Wait—" she called after him.

Footsteps tromped on the metal grate behind her. Laramie wheeled around to find another one of her new allies hurrying up the catwalk, leaving his companion behind to cover the cross platform. He ran past with nothing more than a quick glance at her. Laramie caught a glimpse of the word RESCUE stenciled on side of his yellow CORE helmet.

"Well, that's the truth," she muttered.

She went after him.

The second man was shorter than the one who had pulled her back to safety. He took a firing position near the edge of the next cargo container by the time Laramie caught up. When he didn't fire, Laramie dared to peek around the corner.

Another gun nest sat on the far side of the platform. *Wyatt's side.*

Laramie saw a cloud of smoke from Vector exhaust hanging above the nest. The black-helmeted stranger was crawling along the grating. He would be exposed to fire if the hostiles turned his way. But so far, they were apparently too busy shooting at Wyatt and his squad on the other side.

Her rescuer readied another grenade.

"Wyatt, fire in the hole!" Laramie said, just loud enough for the comm.

The lieutenant would know better than to question a direct warning. The snaps of laser fire lessened as the troopers closest to the cinderblocks put their heads down.

The grenade sailed through the air and exploded just as it passed over the nest. Another flash, another delayed boom that announced a heat wave immediately after.

Laramie realized the thrower had cooked the grenade a few seconds before throwing it so that it would explode in the air over the nest. He knew what he was doing.

Sporadic Vector fire from the RESIT troopers continued for a few seconds before finally stopping.

"I think you're clear," Laramie said into the comm.

"What was that? A grenade?"

"Yes. I have some new . . . friendlies with me. One of them is scouting the gun nest in front of you. Do not fire, I repeat, do not fire."

"Roger."

Laramie glanced at the man next to her. He too wore a hodgepodge of unmatched gear in addition to the yellow Fire & Rescue helmet. Whereas Laramie's vest had insignia patches on the shoulder and back, his were bare. Some sort of radio transmitter was strapped awkwardly to his harness.

"Coming up behind," her earpiece said.

Carlos appeared on the platform, stepping carefully around the remnants of the broken catwalk. He swept the area for threats through the scope of his Vector. When he spied the man next to Laramie, Carlos froze.

This ought to be interesting, Laramie thought.

14

Train
Juliet, Alpha Centauri A
22 February 2272

"Okay, that's who we are," Wyatt said. "Your turn to talk. I get that you're sabotaging supply trains. I'm not clear on who you are, or why. Help me out."

They had all crammed inside the train control room, a leftover vestige from before Julietan law allowed for full computer control. Laramie stood next to Wyatt, ready more than anyone for some explanation.

The man with the arm tattoos sat casually on the pilot chair and rested his helmet on his lap. He had brown hair and green eyes, with a scruff of beard that crawled down to his neck. His companions stood against the wall and rested their arms on their weapons. The forty kilos of military explosives the strangers had with them remained out on the scaffold under the guard of the remaining squad.

He kept glancing at Laramie with a trace of a smirk, perhaps proud of himself for saving her. It made her dislike him. Not that she wasn't grateful, but it almost felt like he was rubbing her nose in it.

"Happy to cover whatever you want, Lieutenant." The man glanced casually at the master display. "I'll point out, though, we've got about twenty minutes before we're in visual range of the city. You said you planned to infiltrate Venice onboard our train here, but take my advice. We don't want to be on it by then."

"Then talk fast."

The man shrugged. "Okay. I'll start with me. Master Sergeant Chris Thompson, U.S. Marine Corps—formerly. Those are Finn and Sid over there. Alonso is outside with our supply of boom. All former Marines. I used to run the security team for Governor Hewitt and his family here on Juliet. Now, I guess we're rebels."

"What's with the explosives?"

"We were going to destroy the train."

"Why?"

"Yakki Mining sends raw material to Venice to manufacture weapons and ammo. We've been putting the brakes on that. We have a couple aerobikes that can match the train speed when it takes the bends in the track, so that's usually where we try to board and wire everything up. Guess the guards were a response to our past success." A sour look crossed Chris's face. "Hewitt's been on a wild tear arming up since he declared martial law. This will be the first train to get through in over a month."

"Martial law—" Laramie said. What was he talking about? She couldn't quite get her head around who these guys were, or why they were doing what they did. "What's going on here?"

Chris turned to her. "A lot of kooky stuff."

She frowned. The Marine watched her reaction with interest.

"Explain," Wyatt said.

"There's been a big . . . epidemic of something. Lots of people getting sick, falling into comas, then waking up . . . different. Empty. Kind of like you'd picture a zombie, I guess. Lots of shambling. Very contagious. Very out of control. Governor Hewitt used that as his basis for martial law."

The revelation hit her hard. Laramie turned and met Wyatt's eyes. She could tell he was thinking the same thing. *Parrell.*

"How far has it spread?"

"I don't know. General McManus is Hewitt's Secretary of Security. He put a bunch of districts under quarantine. Parts of Venice are secure, other parts are wastelands filled with infected people." He chuckled. "Some are just filled with looters and criminals. You can tell the difference if someone's shooting at you."

Laramie felt her eyes narrowing. "Is this a joke to you?"

"No, no joke. I don't think it's funny when your family or friends change into an empty shell. I'm just providing practical advice. You know, so you know whether to run, or duck."

Wyatt brought the conversation back on topic. "So, why are you rebels, Chris?"

The Marine seemed to be considering how much to tell them. He spoke carefully. "How would you picture a quarantine working, Lieutenant?"

"We do this in RESIT sometimes," he said. "You focus on containment so the disease won't spread. Block entrance and egress to an infected area. Deliver humanitarian effort to ease suffering until a treatment can be administered."

A dark smile spread over Chris's face. "Yeah. McManus decided that quarantine meant something a little more aggressive."

"Such as?"

"Proactive extermination."

Laramie wasn't sure she heard right. "What?"

He turned toward her again. "Death squads go in and cull anyone they think is infected. A lot of times, the immediate family tries to stop them. Right? You're not going to let the police kill mom or dad, are you? So, they get waxed too. All in the name of containing a virulent disease. The police have wiped out entire sections of the city."

"That can't be right," Wyatt said.

"Wait." Laramie's brain was racing to catch up. This was insane. It had to be bad information. "You're telling us that the whole Julietan government is complicit in mass murder? That's unbelievable. I served under General Hu when I was in the Army. He'd never let that happen."

"Hu's dead."

For the first time in ages, Laramie was at a loss for words.

"What happened?" Wyatt asked.

"A coup attempt. Hu, by the way, was the Security Undersecretary. He worked for

McManus." Chris's eyes moved to Laramie again. "You're right about Hu. Things were getting crazy really quickly. To his credit, Hu tried to stop it. It . . . didn't work out."

Laramie's mind was spinning out of control. "My God."

Chris looked at her again. She realized he was eyeing her figure—heavy muscles from a heavy planet. "You're from here, aren't you?"

"Yeah."

"Where?"

"West Hadensville."

"I don't know where that is." Chris fingered his beard some more. "Maybe that's a good thing."

Wyatt seemed to be deep in thought. "I assume McManus took over command of RESIT Dagger?"

"What do you mean? I thought *you* were RESIT."

"We're Caustic Team. On station around Proxima."

"Proxima?" The master sergeant seemed confused.

"We came through the quantum gate," Wyatt said. "We were intercepted by Dagger, the RESIT team that handles this system. Their attack craft didn't follow any standard protocol. They butchered the crew of one freighter and opened fire on us."

Chris shrugged. "You're asking if McManus is behind that as well? Maybe. But honestly, I think most of his attention is down here on the ground."

He thought for a moment. "Why *are* you here, anyway? Aren't you, like, deep-space rescue and stuff?"

"We do more than that," Laramie said. Her pride bristled. She wasn't going to take a put-down from some ground-pounder.

Wyatt held up a hand to settle her. "We do a lot of direct-action raids, Chris. Proxima has what you might call a piracy problem."

"Huh."

A repeating chime sounded from the control panel. Laramie felt her bodyweight shift forward as the train started a gradual deceleration.

"Time's getting short, Lieutenant," Chris said.

"Yeah, it is," Wyatt said. "We're about to get off this train and I'm still missing how you went from personal security to hardcore insurgent. You said you were part of the governor's security detail. Why aren't you with him, with all this going on?"

Laramie watched as the master sergeant's demeanor changed. A hardness entered his eyes. "I have a problem with murder. You can justify it any way you want—that the infected are going to die anyway, that they could spread whatever it is to another person. You can say you're euthanizing them for their own good. They're still people. They didn't do anything wrong. So when you round them all up for industrial slaughter, that's murder." Chris spied a stray thread on one of his gloves and started to pick at it. "The governor and his people didn't see things my way, so I left. Unfortunately, he's doing everything he can to find and kill me."

"Because you blow up his supply trains?" Laramie asked.

Chris sniffed a laugh. "No. Because I have his daughter."

15

Venice Mottano District
Juliet, Alpha Centauri A
22 February 2272

The loft office of the old warehouse seemed frozen in time, filled with the leftovers of a busy day brought to full stop. Paper manifests weeks out of date, with coffee rings from empty mugs. A lunch box filled with moldy food. The supervisor's holo monitor, still open to an extranet gambling site. It was as if all of the workers had upped and vanished and left behind their last actions without a care in the world. Wyatt felt awkward as he sat on a swivel chair, as if he were somehow violating the sanctity of someone's final resting place.

Chris had advised getting off the maglev train before it entered the receiving station. Apparently, he and his team had been so successful blowing supply shipments to hell that the arrival of an intact train promised lots of excitement. Wyatt agreed. He ordered Maya to hack the automated pilot from the control room and slow their velocity enough for a quick jump into some low brush. Then they hiked to the deserted storage building in which they now rested, located on the extreme outer edge of the shipping district. The fourth Marine in Chris's ad-hoc squad, Alonso, had remained behind to fly their aerobike the long way back to a safe house.

Now what?

They were technically inside Venice. That seemed like progress. But he was so far outside of his original mission parameters that he wasn't sure where to go from here. Neither he nor Laramie knew the city. They didn't have any contacts other than these Marines. And the hobbies of the Marine leader included blowing up trains and kidnapping family members of the most powerful politician on the planet. Could Wyatt trust someone like that?

Lurking behind it all was the ticking clock. The quantum gate waited for no one.

He would just have to figure out how to go with it.

"Those are some deep thoughts there, LT." Laramie walked up and offered him a meal pouch.

"Just trying to figure out where we go from here." He glanced at the indiscernible green letters on the black plastic. "What flavor's that?"

"Curry something."

Wyatt wrinkled his nose. "Not . . . what I want."

"Why do you think I'm giving it away?"

"I'll find something later. Thanks, though."

With a shrug, Laramie tore open the top and dipped in a spoon herself.

Wyatt studied her while she ate. Laramie was one of the most sarcastic people he had ever met. He knew it was her way of coping with stress, to diminish the deadly seriousness inherent in their business. But ever since Parrell, her tone had taken on an edge that usually wasn't there, as if she was trying a little too hard. He could only imagine what would be going through his own head if his family were at risk in the middle of some epidemic, with no way of knowing if they were safe. As tough as everyone was in his squad, they still needed someone to lead them, to keep them focused on the mission and what they could control.

For their sake, Wyatt had to keep it together.

This is all on you.

A clunking up the metal stair hanger announced the arrival of Chris from the warehouse floor. Prying into Laramie's state of mind would have to wait.

Chris glanced at the meal pouch in Laramie's hands. "Thanks for the rations, Staff Sergeant. We were getting pretty hungry. My boys and I weren't expecting to be out this long."

"Anytime. Glad you liked the curry." Laramie threw a sidelong glance at Wyatt, trying to hide a smirk.

"We have about two hours before dark. We should move out after that." Chris turned to Wyatt. "Before we do, I'd like to understand if we're sticking together or going our separate ways."

Wyatt leaned back in his office chair, squeaking the hinges. "Good question. I'm still not quite sure what to make of you guys."

"Likewise," Chris said. He folded his arms.

Did he open up to these new allies? Wyatt had been thinking about their next steps for the entire time they stalked from the scrub plains to their hiding place. He didn't doubt the military background Chris brought. His team knew how to fight. But what about their motivation? He didn't know anything about these supposed Marines except their words. Did he really buy their story?

Wyatt decided he didn't have much choice. He needed local support, and the card he had been dealt was standing across from him.

"We came to do two things," Wyatt said. "Secure the quantum gate. Then recon the system to get intel on why no shipping is leaving Alpha A. We're a RESIT team, and that's what RESIT does. You understand, Chris, when something disrupts interstellar commerce, it's a big deal. We're talking expensive stuff in transit and expensive vehicles to move it."

He felt his lip twist into a sour frown. "We bungled the first part. Still working on the second."

Chris leaned against a battered office desk. "How do you recon a system from the middle of space?"

"When you're looking at interstellar shipping, where else would you do it from?"

The loft turned quiet. A hungry Laramie fished through her curry meal pouch with clear reluctance. Chris stared out the window at the outlying cityscape. When he turned back, a silent struggle danced across his eyes.

"Something on your mind, Master Sergeant?" Wyatt asked.

"Yeah. Look, Lieutenant, I don't know what's going on *up there*. My guess, though, is that it all has to do with *down here*. All of it." Chris paused. "I think I can help you. Keep in mind, it's not altruistic. I help myself, too. I'm waging a guerilla war against an establishment that governs millions of people. I need stuff. So, I help you, and you help me. Interested?"

"I'm listening."

"If you're after intel, the best kind is the human kind. I know some people. They probably have all the insider information you could want. If they don't, they'll know how to get it. This police state, this . . . cleansing that's developed around us. It has to stop. So, I take you to them, you plead your case, and maybe you get everything you need to blast off and give your sitrep back to RESIT."

Blasting off was still a problem, but Wyatt would deal with that later. "That'd be great, Chris. What is it you want in return?"

"Two things. First, I need weapons and gear. Vests, helmets, Vectors. Chem mags. Everything you've got, handed over before you leave." Chris was gesturing as he spoke, his arm knife-handing the air. "Plus, I want your commitment to drop me a supply container from orbit within the next thirty days that has more small arms and ammo." He gave Wyatt a serious stare. "We need art supplies for our . . . art."

Wyatt scowled. "You've seen the size of my squad. Do you really think a couple small arms will make a difference?"

"When you live on a planet that's basically the wild frontier? Everything makes a difference."

There was no way Wyatt was going to disarm his troopers. Ever. But the opportunity for human intel was too good to pass up. He'd have to figure out how to renegotiate later. "I can't give you everything we've got, Chris, but I'll find a way to make it worth your while. And I can't turn over weapons until we're about to return to orbit. Fair?"

Chris studied him for what seemed like a long time before finally speaking. "Okay. I'm working on good faith, Lieutenant. Don't make me regret it."

"What's the second thing you want?"

The master sergeant took a deep breath. "When you leave, I have two passengers you need to take with you."

"You want us to *what*?" Laramie blurted.

Wyatt held up his hand to silence her. He turned back to Chris. "That depends on who and why."

"No, it doesn't. Nonnegotiable."

"You can at least tell me the details."

Chris's eyes flitted between the two of them. "I will. In fact, I'll let you meet them. But I want your commitment now, Lieutenant. Otherwise there's no point. I'm not asking this lightly and I'm offering you a goldmine of help. I need you to agree. If you don't like it, we can go our separate ways."

Wyatt shared a glance with Laramie. She had stopped eating.

"Okay."

Chris's eyes were burning a hole in him when he looked back. "Don't go back on this, Lieutenant. Do we have a deal?"

"Yes," Wyatt replied. *For better or worse.* "We have a deal."

"Good." Chris straightened up. "Then let's get started. My team has a safe house a few klicks from here, in the next district over. We'll take you there. Be ready to leave in ninety minutes, when it's dark." He looked around. "Remember, we're under martial law. There'll be a curfew. We'll have to move quick and quiet."

"Okay. Let's do it."

Wyatt watched as Chris gave him a nod and left down the stairs.

"Are you really going to give him our gear, LT?" Laramie asked. "You're making me one unhappy *chica.*"

"What else would you have me do? We're stuck here. Anything that gets us back closer to Thermopylae is progress."

"Maybe."

"Yeah. Maybe."

"By the way," she said, dipping a spoon back into her meal pouch, "I noticed you didn't highlight that our Javelin doesn't have its ascent booster. He has no idea we can't take his passengers anywhere."

"Not yet. That's need to know." Wyatt stretched his back. "By the way, any word from Teo?" he asked.

"No. Maya's still trying."

Wyatt nodded. They had had no contact with the Javelin since the train. The problem could be any number of things—weather interference, something wrong with their portable gear. He just prayed the silence wasn't due to some catastrophic failure.

Laramie folded the top of her meal pouch and shoved it into a leg pocket. Wyatt felt a flash of amusement. She was such a spacer—always stowing trash on one's person. The old joke was that if you didn't, garbage would float away and always get stuck in the most critical system at the most inopportune time.

"You know, we're sitting in a deserted warehouse," Wyatt pointed out. "You can just chuck that curry on the floor."

Laramie thrust her chin at him. "Have you ever seen how big a Julietan rat is?"

"No."

She flashed him wide eyes that said, *if you did, you'd understand*, and followed Chris's path down the stairs.

16

Nighttime approached, and Chris laid out the plan to head to the safe house. After a heated debate between him and Laramie over security protocol, they had a final meal and synched up their helmet communications. The good news, Chris explained, was that they would be sticking to side streets and less-traveled routes. The bad news was that the curfew patrols would expect this.

They set out an hour after dark. Finn, the Marine with the yellow helmet, took point. Chris came next, followed by Laramie, Gavin, then Wyatt and the others. Every Marine and trooper wore a CORE helmet with night vision enabled. Wyatt glanced at the sky and noted the thin crescent of Romeo nestled among hundreds of twinkling stars. He recognized a few of the constellations. Pegasus the winged horse. Cygnus the swan. Amazing that the distances between stars remained so great that constellations appeared the same as they did in Proxima, a fifth of a light year away.

The warehouse district had appeared deserted during the day hours. Dark made it even more so. The gaps between each building formed alleys that crammed power transformers and waste dumpsters together into a utilitarian lifeline. Wyatt marched quietly from cover to cover, pausing for a careful listen before following in the path of Laramie before him. The carbon-fiber panels that comprised the buildings' exterior facades lent an exotic, alien air to their trek.

Up ahead, Finn signaled for the column to stop with his fist.

"Team, halt," Chris said in a low voice through the comm.

Wyatt stepped to the side. Up ahead, he could see the greenish outline of Chris slowly working his way up to his point man. Finn had started to peek around a corner when he abruptly turned and dashed back toward the rest of the column.

"Cover! Everyone take cover!" the radio crackled.

A deep, throaty rumble echoed from somewhere in the distance. In the corner of Wyatt's helmet display, an orange threat indicator flashed as sensor telemetry came in from Laramie's position further up their column.

Wyatt winced when he realized he was standing in an empty stretch of alley with nothing but shadows for protection. He spotted a dumpster some five meters away and pushed off toward it in a sprint. Frantic steps and a quick dive sent the back of his helmet clacking against the lift handle. Maya came crashing into him a moment later in a desperate bid for the same cover.

The rumble disappeared for a moment before resurging in volume. Wyatt thought it sounded like a cross between a turbine engine and a growling lion.

"Stay low and still," Chris said. "*No* sighting lasers!"

The rumble turned more aggressive and Wyatt saw a spindly, olive-green vehicle sweep into view. Four outboard nacelles thundered exhaust that suspended a long, narrow body several meters above the street, whipping dirt and debris in all directions. A sensor pod was mounted on the front next to an autocannon. Through his helmet's sensors, Wyatt could see the rapid pulses of electromagnetic energy sweeping the area.

The vehicle moved out of view, but the lull in the noise didn't last long as a second one followed into the intersection. The new arrival paused, hovering above the ground as it searched for the scent of anything out of order.

Wyatt's teeth chattered as the dumpster next to him vibrated in the jet wash. Why wasn't this patrol leaving? Had they been spotted?

After what seemed like an eternity, the vehicle tilted forward and cleared out of the intersection. Wyatt waited a good thirty seconds before he stood up and edged out from cover. Maya remained glued to the dumpster.

"You can get up now," he said.

As if startled, Maya tried to push herself up in the heavy gravity. "Sorry, sir."

"It's okay." Wyatt grabbed her hand and hauled her to her feet. He blinked in surprise that someone so short could be so solid. "You doing all right?"

"Yes, sir."

"Good." He wanted to encourage her, to keep repairing her confidence after Parrell.

"What was that thing, Lieutenant?" she asked.

Chris was walking toward them and overheard. "Those were police Ibex. VTOL patrol craft. I don't think they saw us."

"Were those typical curfew patrols?" Wyatt asked.

"No. That was unusual. They don't scout the warehouses much. I didn't expect us to come across anything until we got to the residential areas." Chris looked over his shoulder. "I wonder if they're searching for whoever waxed their guards on the train."

"Yeah, what a bunch of jerks," Wyatt said.

Chris gave him a double-take. Then he chuckled.

"Right. Let's get back into our spread. We still have a lot of ground to cover."

Their column wound through streets and alleyways that zigzagged toward the city center. Floodlights occasionally swept their path and dispelled the safety of darkness. Wyatt noticed the industrial buildings gradually giving way to more commercial-looking facades, with brick-and-mortar walls, windows, and elaborate porticos replacing the drab and utilitarian carbon-fiber structures of the warehouse sector. He tried to keep focused on scanning for threats, but his mind wandered in wonder at how Venice must have evolved from the first settlers.

He opened a private channel. "Laramie. The buildings are different here."

"Yeah. Looks like middle-period architecture." Her voice had its own twinge of curiosity. "The early settlements all used cargo containers, like you saw in Parrell. Easiest thing to drop from orbit. Then that got replaced by brick and stone as colonists started using local building materials. The last thirty years have all been carbon fiber. You can see the fancy downtown stuff over there."

She pointed at a section of the sky to their right. Wyatt glimpsed a knot of tall skyscrapers visible through the gap of two squat stone buildings. They glittered in the night, with the illumination of decorative floodlights sparkling off their black skin.

"Ever been up in one of those?"

"My dad took me downtown a couple times growing up, before I enlisted. We went on a tour to the top of the Warren Commerce Tower." She walked silently for a moment. "Once was enough."

"Why is that?"

"Because I don't like heights. You know that."

"What? You—what?"

The blank visor of a CORE helmet turned back to look at him. "Wyatt. We've been over this."

"No we haven't."

"I'm sure we have."

"You served in the army!"

"Yeah. Doesn't mean I enjoyed climbing obstacles."

"You're a RESIT trooper!"

"Which is perfect, because there ain't no 'height' in space, LT."

"I just . . . I'm surprised by this. We've never had this discussion."

"Yes, we have."

"Not that I recall."

"Huh. Well, you have a crap memory."

They veered out of the alley and trudged quietly onto one of the larger streets, past a series of five-story shops and restaurants with ground-floor entryways. The night remained silent except for the chirps of exotic insects. Locked shutters covered dark windows. If someone remained in any of the buildings, they seemed determined to stay indoors and avoid the wrath of an Ibex bearing down on them. Wyatt thought it felt like another ghost town, like Parrell, only with no wreckage or bodies strewn about, and no dark shapes in the windows ready to burn away his mind with constriction.

This wasn't what he had imagined Juliet to be like. An amazing Earth-like planet, right next door to Sol in the cosmic neighborhood, ripe with resources and potential and life. The odds were astronomically against such a lucky find. Yet the city reeked of fear, as if the inhabitants regretted humanity's foray into interstellar colonization.

More city blocks. The construction style remained the same, but porticos gave way to entry vestibules and other signs of residential buildings. Each structure shared walls with the building next to it, creating rows of houses and shops that would have appeared as one if not for variations in paint and shutter styles.

Wyatt eyed the street with caution. His helmet fed him a green threat indicator through his neural stub but he wasn't quite sure he believed it. After all, the Ibex had appeared without warning. The constricted hadn't been aggressive, but then they were.

He opened another private channel. "Chris, we shouldn't stay exposed like this. I want to get off the street."

"Not much choice on this stretch. We need to cover half a klick north, and that's not the way the alleys run. When we cross the river, we'll get back to cover."

They passed more buildings and came to a substantial-looking bridge. Ten meters down, a wide river flowed briskly past them and churned against the pylons. Yellow sconces on the embankment fought in vain to illuminate stairs descending into the mist.

"Lieutenant," Chris called. "We head down the stairs here. A maintenance catwalk runs underneath the bridge, so stop at the first landing and swing over the rail."

"Copy that."

Finn disappeared down the stairs, then Chris, then Laramie. Wyatt switched his neural feed to the video from Laramie's helmet. The narrow metal staircase rocked back and forth with each trooper's step. Below the steps, a current slid by with swift menace. Wyatt noticed that Laramie had both hands on the stair rail, and walked at a slower pace than the Marine in front of her.

"Laramie."

"Yeah?"

"Don't look down."

A pause. "Not helpful."

Wyatt reached the stairs and climbed down to the first turnaround landing. The people in front of him were well on their way along the ricketiest catwalk he had ever seen in his life.

He had just hoisted himself over the rail when his leg practically exploded beneath him.

Agony dropped him face-first onto the catwalk. Every nerve, every muscle fiber seemed to contract at once with such force, it ripped the conscious thought from his mind like the rush of a mad river. His hands clenched the expanded metal of the grating, desperate to hold fast, filled with such tension that he was sure he would squeeze holes in the catwalk. The roar of the river filled his ears. The only thing that kept him from screaming was that he couldn't unclench his teeth.

He gradually became aware of his own breathing. At first he didn't know where he was, or why he was on his hands and knees. His arms shook as they held him up. The inside of his CORE helmet felt damp with sweat. Then he realized the anguish was no longer there. The pain was gone—but then, so was all feeling in his leg, the way a deafening noise could rob all sense of hearing.

Wyatt managed a glimpse at his prosthetic. His legs seemed fine. Everything looked normal, no big deal.

What just happened?

Clacking approached from behind. Wyatt turned to see Maya reach the landing. She paused to assess the catwalk, not noticing what had happened to her squad leader.

Wyatt tried to stand up but found his leg with the prosthetic wouldn't respond—not even the part of him that was still organic. He grabbed the railing and forcibly manhandled himself into an awkward, bent-over posture with his good leg. His sense of touch had fled from the artificial sensors wired into his nerves. His prosthetic was a dead weight, frozen into a half-bent position.

Maya swung over the railing behind him.

He couldn't let his troopers see him struggle. Wyatt grabbed the handrails and hauled himself forward to make room for the rest of the squad. A dull ache filled the dead space occupied by his leg. He had to figure out why he couldn't control it.

At least they were sneaking around undetected in the dark.

On cue, Wyatt's threat indicator jumped from green to orange.

"Ground patrol on the bridge," Chris said. "Everyone down."

Wyatt dropped to one knee—a ready-made pose, given his situation. He saw Chris and Laramie exchange hand signals. RESIT had a large vocabulary of gestures for use in the soundless environs of space, but Chris flashed some that Wyatt didn't recognize. Something specific to the Marines, perhaps.

He could hear the engine of a heavy vehicle on the bridge. It stopped with a squeal of brakes. A few more noises preceded a hatch opening.

Laramie turned back toward Wyatt. She made a V with her fingers and pointed at her eyes behind the CORE faceplate. Then she gestured above her head.

Okay, Wyatt nodded. Get eyes on.

Come on, leg. Work.

Laramie gave a thumbs up and waddled around Chris toward the stair hanger at the far embankment. Wyatt switched again to Laramie's video feed. He noticed this time she didn't look down.

At the stairs, she hiked herself over the railing and crept cautiously upward.

Wyatt watched as an armored personnel carrier with six large wheels came into view. The body had a heavy, sloping hull designed to deflect ground blasts. A 25mm rotary cannon sat atop a mounted turret, brooding and lethal.

This was the police? Wyatt thought it looked more like mechanized infantry.

The rear hatch had been popped open and half a dozen armed men milled about. Two figures lined the far railing of the bridge, facing away. Laramie zoomed in. One man seemed to be urinating off the side.

"Stretching?" Wyatt whispered to himself.

He clicked the comm. Laramie wouldn't reply verbally, but she could still listen. "Get a close-up on the vehicle," Wyatt said.

The video feed swept over the APC, recording dimensions for later analysis around armor thickness and speed. An exterior bulge next to the rear hatch caught Wyatt's attention.

"Go to that container housing on the back. What is that?"

Laramie zoomed in. Wyatt scowled as he realized he was looking at a drone pod.

This patrol carried a groundside version of what *Razor* had used on the freighter near the quantum gate. RESIT used it as a last-ditch direct-action weapon. But the housing on this one appeared worn and well-used.

Everything Chris had told them about martial law, curfews, and corralling infected citizens took on a new level of immediacy.

"Break's over, back in!" shouted a man's voice.

The armed figures filed back into the vehicle and pulled the hatch shut. A moment later the engine revved and the truck lurched into a steady pace across the bridge toward the warehouse district.

The noise faded around a corner. Laramie flashed a thumbs up from her observation point and the team silently finished crossing the catwalk to the other side.

Halfway up the far stairs, Wyatt's leg started to tingle. A moment later he found he could move it again. Whatever had caused his prosthetic to fry the wireless connection to his brain had mysteriously resolved itself.

At the top of the embankment, Wyatt tried to partition off his own problems and called Chris on a private channel.

"That group of police didn't look like they were directing traffic, Chris."

A few seconds ticked by without a response. Wyatt started to signal again when the reply came.

"They're not. That was an extermination team. But they're gonna wish they were just traffic cops when I'm done with them."

"Do you—"

"We're almost at the safe house." Chris sounded annoyed. "Let's get there before we run into any more distractions."

The remaining column filed out from underneath the bridge and returned to the cover of narrow back streets. Wyatt couldn't wait for their march to be finished. His leg seemed to be working again, but his entire body ached from the heavy gravity. Whatever was waiting for them at the safe house, he hoped it involved sitting still for a while so he could inspect his prosthetic.

Armed death squads. Airborne patrol vehicles. Military spacecraft quarantining the quantum gate. Chris's explanation of the government's plan made no mention of doctors treating the ill. No research on the nature of the infection. No scientists racing for a cure.

Wyatt bought into the existence of constriction. He had seen it in Parrell. Yet were these the actions of a desperate society battling a health crisis? Were the government's actions really focused on resolving the outbreak? To Wyatt, it seemed like dictatorships had risen from less.

"We're here," Chris said on the comm.

A series of five-story row houses lined the sides of another constricted street. The facades consisted of the same brickwork construction they had seen on the other side of the bridge but with more grime and a dingier appearance. Wyatt didn't see anything interesting or distinctive to draw attention. That must have been the point.

The Marine master sergeant turned to face the others coming up behind him. "We have a security protocol. Finn and I will go in first. Wyatt, when I signal for you, you come in. Then we can file in the rest a few at a time. Anyone who's waiting outside needs to keep out of sight. Sid will stay with you to help pull security. Got it?"

"Copy."

"All right. Let's go."

Laramie dispersed the troopers to the edges of the alley. Wyatt let his Vector drop against his harness but kept his hand on the trigger group. He followed Chris not toward the front door but to a utility cover hidden behind some bushy shrubs.

"Something wrong with the door?"

Chris chuckled as he pushed the cover aside. "Yeah. It's rigged to blow up."

"You seem to like explosives."

The Marine unlocked a metal door half-buried in the dirt. "You make do with what you have. Our team took a supply convoy full of it a couple weeks ago. We're short on small arms, but we've got plenty of boom."

The door opened to reveal a narrow ship's ladder-style staircase that descended into the dark ground. Even with his CORE helmet, Wyatt couldn't see anything in the confined area.

"Keep a couple meters between you and me, Lieutenant," Chris said, taking the first few steps. "These people know who I am. They don't know you yet. And they can have an itchy trigger finger."

17

Safe House
Juliet, Alpha Centauri A
23 February 2272

"Where have you been?" shouted a young girl's voice.

Chris engaged in a heated debate just beyond the door where Wyatt was told to wait. He couldn't see the participants, but the initial speaker sounded incredibly pissed off. The screaming gave way to sobbing. Another man spoke in a voice too low to hear. Then murmurs, followed in a subdued conversation that lasted nearly a minute.

"Lieutenant," Chris said finally. "You can come in."

Wyatt took a deep breath and pushed open the door.

The room had yellow walls, a large oval table in the center, and a cupboard full of dishes in the corner. Five people stood around the table. Chris hovered on the left. Finn stood next to him with a teary, preteen girl clutching his waist. A muscular Hispanic man filled the far doorway with a Vector aimed at Wyatt. A second man stood next to him, overweight and balding.

The pudgy man scowled at him. "So, you're the freaking hero that let the train get through?"

"Elton," Chris said.

"Fine. You want me to be nice, I'll be nice." He glared despite the words. "Elton Forrestal. Deputy Chief of Staff for Governor Hewitt. Or rather, was."

"Lieutenant Wyatt Wills. Havoc Company, RESIT."

"RESIT," Elton repeated, the word sour on his lips. "What, you guys finally turned on each other, too?"

"Wyatt's from Proxima. They aren't the guys who float around Juliet."

"Proxima?"

"Yes."

Elton looked Wyatt up and down, his face filled with obvious disgust. Without another word, he shook his head and shuffled out of the room.

Wyatt arched his eyebrow at Chris.

"You'll have to excuse him. It's been a hard couple of months." Chris's voice betrayed a new, sudden weariness. "Over in the doorway is Alonso—who will be lowering his weapon, thank you. You might remember Alonso from the train. He took the aerobike back after we stayed with you."

Wyatt and Alonso exchanged nods and relaxed their mutual posture.

"Over here," Chris continued, "is Calista, Finn's little girl. Not so little any longer, I guess. She was worried about us."

The girl stood behind Finn's back and eyed Wyatt through strands of black hair. Wyatt guessed she was maybe thirteen.

"You're from Proxima?" she asked.

"That's right."

"Why?"

"They're here to help, Calista," Chris answered. "We'll talk more about it later. Let's let the rest of them get inside."

She seemed to accept this answer. Wyatt wondered privately what defined *help*.

Over the next ten minutes, the remainder of Wyatt's squad filed into the house. Chris vanished to talk with Elton while Finn took over as host. Finn explained they had a number of safe houses around the city that they used to stage raids and smuggle key people to safety. Their current location was nice and quiet, and the neighbors rarely cared what went on so long as it didn't involve gunfire. But the police were relentless. The Marines had established multiple defensive positions on the roof, first floor, and basement. The front door was wired to blow to hell anyone who tried a forced entry.

Finn showed them to a bedroom that was so crammed with mattresses, it might as well have been a giant trampoline. "You can crash here. I'm sure you guys must be beat. I'll ask Calista what we have to eat."

"Thank you." Wyatt looked around at the mattresses. "You have a lot of guest beds. How many of you are there?"

"Enough to cause trouble. We're just one cell. There are more." Finn scratched the reddish stubble on his chin. "But you saw the patrols. We're getting killed off, slowly but surely."

Wyatt studied the Marine. Deep-set brown eyes stared back from a sea of freckles. Finn stood a little shorter than Laramie but had the same stocky build.

"You're from here, aren't you? From Juliet."

"Born and raised."

"Is the rest of your family safe?"

The hesitation betrayed the answer. "Get some rest, or whatever it is you're going to do. I'll check on you in a bit."

A moment later, Wyatt and Laramie were alone.

"What do you think?" she asked.

"I don't know. You?"

"They know how to fight, I'll give them that. But I've been watching them. Chris seems like one of those guys who's angry at everything. You know the type. Sooner or later they lash out, do something stupid."

"Like kidnapping?"

Laramie gave him a careful nod. "Governor Hewitt is the most powerful man on the planet. Are we really falling in with the guy who filched his daughter?"

Wyatt thought for a few moments. The last thing they wanted was to draw attention to themselves on a covert recon. But he also didn't feel like they had other viable options inside a foreign, unfamiliar city. Laramie was a country girl. His RESIT team was trained for space operations.

Without help, they would stick out like a sore thumb.

"We're pretty far out of our element, Laramie. We need to go with the hand we got dealt."

"Let's just be careful, LT."

"No argument there. Set up a rotation for security—with our guys. Two at a time, on our own comms."

"On it." She looked at him again with an odd look. "You should grab some sleep, LT. You look like hell."

"I'm sure we all do." No sooner had he said the words than a wave of weariness fell over him. The heavy gravity tugged at him. Wyatt shook his head, trying to make the feeling pass.

Laramie wouldn't have any of it. "It's okay, Wyatt. I'll get our guys set up. Someone's got to take the first nap shift. It might as well be the boss man."

"No," Wyatt started.

"Really." She gave him a stern look.

The yawn crept out of his mouth before he could stop it. "All right."

"This may be the first time you've ever listened to me."

It was a sign of his exhaustion that Wyatt couldn't remember making a wisecrack back.

***

A field of stars twinkled across the night sky. Wyatt marched over a shallow hill to find a sandy beach, gentle waves rolling to the shore from Lake Michigan. He loved coming here at night, free from the city lights and bustling noise and constant motion. The lake meant escape. Peace. Wyatt popped off each shoe from the heel and pressed his bare feet into the cool sand. It caressed his skin, crawling between his toes, clinging to his feet with each step he took toward the water. When he drew a deep breath, the humid air carried the tang of sea life mixed with the scent of the swaying grasses that clung to the nearby dunes.

Home.

He walked toward the water. The tiny waves poured onto land only to tumble back into the lake without a chance to sink in. Wyatt closed his eyes and listened to the harmony of life and nature. He wished Sara could be here. He could still taste their last kiss from saying goodbye, the salt deep in his lips. Why wasn't she here?

The waves crashed, and Wyatt knew immediately from the frothy aftermath that something was different.

He opened his eyes to a harsh glare that made his stomach drop. The lake had turned black, save for the alkaline foam that floated across the surface. Proxima peeked over a horizon of the broken salt flats and banished the gentle stars with angry flares. The green sea grasses were now the stunted dark weeds of Tiamat. Wyatt felt his face contort with disgust.

The air burned. He turned to move away from the water and felt his feet on fire. Then his ankles, his leg. His leg. *He watched in horror as the sand reached up around his calf like the tentacles of some ghastly octopus. Chemical burns blotted his skin before the flesh tore away in tiny strips. Wyatt's leg disintegrated to the bone, only the bone wasn't white, but rather charcoal gray and stainless steel, studded with mounting points for false muscles and the lies of being whole.*

The ground rushed up, and Wyatt realized he was down on all fours. His body felt so heavy. Elbows wavered under the increasing strain until they suddenly buckled. He fell face-first into the dirt, smothered, unable to even turn his head and take a desperate gasp of oxygen. Then his hips gave. As he lay crumpled against the ground, the crushing fist of gravity squeezed his lungs against his spine and forced out the last of his breath in a hoarse cough. Here he was, a broken half-man, who had rejected friends and family, lovers and comfort, to hurl himself into a repulsive and lonely existence at the mercy of alien planets.

Why?

Wyatt knew he was going to die. The pain, the suffocating weight that bore down on him, left no other end.

At the edge of his vision, two shadowy figures glared at him from next to the wreckage of a burning

Javelin. The first one raised its hand and pointed an accusatory finger at him.

"What do you see?" thundered Major Beck's voice.

"Death," Wyatt grunted. "Pain."

The other figure pointed next. "What do you see?" asked Father Bradley.

"God."

The shadows took a sideways step and became one, their voices joining into a single chorus. "It is the same," they chanted. "It is the same."

Helpless, Wyatt felt the despair flow into his heart.

"It is the same."

Sara . . .

18

"Lieutenant."

Wyatt's eyes popped open. The stars, Proxima, all of it was gone. A lone discoloration from water damage on the ceiling was all that looked back at him.

"Over here." Chris's silhouette stood in the doorway.

He sat up and swung his legs off the bed. His skin felt clammy, his hair damp. He glanced at his prosthetic calf, wondering what agony lurked behind its virtual neurons, waiting for him.

"Everything okay? You were making noises."

"Yeah."

"Can't say that sounds convincing." Chris entered the bedroom but didn't sit. "I brought Elton up to speed on our discussion about getting some human intel. If you're ready."

The truth was Wyatt felt far from ready. But he had learned long ago not to hesitate when it came to accomplishing key elements of a mission. Time killed all things.

He followed Chris down a hall to another room, but this one was configured as a kind of armory. Half a dozen Vectors lined the walls next to a longer-barrel L-6 Viper variant and ARC vests pockmarked from laser blasts. A small carbon-fiber folding table had been set up in the middle with two chairs. Elton waited behind one of the chairs, holding a small tablet computer in his hands.

"Are we gearing up?" Wyatt asked.

"No." Chris sat on one of the chairs. "There are just not a lot of places in this house you can have a private conversation."

"And this does need to be kept private. Even from the others," Elton said.

"Okay."

Wyatt seated himself and did his best to ignore the pain of emptiness in his stomach. Elton remained standing. The deputy chief wore a rumpled dress shirt and gray slacks that looked like they'd been slept in. Dark circles surrounded his eyes. He didn't seem like the friendly sort.

Elton cleared his throat. "Master Sergeant Thompson explained to me a bit more why you're here. You're doing recon from Proxima because interplanetary shipping stopped. Is that right?"

"Yes."

"And you got shot down? That's how you landed on Juliet?"

"Something like that."

Elton nodded. He gave Wyatt a long look. "You stumbled into a hornet's nest, son. Do you know what's happening here?"

"A little, from Chris."

The deputy chief shot a disapproving glance at the master sergeant. He placed the tablet on the table.

"Tell me what you see."

The tablet had an old digital screen that preceded holo monitors by a good twenty years.

Wyatt saw a video still of an older man with a goatee, sitting upright on a hospital bed with his legs swung over the side. The hospital gown had fallen off his shoulders and drooped toward his belly. He didn't seem to notice or care.

"Looks like a patient."

"Yes. This is actually one of my staffers," Elton said. He used his fingers to zoom in on the man's face. "See anything unusual about him?"

Wyatt leaned forward. The man in the image stared into space like he was focusing on something that wasn't there.

"His eyes look funny. His pupils are really small."

Elton spoke from behind his shoulder. "The unofficial name for it is *constriction*, since, as you've pointed out, the most telltale sign is your pupils constricting down to a pinpoint. There isn't an official name."

"So what happens to him? He just sits there?"

"At the beginning. When someone comes down with this, they become very lethargic. They lose the ability to communicate. Soon after, they don't recognize you anymore. What's really happening during this time is the constriction is busy destroying who they are. Everything you might have known about someone—their personality, their identity—it's slipping away. At the end, there's a resurgence where an infected person wakes up and becomes active again. That's when their eyes ratchet down. And all they care about from then on is finding another person to infect."

Wyatt thought back to Parrell and the piercing gaze of the colonists. The shower of golden sparks that filled his vision. The burning pain and the vague sense of his consciousness slipping away.

"Who did your staffer catch if from? Did he know he was infected?"

"You mean, were there symptoms he should have recognized? No. That's probably why it spreads so quickly." Elton shook his head. "How do you notice something's wrong when it's your own mind that's fading?"

A hundred questions flooded Wyatt's mind. Their squad had come very close to those people in the rec facility in Parrell. Had *he* been infected? Had Izzy? Were they going to turn into vegetables like the staffer in the video? Wyatt had so much he wanted to ask, but something told him to keep the questions to himself. He didn't really know how Elton and Chris would react. They had only just met, and Wyatt's mission was too important.

"Help me understand something," Wyatt said finally. "It seems to me a quarantine would be the right thing to do. Not the murderous kind Chris described. One that separates the infected from the healthy until a cure can be delivered."

Fatigue washed through the deputy chief's eyes. He turned to Chris and let out a huff. "*This* is why this is a waste of time."

"Elton," Chris said. The master sergeant's voice remained level. "It's a reasonable question. You need to educate."

The room fell silent. Elton seemed annoyed, as if Wyatt had touched on a raw nerve that had long been burned out. The deputy chief finally turned back to him and clamped his hands together.

"Originally, Governor Hewitt had the same idea," Elton said. "But where do you draw the line? It's contagious. *Very* contagious. How do you know who the carriers are when they're early stage? Are you going to let the police drag away your *child* to what's basically going to be an extermination camp, based on a suspicion? Or a brother? A parent? Quarantine is a death sentence. I'm sure we're just a bunch of foreign objects to you, Lieutenant. You're a spacer. But tell a Julietan rancher you're going to tear apart his family? He'll put a blast hole in your forehead."

His voice dropped to a whisper. "And so, people guess wrong. A wife protects her husband. A brother protects a sister. When the constriction hits, they'll know it was a mistake. But it's still your loved one. Maybe someone you've built your entire life around. You watch as that person slips away, gone forever. Then the next thing you know, your husband, your sister, your whoever—their sole purpose becomes hunting you down so that *you're* gone forever, too. I don't know if that sounds frightening to you, Lieutenant. Let me tell you, it is."

Wyatt glanced over at Chris. The Marine watched him, gauging his reaction.

"Look," Wyatt said. "No disrespect, I'm just trying to understand. Do you know what causes it?"

Elton shook his head. "No. We haven't been able to figure that out. Not from a lack of trying. There've been more autopsies than I care to count. So, with no understanding of what we're dealing with, Governor Hewitt's policy shifted from cure to containment." He looked over at Chris. "General McManus had a very brutal interpretation of that word."

"So I've heard."

"Martial law. Execution squads using 'proactive selection.' Family members torn out of each other's arms."

"And you decided you weren't onboard with that."

"Not just us. Secretary Chavez ran the Office of the Interior and opposed the plan. Hewitt jailed him. General Hu, the Security Undersecretary, attempted a coup. He was executed." Elton suddenly appeared very weary. "The Governorship exists to protect our citizens, Lieutenant. Not eradicate them. But Governor Hewitt is utterly convinced he's doing the right thing and is pursuing it with fanatical zeal. Those of us who didn't agree were going to have a very short shelf life."

Wyatt weighed the story. What level of depth would RESIT want? At a tactical level, neither

Wyatt nor his team had observed any of these events. Important elements always got left out with each passing on of information. And for a response plan that would encompass political, economic, and social initiatives to ensure the well-being of millions of citizens? They'd need more. Much more.

"Thank you for sharing all this," Wyatt said. "I'd like to ask you something. Would you be willing to go with me back to Proxima?"

The familiar look of distaste crept back into Elton's face. "I'm not going anywhere, Lieutenant. If you think I'm going to turn my back on people who need my help, you're out of your mind." He waved a hand dismissively. "I wouldn't be that much help to you anyway. I can talk about a lot of things at a high level. But if you want hard intel, you need someone who knows the details."

"And who would that be?"

Elton and Chris shared a long glance.

"Jack Bell," Chris said.

"And who is that?"

"He's the Chief Analyst at the Department of Health." Elton rubbed his hands together. "You need to understand. Everything Hewitt is doing right now is based on interpretations of how to combat constriction. Bell's team is the group collecting, analyzing . . . *controlling* that data. Get him, and you'll be able to understand all the drivers around what's happening down here."

"All right. How do we contact Mr. Bell?"

Chris stood up and folded his arms. "With a punch to the face and flex cuffs."

"I take it he wouldn't be cooperative, then."

"Depends how hard that punch is."

Wyatt thought he understood. "You want to do a snatch-and-grab. Kidnap a government official. That's not exactly what RESIT is about."

"I thought the *I* stood for *Interdiction*?" Chris asked.

Elton leaned over and put his hands on the table. "Our planet is falling apart. The government is acting illegally, beyond its established powers, to actively harm its citizens. You can put aside any reservations about your own team's boundaries, Lieutenant. If your mission was to recon the situation and bring back intel, this is the only approach to do it in any meaningful way."

Wyatt remained silent. His mind spun through the implications.

Kidnap a state official.

Utilizing a temporary alliance with Chris and his rogue faction was one thing. Asking Wyatt to become a collaborator was another. It had court-martial written all over it.

Did he really believe what Chris and Elton were telling him?

He looked at Elton. The irritation the deputy chief wore belied an earnestness in his voice. A man in deep pain, he had exiled himself rather than act in an illegal and immoral way. If he had an ulterior motive, something to gain other than what he had disclosed in his story, Wyatt couldn't figure out what it could be.

A soft knock thumped on the door. Chris got up, opened it a few centimeters, and spoke with someone in the hallway. "Excuse me for a minute," he said, and left.

Elton still hovered over the table. "What's it going to be, Lieutenant? You say you came here to solve a major problem. So far, I'm not impressed with your conviction."

"You don't seem to like me very much."

The deputy chief stared at Wyatt with tired eyes. "It's not you personally, Lieutenant. It's all of you outsiders. You don't live here. You don't understand who we are, what we had to go through to tame this planet. Julietans are a proud people. Hardy. Clever. Self-reliant." His face softened slightly. "Asking for help is not something we do."

"You're asking for more than help," Wyatt said. "We're talking about taking them hostage."

Elton gave him a long, hard look.

"Chris tells me when you first came through the quantum gate, you said you came under fire. One of your spacecraft crews got killed?"

Wyatt felt his face sour. "A RESIT ship used a boarding drone on a freighter trying to run away. That's not the way it's supposed to work. Lethal force is a last resort."

"We're already at the last resort, Lieutenant. If what's happening here were ever to leave Juliet . . ."

The Deputy Chief left the room, leaving Wyatt alone with the implication hanging in the air.

19

Wyatt found Laramie in the front room sitting cross-legged on the floor. She had a ceramic bowl cradled in her hands and was eating. Again.

"Strange to see you giving up your field rations."

"I do like other things, you know."

A tangy smell hit Wyatt's nostrils. "What is that, anyway?"

"It's called *meesh*. Venetian noodles. I grew up on this stuff." She slurped a spoonful into her mouth.

His stomach reminded him that he still hadn't eaten. "Mind if I try?"

Laramie pulled the bowl away and put her hand over the top.

At first Wyatt thought she was kidding around. The look at her face revealed genuine concern.

"What, seriously?"

"It's spicy."

"I like hot food."

"No." She frowned while trying to come up with the right words. "It's full of silicates. Not Earth spicy. Juliet spicy."

Wyatt stared blankly, not understanding.

"Silicates are in everything here. Crops, grass. Herd animals. Remember the harpoon grass with the barbs on the end? Extreme example. All those particles stay in the food. It'll tear up your insides if you aren't used to it."

"Wait. You're saying you're basically eating ground-up glass fragments?"

"Yep."

"No wonder you're so sweet." He arched an eyebrow.

She flashed a huge fake smile before tucking back into the bowl. "How'd the meeting go?"

"Looks like we're gonna do a little snatch-and-grab."

Laramie stopped her spoon in midair. "Oh?"

"Yeah. I'll tell you more later. How are our guys doing?"

"Kenny's on security. Did I tell you I like him? He's sharp. The rest are fed and crashed. Which reminds me, there are *mild* noodles in the kitchen if you want them. The pot with the red handle."

"Red handle, got it."

Laramie resumed eating. "Want some more good news? We can't recharge our helmets."

"What? Chris said we could use anything here."

"It's not that. Their gear is too old. The connectors they have don't fit ours. Wrong version."

Wyatt rolled his head back and released a groan. Unbelievable. Normally they'd charge up on the Javelin. That wasn't an option right now. And if the batteries ran dry on their helmets, they'd have no night vision, no assisted targeting, no comms.

"How much juice do we have left?"

"Yours was at forty percent. Mine, a little less. Everyone else is about the same range."

"Can't you rig something to make it work?"

"No idea how to do that, LT."

"Any word from Teo, then?"

"Not since the train. Starting to miss that *chico*."

"Yeah."

Wyatt hoped again it was just a comm failure. He didn't relish the idea of peeling off a couple troopers for a search party to find their Javelin. They had too much to do already.

"You know," Laramie said, a sheet of noodles hanging off her bottom lip. "We could daisy chain our helmets together. Charge up some at the expense of others. We'd end up being short a couple, but the ones we did have would be topped off."

Wyatt didn't like the idea of half his team without a key piece of gear, but they couldn't afford to lose their eyes and ears altogether.

"Do it. Drain mine. Keep yours. Buddy up everyone else. I'd rather have something than nothing."

"I'll get it done, LT."

Wyatt watched her some more. "I'm sorry we can't check on your folks."

He regretted the comment instantly. Laramie's chewing slowed as her eyes took on a glassy, distant quality. Not what he was going for. He was trying to show support. Now, all he had done was remind his squad sergeant of the danger her relatives might be in, while they did a recon under covert conditions.

After a moment, she just gave him a nod.

Wyatt's stomach threatened a full-on revolt, so he excused himself before he could put his foot in his mouth again. He went to the kitchen and took a bowl from the drying rack. Two large metal pots sat atop a conduction stovetop. The one with red handles was considerably emptier.

"I was wondering if you'd had a chance to eat," a voice said behind him.

Chris grabbed an empty bowl for himself and dipped a ladle into the pot. He served Wyatt first. The aroma of strange herbs wafted through the air and made his mouth water despite the unfamiliarity.

"Utensils are there." Chris pointed to a drawer. "Eat as much as you like. You never know when you'll get your next meal."

Wyatt stirred the stew-like mixture and slurped up a mouthful of vegetables and noodles. The taste of something that hadn't been freeze-dried made his eyes roll back into his head. Ecstasy.

The two men ate in silence. Wyatt went back for a second bowl while Chris cleaned his in the sink. The master sergeant folded his arms and watched him eat.

"I'm sorry you guys got pulled into this mess," he said.

"Why do you say that?"

"Because it's not your fight." Chris glanced off to the side of the room. "You were on a recon mission about space freight."

"You don't know much about RESIT, do you?"

"What do you mean?"

Wyatt snorted a laugh and put down his bowl. Chris didn't look like he understood. "Space is a big place. Pretty unforgiving. You can die quickly, wouldn't you agree?"

"Sure."

"And if you're in trouble, a lot of times you can't wave your hands and cry for help. RESIT's *mission* is to look for trouble. We make things our fight. We stick our noses into places whether people want it or not. Every single one of my troopers is wired that way. No sheep. Only shepherds."

Chris rubbed the stubble on his chin while his lip curled up. Green tattoos of ancient battles covered his forearms.

"Okay." Chris shrugged. "Marines are the same way. Most people run away from gunfire. We run toward it."

"Where were you deployed?"

"Lots of places. Mars. Africa." His smile slid away. "Mongolia."

"Oh. I've heard stories."

"Yeah. Bad place. China, North Korea, Russia—two hundred years of nonsense that finally came due. That's what happens when you don't address a problem. It just festers."

"Truth. How did you get to Juliet?"

"I guess I just had enough of Earth politics and all the crap. I emigrated. Less people. Less games. Most of your energy just goes into surviving, getting things done. A much simpler life." He let out a sarcastic laugh. "But not anymore."

Wyatt nodded. Weren't his reasons the same for joining RESIT? He had no desire to go back to Earth and its overwrought complexity. For him, fulfillment came from outer space. Solitude. Survival. Such focus was cleansing.

If only his parents could accept it.

"I won't pretend to understand everything you're going through, Chris. But I get it. I'll help however if I can."

The master sergeant looked thoughtful for a moment. "Come with me. It's time you met someone."

The two men walked down a short hallway to a stairwell at the back of the house. Chris led him up a flight and down another hallway until they stood outside a bedroom door. He rapped on the doorframe with his knuckles. When there was no reply, he turned the knob and pushed his way into the dark interior.

"Annika?" he whispered.

Wyatt followed him in. His eyes adjusted as Chris sat down on the edge of a single bed. A small figure was tossing and turning under the sheets. The master sergeant put his hand gently on its side.

"Annika," he repeated.

A small girl popped up from the covers.

Wyatt guessed she was no more than seven or eight years old. She looked at Chris with confusion for a moment before flinging her arms around his neck. Chris hugged her and made shushing noises.

"Hey, it's okay. Another bad dream? It's okay."

Wyatt sighed. It seemed there were enough bad dreams to go around.

Chris drew back from the little girl and turned toward Wyatt. He spoke softly next to her ear. "I have a guest here, Annika. Can I introduce you?"

The girl peeked over Chris's shoulder through tangled brown hair. Her eyes swept over his RESIT uniform until they rested on his name tape.

"Hi. I'm Wyatt. Pleased to meet you." He waved at her, but the girl just stared at him.

"Wyatt's a friend," Chris said. "He's here to help keep everyone safe. You're going to see him and some of his soldiers around for a while. They're all dressed like him, so they're not strangers. Okay? You understand?"

Annika finally pulled her eyes off Wyatt. She gave Chris a nod before throwing her arms back around his neck.

Wyatt straightened back up. He felt indecent, like he was somehow intruding on what should have been a private moment.

Chris rubbed the girl's back. "I woke you up. You want to go back to sleep?"

Annika nodded before finally letting go. Chris turned on a small lamp on the nightstand that struggled to fill the room with a weak light. He made a show of tucking her back into the bedsheets and whispering reassurances. Then he led Wyatt back out into the hallway and shut the door.

"That's Annika Hewitt," Chris explained. "The governor's daughter."

Oh.

"She's very young. Why did you kidnap her?"

Chris frowned and motioned for Wyatt to follow him a few meters down the hall. "*Kidnap*? No. Well . . . no. Call it protective custody."

Wyatt just watched him. Chris grew pensive.

"We were part of a coup, Wyatt. McManus was giving illegal orders. He told General Hu to exterminate innocent people because *their relatives* might have constriction. That's crazy. I swore to protect people, not murder them. We had to stop it. Unfortunately, we lost."

"How does Annika come into this?"

"Part of the plan included securing Hewitt and his family. This was supposed to be a political maneuver. We didn't want them to get hurt. I divided the security detail into squads and assigned them to different people. I had the governor. After his Saturday security briefing, we pulled him into a room with Hu and placed him under arrest. Hu had orders ready to cascade down to his guys to secure other key personnel. But General McManus was onto us. I don't know where the breach was in Hu's op sec, but before we knew it, there were soldiers assaulting the compound."

Chris's face turned dark. "McManus is a bastard. Anybody they suspected of being involved, they shot them. They didn't discriminate. They didn't care about collateral damage. One of my squads had Hewitt's son in tow, Wyatt. Brouard. He was ten. There was a crossfire . . . McManus's guys . . ." He looked down at the floor.

"I'm sorry."

"Yeah." He took a deep breath. "Annika was with her mother. I had a team that was supposed to secure them, but they got engaged en route. I left Hewitt in custody and went to reinforce them. We pushed the government troops back, but when I got to Annika, I couldn't get her to leave. Her mother had been real sick, Wyatt. You know what? It turns out *she* had constriction. Can you believe it? Here Hewitt is, ordering death squads into the city, and yet he's doing the very thing that he claims is so dangerous to the state?" Chris cursed with a few choice words to punctuate his disgust.

"What did you do with the mother?"

"We left her the hell alone. I sure wasn't taking her with us. But we got Annika out. Obviously."

"And what about Hewitt?"

"Yeah." Chris snorted in disgust. "McManus came in force, stormed the room where we were keeping the governor right after I left. The decision to go get Annika probably saved my life. Cost my Marines theirs, though."

Chris glanced back toward the bedroom. His eyes stared into nothing with a look Wyatt recognized well.

"I've spent two years of my life watching after the Hewitts, Wyatt. They weren't just some assignment to me. They were family. I still have trouble processing all this madness."

The hallway stewed in silence.

What a mess.

"How much of this does Annika know?"

"She knows her mom was infected. That's traumatic enough. She doesn't know about her brother getting killed, or the blood on her father's hands. There's no good that can come of it."

He took a few steps toward Wyatt until he stood almost uncomfortably close. "Annika's one of the passengers I need you to take away from here, Lieutenant. Her, and Calista, and Finn. Finn won't like it. I'll have to order him to go. But they deserve better. It's bad here. It's bad, and it's going to get worse."

20

Over several days at the safe house, Laramie helped Wyatt and Chris sketch the outline of how to abduct Jack Bell.

The RESIT team had experience snatching injured crew from damaged spacecraft just in the nick of time, so no shortage of ideas there. Elton provided the insight around staffer schedules and movement patterns. Chris planned the tactical approach using satellite maps and his local knowledge from his role as head of security.

Now they needed to case the area in person.

They decided on three teams of two, each with a trooper from RESIT and someone who knew Juliet. Chris and Wyatt formed the command element. Carlos and Sid, one of Chris's Marines, made the second pair. Laramie and Kenny were the third even though they were both RESIT. That suited Laramie fine. Even though she was a country girl, she knew her way around Juliet, and she didn't quite believe all the lines Chris and his team kept feeding Wyatt. She'd be happy to stick to their own for this patrol.

In any event, their flexibility with manpower was about to get worse. Wyatt desperately wanted to find Teo and the Javelin. So after much thought, he decided to send Gavin and Rahsaan on a scouting patrol outside the city. They prepared immediately to head out with one of Chris's aerobikes.

Laramie saw Gavin off at 0400. "I want an update when you make contact. Location, status, and mobility. Make sure all transmissions are encrypted. Got it?"

"Yes, Mom. We've done this before."

"I know. It's still my job to make sure you morons don't get killed. Do a comm check."

Laramie pulled one of the few operational CORE helmets over her head. Gavin switched on his mike. "Check, check," he said. "Battle One Actual, over."

"Acid One reads you. Over."

"Copy."

Laramie removed her helmet. "Good comms. Be careful, Gav."

Gavin frowned, his face becoming serious. "I will, Laramie. Relax. We'll find them."

Laramie and the other observation teams prepped for their own departure at 0450. Everyone traded in their tactical gear for the urban camouflage of local garb. Chris and Sid tried to guide the RESIT troopers around how to best mimic current Julietan fashion using the small trove of mismatched clothes they kept at the safe house for disguises. Wyatt donned a business suit that his narrow build didn't quite fill. Kenny picked some trendy clothes worn by the young crowd. The other troopers did what they could so they wouldn't stick out.

Laramie found a set of field trousers and a gray rancher's tunic. She pulled them on, along with a work poncho that made her feel like she was back home.

Chris made a quick inspection to make sure nothing looked unnatural. His eyes stopped on Laramie. "You didn't want the cocktail dress?"

"Master Sergeant Thompson, there aren't enough cocktails to get me into a cocktail dress."

"Huh."

Laramie stopped cold, one boot on her foot, the other in her hands. She glared at him watching her. "I ain't one of your girlfriends, jarhead."

Chris put his hand up. "Fair enough," he muttered, and moved to inspect the next trooper.

When the team had finished prepping, they assembled in the front room of the safe house.

"Okay, ground rules," Chris said. "RESIT guys, this isn't outer space. People will be watching. *Cameras* will be watching. Don't draw attention to yourself. You're just regular Venetian citizens going about your business. Relax, act like you belong here. Blend in.

"We've already reviewed mission objectives. You each have your coordinates for your observation posts. Take video footage of your assigned areas around the Department of Health complex. Pay close attention to ingress and egress, police strength, any fixed positions. That's what we're going to have to deal with on our next mission.

"Use these to keep in contact." Chris handed each of them a small earpiece that clipped around the earlobe. "Audio is via bone induction and will pass along everything you say—no *Send* key. The transmitter clips to your belt. All teams are to provide sitrep updates in fifteen-minute intervals.

"The city curfew isn't over until 0600. Stick to cover and stay out of sight until then. Any questions?"

Five faces looked back at him, silent.

"Then let's get rolling."

Chris and Wyatt left first. As Laramie waited for her team's turn, she passed the time by worrying over her partner, Kenny.

"You ready for this, kid?"

"Yes, Staff Sergeant."

"We'll take turns grabbing the video when we get into position. You'll go first while I watch our perimeter."

"Yes, Staff Sergeant."

"I grew up here, so just follow my lead."

"Yes, Staff Sergeant."

Laramie lobbed more orders at him as she mentally worked out the details of their route. Kenny was a boot trooper on his first deployment. So far she thought he was solid. But how old was he? Twenty-one? Laramie had just turned thirty. What a world of difference nine years made in the experiential learning of one's life. She wondered how solid this kid would be under fire. Would he panic? Fail to shoot straight? How would he adapt to a recon mission under heavy gee when his limited training had concentrated on inspection and boarding actions in the weightlessness of space?

She searched his face for uncertainty, any twinge of fear, but found only focus in a pair of youthful brown eyes. Everything would be fine, she told herself.

When their turn came, they exited through the basement ladder and hiked through a succession of deserted streets and alleyways. The air felt cool and reminded Laramie of growing up on her family's ranch, waking early to tackle the boatload of chores that came with country life. She loved being outside before sunrise. The crisp air, the solitude, with only Romeo looking down from the sky for company. She glanced up. The brilliant white of the moon peeked back through the rooftops like an old friend playing hide-and-seek.

She laughed to herself. *A friend*. She may live and work in space, but Juliet was home. She hoped whatever they learned on this mission would help protect it.

Dawn came and dispelled the chill around them. By 0700, Laramie and Kenny had slipped into the hustle and bustle of metropolitan commerce. Men and women wearing business suits passed service workers in utilities as everyone rushed to their place of work. Electronic billboards flashed tailored advertisements at the passing foot traffic. Aerobikes and wheeled vehicles mingled with the foot traffic pushing its way through intersections.

It was as if a hidden gate had opened and suddenly disgorged the lifeblood of a city populace.

It almost seemed perfectly normal.

Almost.

Police teams were set up at every major intersection, filled with armed men in riot gear who watched carefully into the crowds. Ibex patrol craft circled overhead with a distant whine. She even saw another extermination team activating the drone from their APC, terrifying any passersby as it tromped toward the street on mechanical legs made for heavy gravity.

Laramie could feel the anxiety from the people around her. Downcast faces moved past them a little too quickly and with a wide berth. Men wearing the clothes of tough, blue-collar professions threw nervous glances at the police patrols. Even the street vendors seemed tentative as they called out to grab a bowl of stew, extra noodles, extra spicy.

At the corner of one intersection, she pulled Kenny close as they waited for the vehicle traffic to stop. "Everyone seems really nervous," she whispered. "Try to act the same."

Their eyes met, and Kenny gave her a small nod.

At 0720, they reached the target location for their observation post. Laramie dipped into an alley and spotted a fire escape hung on the side of an old masonry building. They needed to get to the top.

"Give me a boost, Kenny."

ESCAPE VELOCITY

The lance corporal laced his fingers together and with a great heave lifted Laramie by her foot. She grabbed the telescoping ladder and pulled it down to ground level.

"That was easy," Kenny said.

"Yeah. Need to teach these people a thing or two about keeping their buildings secure."

They climbed the fire escape, flight after flight, until they reached the top of the fifteen-story building. Laramie glanced below to make sure no one had seen them, then swung her body over the top of the ledge. Kenny plopped down a moment later. They crouch-walked across the rooftop until they came to the far edge.

"Battle One in position," she said, her earpiece transmitting her report to the others.

"Copy."

"Chemo copies."

Across the street, Laramie looked down at a fat, ten-story building with a sleek carbon-fiber structure. Some kind of landing pad for aerial vehicles perched atop the roof. She slipped a pair of binoculars out from underneath her poncho for a better view. Kenny moved alongside her with a small digital video recorder.

Her heart sank. The police had built a substantial fortification around the building. Razor wire stretched around the perimeter under the watchful gaze of heavy weapons set up in reinforced positions. Manned checkpoints straddled the main entrance. Inside the wire, Laramie saw a service road that seemed to lead to a garage underneath the main structure. An APC with an open drone cover idled off to one side.

"Wow," she whispered.

Kenny said, "Maybe that's why they don't care about the fire escapes."

"Acid One, any ideas why security's so tight?"

"Name it," Chris's voice crackled. "Constriction. Protestors. Saboteurs."

"Saboteurs like you?"

"Huh. Yeah, like me."

The morning wore into midday. Laramie and Kenny watched a guard shift at 0930 and another at 1132. Foot patrols walked the block every ten to fifteen minutes. Laramie saw the police carried L-6 Vipers, which had better accuracy and kill power than RESIT's stubby Vectors. The police obviously wanted to keep people away.

At 1448, a sudden flurry of activity at the checkpoints caught Laramie's attention.

"Kenny, get the video going."

A light truck with a square blue cargo pod drove up to the fortifications and stopped. One of the guards approached the driver and motioned for him to lower his window.

"What's that? A delivery truck?" Kenny asked.

"Looks like it." Laramie peered through her binoculars. The driver appeared calm, like this was just a routine route and no big deal. He handed credentials to the guard.

"Get a close-up of the driver."

"Yep." Kenny rested the video recorder on the railing to keep it steady.

The checkpoint guard reviewed the documents. Then he handed them back and waved for another guard to raise the barricade. Laramie could barely hear the engine rev up before the truck lurched forward and rolled slowly toward the underground garage.

"That was interesting," Laramie said. "Acid One, did you see the delivery man?"

"Affirmative, Battle," Wyatt replied. "We didn't get a good view of the security challenge."

"We have it on video."

"Good job. Keep your eyes open."

"Copy."

At 1519, Kenny took the binoculars while Laramie tore into a meal pouch. It took one whiff for her to realize she must have grabbed the wrong one. She scowled for a moment and forced the spoon into her mouth. Another bite and she couldn't do any more.

"Kenny, you want this?"

"What kind is it?"

"Cheese and veggie omelet."

No hesitation. "No."

"You sure?"

"Yes."

"I thought you were hungry?"

"Wouldn't matter if I were starving. Hey—that truck is leaving."

Laramie peered over the ledge just in time to see the barricade open. The truck slowed but didn't stop as it exited the perimeter. One of the guards appeared to be yelling at the driver, tapping his wristwatch in an exaggerated, scolding motion.

"That cargo box was green. Didn't it go in with a blue one?"

"Yeah, it did," Kenny said.

"Huh. They must bring supplies, drop them off, then haul off the empties." She thought for a moment. "How long did they spend in there?"

"About thirty minutes."

Thirty minutes to unload and load. That seemed like a long time to just change out cargo boxes. Apparently the guard felt that way, too. But they had tolerated it. The wheels in Laramie's head started spinning.

"Acid One, Battle One. What floor are the target's offices on?"

A moment of silence before Chris answered. "Six. The big conference room is on seven. He'd probably be on one of those two floors during most of the day."

Half an hour between entrance and exit. Would that be enough time?

"Okay," she said, "I have the beginnings of a plan."

"God help us," said Wyatt's voice.

"Hey, if you have something bet—"

"Chemo One is on the move," came a low, terse voice. Carlos.

The hairs on Laramie's neck stood up. No one was supposed to displace until 1600.

"Copy, Chemo," Wyatt said. "What's your status?"

"We have a tail."

21

Department of Health Campus
Juliet, Alpha Centauri A
26 February 2272

Kenny glanced in her direction.

Laramie scowled back at him, pointed to her eyes, and snapped her wrist back toward the Health Department building. Watch the target. They still had a job to do, at least, until they didn't.

She pulled out a dog-eared street map Finn had given her. A moment later and she had it unfolded to the square that showed their immediate area. "Chemo. Call your position as you move."

"Copy. We're on Fourteenth, walking south. Sid is in front and picking the route." The words were careful, almost a murmur.

"Who's following you?" asked Chris's voice.

A few moments passed with no response. "Two men. Black tactical gear."

Laramie found Fourteenth Street on her map. Moving south would take them close to her observation post. Chris and Wyatt were on the other side of the compound. She wondered what happened to have attracted attention. Sid was a native. He knew his way around the streets and would have worked hard to avoid being compromised.

"Can you tell if they have radios?" Chris asked.

"Unknown. Turning left on Palazzo."

Laramie raised her head and peered over the ledge at the guards working the Health building perimeter. They had dark vests and closed helmets. They didn't seem any more alert than before. Had one of them noticed a stranger casing their building?

"Palazzo leads to Alexandria Square," Chris said. "It's near the end of lunch. Sid—lose them in the crowd."

"Copy," said a different voice. Sid's.

"Kenny," Laramie hissed. She pointed to their flank. "Alexandria is that way. See if you can get eyes on."

"On it." He hurried to the far railing with binoculars in hand.

Laramie listened to the tense silence, staring at the street map, visualizing Sid and Carlos threading their way past busy citizens hurrying back to their offices. She suddenly felt very over her head in her knowledge of the big city.

"Entering the square," Carlos said.

"Staff Sergeant?" Kenny's voice had a tinge of alarm. "I have eyes on Alexandria. An APC just parked at the far edge, the right edge."

Great.

"Did you get that, Chemo?" Laramie asked. "APC on the . . . east edge of the square."

"Copy," said Carlos.

Kenny was counting quietly to himself, but the comm picked up every word. "Troops unloading from the vehicle. Six. Seven. They're fanning out, Staff Sergeant. Active patrol."

"Acid to all elements, we are scrubbing the mission. Displace and evade. Do not return to the safe house until you are sure you are clear."

"Acid, Chemo, they are still on us." Carlos's breathing was heavy, as if they were running an obstacle course. "Turning on Magellan."

"How many pursuers?" Wyatt asked.

"Still see two."

"Staff Sergeant." Kenny had turned ninety degrees and was looking off the adjacent edge of the building. "The APC from the Health building is loading up. Looks like they're getting ready to roll out, too."

Laramie looked over the ledge and watched half a dozen police in full tactical gear board the armored truck. She glanced down at her paper map again. Magellan Street ran diagonally away from the Health Department. It was parallel to Alexandria Square. She could see the pincer move in her mind. If the agents trailing Chemo kept providing radio updates on their position, Carlos and Sid would be cut off.

"Chemo, Battle," she said. "You need to take out that tail."

"Say again?"

"Belay that," Chris's voice interrupted. "Your orders are to escape and evade. Battle, you too."

Laramie cursed their lack of understanding. "We have eyes on reinforcements from two APCs. They're going to get encircled."

"Your orders are to *escape and evade*."

Laramie looked over at Kenny. He wore a grim expression, fully aware of the danger Carlos and Sid were in.

Her lips twisted into a snarl. "Carlos, *elimina los que te están persiguiendo o no habrá un después*."

"*Afirmativo, chica*."

Kenny stared back at her, puzzled.

She glared hard at him until he got the message.

Chris's voice filled the comm. "Say again, Battle?"

"Battle is displacing. Out."

But the truth was, they weren't running. They were engaging.

They hurried down the fire escape. Laramie thought briefly on the irony of knowing Spanish. Many ranchers in West Hadensville were descendants from Mexico. She'd learned it growing up in the fields. Her first boyfriend was third-generation Mexican. But no one expected a tall, blonde tomboy from Juliet to speak it. It was her little secret.

But Carlos knew. And he was in trouble.

The alley at the bottom remained clear, but the absence of contact didn't make Laramie feel better. She hoped the crowds might frustrate the tail. But she also didn't have any illusions about how quick civilians would be to scramble out of the way of armed police.

"Moving off Magellan," Carlos said. His voice was low, still out of breath. "In the alleyway by the red dumpster."

He was signaling where they were going to lay their ambush. She hoped Sid was onboard. Carlos had no doubt made it clear what he intended, but that didn't mean Chris's Marine would disobey his boss.

Laramie set the pace for her and Kenny. The back streets were largely deserted save for blue utility cabinets and the smell of trash. They had just slipped past a power transformer between two old brick buildings when Kenny let out a stifled cry. Laramie turned to see a rat the size of a small cat scurrying across the pavement.

"Did you see the *size* of that thing?" Kenny asked.

"Heavy gee makes 'em bulky. Come on."

They rounded the back corner of what appeared to be a bank. Laramie's earpiece suddenly filled with the sounds of a scuffle.

She started running and came to Magellan. Throngs of people flowed past the maglev track in the center of the road while a mass transit train squawked *Stand Clear* warnings to their left. Laramie scanned the crowds but didn't see any hostiles.

More struggling noises. Laramie thought she heard Carlos growl.

"Hurry!" Laramie hissed.

"There, to the right," Kenny said. He pointed at a side alley and a barely visible dumpster in the distance. A red dumpster.

Laramie darted through the crowd, barley dodging a businessman in a peach-colored suit who was clearly paying attention to his neural stub instead of where he was going. She leaped over the safety railing that bordered the maglev track. The dumpster sat fifty meters ahead, beckoning. She hurried past more pedestrians, desperate to close the distance.

A cry of pain filled her earpiece. "No, don't—"

Laramie heard the dual echo of a laser shot from both the alley and her earpiece. She broke into a sprint. As soon as she reached the dumpster, she slowed down and drew the pistol from underneath her poncho. Around the corner she could hear more noises, grunting. *Thumping*.

She peered past the edge of the dumpster. In another side alley, two policemen were hunched over the ground pummeling something with their pistol butts. Both wore ARC vests, their heads protected by open-faced helmets.

Fury filled her.

The space between them collapsed. Laramie launched herself through the air until she was suddenly upon the police officers. She brought down her own pistol butt square on the exposed cheek of the closer one, connecting solidly and shattering bone. The officer immediately fell to the ground, dazed.

The second man, momentarily confused by the sudden attack, moved out of striking distance and locked eyes on Laramie's pistol. He lurched forward with a massive bear hug and staggered her backward, pinning one arm to her side. Laramie barely kept her footing and almost toppled over. But she managed to keep her right arm free and delivered a vicious elbow into the officer's throat. He coughed a horrible, wet croak and his arms slackened. A head-butt to the bridge of his nose released his grip altogether and sent him to his knees.

She wheeled around just in time to see Kenny deliver a boot to the first man's face. He went down flat. Thinking that seemed like a good idea, Laramie put her own foot into the bear hugger's nose and he went down as well. She kicked away the pistol that fell out of his hand.

Her ears roared with her own heavy breathing. When she finally looked around, her heart sank to her feet.

A crumpled heap that used to be a person lay a few meters away. Kenny knelt next to him, his hands resting lamely on an unmoving arm. Laramie knew why he wasn't taking a pulse. She could see the fresh steam from the laser hole rising from Sid's neck.

A pitiful moan next to her snapped her out of her daze.

"Jesus Christ."

The police had beat him brutally. Laramie grabbed his tunic and pulled him into a sitting position. Carlos let out a moan of anguish, his eyes rolling in random directions as they meandered on the border of consciousness.

"How bad?" she asked.

The sergeant's eyes were scrunched shut. "Ribs . . ." he grunted.

The radio of one of the police officers crackled. "Orange Team, do you have control of the suspects? Over."

Laramie smacked Carlos's cheek hard. His eyes snapped open.

"Can you walk?"

He struggled with the concept before giving a stilted nod.

"Help me," she said to Kenny.

They each took an arm and hauled Carlos to his feet. His face contorted into a parody of itself, agony spilling forth from the unrestrained beating he had endured moments before.

Laramie wrapped Carlos's left arm over her shoulder, propping him up. "Kenny, you're on point. Ten meters. Carlos, act like we're boyfriend and girlfriend. We've had too much to drink and you need to hold on to me. Got it?"

"Uh-huh."

Carlos leaned heavily against her as he clutched his side. He didn't even attempt a crack about playing lovers with his boss. Not a good sign.

"How do we get out of here?" Laramie asked.

Kenny's eyes darted from alleyway to alleyway. "We have to get back on Magellan. These back paths loop back around and are all dead ends."

"You're sure?" Laramie didn't like the idea of merging back into the main thoroughfare.

"I spent a lot of time looking at those maps."

"Okay. Let's move."

Kenny went to the end of the side alley and peeked around the corner. He beckoned them forward. Laramie forced Carlos to walk with her and followed Kenny onto the main road. They stumbled with every step, and Laramie struggled to steer him. At least their intoxication act would be convincing.

They wove through a maze of people and emerged into a temporary clearing next to an aerobike. Kenny dodged a food cart vendor who had just packed up and veered off the sidewalk into him. The sudden altercation caught the attention of a number of passersby.

"Kenny," Laramie whispered so that only her comm would pick her up. "Slap the cart hard and yell *eeyah*. Do it now."

The young trooper stared at the vendor, a stout, balding man a third of a meter shorter. Even from a distance, Laramie could see the blatant disregard in the vendor's face.

Kenny made a big windup and smacked his hand on the plastic shell covering the food bins. "Eeyah! Eeyah!"

The vendor jerked his head back. His expression changed to annoyance as he muttered a curse and turned his cart. The other pedestrians quickly lost interest and refocused on scurrying past the watchful eyes of security officers.

"Can you explain to me what I just did?" Kenny muttered on the comm.

"You told that bastard to watch where he was going. Slang for *eyes up*. Otherwise you'll draw attention for not acting tough. This is Juliet."

"Got it, Staff Sergeant."

"*Shhh*. Call me that again out here and I'll stomp your guts out, Kenny."

The young trooper kept walking, staying ten meters ahead. He looked back over his shoulder. "I see police way behind you. At least four. They're moving fast, on foot, like they're on a mission."

They stumbled further down Magellan. Most of the civilians ignored them, eyes down or absorbed in their own agenda, universally unconcerned with a drunk couple who had apparently enjoyed a very early trip to a bar. But one couple, a young man and a woman dressed in casual garb, slowed their pace. The man's eyes flicked between Carlos and the approaching police detachment shoving citizens aside.

His eyes went to Laramie. He stared.

Laramie flashed him a lecherous grin. "Buy me a drink? We could make this a group thing."

The young man seemed to actually consider the offer. The woman with him turned red. An angry slap snapped him out of the fantasy and they quickly hurried on.

"Yeah, I didn't think so," Laramie smirked. "You're all mine, Carlos."

The mention of his name made Carlos stagger. He almost went down to the ground. It took everything Laramie had to hold him on his feet.

"Come on, buddy, you can do this."

Pain tortured Carlos's features as he tried not to gag.

"Blue Team, status," a police radio crackled over the crowd.

Laramie focused on the simple act of hauling Carlos along one step at a time. He was heavy and unbalanced. She hoped their drunken show was a convincing ruse. Nothing in the RESIT curriculum taught active camouflage, let alone disappearing into a mass of tough-love Julietans bristling under martial law. This was all her. The art of blending in was a personal skill honed during teenage years filled with filching drinks, racing aerobikes, and dodging the law. God help her if she couldn't get this act right.

A series of shrill whistle blasts sounded from behind them.

"Maglev coming," Kenny said. "Do we get on?"

"How close are the cops?"

"Close."

"Do it."

Kenny veered to the elevated platform that straddled the middle of the street. Carbon-fiber awnings extended from vertical poles to shield pedestrians from rain and sun. Laramie followed, propping Carlos up against a pole that helped anchor a city diagram.

The mass transit train slowed to an eerily silent stop underneath the awning. When the doors opened, Laramie took the lead and dragged Carlos along with her. The interior of the passenger car showed the wear and tear of heavy use, with bits of trash discarded on a blue-black rubberized deck. She plopped Carlos on the seat vacated by an older woman who had just exited the other side. Then she sat down next to him and watched Kenny board along with half a dozen other passengers.

The sliding double doors remained open.

Come on, Laramie thought. *Let's go.*

Outside the car, an authoritative voice erupted on the platform. "Stop! Do not leave!"

She glanced down the length of the train car and saw multiple passengers turn their heads toward the shouting. Kenny was holding on to a hand loop and looking back at her. His eyes mirrored her own thoughts. *Not good.*

On a hunch, Laramie turned her body around and sat across Carlos's lap. He grimaced as she pulled her knees up and draped her arms around his neck.

"Huh, wha—?"

"Shhh, boyfriend," she whispered.

He stared at her, not understanding. But Laramie couldn't be bothered to explain. She only had eyes for the door.

A heavyset figure in a police uniform and tactical vest stepped onto the train.

Laramie's blood ran cold. She stole glances at the faceless visor of a CORE helmet sweeping across the passengers. No doubt his helmet cameras were scanning faces against some kind of registry. The officer moved forward to make room for a second man behind him. Both of their hands rested on the service weapons on their hips.

The lead officer walked slowly down the aisle, his helmet evaluating the passengers. Some looked back with restrained indignation. Others stared at the floor or into space. None tried to hide, though.

She lifted her head in feigned curiosity, pretending their arrival was a small inconvenience to cuddling with her lover. She tried to keep her expression as bland as possible.

The officer stopped directly in front of them.

For an agonizing moment, Laramie wondered if the cops they subdued in the alley had somehow tagged Carlos. Even if that were true, would their central headquarters have been able to process and distribute a digital face match so quickly?

Someone further down the train coughed. The policeman continued to stare through his visor. Laramie's heart beat madly in her chest.

Then the officer's attention abruptly shifted to the passenger next to Carlos. And then the next.

Laramie held her breath as the police went down the aisle and checked the remaining passengers. They stopped near the door and looked back down the compartment.

A long, tense moment passed. Then they stepped off the train. The doors sounded a warning chime and slid shut.

Laramie turned her head and saw Kenny still standing next to his hand loop. He seemed paler. As the train began to slide away, she was reasonably sure her complexion had him matched.

22

Safe House
Juliet, Alpha Centauri A
26 February 2272

"You didn't follow orders. You were supposed to evade the police, not engage!"

Chris slapped his hand down hard on the table. Laramie flinched as the carbon-fiber structure wobbled back and forth. Their Marine host was absolutely pissed. Wyatt watched her from a few meters away with his arms across his chest.

"Engaging was the only option," she said matter-of-factly. "Their tail was radioing in reinforcements. We watched two APCs dispatch with police. It was just a matter of time. The *only* possible choice was to take out the men transmitting Carlos and Sid's position."

"No." Chris's face was a light shade of crimson. "We've done this game before with the cops. We know what we're doing. I gave you orders and you willfully disobeyed them, and now one of my men is dead, *Staff Sergeant*."

Laramie couldn't believe what she was hearing. Was he trying to pull rank? "And one of mine was beaten within an inch of his life. They'd both be dead if I'd let them follow a bad call."

"They'd both be alive in this safe house! This is my turf. I'm the one that knows how things work here."

"I've lived longer here than you have, pal."

"On Juliet? Sure. In Venice? Hardly. Check your ego, Staff Sergeant. It's clogging your ears."

Really? Check my ego?

"You weren't there, Chris. Kenny and I were—we had eyes on the whole net closing around them. It was the only possible choice. Even Sid knew it. He obviously went along with the plan to lay an ambush."

Chris's expression darkened. "Sid stopped because *your guy* stopped. He wasn't going to abandon him. That doesn't make it good judgment."

"And what would you have had them do?"

"Hide!" he exploded. His voice was very loud, and the outburst made Laramie take an involuntary step back. "There are literally a thousand places to duck into and disappear. We do it every time. It works *every time*. Sid knows the drill, but *you* preempted his ability to do his job, Staff Sergeant."

"I disagree. You weren't there."

Chris stiffened. They locked eyes, and Laramie could see the anger behind them. When he stepped around the table and started toward her, it was all she could do to hold her ground.

He stopped next to her, standing well into her personal space and glaring down at her.

Laramie forced herself to keep eye contact. Her stomach was twisting into knots.

"Sid had a family," he said softly.

The words, the change in volume, caught her off guard. Unsure of a retort, she stared back while the silence stretched out.

Chris finally stepped back. He turned and threw a cold look at Wyatt. "Lieutenant. My team can't work with people who won't coordinate with us. The deal's off."

Wyatt blinked. "What?"

Chris had already yanked the door open and was storming into the hall. Wyatt gave Laramie an alarmed glance and went after him.

Alone in the meeting room, Laramie's mental defenses fell away like discarded pieces of junk. She collapsed into a chair and clutched her stomach.

She had made the right call. She *knew* it. She and Kenny had watched the police deploy additional forces into a giant net. Carlos and Sid were going to get flanked, cut off, and then captured or killed. Or maybe Carlos would be sitting in an interrogation room right now, pumped full of drugs as multiple detectives worked him for information.

The *only* chance they had was to keep the initiative and silence the cops calling in their position. It had been a calculated bet. But it had been the best choice of any of their poor options.

Hadn't it?

The deal's off, Chris said.

Had Laramie just botched their entire mission?

Wyatt needed intel. Chris had made an offer to help secure a high-value target. If they were able to get back through the quantum gate, RESIT would be able to question this health analyst and develop a response plan for the crisis unfolding around them. And the clock was ticking.

Now Chris had withdrawn his proposition.

What now? Maybe he'd throw them out into the street, tell them they were on their own. What would that mean for Carlos? They had pumped him full of painkillers to help with six broken ribs. What would it mean for Izzy getting help?

She already knew what it meant for Sid. Laramie closed her eyes, the guilt swelling up inside.

Sid. She hadn't dealt with him in but a few small interactions. He had a friendly face, a bright smile. White teeth that blazed against dark-brown skin. Tactically competent. A former Marine, like Chris.

Now she thought of Chris's last words. Sid was gone. Who did he leave behind? A wife? Children? Why weren't they here, like Finn's daughter? How would they find out that Sid was gone, lost to a stupid altercation with a couple of trigger-happy thugs masquerading as police?

The door opened. Wyatt stepped inside and closed it quietly behind him.

Laramie stood and shifted back into business mode. She made a quick dab at her eyes and hoped it looked inconspicuous.

"You okay?" Wyatt asked.

"Yes, sir."

Wyatt gave her a disapproving look. She knew he didn't like the formality. He pulled one of the empty chairs from the table and sat down.

"I have faith you made the right call, Laramie. It was a tough decision."

She said nothing.

He paused for a second, considering her. "I wouldn't be here today if you couldn't make tough decisions."

"Yes, sir."

"Stop that."

Laramie turned her head away. Her eyes were starting to sting again.

"I talked to Chris, spun him down. We're still a go. Take a couple hours and unwind. Eat. Rest. We'll get back together at 0700 and start planning the op."

She gave him a nod. "Yes—" She cut off the *sir*, realizing her voice might buckle. Now her throat was getting tight. What the hell was wrong with her?

Wyatt got up and walked to the door. He seemed to want to say something more to her. But perhaps thinking it was best just to allow her some space, he gave her a sigh and a nod and excused himself.

Laramie remained at attention in the middle of the room, suddenly alone except for the thoughts of Chris yelling, Carlos in pain, and a dead Marine whom she'd barely had a chance to know.

***

Annika sat at the dining table and focused on her bowl of meesh. It was hard to ignore all the yelling. Chris could be scary to lots of people, but to her he had always been big and cuddly. Not now, though. The whole house shook when he stormed down the hall and slammed the door behind him. That Wyatt person had been running back and forth between rooms ever since, looking as worried as Annika felt.

It scared her to see Chris like that, red and loud and ready to smash things.

The meesh was too hot. Annika swirled it around with her spoon and blew across the top. She didn't really feel like eating. Her hands were shaky and her head seemed to hurt all the time. She didn't even want to play with Calista. All she wanted to do was sleep.

Wyatt came back out of the meeting room again and gently shut the door. He seemed to be calmer, relieved. Annika saw him look over at her and give her a tired smile. Was he the one that Chris was mad at? She looked back at her bowl of food, suddenly self-conscious.

Footsteps let her know that Wyatt was walking toward her. She stole a glance just as he pulled out a chair and sat on the other side of the table.

"Hi there," he said.

Annika's breath went across the meesh and flipped over a green herb sitting on top.

"A lot of shouting, huh?"

She nodded. Yes, it was.

"I understand if you didn't like it. I didn't like it either."

Okay, she thought.

Wyatt lowered his voice. "Does he get angry a lot?"

Annika kept staring at the table. Sure, Chris got mad. All of them did. They had to hide and sneak around all the time. But that was their business. Not some outsider's.

Wyatt leaned over the table toward her. "It's okay. Grown-ups can argue a lot. It doesn't mean we won't work it out."

Annika moved her spoon around some more.

"You don't say much, do you?"

No, Annika thought. She tried. But ever since the night they left home, words just wouldn't come out.

What a terrifying night. Explosions rocking their house. People with guns, shooting in the halls. Annika ran to her parents' bedroom even though her mommy was sick, lying there in bed for days and days. Somehow, she knew mommy would still protect her.

And she'd been right! Mommy heard her come in and looked right at her, her beautiful eyes inviting her to come close, the little golden fireflies dancing around like a wall that would surround her and keep her safe.

She's been so close to being safe forever. Annika remembered how wonderful and warm she felt as the fireflies did their dance, making their nest that would live inside her and protect her forever. Nothing would be able to hurt her. Not the guns. Not the explosions. Not her own muscles, shaking and tight.

Then, before the fireflies could finish, Chris had come and dragged her away. No safety. No nest. Just an empty, half-finished dirt clump.

Thinking about it made Annika start to cry. Tears welled in her eyes and she raised her chin to dry them. She noticed Wyatt again, sitting across the table, watching closely.

She took a deep breath and tried to be brave. Annika lifted her chin and met his gaze. His face seemed friendly enough. Kind blue eyes. He had tinges of gray in his dark hair.

Wyatt gave her a smile like grown-ups did when they wanted kids to feel better.

Part of her wanted to smile back.

But she knew. She could see the little scabs in his mind. They were like pockmarks on the street after a heavy storm, with bits and pieces of rock left behind that made it hurt to walk on the surface with bare feet.

Wyatt had met the fireflies, too.

They had tried to hurt him.

They tried to hurt anyone who didn't let them build their nest.

23

To evade security and gain access to the Health Department, Wyatt, Chris, and the rest of the team would rely on a trick that dated back nearly to prehistory. A Trojan Horse.

Laramie had hatched the idea. Supply trucks made deliveries every two days, with some variability in schedule and route taken. They would ambush one of the deliveries and commandeer the vehicle. Then, after chucking the supplies from the cargo container, their team would climb inside and drive into the garage just like they were making the normal supply run.

Chris and Wyatt decided on three fireteams of two people each. Finn and Maya made up call sign Chemo and would control Building Ops, cutting any alarms and allowing them to use the security equipment to locate Jack Bell inside the building. Laramie and Kenny were call sign Battle and were responsible for securing the garage—and their escape route—once they made it inside the compound. Finally, Wyatt and Chris comprised call sign Acid and would be responsible for the actual abduction. They would *secure Dr. Bell's cooperation*, as Chris put it, escort him to the garage, board the truck, and drive back out with no one the wiser. From building entry to egress would take less than thirty minutes. Shipping and Receiving wouldn't even have time to swap out the outbound container.

When it was time to go, Wyatt assembled their patchwork team in the living room of the safe house. The troopers and Marines jostled burly shoulders and bristling weapons to make room for themselves.

"You all know what we're about to execute," Wyatt began. "We're going to infiltrate a high-security area and forcibly remove a High Value Target. This person has intel that may be vital to the future of Juliet. Now, several of you grew up here. Some of you immigrated here. Others, like me, were brought here under orders. Our branches of service are different, some Marines, some RESIT. It doesn't matter. We're all here now. We're all on the same team. We're all obligated to make this happen. If we don't, we leave twenty million people to a choice between an epidemic disease or a totalitarian regime. That's not an option.

"We will attempt to accomplish this task with stealth. I will be honest with you—this may get ugly. As valuable as our target will be to us, he is equally valuable to the current government. We may be met with significant resistance. If that's the case, everyone needs to be prepared to fight. We must have faith that our cause is true and we must not hesitate, for our own sake, and for those around us.

"We're only going to have one shot at this. If we fail to capture the High Value Target, we will be hunted down. If we do not execute the extraction plan, we will be hunted down. Stay switched on. Our lives may depend on it."

Wyatt looked around the room. "Any questions?"

Much to his surprise, not a single hand went up. He glanced at Laramie and Chris in turn, each of whom gave him a level look.

"Then may God help us," he finished. "Get ready to move out."

The teams looked over their weapons and did a final comm check. Wyatt noticed Chris kept wearing a smirk, like something was funny. "What is it?" he asked.

Chris cinched up the laces on his boot. "Nothing. Just that little bit about God at the end."

"Not your thing?"

"No."

Wyatt picked up his Vector. "We don't have to have the same beliefs."

"It's not about belief."

"What do you mean?"

"Study your history. Religion isn't about salvation. It's a tool for oppression."

"I was praying to God, not to a religion."

"Same thing."

Wyatt shook his head. "Maybe after we get through this, we can share theology over a couple beers."

"I might have been open to that once. A long time ago." Chris finished with his boot and gave him a sanctimonious smile that said *you poor, dumb fool.*

Wyatt felt a flash of disappointment as he watched Chris walk away. If anyone needed some reassurance of a higher power right now, he was sure it was the master sergeant. He hoped Chris could find someone to help him with his anger.

Wyatt hoped he could find the strength *he* needed.

The teams readied to leave and pulled on rancher ponchos to help conceal their tactical gear. At 1007 hours, they exited the safe house and hiked along alleys and back streets toward the Health Department compound. Foot traffic was light, and the only police presence they saw was an Ibex VTOL patrol craft circling high above the rooftops.

An hour later they reached the staging site for the supply truck ambush. The old brick building had previously been a popular restaurant. Now it sat abandoned, its owners and clientele long since evicted as part of a martial cleansing of the neighborhood. Broken glass littered the street in a final rebuke of the police action.

Wyatt managed to shove aside an old utility panel that had been used to fill a busted window front. They climbed through the opening and found a dimly lit dining area. A few of the tables were tipped over and damaged. The majority still had place settings spread out on patterned tablecloths that waited for noontime diners who would never come. A large antique bar filled the side of the room with a giant mirror behind it, amazingly still in one piece.

"Dragon One, this is Acid Two, do you copy?" Chris said on the comm.

"I read you," Elton's voice crackled from the safe house. "Are you in position?"

"Affirmative. Your signal's weak."

"A lot of storm clouds overhead. They must be interfering with our roof transmitter."

"Copy that. Do you have eyes on the street?"

Wyatt listened as Elton gave a rundown of multiple intersections and side streets. They didn't know the exact route or timing of the next supply delivery, but the Marines had long ago hacked into the city's traffic camera network. Now Elton acted as their analyst from the makeshift NOC back at the safe house. So far, no sign of the truck.

"Is Acid One on the line?" Elton asked when he was done.

"I'm on," Wyatt said.

"You'll be happy to know your team found your spacecraft. They made radio contact right after you left."

Relief swelled inside Wyatt's chest. "Outstanding news. What's their status?"

"En route to the city outskirts as we speak. Your pilot said something about casualties, but I don't have the details."

Chris's head turned toward him, watching carefully.

Wyatt took a deep breath. "Understood."

He wondered what happened, who was hurt. But Wyatt knew he would have to wait. He needed to stay focused in the meantime.

Elton began a regular update of vehicular traffic on each of the monitored routes. Chris pulled on his jet-black CORE helmet and watched the camera feeds firsthand through his neural stub.

Wyatt couldn't figure out how the Marines made the networking all come together—multiple systems, different protocols, any number of hacks to get access. Then it hit him. The word POLICE traced the jawline of Chris's helmet in faded letters. Chris had a law-enforcement helmet that would allow native access to the traffic camera network. He wondered suddenly if he hadn't given the Marines enough credit for staying ahead of the government with their resistance efforts.

"That's interesting," Chris said out of nowhere.

"What?"

"A hunch. Alonso's running the perimeter on an aerobike, and he thinks he may have found our inbound supply delivery. I'll go check it out and contact you if it's our guy. Otherwise, no point in risking all of us moving around in the open."

Chris and Finn took off down the street and left the others behind in the abandoned restaurant. Suddenly idle, Wyatt sat down on a chair near the window and pulled out one of the precious few paper street maps they had of the city.

A noise caught his ear as Kenny rummaged behind the bar. He picked up a glass and one of the fountain guns. "Too bad the drinks are turned off."

Laramie glanced over from the far wall. "It figures they shut off everything before they boarded the windows—*whoa*. Is that bar made out of *wood*?"

Kenny rapped on it with his knuckles. "Sounds like it. Why?"

Laramie shuffled across the room and spread her hands over the bar top, caressing the surface in amazement. "You don't see wood here, hardly ever."

"Why not?

"Because there ain't no trees on Juliet, Kenny. Lots of different grasses and stalky-things, but no trees."

Kenny cocked his head like a dog that heard a strange noise. "Juliet doesn't have trees?"

"No."

"What about paper?"

"Grass pulp." Laramie rested her cheek against the bar, eyes closed, a wide smile forming on her lips. "The import tariffs on this must have been huge. Oh my God, this is neat."

Wyatt eavesdropped on the exchange as he traced routes on his folded street map. Paper manufactured from grass pulp. He thought of harpoon grass and shrugged away the image of a paper mill worker getting shredded to death as he cleaned out some giant machine.

Two uneventful hours went by. Each of Wyatt's troopers took turns keeping watch by the window. Kenny eventually found a carbon dioxide bottle in storage and Maya helped him get the fountain drinks running. It didn't take long before all of them were exceptionally hydrated. Wyatt visited the restroom twice.

"Everyone, this is Dragon," Elton's voice crackled. "Confirming we have eyes on our supply truck at Gervais and Marconi, heading northwest. Acid, if they keep going straight, they'll be one block east of your position in about three minutes. Over."

"Roger." Wyatt held his map out, studying the nearby intersections. "Chris, did you copy?"

"We copy."

"Can you get us a blocking position at Gervais and Cleese?"

"Affirmative, on our way."

"Let's go, people."

The team grabbed their gear and hustled back out to the street. Wyatt set a quick pace, passing abandoned vehicles and empty buildings and wondering what happened to the people who had once lived there. The intersection where they would spring their ambush lay two long blocks from the restaurant. They had to hurry if they were going to intercept the truck.

"Truck is now at Gervais and Zapata," Elton said.

Laramie pulled on her CORE helmet, which gave her voice a clearer tone on the comm. "How much further, LT?"

"One block," Wyatt said, panting. "Acid Two, what's your position?"

"Coming up on the intersection now."

"Copy," Wyatt acknowledged.

They rounded a corner with an old bicycle discarded against a streetlamp. The ambush point lay a block ahead of them. Wyatt could see a maglev track running down the middle of Gervais, which was a large road that approached downtown perpendicular to Magellan, the other main artery. The street looked very wide even from a block away. Wyatt had a sudden pang of doubt that they'd be able to stop the truck. Maybe they'd just spook the driver and cause him to make an evasive maneuver around them.

"I see the target approaching," Chris said. "Twenty seconds."

"Copy."

Wyatt realized they were moving too slow. He broke into a sprint. They couldn't miss the truck.

Up ahead, the whine of a methane-turbine engine echoed off the walls of the buildings. Wyatt pulled back his run just in time to avoid darting into the middle of the intersection. He careened instead into the doorway of a ransacked shop. To his right, the supply truck rumbled along the deserted street, oblivious to the impending interruption.

"Laramie, Kenny, get ready on my mark!" Wyatt barked.

"Ready."

"We are in position," he signaled.

"Acid Two in position," Chris replied. "Ten seconds."

Wyatt peeked around the corner. The truck was bigger than he expected, with a cab floor that sat a good two meters above the street. The cargo bed looked like it could easily accommodate two containers side-by-side rather than just the smaller pod currently mounted on its back.

"All elements, stand by," Chris said. "Acid Three, on my mark."

Wyatt blinked. Who was Acid Three?

The truck cruised closer toward them.

"Acid Three, go."

A turbocharged engine shrieked from the other side of the street. Wyatt watched as Alonso burst into the middle of the intersection and stopped his aerobike right in the path of the truck. It seemed such a foolhardy challenge. The light frame of the bike hovered like a dragonfly, its vectored nozzles howling at the pavement, while the cargo truck rolled forward like a rhino in the middle of a charge. For a moment, Wyatt wondered if the truck would bother to stop at all.

Then he heard the hiss of air brakes. The truck visibly slowed, its driver startled at the sudden blockage.

"All teams, now, now, now!" Chris yelled.

In an instant, Marines and RESIT Troopers swarmed around the cargo truck with Vectors aimed at the crew cab. The driver was a young man with blond hair hanging over his forehead. He saw them and jerked back into his seat, his eyes growing wide at the array of weapons pointed at him. A second man, about the same age but with a shaved head, sat on the passenger's seat. The vertical barrel of a Viper was visible in front of him.

Wyatt approached, waving his arm at the driver to stop. Laramie, Kenny, Chris, and Finn glided to the sides of the cab, their CORE helmets feeding targeting telemetry to their weapons.

The truck still moved forward.

"Stop your vehicle now!" Wyatt shouted. He waved again, praying the driver or guy riding shotgun didn't freak out. The interior of the cab would get spackled by the charred remnants of their skulls.

The driver wisely decided he wanted to see his next birthday. Air brakes squealed louder and the six-wheeled vehicle rumbled to a stop.

"Turn off the engine and exit the vehicle. No sudden moves."

The turbine spun down, ending the stereophonic symphony with the nearby aerobike. Two pairs of hands rose above the dashboard and unlocked the cab doors in exaggerated slow motion. Kenny and Finn climbed the truck and guided the two men down to the street. Flex cuffs graced their wrists a few moments later.

"Get their ID badges," Chris said. "We'll need to doctor them for the checkpoint."

While the others handled the detainees, Wyatt circled around to the back of the truck. They needed to clear space for the team to ride. The steel cargo pod sat mounted on the end of the bed with a bright orange biohazard tag looped around the door latch. He tried untying the lanyard with no success. Frustrated, Wyatt pulled the utility knife from his vest sheath and sliced it off.

Footsteps sounded on the pavement. Chris appeared from the other side of the pod, his black CORE helmet fixated on the tag with an eyeless gaze. "What is that?"

"Let's find out," Wyatt said. He grabbed the latch handle and forced the mechanism to release the door.

The interior of the pod was cast in darkness. As Wyatt's eyes adjusted, he saw the outlines of dozens of bundles slowly come into focus. Large, bumpy yellow bags stacked one on top of the other, with some kind of zipper along the length. By the time Chris uttered a curse, Wyatt had already stepped back from the door in disgust.

"Jesus. These are body bags. What the hell?"

Chris stormed around to the prisoners. He stood over the prone driver and grabbed a fistful of hair, hauling him half upright by his head.

"What's the deal with the corpses in the back?"

"It's just the weekly shipment from the Justice Department—"

"*Justice*? Wait. You mean a death squad killed those people?"

"I just drive—"

Chris ripped off his CORE helmet. "Where did they come from?"

The driver started to panic. "I-I don't know. From Justice. I'm just the driver."

"*Where*?" he roared.

The boy lost it. "I dunno, I dunno! The pod's already loaded up when we get it. We just put it on the truck. It comes from the Justice Department. I don't know anything else!" He burst into sobs.

Chris threw him back onto his stomach, furious. Wyatt reached for the Marine's elbow and tugged him away from their prisoners.

"They're culling neighborhoods. I know it," Chris fumed. "Then sending them to the Health Department for some kind of science project. *Damn* them, Wyatt."

"What if they already died? You don't know what put them in those bags."

"They wouldn't be coming from Justice if they were lying on the street."

Finn approached them from the sidewalk with a shiny pair of cards in each hand. "IDs are done—" He cut off his words when he saw Chris's expression. "Did I miss something, Top?"

"No," Wyatt said preemptively.

In the Marine's hands were the same identification cards they'd confiscated from the truck crew, only now each had a new picture.

Wyatt spied a cleaned-up version of Chris behind a holographic sticker. He wondered how long ago that must have been, whether it had represented a happier time.

Finn waited a beat, skeptical at Wyatt's deflection, then plowed on. "You're the driver, Chris. I'm the meat with the Viper."

Chris took the badges and inspected them. "OK. These are good. Grab the shirts off those two and let's get into costume."

"Aye, aye, boss."

Finn started back toward their prisoners. Wyatt glanced at Chris and saw the anger in his eyes had given way to an immense sadness.

"You okay?"

"These people deserve better. Help me end this. Please."

"I'll do everything I can, Chris."

The master sergeant turned to face the open pod door. He inhaled a deep breath, his shoulders sagging at the end.

"Pull some of these bodies out to make room."

24

Truck
Juliet, Alpha Centauri A
2 March 2272

The truck rumbled down the street and jostled everyone inside the storage pod. Wyatt and the others clung to wall-mounted anchor points meant for cargo nets instead of human hands. One large bump sent the beam from Wyatt's tactical flashlight dancing across Laramie and Maya in their CORE helmets. A morbid thought passed through Wyatt's mind that maybe they should have left a couple cadavers inside for padding.

"We're approaching the Health Department campus," Chris said over the comm. "Radio silence from this point on."

"Copy," Wyatt said.

Their forward movement slowed for half a minute before finally coming to a complete stop. The turbine engine vibrated in protest at being forced into idle.

"Hope this goes okay," Laramie said.

"Me too. Don't really want a shootout with an APC cannon."

"Copy that, LT."

The troopers stewed in confinement while they mentally followed what would be happening outside. A guard challenging Chris to roll down the window. Chris turning over his forged ID card.

Possible questions about where was the usual driver, or the cargo, or their route. Wyatt prayed that nothing was out of order, that Chris knew his way around government protocol well enough to bluff their entry into the garage.

The whine of the engine suddenly disappeared, taking the gentle thrum of vibration along with it.

"They turned off the engine," Maya whispered.

A muffled voice sounded outside the pod wall. Was someone walking around back?

Wyatt felt the hair on his neck stand up.

"Firing positions," he said softly. "On my order only."

Multiple bodies scuffled quietly inside the cargo pod. Wyatt raised his Vector and kept his tactical light on, pointing it at the rear door so that his eyes wouldn't struggle if it opened and let in a blast of sunlight. The round circle of light jiggled as he took a deep, steadying breath.

More voices from the side of the truck. A stifled laugh that moved aft.

The soft *tick* of safeties clicking off filled the interior.

Wyatt cleared his throat. "Be ready to displace. Find cover from the APC."

"Yes, sir."

Stifling silence. All Wyatt heard was his own pulse in his ears. Sweat trickled down the back of his shirt.

A sudden, high-pitched whine announced itself from the front of the truck. Wyatt jumped. It took a moment before he realized the engine had started. Seconds later, a guttural scrape signaled that the truck had slipped into gear. The pod lurched forward and pitched Wyatt to his hands and knees.

They rumbled slowly ahead. Wyatt felt the front of the truck dip downward and had to grab at a cargo hook. They were headed underground, into the garage. A minute later they leveled out and stopped, the engine once again spinning down to off.

One of the cab doors opened and closed with a distant *whump*.

Wyatt still wasn't sure what to expect. Maybe Chris and Finn had been detained, and one of the police guards had driven the truck inside to the freight dock. He motioned for Laramie and Kenny to move close to the door. Kenny kept his Vector ready. Laramie put her hand on the hilt of her combat knife.

The latch clacked and the door swung open. The harsh white of overhead garage lights flooded into the pod interior.

Wyatt saw Chris standing at the tailgate and they all visibly relaxed.

"Okay, we got through the opening act," Chris said. He looked over his shoulder. "Time to do some damage."

The troopers jumped out of the pod, with Wyatt crawling out last. The parking garage extended across the entire footprint of the building. Heavy white pillars that smelled of fresh paint shouldered the ceiling, while another ramp on the other side of the space appeared to descend further underground. Commercial vehicles filled most of the spaces not occupied by cargo containers.

"Why did you turn off the engine? I just about had a heart attack."

"Sorry. The guard asked me to. He was hard of hearing." He dragged a duffle from the back of the cargo pod. "Clock's ticking now. Let's get busy."

The two Marines changed back into their tactical gear while Maya and Kenny covered the entrance ramp. Laramie hustled to the fire door near the stairwell and made sure it was clear. Wyatt followed her, checking the chem mag in his weapon to busy his nerves.

"Fire door's ready," Finn said. He turned to Laramie. "I've got a block of C-X on the backside, Staff Sergeant. If you need to displace, slam it shut and hit the arming switch. Then get the hell up the stairwell, because it'll be nasty when it goes off."

"Thanks, Finn. We'll try not to kill ourselves."

"Please don't," Wyatt said. "Chris, lead the way."

The four of them climbed the staircase and left Laramie and Kenny—Chemo—in the garage to secure their exfiltration route. Wyatt watched Chris scan for heat signatures with his helmet sensors. They reached the ground level without any trouble and stacked up next to the interior door.

"Check the hall," Chris said.

Finn put his hand on the latch underneath a keycard reader. "Locked."

"Burn it."

With the gain on his Vector turned to minimum, Finn pointed the barrel at the latching mechanism. He pulled the trigger and a smoke plume began to appear from the metal. A barely audible hiss quickly indicated the tumblers had been reduced to slag.

Finn tugged on the latch again. This time the door cracked open. He peeked past the edge.

"Clear."

"Move."

The door swung wide open and four bodies flowed into the hall, each with a hand on the shoulder in front of them. They were in a utility area separated from normal traffic. It had been a long time since Wyatt had been inside a groundside office building. The coziness of bland walls and a carpeted floor felt alien and unfamiliar.

"Security should be forward, then left," Chris whispered through the comm.

Finn led the way. They passed several closed doors and one open arch that revealed translucent boxes full of office supplies. A moment later they came to a hallway intersection with a heavy door on the far side. A black camera bulb protruded from the ceiling above it.

"Camera. Stack against the wall by the door, move!"

They split into two groups and hugged the walls on either side of the security door. Wyatt saw another keycard mounted above the latch.

"Finn, go," Chris said.

The Marine repeated the process of melting the lock mechanism.

"We're in the open. Can't they see us right now?" Wyatt said, eyeing the camera bulb.

"It's probably pointed at the hallway we came from. Just be fast. Get ready."

Wyatt tried to slow his breathing and manage the adrenaline.

"Lock's gone," Finn said.

"Go!"

The security door swung inward and the four of them moved silently into the building operations center. Wyatt was third in the stack behind Finn and Chris. In front of them, an L-shaped desk stretched out underneath a bank of ancient flat panel displays with video of the campus and garage. A lone guard in a private security uniform had his feet up on the desk, sound asleep.

Chris didn't miss a beat. He glided over to the guard, grabbed his jacket in one hand, and punched him square in the mouth. Arms and legs flapped out into a giant X as the man flew out of the chair. A few seconds later and Chris had him on his stomach, flex cuffs around his wrists.

"Keep your head down and mouth shut," Chris told him. He raised his head. "Clear."

"Clear," said Finn and Maya.

"Clear," Wyatt repeated. He lowered his weapon and walked over to the monitors. He spotted the feed in the garage below them, a truck and cargo pod filling most of the image.

"Nice parking job. You can't see anything."

"Uh-huh," Chris said. He scanned the other monitors. "A single guard at the front desk. Don't see much else."

Wyatt walked back toward the security room door. "Chemo One, Acid One. Status check, over."

"All clear, Acid One," Laramie said.

"Copy."

He turned back to find Finn sitting on the guard's chair. He was cycling the cameras through the building, searching for their target.

"Who are you people?" the guard asked from the floor.

"Shut up," Chris said. He gave him a kick.

The guard persisted. "You know there's a ton of security here, right?"

Chris crouched down over him. The guard was an older man but had the blond buzz cut of someone who had never let go of a prior military career.

"Hey there, pal. Let me explain how this is going to work. You're going to be still and study the dirt on the floor. I'm going to leave one of my guys behind here to watch the cameras. If he has to watch you, he won't be watching the cameras. That's bad. He might have to kill you. So don't distract him and just study dirt. Understand?"

The guard's expression remained the same, but his color paled a tiny fraction. "Yes."

"Good boy." Chris turned and glared at Finn. "Well?"

"I think I found him." In the monitor in front of him, a black man in a lab coat was sitting at a large desk, talking with an older woman standing on the other side. He seemed to alternate between gesturing at the door and rubbing his eyes with his fingertips.

"Can you get a better view? We can't see his face from behind."

"The camera is where the camera is," Finn said. "But I'm sure that's him."

The Marines stared at each other for a long moment, as if sharing some secret insight that was only known to them. Chris finally nodded. "Where is he?"

"Fifth floor, west side of the building."

"Okay." He turned to Wyatt. "You ready?"

"Let's do it."

Wyatt unsnapped the buckles of his ARC vest and pulled it over his head. Chris shrugged off the small duffle bag at his waist and did the same. Underneath, they had each dressed in a button-down business shirt. Chris unzipped the duffle and produced two white lab coats, each rolled neatly into a tight bundle.

Wyatt pulled the coat on one arm at a time. "Do I look official?"

"Works for me," Chris replied. "Side arm?"

"Check." Wyatt patted the holster where his Beretta R-40 was snuggly strapped in, either the largest pistol or the smallest laser weapon in use in RESIT.

"Acid on the move," Chris said.

Wyatt and Chris exited the security room and traced their path back through the hallway until they came to a different stairwell, one that climbed upward without garage access. This fire door was unlocked and opened easily. Then they began the ascent up multiple flights of stairs until they reached a door that said *Floor 5*.

"Exiting the stairwell," Chris muttered.

"Copy," came Finn's voice through the comm.

They opened the door and entered an administrative area. Offices lined the exterior walls, most with closed doors. Carbon-fiber cubicles stretched through the open space with the low buzz of workers talking on video circuits or with each other. The white walls offered a clean, clinical contrast to the dark gray of the carpeted floor. Wyatt glanced at several of the people moving about and felt a knot of angst at the realization that he and Chris were the only ones wearing lab coats.

Chris moved forward with a purposeful gait. Wyatt followed, scanning the room for anything that seemed like a threat. A young woman with her dark hair pulled into a ponytail stood up from her cubicle and made inadvertent eye contact with him.

He smiled and gave her a nod. She smiled back, quickly looking away.

They continued through the hallways, navigating twists and turns while checking name plates outside each office door. When they came to the one that said Jack Bell, Chris paused and looked over his shoulder at Wyatt.

"At target location."

"Copy," Finn said. "Cameras show he's still sitting there. No security spotted."

Chris looked at Wyatt. "Ready?"

"Ready."

Without any further hesitation, Chris put his hand on the door latch and pushed it open.

25

Department of Health Campus
Juliet, Alpha Centauri A
2 March 2272

Laramie heard the ding of an elevator before she saw anything.

She waved her hand at Kenny and the corporal pressed himself flat on the pavement. She crouched behind a gray cargo pod. They had set up their defensive positions about ten meters apart, Laramie watching the entry ramp, Kenny remaining by the hijacked truck. She couldn't see the cargo elevator, but the sound of two voices had already intruded into the garage.

". . . still can't believe Jensen got promoted."

"I can. He kisses so much butt, he's going to need a lip transplant by the time he's thirty."

"I know, but . . . I just figured Director Horst could see through all that, you know?"

"Yeah. Look at it this way, though. At least you don't have to work with him anymore."

"I guess." A pause. "Where's—oh, there it is."

Leaning around the edge of the pod, Laramie saw two men wearing maintenance coveralls dragging a cart toward Kenny's position. They didn't seem in any hurry and were too caught up in their conversation to be particularly observant. But Kenny was boxed in between the garage wall and the truck. He couldn't displace without being exposed.

"I see them," she whispered into the comm. "Stay low."

One of the men bobbed his head side to side like he had a stiff neck. "I tell you, Jensen's good at bending ears. He's going to start empire-building. Next thing you know, we'll both be reporting to him."

A laugh. "That will be the day."

"It'll happen. Just you wait."

"Well, he might have to have an accident with something heavy."

The two men chuckled. Laramie watched them walk toward the back of the cargo pod. One of them was taller than the other and had some sort of metal hook in his hand. The shorter one grabbed the latch on the pod door and opened it. He abruptly looked over his shoulder in confusion.

"This isn't it. Is it?"

Both men peered into the dark interior.

"Where are the bodies?"

The hairs on the back of Laramie's neck stood up. The team had stuffed all the body bags in some alleyway. They thought the shipping and receiving crew would exchange the incoming and outgoing pods, not unload anything.

This was bad.

The shorter man keyed a transmit button on an earpiece. "Bobl to Fitz. You there?" A pause. "I thought you said the last field collection rolled in?"

The taller man wandered around the truck and scanned the garage, clearly wondering if they were looking in the wrong place.

Laramie raised her Vector. Her CORE helmet painted each of the targets. "I have the guy talking," she whispered to Kenny. "You take the other."

". . . no, I'm looking at it right now, and the pod's freakin' empty."

The tall man's eyes drifted to his right, past empty pods sitting on the cement floor.

". . . well, call Security, because whatever they said they let in, it ain't here and there ain't no flippin' bodies to unload."

Laramie clicked her safety off.

The tall man took a couple steps around the end of the truck. He rubbed the hook absent-mindedly in his hands. His eyes drifted across more cargo containers. Kenny lay four meters in front of him in plain sight, his weapon aimed.

"Good. We'll wait here," Bobl said.

The tall man finally turned toward the garage wall and saw Kenny. He froze.

". . . they're sending some guys down to take a look," the shorter man said to his companion. "Fitz says they're positive the delivery truck came through, though."

It happened in almost slow motion. The tall man stared right at Kenny, uncomprehending that another human being was lying on the garage floor with a weapon pointed at him. Then the realization hit.

He took a startled step back. The arm holding the hook stiffened with an impulsive, defensive gesture.

Laramie stepped out from behind the cargo pod with her Vector raised. "Hold it right there, pal. Both of you. Hands in the air."

The two men froze. Bobl's eyes locked on Laramie. "Who are you?"

"Shut up." She walked toward them. In her optic nerve, a square red reticle hovered over each of their torsos. "I said, put your hands in the air."

Kenny got to his feet and approached the taller man. "Drop the hook," he said, motioning with his Vector.

The tall man let the unloading hook fall to the ground. It clattered noisily against the cement.

Bobl raised his hands to the side but took a step back. He was older, maybe fifty, with receding bushy hair. "You guys aren't supposed to be in here."

"Stop moving and get down on your knees."

Laramie hurried her pace to close the remaining ten meters between them. This was *really* bad, she thought. The workers weren't armed combatants. They were civilians doing their job. She needed to subdue them and get them out of sight.

"Hey, *chica*, we don't want any trouble," Bobl said. "We're just here to unload the truck." Another step back.

Five meters now. Bobl took two more steps, each with more urgency. The stairwell lay just on the other side of him. She couldn't let him raise an alarm, retrieve a weapon, or stumble into Finn in the security room.

A clatter rattled behind her, followed by an electric whir. Laramie's brain raced to match the sound with the implication.

Kenny did it for her. "The garage gate's opening!"

She turned her head a fraction toward the entry ramp. Toward where Fitz's people were entering. Toward police who might be armed.

"*Get down on your knees!*" Laramie commanded.

Bobl broke and ran.

It took only an instant for Laramie's finger to squeeze the trigger. The chem mag snapped its tiny explosion and sent its energy into the reaction chamber of her Vector. An intense beam of lazed light sprang from the end.

Bobl fell with a splash of pink mist.

The taller man let out a gasp, his body language screaming flight. "Gill . . ."

A stream of curse words shouted their frustration in Laramie's head. Why hadn't he listened? What a stupid waste of life.

"Get down, now!" Kenny yelled.

The remaining worker complied and lowered himself into a prone position.

Laramie twisted toward the garage entrance. The security curtain had retracted two-thirds of the way into the ceiling. A pair of figures stood frozen in the middle of the ramp. One of them was pointing in her direction.

Bad, bad, bad.

"Find cover, quick!" she said.

She hurried behind a pylon. Kenny stayed low, covering their new guest. "What about this guy?"

Laramie hissed at him. "Hey. You."

The man turned his head toward her.

"Don't be stupid like your buddy," she said. "Do what I tell you. Stay down on the ground and don't move. Understand?"

"Yes." His voice held a twinge of grief. Laramie peeked around the pylon and saw that the figures in the entry had disappeared. She felt her lips twisting into a snarl. *Damn it.*

She opened the squad channel. "Chemo One to all elements. We've been compromised. Moving to defensive positions."

Maya's voice hit the comm. "Copy that, Chemo. What happened?"

"Building admin sent some guys to unload the bodies we took out."

Several seconds went by before any reply. "Understood."

Kenny installed himself inside the stairwell doorway and sighted his Vector at the descent ramp. Laramie left her pylon and set up next to a concrete construction barrier that lined the pedestrian walkway. She studied the ramp and thought through the angles of their respective vantage points, visualizing different fields of fire.

"You cover the left side," Laramie said. "I'll cover the right. If I say displace, we go through your door, shut it, and arm it. Then up and out on floor one. Got it?"

"Got it, Staff Sergeant."

An eerie silence fell over the garage as they waited. A minute went by before Laramie noticed a strange, intermittent whimper. She realized it was the dock worker.

"Hey, tall guy," she called out.

Several seconds passed before a weak voice replied. "Yeah?"

"You know your buddy? He'd still be with us if he'd just followed directions. Don't you make that mistake. Stay put where you are. You understand me?"

"I understand."

"Good."

Deathly stillness. This was the worst part, Laramie thought. Anxiety always built up before combat. Once things got rolling, it just became act and react, fire and move, attack and counterattack. She didn't have a problem when the world was falling apart around her. But the anticipation of the start? It never failed to gnaw on her nerves, a sinister shadow that lurked underneath an ocean of fear and doubt.

She caught a glimmer of movement at the edge of the ramp. Shadowy figures were hugging the wall. Off in the distance, the growl of a turbine-driven engine echoed from somewhere beyond.

Laramie scanned the area to find threats and let her helmet mark them. A line of sweat trickled down her back and she forced herself to push the sensation out of her mind. She was a professional and had no room for distractions right now. It was time to go to work.

26

Chris and Wyatt strode into an elongated office with steel-blue walls and light carpet, accented with plants in an array of clay pots in the corner. An expansive cityscape filled the view beyond a set of floor-to-ceiling windows. White noise speakers hissed softly from the ceiling.

A man with dark skin and graying black hair looked up at them from behind a desk near the far wall. "Who are you?"

"Dr. Bell?" Chris asked.

"Were you expecting someone else sitting in my office?"

"We need to borrow you, sir. Please come with us."

Dr. Bell sighed with annoyance. He reached for the tablet on his desk. "I told Gretchen I didn't want to be disturbed, and here she is, sending in the whole blasted department. Let's clear this up right now—"

Chris closed the distance in a heartbeat, flowing around the desk and smacking the tablet away. Then he punched Dr. Bell hard in the cheek. The doctor went sideways in his chair and let out a grunt. Wyatt provided security by the door and listened for any sounds in the hallway that might indicate someone had heard.

"You're not calling anybody," Chris said.

"What the hell?"

Chris grabbed a fistful of Bell's shirt, drew his pistol, and shoved it into the man's face. "Do I have your attention?"

His eyes stared at the weapon. "Oh, you have my attention."

Chris glanced at the desk. Large diagrams of city streets filled the tabletop, each with an array of colored marks drawn in seemingly haphazard patterns.

"Whatcha working on?"

"City planning."

"My ass." Chris reached up and picked off the neural stub adhered to Dr. Bell's temple. "You're a bastard, you know that? How many neighborhoods are you going to murder today?"

Bell's eyes showed defiance. "Do you think I like what we have to do? Do you think I enjoy this?"

"Maybe you do, all safe and cozy in this little building here."

Wyatt began to feel uncomfortable with the exchange. Chris was amped up in a way that didn't fit their mission. They needed Jack Bell to come with them. They needed him to cooperate. Chris seemed to want to hurt him.

"Being here is not a choice." Even though he had a pistol next to his nose, Bell showed remarkable composure. "It's the only option we have. And the fact of the matter is, if I'm not the one directing things, someone else will—someone who maybe isn't as humane."

"You think murder is *humane*?"

Wyatt took a worried step away from the door. "Chris."

Bell was busy shaking his head. "We're managing constricted people who are already going to die. The only way to save those who *aren't* infected is to remove the ones who are."

"And what are you removing?" A dangerous edge crept into Chris's voice. "*People*, Bell. Not cattle. Not crops. You're taking away children. Brothers. Sisters. Friends. You should be finding a cure, not destroying our society."

"*Constriction* is destroying our society. The only way to survive is to cut it out."

"Said every despot in history."

"I don't think that's an apt comparison."

"Chris," Wyatt said again. They were making too much noise. He wondered if anyone could hear them from the hallway.

The Marine ignored him. "*I* think Hewitt has an obligation to help the people who elected him, not kill them off."

"Well, Hewitt's dead, so he doesn't really count."

"I—what? What did you say?"

For the first time since Wyatt had met him, the Marine seemed at a loss. He stood by the desk and just stared at Dr. Bell.

Bell's eyes flicked back and forth between Chris and Wyatt. "You're not Department employees. Who are you?"

The menace suddenly returned, more dangerous now. Chris tightened his grip on Bell's shirt and jerked him upward. "What happened to the Governor?"

"That hurts."

"Talk!"

"Get that gun out of my face and maybe I will."

"*Chris!*" Wyatt spoke with heavy emphasis on each word. "This is *not the best time* to be having this conversation."

A few tense moments passed. Chris released Bell, leaving a rumpled knot in the middle of his shirt. He lowered his voice. "Keep your hands on the desk, or you might lose one."

"Don't worry," Bell said, unflustered. "I don't have any spy controls or secret panels. You know, government budgets and all."

"Now, quickly. Hewitt. I saw him on the news vids yesterday."

Bell sighed. "Those are computer generated. It's all about keeping the populace calm. The illusion of control, that sort of thing. Governor Hewitt died a month ago."

"How? Constriction?"

The Secretary's eyes narrowed. "You need to tell me who you are first."

"Talk."

"No."

"You've got a lot of nerve for someone with a gun pointed at them."

"Yeah, and if you wanted me dead, you'd have done it already. Look, the odds are pretty high right now that constriction's going to kill all of us. Your scare tactics are sneezing into a hurricane. But I *might* talk to you if you answer some of my questions."

Chris seemed like he might punch him again.

Wyatt had had enough. "This is my mission, Dr. Bell."

"And what mission is that?"

"Recon. All the interplanetary shipping from Juliet has stopped. Let's just say that people outside of Alpha A took notice. My team came here to scout it out and find out what's going on. A bunch of those roads led to you."

Comprehension dawned on Dr. Bell's face. He nodded slowly. "You're not from Juliet."

"No. Come with us and we can have a nice long chat about it."

"I want the answer to my question first," Chris growled. "The governor."

"You sure you want to know?"

"Try me."

The room was still except for the sound of white noise.

"Operation Firebreak," Bell said finally.

"Which is?"

"*The solution*, according to some. According to Commissioner McManus." Bell stared at his desk, seemingly resigning himself to something. "Do you know what happens if you try to hurt a person with constriction?"

"They try to infect you," Chris said.

"No. They attack."

Chris narrowed his eyes.

"Ever notice how you don't find constricted persons by themselves?" Bell continued. "They're always in groups. Not that surprising given how contagious it is. It only takes one infected person to spread it. And if someone happens to stay too close, that's exactly what happens: one person tries to spread it.

"But if they get accosted, it's not the individual that responds. *Every* nearby constricted focuses on you. And when you have multiple constricted propagating the infection at the same time, the effect is devastating. They burn you to a crisp from the inside. Your mind shorts out and you're turned into a vegetable."

Wyatt felt his insides twist. He thought back to Parrell, to the constricted woman who had stared at Izzy. Wyatt had shot her. And then the other constricted woke up and his mind flooded with painful, golden specks.

Bell's voice took on a weary quality. "Every attempt to corral or drive constricted citizens to a controlled area has resulted in an attack. It didn't matter if we used nonlethal means. They still turned hostile. We had squads of police in full riot gear drop to the ground and die, massive convulsions shaking their bodies, no way to shield them. We absolutely failed to contain it.

"So, that's where General McManus comes in. He was born here. He knows the Julietan mindset better than anybody. Julietans stick together in adversity. They don't abandon friends or family. That's how this planet got colonized.

"But he knew it was also killing us. Parents wouldn't leave children. Brothers wouldn't leave brothers. Sometimes they wouldn't even realize constriction was happening until they were already infected themselves. The only way to stop constriction from spreading was to get ahead of it. To *kill* ahead of it."

Bell looked out the window for a moment. The sky had darkened with storm clouds overhead.

"Governor Hewitt disagreed with how to contain it. Hewitt was a compassionate man. I'm not sure exactly what went down, but it cost him his life. And now you have what we have today. Firebreak. A terrible, terrible thing. But if it saves us from extinction . . ." He let the words trail off, staring at his desk.

Wyatt thought back to growing up in Michigan as a young boy. Scouts. Lots of camping, fishing, time outdoors. Being careful and deliberate. But many who enjoyed nature were not, and a shoddy fire pit or careless cigarette butt easily started a wildfire that swept through dry brush and ground cover.

How did firefighters contain a perimeter filled with combustible material? What could they do against a wildfire that could easily outpace any possible resources thrown against it?

By clearing a gap in the unburned vegetation. By denying the fire its fuel.

God, what a mess.

"I ought to kill you right now," Chris said.

He jerked Dr. Bell's shirt and hauled him to his feet. Wyatt watched the pistol swing up to Dr. Bell's chin.

"What's the alternative?" Bell said. "Let someone who might be infected loose? It only takes one, and everybody dies."

"You're a murderer."

Despite the threat of Chris's weapon, Dr. Bell yanked himself free. Anger spilled over his face. "Do you think I asked for this? *Do you*? I spend *every hour* of *every day* making these horrible decisions. Me. My staffers are in the dark. They think they're analyzing data usage, fixing blackouts for better police response. They don't have any idea that a blackout means a new outbreak, that no one is using technology anymore, that everyone there is going to get shot."

"Not good enough."

Wyatt could feel the tension in Chris's trigger finger.

He took a step into the room and spoke in the best command voice he could muster. "Master Sergeant Thompson. Lower your weapon."

The Marine turned his head a fraction. His pistol didn't move.

"Are you going to kill the one man who actually understands how constriction spreads?" Wyatt asked. "I need him. We need him. If anyone's going to come up with a nonlethal approach to get ahead of this—*those* people need what's in his head."

"He needs a laser blast in his head, is what," Chris said.

"Do that, and every colonist is going to die. Constriction or police action, one way or the other."

A long, anxious pause filled the air. Chris remained frozen with his pistol underneath Dr. Bell's chin.

Wyatt remained on the offensive. He turned to the doctor. "And you, Dr. Bell. I get that Juliet likes to keep problems in the family. But you're absolutely complicit in these preemptive deaths. You can complain about the burden on *you*. You still told the police where to go. For you, your absolution is going to come from me."

"And how's that?" Bell asked.

"I'm taking you off-world. You need Proxima and you need Sol. You need every resource we can throw your way. This is too big, for you or anyone. It's going to take everyone. That is the only way to salvage this situation. To atone."

Jack Bell stared hard at him. Perhaps he was judging whether a complete stranger really offered a viable alternative to something reprehensible. Or maybe he thought Wyatt was out of his mind and was going to just get more people killed, like Hewitt.

After what seemed like forever, his eyes softened an infinitesimal amount.

"Okay."

Chris lowered his pistol.

Wyatt stifled a sigh of relief. "Now can we please get the hell out of here?"

The comm crackled with an incoming message from Laramie. "Battle One to all elements. We've been compromised."

27

Laramie watched armed figures walk in a skirmish line down the garage ramp. How much had they seen? Did the police know Laramie and Kenny were armed? She hoped she and Kenny still had the advantage, that the troopers who spotted them hadn't been careful in observing details. Regardless, the odds of leaving the way they arrived had dwindled almost to zero.

A police trooper in a black CORE helmet leaned around a structural pylon. Laramie sighted him with her Vector.

"Staff Sergeant?" Kenny's whisper sounded crisp over the comm. He looked at her from behind his construction barrier, ready to shoot.

"Hold your fire."

Her helmet picked up two more police officers creeping out of the entry ramp, moving to cover.

"Chemo," she said. "We have multiple contacts in the garage."

"Copy, Battle." The sound of Finn's voice was a surprise. "Chemo Two is moving your way." *Maya.*

"Do not enter the garage. I repeat, do not enter the garage. You'll expose your position. Stay in the stairwell."

"One copies."

"Two copies," Maya said. She was breathing heavy, probably rushing down the stairs.

The police troopers darted from pylon to pylon, pausing at each one to scan their surroundings for the mysterious figures spotted by the cargo truck. Laramie noticed the long barrels of L-6 Vipers in several of their hands. One policeman, perhaps the commander, carried a pistol. None of them appeared to have visors with integrated targeting.

"Chemo Two in position," Maya said.

A burly officer with an open-faced helmet shifted to Laramie's far left and ducked behind a payment kiosk. The construction barrier lay just a few meters beyond. He was moving dangerously close to Kenny.

"Stand by," Laramie whispered. She painted the officer with her targeting system.

A trooper dashed wide right and past the edge of the cargo pod she was using as cover. The pod edge touched the garage wall, so Laramie knew she couldn't be flanked, but only Kenny could cover the approach from that side.

The kiosk trooper raised a Viper and covered the area.

Another officer, skinny and short, peeked around a pylon. She could hear one of them issue a hushed command on their own comm net. Then the skinny officer left the pylon and made a dash toward the construction barrier.

The adrenaline flush hit Laramie like a ton of bricks. She recognized the bounding overwatch pattern. With the next advance, the skinny officer would reach the construction barrier and clear the opposite side to make sure there wasn't an enemy hiding. An enemy like Kenny.

Training took over.

"Weapons free!"

Laramie's Vector jumped as it snapped out bolts of lethal light. The skinny officer took a shot in his shoulder. He pirouetted sideways into the wall and left a red smear as his equipment clacked against the cement.

The kiosk trooper swung his rifle toward the incoming fire, but Laramie's targeting system beat him to the punch. Instead of relying on human precision, the computer automatically knew when to release the laser blast as the aim of the barrel passed over the predesignated reticle. Laramie put two shots on her second target. The puff of vaporized resin filled the air as he fell backward, stunned but still alive. Still dangerous.

The maintenance worker from earlier began to wail in terror as the police exchanged laser blasts.

A shot hit the cement wall and sprayed sizzling dust into the air. Laramie knew she had to call it. "Battle One to all elements. A is a no-go. I repeat, Plan A is a no-go."

Kenny snapped off a number of shots in front of Laramie. She heard a clatter of someone in tactical gear either diving or falling to the ground. More blasts from her left announced Maya's presence in the stairwell.

Frantic shouting echoed off the far wall of the garage. The throaty sound of an APC signaled its displeasure from somewhere in the parking lot above.

"How many still up?" Kenny said.

Laramie swiveled her head and let her helmet computer show the last known location of each target. She counted two down, including the wounded officer by the parking kiosk. Maya's telemetry added one on the ramp and another crawling to cover on the other side of Laramie's cargo pod. That would be the clatter, she thought.

"Two in the middle," Laramie answered, finishing her tally. "Near the ramp entrance. Number three by the kiosk. Number four to my right."

A burst of fire flew back and forth between the garage ramp and the door to the exit stairway. Maya dropped flat in the stairwell, landing as chunks of wall crackled into brittle shards. Kenny popped over the construction barrier and shot several times at the ramp. Laramie leaned around the cargo pod and did the same, worrying less about actually hitting a target than providing cover fire for Maya. That's when she heard the whine of a turbine engine and the light suddenly darkened around the ramp.

"APC inbound!" Kenny yelled.

Laramie snapped off more shots. "Maya, you OK?"

"Okay!"

"Kenny, displace to the stair—"

A blinding flash. Laramie suddenly felt like she was floating in microgravity, her hands and feet batting at nothing but the air. Her ears registered noise, but it was all indistinct and unclear. Then the light faded to darkness and the floating sensation ended. A thud knocked the air from her lungs in a single, forced exhalation.

"—ramie! Laramie!" a woman yelled with a muffled voice. A distant rattling echoed in the void beyond.

Still black. Something instinctual lifted Laramie's hands to her head. She pulled on her chin, could feel the tugging, yet the world remained as dark as deep space. Then her fingers closed into a strange, square shape and squeezed. A pop released the blackness.

An intense smell of ozone hit her nostrils as she lifted the helmet from her face. Laramie blinked several times at the sudden light. Rows of LED lighting shone down at her from the ceiling fixtures.

She was lying flat on her back.

"Laramie!" the woman's voice said again. Maya.

"I'm . . . okay," she managed. Laramie scrunched her eyes shut and opened them again. Her hands held what was left of her CORE helmet, a blackened indentation the size of her forearm carved into the left temple.

"Maya, I said *cover me*!" someone shouted.

A jumble of *snap-snap-snap* echoes ricocheted off the walls and reminded Laramie that her own weapon should be in her hands. Where was it? She looked toward her feet and saw her Vector lying against her waist. As her hands clasped around the stock, her brain began screaming at her to get to cover, get to cover, that rumble is an APC . . .

A flash of dark swept past her and the next thing she knew, Kenny had grabbed her by the collar and was dragging her to the stairwell. A moment later they were inside the landing. Kenny's face filled her vision, desperately searching for signs of injury.

"You okay, Staff Sergeant?" he asked, urgency in his voice.

"Your breath stinks. Now help me up."

"APC! APC!" Maya yelled. *Snap-snap-snap*.

Kenny pulled Laramie to her knees and rushed back to the door. Her body felt like it weighed a thousand kilos as she pushed herself to her feet. But her mind managed to click back into gear, and she knew they had only moments to get away before either a rotary cannon or a squad of reinforcements erased their position.

"Displace and shut the door!" Laramie ordered.

A furious exchange of laser fire filled her ears as Kenny and Maya backed into the landing. Little puffs of dust danced off the thick cement wall from the laser blasts on the other side. Laramie moved to the right of her two squad mates and grabbed the metal door with both hands.

"And . . . now!"

The troopers rolled left while Laramie slammed the door shut and wheeled to the side. Several laser blasts made loud pops against the metal like an angry drunkard smashing his hands into a tin roof.

A block of C-X explosives on the fire door's backside caught Laramie's eye. Finn's insurance policy from earlier. She hit the arming trigger.

"Up the stairs. Move!"

The three of them stormed upward. At the first turnaround landing, Kenny fought to speak between gasps of air. "Wyatt's going bonkers on the comm. Acid is heading our way."

"Negative—tell them to meet us at the security center. We are on Plan B."

Kenny relayed the instructions as they made it to the ground floor. Laramie unceremoniously yanked open the security door with the melted latch. The office corridor on the other side appeared to be deserted.

"In the hall . . . left, then straight, copy that," Kenny said in response to a radio communication Laramie couldn't hear.

Thirty seconds later and they opened the security station door.

"Friendlies coming in!"

Finn was sitting at the control console and had camera feeds of the garage displayed on a set of flat panels. Chris stood behind him and studied the display. Wyatt was the only one who turned toward them as they entered the doorway. He lowered his Vector and went back to pulling an ARC vest over his head.

"What the hell happened? We couldn't get you on the comm."

"Got shot in the face."

Wyatt visibly jerked his head. "What?"

"I'm okay. Helmet got toasted."

He seemed to accept that for the moment and finished cinching the straps on his vest.

A deep rumble sounded from below their feet. The lights in the security room dimmed while the video images rippled on the monitors.

"Charges at the stairwell just went off," Finn said.

"What charges?" asked a voice Laramie didn't recognize.

She moved to the left and saw a thin, older man with chestnut-brown skin. His attention shifted from Finn to her as she approached.

"Is this our guy?" she asked.

"Apparently, I am," the guy said. "Doctor Jack Bell. You?"

"Staff Sergeant Laramie McCoy."

The man stared at her for a moment like he was trying to memorize her face. Then he gave her a nod. "There better not be a quiz later. I'm not going to keep all of you people straight."

"Just call me Laramie. There aren't too many of those."

"Then I'll just be Jack."

Laramie thought Jack Bell seemed awfully calm for everything going on around him. She wondered if constant police actions had desensitized him to violence. Or maybe he was just high. People found escapes in different ways.

Finn pointed at several spots across the flat-panel displays. "Three targets down. The APC's secured the exit. Looks like they're going to wait for reinforcements."

"What sort of reinforcements?" Wyatt asked.

Chris's face had turned dark. "A crisis response squad—heavy gear and weapons. Our door charge may have stopped the B-team, but we won't last against who's coming."

"How long until they get here?"

"Five minutes, maybe. Rimini District station has a CRS and they're only a couple blocks away." Chris leaned back over Finn and swept his fingers across the control tablet. The cameras switched to the street-level entrance, where police officers with weapons out were scrambling around the perimeter. "Looks like they got the alert out to the guards. We're not getting out the main entrance, either."

"Forty minutes, and we're already on Plan C," Wyatt said.

"We have a C?"

Wyatt grabbed his Vector and went to the security door. "Maya, switch with me. Hit the building transmitter and patch me with Dragon."

"On it, boss," she said. Maya moved her small frame against the wall, her head drooping as she sent neural commands to her CORE helmet. The *last* CORE helmet, Laramie realized with a start.

"I've got Dragon. What do you want to tell him?"

"Open the comm so I can talk."

"Done."

"Dragon One," Wyatt said, pressing his earpiece against his head. "Do you copy?"

"Wyatt? I mean—Acid? What's going on?"

"Bad things. Contact Teo and reroute the Javelin to our position. We need a roof pickup ASAP."

"Okay, will do. What channel are you broadcasting from? I don't recognize the source."

"We're using the Health Department transmitter."

Several seconds passed on the comm. "They'll be able to trace that to the safe house. You just compromised our location."

Chris moved next to Wyatt and took over the conversation. "We have other houses, Elton. Have Teo pick you up on the way. Get out of there and take the girls with you."

"Okay," Elton said. His voice sounded heavy, resigned. "I'll do it."

Laramie watched as Wyatt and Chris shared a long look. Then Wyatt moved back to the door and spoke with Maya. It took a moment for Laramie to realize Chris was staring at her.

Her gut wrenched into a knot. His tirade over Sid still stung. Chris had made it very clear he felt she was responsible for his losing a brother Marine. What was coming next? Blaming her for how she handled the garage?

Instead of a rebuke, he gestured at her forehead. "Are you all right?"

"Huh?"

"Your head."

Her fingertips went up to her temple and brushed blistered skin. "Oh. Yeah. It's okay."

He watched her in silence. Surprisingly, Laramie didn't see anger in his eyes. Then he just gave her a nod and turned back to the security monitors.

"We've got company," Finn said in alarm. He made gestures over the control tablet to adjust the images on the flat panels. "CRS is rolling up. West side, multiple vehicles."

Wyatt started barking orders. "Okay, let's get going. Maya, you're on point. Everybody else stack up. We'll move to the roof and fortify a position until our pickup. Dr. Bell, you stay behind me."

"No argument there," Bell said.

The power suddenly went out and the room plunged into blackness.

Laramie switched on the tactical flashlight mounted to her Vector. Nervous faces glanced around, some looking for the exit, others instinctively scanning for threats.

Wyatt's voice boomed in the silence left behind by the lack of ventilation. "Let's *move*, people!"

28

Laramie took fourth position in the stack behind Maya, Finn, and Chris. She drummed her fingers against her Vector's trigger group and wished she still had her CORE helmet. The police had cut the power and blinded them for a reason. This wasn't good.

The team flowed out of the security room single file. The interior corridors were dim, with no exterior windows and only yellow emergency lighting to replace nonfunctional light fixtures. Each trooper put their hand on the shoulder of the person in front of them to stay together. Laramie heard Wyatt instruct Dr. Bell to do the same.

"Back stairwell," Finn said. "Not the one to the garage."

Maya led them through a maze of hallways until they reached a heavy fire door. She grabbed the latch and carefully swung it open. Once sure no one was on the other side, Maya started up the stairs with the rest of the stack trailing.

Emergency lighting cast an otherworldly glow from battery-powered boxes on the walls. At the first landing, Finn pivoted to cover the back angle while the rest of them continued up. More stairs and a second landing. As they approached the third floor, Laramie heard a door latch release. A cacophony of voices filled the landing as office workers moved into the stairwell to evacuate the building. At almost the same instant, a dull rumble thundered distantly below them.

"Security room charge went off," Finn yelled.

Just like with the garage door, Finn had booby-trapped the security room with an explosive device. Laramie realized a detonation meant that police officers were in the building—and whoever hadn't been killed by that blast would now be incredibly pissed.

An older woman wearing a teal jacket noticed them from the landing above. She gasped and clutched her chest at the sight of an armed team. A throng of additional office workers surged from behind her, completely blocking the way up.

"Step aside!" Chris yelled. "Coming through! Step to the side!"

The woman stepped backward into a middle-aged man with a shaved head and goatee. He caught her to keep her from falling. "Who are you?" he asked.

"I said, step aside! Police business!" Chris motioned with his Vector.

The man glanced at Chris's battered CORE helmet, eyeing the faded POLICE letters on the side. He appeared dubious but pressed himself against the wall anyway, hauling the older woman with her. Their effort was quickly nullified by a dozen more office workers who pushed from behind them in what must have been a standard safety drill for building emergencies.

Maya and Finn stormed upward and began to aggressively motion for people to move against the wall. Some of the Health Department employees got the message right away. Others saw the weapons and either froze or wailed in alarm.

Their progress slowed as Laramie and the stack waded upstream. For every worker that tried to clear a path, another one seemed to spill in from the fire doors from above. Confusion and fear added to the impediment.

"Director Bell! What's going on?" one of the workers asked, spotting the director behind Wyatt.

"Security issue," Jack said.

"Why are you going up? Aren't we supposed to follow evacuation procedures?"

"Don't worry about me. Worry about you. Head toward the lobby and move slowly. Do whatever the police tell you."

That was smart, Laramie thought. The officers below them would have a hair-trigger temper after the explosive charges. Dr. Bell didn't want any of them to get waxed just for showing up.

Crowds of gaggling people filled the stairwell now. Even with Maya and Finn's forceful crowd control, the stack's upward progress had virtually frozen. People Laramie couldn't see began to question loudly why the throng was no longer moving.

A voice behind her yelled to get her attention. "Laramie! Get us to the central stairwell," Jack said. "It's bigger and has roof access."

Chris heard. "Finn, Maya, exit third floor. Push 'em out of the way if you have to."

More shoving. A woman screamed from above, pointing at Maya and the frightening exoticness of her CORE helmet. Curses of surprise followed as more eyes trained on their stack.

Despite being small, Maya apparently knew how to use her bodyweight. She shoved her Vector into the obstructing bodies and forced them out of the doorway. Finn barked at them to remain back while the rest of the stack pushed through the gauntlet. Laramie passed through the threshold and saw a corridor flanked by laboratory spaces, each encased in glass walls and filled with robots and testing vessels. The number of people thinned rapidly in what was a wider space to move.

"Let's go!" Chris growled. "Central stairs, *now!*"

They flowed around a corner and left the remaining workers to stew in their confusion and fear. Laramie spotted a lab with several gurneys lined up against the wall. Each had a body draped in a white sheet on top.

Chris glared at them as they passed. "Were those people culled, Bell?"

"Probably," came the matter-of-fact reply.

The corridor opened into an open workspace filled with cubicles. Tinted windows revealed a threatening-looking storm cell that blocked out the afternoon sun and threw raindrops against the glass in a staccato patter. The office area seemed abandoned, its normal occupants having already evacuated to the stairwell behind the troopers, but Maya and Finn swept for threats just the same.

The walls lining the interior of the office area were made of glass. On the other side Laramie saw an expansive atrium that stretched up and down across multiple stories, with a series of balcony walkways lining the perimeter of each floor to allow movement between offices. In the center of the atrium, a large, open stairwell curved around a central elevator shaft and allowed access to each level via a narrow foot bridge.

"There, in the middle. See the stairs?" Chris called up to the front of the stack.

"See it," Maya acknowledged.

They moved through an exit door and found themselves on the walkway. Laramie heard the gurgle of a fountain from somewhere on the ground floor. She broke from their column and peeked over the edge of the railing.

"Wyatt, we've got at least fifty people on the bottom floor, all flat on the ground."

"What?" Wyatt edged over to her position. "Are they shot?"

"I don't think so." She looked more closely. "Their hands are folded behind their heads. Prisoners?"

No sooner had she said the words than her brain caught up to the implication.

The police must have ordered the fleeing workers to lie down.

Which meant the police had already been through the lobby, and could be coming up the central stairs . . .

Movement caught her eye on the central stairs just one level below.

"Get down!"

Laramie hauled Wyatt away from the railing just in time. She felt rather than saw the blast. Invisible light ionized the air in front of her in a flash of heat.

"Contact below!" she said. "Police in the atrium!"

"Any hostiles above us?" Wyatt asked.

"Nothing yet," someone said.

Chris hustled over. "They're going to push up both sides—the central stairs, and the ones we came up," he explained. "We've got to get to a defensible position. We'll get flanked here."

"Maya, any ETA on our Javelin?" Wyatt barked.

"Dragon says they haven't been picked up yet."

Wyatt looked hard at the central staircase, studying it. "Okay. We'll move up. I don't think they have an angle on us from the ground if we climb."

Chris seemed to agree. "Let's hope they don't. It'll be hard for us to return fire if we don't want to hit those civvies all over the floor."

Laramie felt herself frown. Had the police thought of that? Using office workers as human shields . . . this wasn't the Juliet where she had grown up.

"Okay, let's move," Wyatt said. "Change the order. Move Bell to the middle of the stack. Laramie, cover our six with Kenny. Might get hairy."

"On it." Laramie moved to the rear of the order and checked her chem mag. Half charged. She had six more around her vest, but if they got into a sustained firefight, it wouldn't be anywhere near enough.

The stack moved along the atrium walkway, hugging the railing until they reached the footbridge to the central stairwell. Maya stayed at the front. Laramie shuffled around until she was next to Kenny.

"Get ready to duck-walk backward, Kenneth," she said.

"I was born to duck-walk, Staff Sergeant."

The squad stretched out as they began up the stairs. A few tense seconds went by while she waited with Kenny for everyone to pass.

In the office space behind the glass wall, a faint jangle caught her ear. She thought it sounded like someone with poorly secured tactical gear hurrying to cover. She hit Kenny on the shoulder and pointed. Possible movement.

A bulky shadow edged up to a corner, crouched and alert behind the arms of a floor-mounted lab robot. Laramie spotted the long barrel of a weapon.

Her own Vector was up and unleashing a barrage of shots before she realized it. "Contact rear! Move, *move!*"

The figure ducked back. Laramie scrambled up the open central stairs until she reached the turnaround landing between floors. She reset her position and watched as the bulky figure edged again around the corner. Her heart sank as she spied the hardened ceramic plating of powered assault gear.

Oh no.

There was no way their Vectors would penetrate that armor.

"Heavy!" she yelled. "Heavy, behind us!"

She turned and sprinted up the next flight. The railing around the open stairs provided poor cover. Chunks of plaster exploded nearby as laser fire connected far too close to her position.

She made it to the fourth-floor landing. Kenny was crouching down by the turnaround and joined her to provide covering fire. Two more police figures in black tactical gear emerged from the fire stairs corridor and were trying to conceal themselves behind the lab equipment. She had lost sight of the officer in assault armor.

Kenny was hurling a barrage of laser fire at the other figures, punching blobs of slag out of the glass panels. Laramie joined in. One of her shots hit an officer's rifle and sent a sizzling chunk of metal flying over his shoulder.

The electric hum of power-assisted limbs filled the landing below them.

"Displace!"

Laramie and Kenny moved up the stairs just as the terrifying shape of the assault armor rounded into view. She didn't even try to shoot. Her Vector wouldn't penetrate the torso or even the black, opaque dome that substituted for a helmet. The only chance they had was to stay ahead of it and the long-barreled cannon it carried.

"Contact on the stairs!" Kenny shouted up. "Heavy, heavy!"

"Get to the top, *now!*" Chris said across the comm.

Laramie saw more police scrambling two floors down. They would all be on the stairs in a moment, putting more guns in the fight than her team could possibly hope to match. She raced up to the next turnaround and narrowly avoided plowing into Finn, crouched against the solid banister.

"Heavy is right below us. Let's go!"

Finn had set a small gear pack against the inside railing and was pulling a fine filament across the stairs. "Almost."

Explosives. How much of this stuff did Chris and his team have?

Hummmmmmm.

The assault armor rounded the turnaround below. Laramie pulled her trigger and landed six shots on the shoulders and dome helmet. Tiny ceramic shards popped into the air with puffs of superheated ash, but the police officer didn't miss a step and raised his weapon toward them.

"Get down!"

The loud *boom* of a ballistic weapon rang out. Laramie and Finn fell onto each other and hugged the ground, flattened beneath the Heavy's field of fire. The staircase structure exploded all around them. Another boom, then another.

Laramie smelled a sudden whiff of ozone. She glanced up and saw Maya on the stairs, Vector trained on the steps below them, blasting away with the enhanced accuracy of a CORE helmet.

A sharp crack reverberated from below. The booming of enemy fire momentarily ceased.

How? Laramie thought. There was no way Maya could have taken out assault armor with a Vector.

"Staff Sergeant, come on!" Maya yelled.

She pushed up and saw a splash of red against Finn's vest. Laramie grabbed an arm and dragged him up the stairs, crawling on all fours to keep her balance. Maya grabbed Finn's other side. The Marine tried to stand and move under his own power and almost fell over.

Laramie caught a glimpse of the Heavy. He was assessing his weapon, now a fractured tangle of metal with a smoking hole in it.

Good shot, Maya.

The three of them staggered upward. Laramie felt a faint, desperate twinge underneath the shell of concentration that kept her in the moment. She had to get her squad mates out. If Dr. Bell could stop this outbreak of . . . whatever it was . . . if they could get some alternative underway that didn't involve this insane, police-led massacre, then she could feel like her family would be safe.

Her family. How she would have loved to see them again. Would she ever get another chance? Were they living on borrowed time? Were they even alive?

I have to get my squad mates out.

They reached the last landing before the topmost floor. Kenny was leaning against the railing and burning through chem mags as he lay suppressing fire. Maya, the smallest one of the them by far, was somehow manhandling them forward. "Roof exit! We need to get to the roof exit, Staff Sergeant—"

One level below their feet, a blinding flash filled the air as Finn's rigged explosives detonated across the stairs.

The world turned strangely and suddenly silent. Laramie blinked repeatedly but couldn't quite make sense of what she saw. A gaping, charred hole where the stairs used to be. A bulky assault suit with no legs, tumbled into a heap. Her own hands, pushing herself up and hauling Finn to his feet. Every movement felt surreal and disconnected, as if Laramie was watching through someone else's eyes as her body and her troopers moved of their own accord.

She reached the top of the stairs and tumbled onto the uppermost landing.

Kenny was waving at her from the walkway by the end of the footbridge. He was shouting something that couldn't make it past the ringing in her ears.

"What?"

Kenny pointed down a hallway at a fire door.

Get to the door. Got it.

She gave him a thumbs up and looked back to Finn and Maya. They were pressed against the railing, Maya training her Vector on the staircase behind them, Finn looking around as if he had lost something. Laramie realized he no longer had his weapon.

"Get moving!" Laramie yelled. "I'll cover!" Her own voice sounded muffled, like she was holding a blanket around her ears.

Finn nodded and staggered away, holding the side where Laramie had seen the blood.

Laramie and Maya hurried along the footbridge, weapons up, covering their withdrawal. Her vision seemed extra sharp. But why couldn't she hear? She thought she should know, but thoughts came slowly to her brain, and she couldn't put her finger on it.

They reached the walkway that encircled the top level of the atrium. Kenny stood by himself, covering the landing with his Vector.

"You okay?" he yelled, barely audible. His face contained a strange grimace, as if holding back pain.

"I'm fine." She did feel good. At least, not bad. Maybe numb. Or euphoric? "What about you?"

Kenny gave her a nod that didn't jibe with his expression.

"Do we have an ETA on our ride?"

"Nine minutes—"

Laramie saw movement the same time Kenny started firing. A group of police crouched near the top of the central staircase. They must have jumped across the hole from the explosion.

An explosion. That's why she was deaf. She had been lying right next to it, on top of Finn.

She dove to cover as return fire snapped into the wall by her head. On impulse, she reached up to her earpiece and turned the comm volume all the way up.

Wyatt's voice filled the air around her. "Chris, coming up behind you from the stairs, we're coming in hot!"

"Copy. We can't get on the roof."

A flurry of snaps from the Vectors covered the top of the stairs, forcing the police to keep their heads down. Laramie's trigger locked on her next pull. She dropped to her stomach and fished out a fresh chem mag from her vest.

"Say again?" Wyatt barked.

"We are *not* on the roof. The access door is motorized and the power is still cut."

"Can you get it?"

"Working on it."

Laramie didn't hear any more as she shot at the police. She really didn't need to. The police obviously had a response plan for this location.

Swarm the regular doors with personnel. Cut the power on any other exits. Trap your prey and hunt them down. All she could do was focus on her job, which right now was to hold off enemy combatants and trust that Wyatt would earn all that fancy officer pay and not let them all get killed.

Laser bolts popped chunks of plaster and ash out of the wall to her left. Laramie tried to return fire but another barrage forced her to press flat against the floor. Dust from more impacts swirled around them in a white cloud, obscuring their attackers.

"The lock is free," Chris said on the comm. "Come on, Finn . . . push . . ."

More blasts. Laramie tried to locate their origin, but a quick peek was met with an electric *zing* that almost shot her in the face again. For some reason, she found herself laughing. Why imminent death seemed funny, she wasn't sure. But it seemed to pair well with the ringing still in her ears from the explosion.

Kenny's voice filled her ears through her comm earpiece. "I'm on my last mag."

Laramie managed to tug her Vector a few centimeters off the floor. "Maya, can you see them?"

"No. I can't get a shot."

A laser blast hit a nearby potted plant, exploding it into a cascade of clay fragments that showered them in debris.

"Roof door is open!" the comm said.

"Move!" shouted another voice.

But all Laramie could do was stay flat. She and Maya were hopelessly pinned. A tiny voice told her that more police were flanking them while the first group kept up the suppressing fire.

She shrugged up her Vector anyway. If she was going to get waxed, at least she was going to go out shooting. Curiously, she didn't feel bothered by this.

"Laramie, get your team to the roof!" Wyatt said on the comm.

"We're pinned," Laramie said.

She glanced at Maya, lying flat on the other side of the hallway. She couldn't see Kenny. A barrage of shots eviscerated the rest of the wall.

Laramie's hand slid off her Vector. She readied her body to push herself up. She was sure she could get off a couple shots, just enough to the others Maya retreat. That was all she needed to manage. It would very likely be the last thing she ever did.

"Maya, Ken, when I say, shoot and fall back. Got it?"

"Got it."

Another blast electrified the air over Laramie's head.

"Ready?"

Before Laramie could commit herself, multiple laser shots ripped holes in a seemingly random pattern on the wall in front of Maya. At first she thought the police must be shooting through the wall at them. But that wasn't right. The shots had come from behind her.

One of the hostiles, a body in black tactical gear, rolled face-down at the end of the hall with a large hole in his shoulder.

"To the roof! Now!" Wyatt shouted from behind them, his face red from exertion.

He had come back for them.

The corridor was literally disintegrating. Laramie scrambled to get to the cover while Wyatt laid down suppressing fire from the fire door, snapping his trigger as fast as he possibly could. A picture frame filled with corporate art shattered from a laser blast and sent a fine glass mist into her face just as she crossed the threshold of the fire stairs.

They turned and ran. At roof level, the top of the fire stairs exited into a wide landing with stacks of cargo crates in front of a nonfunctional freight elevator. A large metal door sat ajar at the far end, pushed open just wide enough for a person to squeeze through.

Wyatt ran for the door. "Friendlies coming out!"

Maya followed, then Kenny, then Laramie. Her ARC vest felt loose as she ran. She glanced at her chest and saw pieces missing. One of the ablative pucks was completely gone. When had that happened? She tugged on a loose piece of fabric just before she wiggled through the open door.

Then they were outside.

The fresh air felt overpowering. Rain fell from a dark sky, pushed sideways by gusts of chilly wind that raked across the roof, yet streams of orange sunlight peeked past the edge of the storm cell to cast a surreal glow from the horizon. A raised, reinforced carbon-fiber platform occupied the middle of the area and was clearly some sort of landing pad. Large metal boxes, transformers, and HVAC ductwork filled the remaining space around the platform.

"Keep moving!" Wyatt shouted. "Get to cover and get your guns on that door."

Laramie scrambled behind a large metal evaporator painted in an industrial gray. Wyatt tumbled past her a split second later, just before a laser bolt ticked off the edge of the box by his head.

"Contact, five o'clock!" Maya said. Her CORE helmet would easily pick up the invisible light of the laser shots. "By the freight door."

Four Vectors went up. Four Vectors released a volley of death. When an empty magazine froze her trigger again, Laramie thought for a moment that surely the police knew they better leave them alone.

She slapped the fresh mag in her weapon and peeked around the edge of the evaporator. The freight door stood silently in its track, a spray of pockmarks on the outer face around the opening.

Laramie almost didn't see the streak of the rocket motor.

"Incom—"

The evaporator exploded. Laramie and Wyatt flew backward from the force of the blast. Laramie's head hit the roof surface, filling her vision with stars.

"Contact—multiple Heavies!" Kenny was shouting. "Repeat, multiple Heavies moving on your position. Lieutenant, displace!"

Wyatt had rolled onto his side and was trying to get up. "Copy," he replied, his voice groggy.

Another exhaust trail from a sleeve-mounted rocket streaked past them.

Laramie blinked hard to clear her vision. Somehow she had gotten herself into a kneeling position. Her mind raced to catch up with events. But for some reason all she could think about was the explosives Finn had set back on the central staircase. He always had a lot of explosives.

"Finn . . ."

"Say again? Didn't copy?"

"Finn. We need help." Her voice sounded alien to her own ears.

"We're pinned!" came the reply on the comm. "You need to displace, they're advancing on you!"

"*This is Savage Echo One, inbound. Someone say they needed help?*"

Wasn't that their Javelin's call sign?

"Teo!" Laramie blurted. She frowned, trying to focus. "We've got . . . multiple contacts in assault armor . . . on the roof."

"Roger. Turn your strobes on. Coming in hot. ETA thirty seconds."

They had to find a way to last half a minute. She glanced at the next evaporator a few meters over.

"Wyatt!" she yelled, pointing.

"Copy," Wyatt said. He shot at several shadowy shapes near the freight door. "All teams, turn your strobes on. Repeat, strobes on."

"Wyatt, we don't have strobes," Chris said.

The Lieutenant paused. "Where are you?"

"West corner, next to the vent—"

A hollow *foomp* announced a Heavy firing another rocket. Laramie weaved around several knee-high air ducts and saw Chris and Finn taking cover behind a low cement reinforcement. The rocket streaked past them and into a power transformer, creating a brilliant explosion that sent a shower of rock and metal into the air.

One of the other Heavies—there were *three*—was shooting an autocannon as he moved from the other side of the landing platform. He was advancing on the Marines' position, flanking. A stack of four officers in helmets and ARC vests trailed close behind, using their armored comrade as cover.

"Chris, say again, what is your position, over?" Wyatt said again.

Static.

"Fifteen seconds," Teo's voice crackled.

Still wrapped in a cloud of muffled sound, Laramie watched as the police moved closer to the Marines. Yet her mind screamed at her that the real threat was something else.

Why was her mind so slow?

She knew the answer. It seemed like it was just out of reach though.

Then it hit her. Teo's Javelin was coming in with guns blazing. RESIT ARC vests all had strobe beacons for locating positions in deep space, but the Marines' vests didn't. Chris and Finn would get waxed along with the hostiles.

Laramie's instincts made the call for her.

"Wyatt, cover me!"

His head turned in alarm. "What?"

She didn't wait. Laramie launched herself from cover, her feet finding the edge of the roof and carrying her at full speed around the ledge that traced the perimeter. The ground taunted her from ten stories below and threatened to pull her off balance. A part of Laramie's brain reminded her that she hated heights. She was supposed to be afraid. What if she slipped? What if a gust of wind pushed her sideways? She would plunge to her death in a stupidly terrifying end.

Yet, curiously, the idea of smashing into the ground as a crumpled pile of bones didn't frighten her. Neither did the hostile gunfire. All she could think of was counting the seconds left to reach the Marines before a RESIT Javelin obliterated them along with the enemy.

So she ran.

The wet air turned crisp near her face. Someone was shooting at her.

She turned the corner, leaning away from the vertigo caused by the sudden change in direction. Her foot landed in a puddle of water and she almost slipped.

Five seconds.

Laramie saw two figures huddled behind the jagged remains of an air conditioning shroud. Hostile fire had them completely pinned down.

She raised her Vector and took a few wild shots. Two of the police trailing the Heavy hit the deck. Another thumped the armored officer on the shoulder and pointed at Laramie.

"Friendly!" she shouted. She dove at the two Marines.

A distant rumble suddenly transformed into the thunder of four rocket engines. The Javelin screamed past the edge of the rooftop, and a split-second later the chin turret blazed a shower of death.

29

The chemical reaction that powered the laser blasts in small arms was loud. The Javelin's proved to be deafening. Even with her muffled hearing, Laramie had to cover her ears from the screech of venting gas as laser bolts raked the rooftop. Multi-megajoule bursts vaporized the flesh and equipment of the advancing enemy.

The Javelin circled above for a few moments and searched for hostiles. Teo finally came on the comm. "Roof is clear. I'm setting down on the pad. Get ready to move, we're tracking hostile air assets inbound."

Laramie pulled on the back of Finn's collar. "You okay?" she shouted.

Finn gave her a thumbs up. But when she turned to Chris, she saw him grasping his arm instead of his weapon.

"What happened?"

"One of those rockets hit our cover. Threw a chunk into my elbow." He pointed at the twisted metal of a nearby evaporator unit.

Laramie saw blood streaming down the green tattoos of his forearm. "Is it broken?"

Chris grimaced and gave her a nod.

Laramie helped him up. A cloud of dirt raged over their heads as the Javelin's engines set it down on the landing pad. As they moved, she couldn't help but glance at the remains of the advancing police squad. Pieces of bodies lay strewn about, charred and sizzling as they cooked in haphazard locations. What a terrible way to go. Laramie knew those police troops were just doing their job, even if that job had been to try to kill her companions.

The comm crackled with Teo's voice. "Lieutenant, we need to dust off *now*."

Wyatt waved everyone to the vehicle and they clambered through the side access hatch. A moment later the Javelin abruptly lifted into the air, sending Laramie to hold on for dear life.

She fought to keep her feet on the deck. The Javelin accelerated, and the next thing she knew, she was practically dangling in freefall. She looked to the crew chief to ask what the hurry was, but the seat across from Wyatt was empty.

Her eyes darted around the compartment. Chris and Finn sat next to Elton and the girls from the safe house, both of whom had death grips on their safety harnesses. Toward the front, an unconscious Izzy lay strapped against the deck with a medical immobilizer around his neck. Next to him was a figure with heavy bandages covering his face and hands. No, strike that—not hands. *Stubs*. Red soaked through portions of the gauze around his neck.

The realization had just dawned on her that she was looking at the crew chief when another figure caught her attention.

"Gavin!"

The trooper sat on the other side of an aerobike lashed to the deck. He flashed a smile behind his dark beard. "Hey there, Staff Sergeant. You like the limo?"

"Yes, I do!" She saw that his face looked like it had been dragged across rough pavement. "What happened to you?"

"Long story. It'll require alcohol."

"And the short version?"

He frowned, fumbling for words. "Groundhogs with big teeth and no head."

"Hopper nest? Oh, no." She shook her head at the dumb luck. A nice, big field might have looked like a good LZ, but the Javelin's engines would have certainly stirred up Juliet's most notorious predator. "I'm glad you found them, Gav. It could have been a lot worse."

He arched an eyebrow, apparently trying to picture *worse*. "Thanks."

Teo's voice trampled their discussion from over the comm. "Buckle up, it's going to get rough."

"*Going* to get." Gavin balked. He pulled on his safety harness.

Laramie hauled herself by the grab bars until she reached the crew chief seat. Wyatt sat at his own station on the other side of the cockpit hatch. A sudden lurch left her stomach on the wall of the fuselage. She didn't waste any more time before strapping in.

"What's going on, Wyatt?"

He tapped the wired headset over his ears and pointed to a compartment above her head.

Laramie got the picture. She opened the locker and retrieved another headset. It took only a second to plug the cable into the control panel and fill her ears with a stream of chatter from the flight deck.

". . . second contact, aft, seven o'clock high," the copilot said.

"I see it," Teo replied.

The Javelin banked to the right, sloshing around Laramie's insides.

"What are they?" Wyatt asked.

"Patrol drones. The threat computer says they're AV-8B Ibex. Two of them, coming in fast."

"We saw one up close when we were in the city. There's a nose-mounted autocannon."

"Do they have air-to-air?"

"Don't know."

Laramie saw Wyatt turn on his station's holo monitor and realized she could do the same. She groped around the perimeter until her fingers closed on the power toggle. After a second to power up, a shallow, three-dimensional display appeared in the air between her and the bulkhead.

She changed the screen to an overhead tactical map, with the Javelin represented in the center by a triangle embedded in a circle. Two red squares with carats above them bobbed nearby. Another few taps and the right side revealed the visual feed from the nose camera.

The red squares were lining up single file behind Teo. Laramie heard the defense computer narrate threat information as it analyzed the attack pattern.

A noise that sounded like hail reverberated off the back quarter of the Javelin, quickly followed by the bleat of a computer warning.

"Hit, port side," the copilot said.

They banked hard. Gravity tugged with renewed ferocity and Laramie grasped a nearby handle. The computer went momentarily silent as they rounded a city block and broke line of sight.

"Can you light them up?" Teo asked.

"Too close. I need some space," the copilot replied.

"Why don't we just outrun them?" Laramie said. "Javelins can go fast enough to make orbit, right?"

Wyatt pointed at her screen. "Telemetry is in the corner. They're faster than we are. Without an ascent booster, we're just a big, slow-lifting body."

"Slow, but slippery," Teo said. His voice was cool to the point that he could have been talking about mud drying. Quite a contradiction to the panic in Laramie's gut.

On cue, they pitched nose down and picked up speed. She clutched harder at the grab bars. Someone made a retching sound further back in the cargo bay.

The video feed showed the Javelin slotting between the blur of carbon-fiber skyscrapers. Teo flew them down near street level. Laramie saw throngs of panicked people running for cover. The red squares on the left slid further behind, but with the extra distance came a smaller angle of attack, and that meant easier targeting.

"Still behind us," said the copilot. "Both high, negative closure."

"We're going to run out of buildings for cover," Wyatt warned.

Teo pushed his control stick and sent the Javelin into another hard bank. The stream of skyscrapers in the holo monitor made Laramie dizzy. But each turn broke line of sight with the pursuing Ibex. Their optical targeting would have to reanalyze and retarget every time they came back into view.

Unfortunately, Wyatt's comment proved spot-on. The video feed showed a rush of high-rises give way to the five-story buildings of a different construction period.

A barrage of ugly, metallic *whumps* rattled the spacecraft this time. The Javelin seemed to drop several meters before flattening back out. The contortions of her teammates suggested they wanted to be anywhere but here.

"Another hit on port. Engine C is shutting down."

"Range?" Teo said.

"Two hundred meters."

Laramie glanced over at Wyatt. He was staring hard at his own holo monitor.

Teo pulled back on the stick and the Javelin shot upward, gaining altitude. A moment later he leveled out.

"I have Optical Target Lock," the copilot said. "Othello, Othello."

"Weapons free."

The deck of the Javelin shuddered as the laser turret fired underneath their feet.

Laramie saw one of the rectangles turn a flashing white. She guessed what happened. In his eagerness to take a shot, the Ibex's remote pilot had lined up right behind the Javelin and into their field of fire. Teo was right. None of these guys knew what a Javelin was, or what sort of armament it had.

The rectangle flashed one last time and disappeared. In the holo monitor, a cloud of smoke appeared as the Ibex smashed uncontrollably into a brick building.

"Good hit," Dave said. "Target one down."

The second red rectangle drifted further back in the threat display until Laramie had to adjust the zoom. Apparently it didn't want to play the same game.

"Target two is still shadowing us."

"Any fast movers showing up?"

"Negative."

Laramie peeked in the cockpit. She suddenly realized how hard Teo was fighting to keep the Javelin's flight path level.

"How badly are we hit?" Wyatt asked.

"Once we set down, we're not getting back up."

The Lieutenant thought for a long moment. "Can you reach the spaceport?"

"I'll try. If I can, do you want to put down easy, or hard?"

"Easy, please."

"Sorry, was kidding. Hard is all we've got."

Wyatt glanced over at Laramie. His eyes betrayed his thoughts of another hard landing many months ago. She knew he was thinking of Tiamat.

"You know," she said, "you don't have to keep doing this just for me."

Wyatt blinked in surprise. A wry smirk started to form on his lips. "It's hard to teach an old dog new tricks, isn't it?"

"Yet I try, and I try."

They shared a long look. Laramie could see that he understood, and was glad. She would be in it with him, together, no matter what.

Her eyes drifted back to the video feed from the nose camera. The buildings in the nose camera were shorter here, further from downtown, with the blue haze of water visible in the distance. She focused her energy on staring at their failing altitude. If they were about to crash—*again*—she at least wanted to see the end coming.

30

Harrison-Munroe Spaceport Complex
Juliet, Alpha Centauri A
2 March 2272

Wyatt's leg was on fire.

It had started with a dull thumping as they pushed up the central stairwell at the Health Department. By the time they cleared the roof, a shock of pain seemed to shoot through his calf every minute or two. Now it had ignited into a slow burn that made it incredibly difficult to concentrate on the command decisions he was making.

While Teo strained with the controls of the Javelin, Wyatt tried to distract himself from the phantom pain with anything he could think of. An imminent hard landing was unfortunately the easy choice. He looked down the fuselage at his team and said a silent prayer. How similar this felt to the crash on Tiamat. So many of those faces were gone from this life.

Wyatt pleaded to God to avoid a repeat. His prosthetic howled in its own silent prayer.

Assuming they survived, things were about to get even more dicey. The original plan had been to smuggle Dr. Bell out of the Health Department inside the supply truck. Figuring out the plan to get to orbit was supposed to come after that. But now, *after that* loomed in front of Wyatt like a maglev train. There would be no hope of refueling or repairing their Javelin once they landed at the spaceport.

This wouldn't be a discrete entry. They couldn't blend in with other passengers, perhaps buy tickets and take the next catapult up. They were about to crash-land a military spacecraft full of fugitives and wounded, with the city police tracking them and mobilizing for their next engagement.

A warning chime bleated from the cockpit. Wyatt switched to the onboard channel. *God, my leg hurts.*

He had to push it aside. He had to focus.

"How are we looking, Teo?"

"Almost there. I've got my eye on a potential LZ. It's going to be a big belly flop."

"How long?"

"On the ground in sixty."

The tactical screen beckoned with a static-filled video feed. The Javelin approached a freight receiving yard on the edge of the spaceport campus. Wyatt hoped it would be unpopulated enough that police in riot gear didn't immediately swarm them.

One of the engines sputtered, breaking the steadiness of the background whine.

The cargo bay was absent of any conversation. He spotted Laramie staring at the fuselage in a daze. He worried about her behavior. One minute she seemed lucid, the next she was out of it. Was it a concussion? Adrenaline? Either way, if it was the same thing that drove her foolhardy behavior on the roof, she might not be so lucky the next time around.

"We're coming down," Teo announced. "Everybody brace."

The whine flared in volume and the Javelin slowed its forward momentum. Wyatt felt the gyrations of landing adjustments through the fuselage. Then the spacecraft dropped from underneath them, throwing Wyatt against his safety harness.

Floating.

A last, desperate burst from the engines fought the draw of Juliet's heavy gravity.

They hit the ground with a crunch. Wyatt's teeth jarred against the inside of his skull as the engines died. Then the Javelin pitched forward as the tail of the spacecraft rose some thirty degrees into the air. An eerie silence descended around the cabin.

"Everybody okay?" Wyatt called out.

A number of aye, ayes. A few groans. Wyatt unbuckled his harness and grabbed his weapon. "Gavin, out the side hatch. Make a perimeter."

"On it."

Laramie shot him questioning look. Normally he'd give her the order.

"LT?"

"Come here," he said. As she moved closer, Wyatt studied her face, looking for any signs of brain trauma. "You okay?"

"Yeah. Why wouldn't I be?"

"Follow my finger."

He swept his index finger from one side of her face to the other. Her eyes seemed to track well enough.

"What day is today?" he asked.

"No idea."

"How many fingers am I holding up?"

"Two and a thumb."

"What's your favorite color?"

"Camo."

Wyatt felt some relief. She still had her wits. He still couldn't believe she had sprinted along the roof ledge to cover Chris and Finn. But if Laramie was anything, she was brave.

She stared at him expectantly. "LT, what gives?"

"You scared the hell out of me, running on that ledge. I thought you didn't like heights."

"I don't," she said matter-of-factly.

"Just want to make sure you're okay. You got shot in the helmet. You ate an explosion on the staircase."

"LT, I'm fine."

"I want to believe you. Let's just make sure. Gav can cover."

Laramie's eyes took on a severe intensity.

The sense of hurt was palpable. Laramie was as proud as they got, and that pride drove an incredible work ethic. But Wyatt couldn't take any chances. He waved toward the back of the cargo bay. "Let's get a marching order for the civvies and wounded."

Laramie slipped stiffly into business mode. "I'll get it done," she said, a bit too formally.

Wyatt pushed the friction aside for later and jumped out the forward hatch. His boots crunched into the crushed granite of a wide industrial lot. He could tell from the smell of the salt air that they were near the coast. Low buildings enclosed two of the sides, each with a receiving dock and freight door placed one meter off the ground. A covered breezeway wide enough for a lift loader led off to the east. Above, the storm cell that pelted them at the Health Department had mercifully blown inland. A cascade of color splashed the sky as the sun sank toward the horizon.

He scanned the area. He didn't see any people. He didn't see anything. Everything appeared dead and abandoned.

Wyatt's eye gave an involuntary twitch at a sudden spike of heat from his prosthetic.

"Gavin, sitrep."

"Emptier than Carlos's head. I don't like it."

Wyatt studied the perimeter again. "Yeah. We drop a spacecraft from the sky into their backyard. You'd think somebody would notice."

"Or at least have security come to see what the ruckus was all about."

Something told him not to waste any more time than necessary. "Gav, recon the breezeway. The tactical showed the main facility to the west. Let's get moving."

"Roger that."

Gavin sent Maya and Kenny to scout ahead. Wyatt turned his attention back to the Javelin. The aft ramp hung open about a meter off the ground, with Elton and Laramie helping the two young girls drop off the back. Dr. Bell was assisting Chris with a makeshift sling for his broken arm. Corporal Rahsaan had joined Finn at the back half of the perimeter. Teo stood by the forward hatch near the buckled landing gear. The pilot gave the side of the Javelin a pat on the fuselage, as if it were a faithful mount who had just made its last charge into battle. He held a small zero-gee bulb in his other hand. Wyatt thought he spied the cactus Teo kept in the cockpit.

"LT," Laramie said. "Looks like Izzy's up."

That got his attention. Wyatt jogged toward the aft of the Javelin. Carlos was moving down the ramp with a pained expression. Izzy sat on the ground just below him, awake and apparently lucid.

"Nice of you to join us again, pal," Wyatt said. He knelt next to the trooper. "How are you feeling?"

"A bit lost," Izzy replied. "Where are we?"

"We're making an exit."

The corpsman glanced with dark eyes at their surroundings. He nodded blankly. "What do you need me to do, sir?"

"Can you walk?"

He thought for a moment. "Yes, sir."

"Good. That's all you need to worry about right now."

The group made a hurried assembly while Wyatt pulled Chris over for some quick route planning. "Do you know anything about the layout of this place?"

The Marine shook his head. "Hewitt's job was groundside, not out in space, so we didn't exactly come here. But I've been on enough military bases to make some guesses. I think that breezeway must go to the operations building." He pointed with his good arm. "The main concourse should be on the other side. If we get there, we can find the boarding area and get you aboard a catapult pod. Then you can bolt out of this place."

"Hopefully before we draw too much attention," Wyatt said.

Chris raised his eyebrows. "Oh, I'm sure we'll draw attention."

A minute later, the call came back from Maya that the breezeway approach was clear. Neither she nor Kenny had seen a soul.

They lined up into formation, seventeen people divided into four groups. Maya, Wyatt, Chris, and Finn comprised the lead element. Gavin, Rahsaan, and the flight crew came next, carrying the bandaged body of the crew chief in a makeshift stretcher. They were followed by the noncombatants—Elton, Annika, Calista, and Dr. Bell. Laramie and Kenny brought up the rear with Carlos and Izzy. The moved along, quickly but carefully, keeping a watchful eye for anybody that might notice them.

As they approached the breezeway, Chris unholstered his pistol.

"This is wrong," he muttered. "No security guards, no alarm. This is bad."

Maya turned her head and looked at Wyatt, no longer wearing her helmet after finally running out of charge. He saw her face and instantly knew what she was thinking.

Parrell.

A simple badge reader secured the door of the operations building. Finn shot a hole in the lock and they moved inside to find an administrative office. A number of holo monitors and consoles lined one wall, with camera shots displaying the Javelin nose-down in the receiving yard. The room was abandoned.

"This is very, very wrong," Chris repeated. "Watch your corners."

"Move up," Wyatt said.

The office had an interior security door as the only other exit. Finn and Maya edged to one side, covering each other. Finn peeked through the small window above the latch. Then he pushed it open with his Vector. A service corridor extended further into the complex.

"Clear." Finn's voice was low, careful.

Wyatt gave a hand signal to push forward. They entered the corridor and followed it to a T-intersection. Instead of the hustle and bustle of a busy spaceport, the only noise came from the echoes of their boots off the tile floor. Stripes of different colors ran horizontally on the wall, indicators of what to follow to reach different operational destinations. A yellow band marked the path toward Flight Control.

"I don't think we're going to find an agent to book your boarding passes," Chris said.

"No, I don't think so either." Wyatt eyed the yellow stripe. "Looks like this is going to be self-serve. Let's head to Flight Control and see what our options are."

They passed an open doorway that revealed a deserted employee breakroom. Up ahead, a set of double doors obscured the corridor on the other side. Finn and Maya hurried up to one side and waited for the nod to push it open.

Wyatt gave the hand signal. Maya released the latch and began to press through slowly. Then she suddenly froze with her weapon up.

"What is it?" Wyatt said.

Silence.

"Maya?"

She cleared her throat. "People face-down in a ring."

The hairs on the back of Wyatt's neck stood up. "How many?"

"Six."

"Are they moving?"

"No movement yet."

Chris turned toward him as recognition slid across his face. *You've seen Constricted before. You didn't tell me.*

Wyatt nodded. Part of him felt dishonest, but there wasn't a lot he could say at the moment. He'd have to explain later that he hadn't been ready to share all his cards with someone he'd just met.

Chris wore his disapproval openly as he spoke. "Finn. Is there a path around them?"

"On the left. Maybe two meters wide."

"I guess it's your show, Lieutenant," Chris said.

"Okay. My show. Let's move. Everybody walks on the left, single file."

Maya held the door and they carefully stepped through, one at a time. Wyatt saw six people kneeling in a small circle, arms to their sides and foreheads touching the ground. Five men. One woman. If he hadn't known better, they could have simply been asleep, or perhaps praying in the formation of some obscure religious sect. He still didn't understand what this was. But he knew it was dangerous.

As he passed Maya, he felt the tension in her to match his own.

"Steady, Maya," he whispered.

"Yes, sir," came an unsteady reply.

He made it beyond the strange ring of constricted people and stood aside to let the others pass. Dr. Bell looked thoughtful as he moved alongside them. Calista kept her eyes on her feet.

Then Annika's turn came. She walked more slowly than the others, her attention drawn to the ring of people with unusual intensity. Wyatt saw her eyebrows furrow the way someone might react in spotting a familiar face across a room full of strangers. Her steps slowed. She might have stopped altogether except that Laramie grabbed her arm and forced her onward.

As the last of their squad came through the door, Wyatt moved up toward the front of their column. Finn pressed down the corridor to another T-intersection. Here, the colored lines diverged into different paths on the walls. Flight Control led off to the left. A green line to the catapult terminals went right.

More constricted lay along the floor of both corridors, strewn about in individual sprawls of one or two.

Finn motioned with his Vector at the prone bodies. "This isn't a good sign," he said, his voice low. "There's going to be a lot more in the concourse."

Did constricted react to sound? Wyatt tried to be as silent as he could as he cleared his throat. "How many more?" He wasn't sure he wanted to know the answer.

"Hundreds. At least."

How were they going to sneak a eighteen people past hundreds of constricted? He looked at Maya by the door. Her body screamed anxiety. She pointed her weapon at the ring of bodies, fearful they might jump up at any moment.

Wyatt turned to Chris. "Maya's the one we need to get to Flight Control. She's our tech. She can configure a catapult launch. Let's move everyone else directly to the passenger terminal. Does that work for you?" He threw his chin toward Annika and Calista. "For them?"

Chris scowled, clearly still not happy from before. But he nodded in agreement. "Yeah."

He looked at Maya again, how stiffly she stood.

"I'll escort Maya and pull security. Help Laramie and Gavin get the others to the right terminal. I'll honor our bargain—you, Finn, and Elton can have our weapons, and we'll take the girls with us off this rock. You can be on your way."

Chris arched an eyebrow. His anger seemed to diminish slightly.

Wyatt looked back in their ranks until his eyes fell on Jack Bell. The Director was watching him with interest.

"Doctor Bell, a word?"

Bell shuffled forward with clear reluctance, perhaps afraid he was going to get assigned some military task. "What?"

"These people—these constricted. If we don't interact with them in any way, will they stay like this?"

Bell's eyes drifted toward the body closest to them, a heavyset woman with a bundle of long, braided hair obscuring her face.

"There's a lot we don't know," Bell said. "Probably, yes. When they make these rings, it seems to be some sort of recuperative ritual. But it doesn't last forever. Eventually they'll wake up and . . . hunt."

"Well, that's encouraging."

Bell regarded him strangely. "Is that an optimistic comment that they might stay dormant, or a sarcastic one that they won't?"

"Whichever keeps us alive longer."

The director's lip curled into a half-smile. It disappeared a moment later. "Remember, Lieutenant. Even if they wake up, infection doesn't happen instantaneously. There's a window—a small one. Just get away before it has a chance to take hold. Whatever you do, don't provoke or injure them. It would be the last thing you ever do."

"I understand."

They divided up the team. Maya knew a programming assignment was coming, since all the operational personnel were motionless and inert on the floor. Her eyes betrayed her feelings about splitting off from the main group.

Wyatt tried to get her mind off the constricted. "How long do you think you'll need to set up a script?"

"Sir?"

"Maya. Focus."

"Okay." She took a deep breath. "It depends on which version of software they're on. I'm going to guess fifteen, maybe twenty minutes."

"Fifteen minutes. It'll go by like nothing." Wyatt clasped her shoulder. "You've got this."

"Yes, sir."

"Okay." He turned to find the others huddling at the intersection. "Everybody, be careful. There are no points for being reckless. Stay clear of the constricted. Get to the terminal. Chris will take the front, Laramie the back. Don't do anything stupid. Questions?"

The hum of a ventilation fan was all that broke the silence in the corridor.

Another phantom shock sent pain through nerves that were no longer there. Wyatt grimaced. It took him a moment to collect himself, to get back the focus of a RESIT officer.

There wasn't room for any mistakes.

"Let's move."

31

Maya and Wyatt crept slowly through the complex, Vectors up, following the yellow line that led to Flight Ops. Constricted bodies lay on the floor every five or ten meters. Almost all were in pairs, perhaps one person a carrier, the other the recipient of the infection. Wyatt couldn't imagine something so virulent. It was as if constriction had stopped time for these people, dropping them in their tracks as they transformed into whatever it was they now were.

The corridor terminated in a security door with an industrial-looking bio scanner mounted in the wall. The heavy construction rivaled any reactor room hatch found on interstellar spacecraft. It hung slightly open, beckoning.

"I was kind of hoping there'd be good guys barricaded in here," Maya said.

"Me too. Keep your guard up."

He tugged on the security door. It swung open silently, without protest.

Maya entered first and swept to the left. Wyatt covered the right. He saw a wide, multi-tiered operations room with multiple banks of control stations. Blinking lights and holo monitors relayed launch system status for the benefit of anyone without a neural stub. On the far wall, a series of giant windows revealed a brilliant stretch of blue water sparkling in the evening sun. Remnants of storm clouds clung to the coastline. Underneath them, the maglev rails of an orbital catapult ran along the rocky coastline.

"Lieutenant." Maya gestured with her weapon. "Four on the floor."

"I see them."

The constricted had arranged themselves haphazardly behind the operations consoles. Each had the same posture—kneeling, head down—but their orientation was different. Perhaps they tried to make one of their rings and ran out of space.

He stepped carefully around the console. "Two more over here."

"Copy. I've got three up against the window."

"Can you get to a control deck?"

"I think so."

"Get on it."

Maya took careful steps around to the console, as if she were testing her away across a frozen lake. A moment later she punched up a holo monitor. "Maybe our luck's going to turn, Lieutenant. The last flight operator was still logged in."

"Copy. You know where you're sending us, right?"

"Gateway Station."

"You got it."

Wyatt eyed the prone figures sprawled out across of the room and busied his mind to keep it off the phantom pain from his prosthetic. Such a strange behavior, trying to form a ring. Why did they put their heads together like that? Gavin had told him stories about ranching in Texas, how horses would huddle up in a circle to shelter each other from the cold. They did it head-first to maintain social connection. Very different than cows, who went head-to-rump. Cows apparently weren't very smart.

He scanned the room. Nine people total in Flight Control. Most wore business-type clothing. One had security apparel. None of them seemed injured—no blood, no signs of a struggle like in Parrell. Wyatt wondered what the end must have been like, whether anyone had been able to hold their wits long enough to even attempt to seal the security door.

The comm came to life with Chris's voice. "Acid One, Acid Two. Come in."

"This is Acid One."

"We've reached Passenger Embarkation, Terminal Six, with no incidents. What's your status?"

"All quiet here. Everybody's sleeping."

A beat of silence. "How's the script coming?"

"Good," Maya responded, overhearing. "I've got a standard launch package up that I can automate the hold gates in the countdown. Five more minutes."

"Okay," Chris said. "Just so you know, there's no shuttle pod at the gate."

"There won't be anything served up until I kick off the sequence." Maya spoke with distraction in her voice, and kept her eyes glued to the holo monitor.

"Copy. Signal us when you're moving out."

"Roger that," Wyatt answered.

He glanced at Maya hunched over her keyboard. Behind her, the blues of the ocean battled the growing red of sunset.

"You sure are taking your time, Sergeant. You making a shopping list over there?"

An absent-minded laugh. "You want to sit in a nice, lonely orbit and play cards until the O2 runs out, Lieutenant?"

"Fair enough." The nerves around his leg danced in a slow smolder. He gazed out the window and saw whitecaps. "Looks windy."

"I don't handle that part. The catapult makes those adjustments."

Wyatt nodded and went back to watching the bodies. He felt optimistic with how things were coming along. He had only known Maya through this mission, but there was no doubt around what she could do with computers. Maybe that would be just enough to get them back to Proxima alive.

Some final adjustments and Maya stood up. "All done. Give the word and we're ready."

Wyatt signaled Chris on the comm. "Acid Two, we're about to move out. Over."

"Copy, Acid One. When the passenger shuttle comes up, Finn and I will make sure everyone gets onboard."

"You sure you won't come with us?" Wyatt said.

"Sorry, Lieutenant. Our fight is down here."

"Understood. Stand by." Wyatt looked around and mentally plotted his path around bodies to the door. He nodded at Maya.

"Ready?"

"Ready."

Maya tapped one of the screens to begin her script.

Nine kneeling bodies sat suddenly up on their heels.

It happened in absolute silence. Wyatt yanked his Vector up. The constricted didn't move any further. They just stared emptily into space like they were in a trance.

Maya's eyes grew wide in alarm. "Lieutenant?"

"*Psst.*" Wyatt pointed at the figure to Maya's left. He motioned for her to come toward him in a wide berth, aiming his weapon at the kneeling shape.

She took small, fearful steps. Wyatt had to focus on his own breathing to keep steady. He remembered Parrell, feeling like he was sliding into a burning hole, losing himself. He understood what Maya was feeling. She had been there with him in the building.

The comm crackled to life with Laramie's voice. "LT. Something just woke up all these people lying on the deck."

"Copy. Same here." He started to move backward toward the door, covering the constricted with his weapon, making sure none of them tried to do anything to his partner.

"Doctor Bell says you need to get out of there, fast."

He crossed the threshold into the corridor. A moment later, Maya stepped out of the room, her face pale. Wyatt grabbed her elbow and pulled her down the hall. "We just exited Flight Control. Script is running. En route to the concourse now."

They reached the end of the corridor and pushed open a set of double doors. The main spaceport concourse ran left to right, a tall and airy structure made of tinted glass and dark carbon fiber. They stood in what was obviously the commercial wing. Multiple freight staging areas divided the floor space, with overhead winches and powered hand lifts strewn about for loading pods. Wyatt's eyes searched the pallets until he found a map placard on a nearby column. Terminal Six, in the passenger wing, was to the right.

"This way," he said, and again had to tug on Maya's arm.

"They're watching us." Her voice trembled.

She was right. A freight worker in a hard hat stood near a column and stared directly at them. Even from twenty meters away, Wyatt could see the pinprick pupils in the man's blue eyes.

They had to keep it together. "Keep moving."

A new voice came over the comm. "Lieutenant, this is Jack Bell. You have maybe two minutes, tops, before all these dormant constricted become fully active. You need to haul ass."

"Roger that." His thoughts ran in all directions as more eyes followed them. For a second he forgot where they were going. "Confirm your position."

"We are at Terminal Six, standing outside the—wait, a shuttle just moved up the track and is approaching the gate."

Maya's script seemed to be working. "Get everyone onboard and stand by. We are headed toward you."

They approached a wide cargo hatch with the words Terminal Two stenciled above it. A nearby monitor rotated through warning messages about the high-gee loadings used with commercial freight. This area seemed empty of constricted. A few cargo pods lay strewn about, along with a large, cylindrical container with a red inspection tag wired to the end.

Why Terminal Six? Wyatt thought. *We couldn't catch a ride at a closer dock?*

He was breathing heavy now. They left Terminal Two behind and hustled down the concourse, passing stacks of cargo boxes waiting to be loaded from areas marked off in yellow tape. At Terminal Three, however, they had to stop. Tall pallets of cargo boxes stretched across the thoroughfare and completely blocked progress forward.

"Did they try to build a barricade?" Maya asked. She motioned toward a nearby lift loader parked to the side.

Wyatt scanned the concourse for a solution. A narrow path looked clear near the exterior window. Four gaunt figures stood in front of it, watching.

"Um, we have a problem. Three is blocked."

"Copy," Laramie said back on the comm. "Look for a cleared area on your left. That's what we used."

"A couple of our friends are standing in the way."

A pause. "Okay. We're sending a team back to you."

"Negative," Wyatt said. He fought down the tension that tried to creep into his voice. "Everyone stays on that shuttle. That's a direct order. We'll figure it out."

Maya aimed her Vector at the constricted. Wyatt did the same. The constricted stared back with hollow eyes.

"You're sure we can't shoot these guys?" Wyatt asked.

"*No!*" Jack Bell's voice cut through the comm. "Don't engage. You'll trigger all of them to attack. Just get around them somehow."

Wyatt thought back to how his laser blast in the Parrell rec center set off a chain reaction of crippling mental pain. He lowered his weapon in frustration. Maya didn't.

"Hold your fire, Maya."

She stole a glance at him, pale as a ghost.

Come on, keep it together, trooper.

The burn in his leg intensified, starting to scorch.

Wyatt looked for another way around. He pushed against one of the crates to gauge the weight. It didn't budge. He tried again, this time using most of his body mass, but he might as well have been trying to heave a traffic barrier.

His eyes wandered to the lift loader. Instinctively, he made a dash toward it.

Metal bars formed the rough outline of the loader's cockpit. Wyatt swung himself in and pushed back onto the padded stool that passed for a seat. The controls seemed simple enough—a steering wheel and a pair of levers. The thumb grip of a keycard extended from the dashboard. Wyatt thanked God it wasn't biometric and switched on the power.

A moment's hesitation gripped him. He was about to make a hell of a racket. Would the constricted take it as a threat? Would a hundred minds suddenly come to bear in an attack designed not to infect, but to destroy?

A tiny, golden speck winked at him from his peripheral vision and made his decision for him.

Wyatt stepped on the accelerator pedal.

The loader glided forward with the hum of an electric motor. Wyatt picked up speed and rammed the barricade, crashing into the heavy pods and sending them tumbling from the top of the pile. He kept his boot jammed on the accelerator and could feel the wheels spinning beneath the footplate. As the loader struggled to push aside the metal containers, the faint smell of burned plastic wafted from the motor housing.

A rectangular crate tumbled free and the loader lurched forward. Wyatt plowed another three meters past the obstruction before he came to a stop. Straight ahead, a dozen spaceport employees stood in a circle. Their piercing gaze turned slowly toward him.

He bolted from the driver cage. "Maya, let's go!"

No answer.

"Maya—" he yelled again, but he was already stumbling back through the gap with his Vector against his shoulder. He could feel the constricted coming awake. He could feel the eyes on him.

Maya stood rooted to the same spot, her weapon trembling in her hands. Three figures walked toward her with a haunting gaze that burned the air with wisps of gold. Wyatt knew the specks were coming. He could *taste* them. He lunged forward and grabbed the back of her collar. As he pulled her away, he caught a glimpse of her face and saw the abject terror of someone about to lose it.

He threw her through the gap in the barricade.

She tripped and fell on top of her Vector with a clatter. Wyatt stumbled over her and grabbed her vest in a single, unbroken motion.

"Come on!"

"I-I . . . they're . . ."

Wyatt dragged her forward with his momentum just as another wisp of gold darted across his vision.

"We need to move!"

"I *can't* . . ."

Wyatt thrust his face next to hers and shouted at the top of his lungs. "*Maya, you are RESIT! Now move!*"

The volume seemed to snap her out of it. He shoved her to her feet and ran next to her, his equipment rattling with every step. He could see the signs for the next terminal in the concourse. But numerous figures now loomed from the shadows, lining the walls and the grand picture window with the coast behind it, gazing in silent menace. Golden specks darted with more frequency along the edges of his vision. Each little fleck seemed to nudge Wyatt in a different direction, nipping at his consciousness with an accumulation of distractions. He fought to ignore them, to stay focused on the goal of reaching the shuttle.

A burst of agony flared in Wyatt's calf, worse than any cramp or muscle tear he had ever experienced. He nearly collapsed to the deck. A memory loomed from the shadows of sneaking to the safe house under cover of night, creeping along the catwalk under the bridge with a police patrol above. The phantom pain of a long-lost limb had immobilized him. *Not now, God, please, not now.*

Wyatt forced himself forward, stumbling. His teeth clenched so tightly he thought he might crack them.

They passed another cargo terminal, dodging shipping crates and cargo pods strewn about the concourse. A dozen people watched from the windows as Wyatt and Maya ran.

Wyatt sputtered words into the comm. "At Four!"

The constricted were moving now. Several maintenance personnel walked toward the middle of the thoroughfare. One spaceport employee, a young woman with black hair pulled into a bun, took several steps forward and put herself directly in their path. The irises of her green eyes loomed brightly on her face.

Don't look. Don't look . . .

Wyatt squinted at the walkway, at the reflective tape that said RESIT on the back of Maya's ARC vest, at his own feet as they chugged one in front of the other. He steamrolled past the woman at full speed just a meter behind Maya. But he could feel the tug on his head, a firm pull that wanted to draw his face to the left so he could stare into the gaze of those magnificent green eyes. They called to him with a thousand shiny flecks of light.

"Acid One, what is your status?" crackled the comm.

"Passing Five!"

His leg howled in agony. Wyatt missed a step and stumbled, barely keeping his feet.

They sprinted under a truss structure supporting a large sign that read *Passenger Terminal*. Kiosks and shops announced the changeover to human cargo with supplies on sale for upcoming shuttle trips. An overturned carbon-fiber display lay in Wyatt's path, an array of zero-gee drink pouches spilled across the concourse.

Maya was slowing down. Her head drifted toward a bearded kiosk cashier who had his gaze locked on her.

"Wyatt, run!" someone shouted, not over the comm. It was a human voice from somewhere up ahead.

You don't need to run.

The urge to slow down slipped its arms around him. Why was he breathing so hard? So unnecessary. All he had to do was stop and let one of the nearby people comfort him.

Stop running. Stay with us.

He felt a vague and easy warmth. The burning from his prosthetic seemed more distant now, anesthetized.

A dozen figures with constricted eyes crowded in front of the last terminal gate. They formed a tight gauntlet, as if all of Wyatt's family and friends had gathered to encourage him to stay just a little bit longer.

Maya was slowing down, too. "I can't . . ."

A mistimed step made Wyatt stumble again. His face scraped against the back of Maya's vest, the edge of a loose ablative puck poking into his chin.

A tiny scrape to prick the cocoon enveloping them.

It was enough.

"Move!" he shouted, for both of them.

Thighs pumping. Heart thrashing. Lungs on fire, his prosthetic seemingly ready to rip apart. They thundered toward the wall of constricted as the golden flecks tried to smother him, dipping into his mind and darting away with his thoughts. Wyatt grabbed Maya's collar to keep them together. He squeezed his eyes shut, lowered his shoulder, and braced himself like he was about to take out the opposing team's quarterback.

He rammed into something. A body, perhaps several. A brief resistance, then open air as obstructions flew aside and he rumbled along the downslope of a passenger walkway.

The warm cascade of golden flecks turned sharp, sour. He blinked and realized he had Maya in both hands. Wyatt desperately tried to stay in stride and not fall.

But the sparks were receding. The agony of his leg was coming back.

Wyatt and Maya lumbered down the access corridor that led to the shuttle hatch, toward the desperate, waving arms of his squad mates.

32

Catapult
Juliet, Alpha Centauri A
2 March 2272

The catapult may have been tailored for human passengers, but the acceleration of the shuttle still pressed everyone into their launch chairs like the packaged cargo they really were. Three gees tugged at body parts inside and out as they shot down the maglev track. Two hundred kilometers away, the vacuum tube would terminate and eject them into the atmosphere with enough velocity to reach low orbit.

Wyatt rolled his head to the side. Annika sat next to him in the eight-seat-wide configuration, teeth clenched, eyes front, looking like she was on a thrill ride at an amusement park. She seemed so little in her safety harness. Did she understand what was happening around them? Wyatt didn't know how much information Chris shared with her, but she seemed like a brave girl. He hoped she would be brave enough to deal with the news of what happened to her family.

Warning chimes sounded from the cockpit. Teo's voice crackled over the shuttle's comm system. "We're about to hit atmo. There'll be a bit of a bump with the transition."

Wyatt watched as the light disappeared from the portholes. Then the entire vehicle shuddered as they ejected into the thin air of a much higher elevation. Somewhere behind them a sonic boom echoed over the coastal mountain range. The shuttle's onboard engines fired, taking over from the maglev track and shaking the interior with a mighty rattle.

He lifted his eyes and looked at Chris sitting on the other side of Annika. The Marine stared out the porthole with a sullen expression.

Wyatt could feel the tension. Chris and Finn leaving Juliet wasn't part of the plan, but the horde of constricted at the spaceport hadn't given them much choice. Remaining behind would have been a death sentence. Yet despite having only one escape route via the shuttle, Chris had always been very clear that his fight was down on the surface. He had other cells of resistance Marines hidden around the city. His top priority remained the struggle against a government bent on wholesale murder. Wyatt wondered how long it would take for him to start negotiating his return to the surface.

The passenger bay remained silent as the engines continued their burn. Outside, the noise of air rushing past the fuselage lessened. By the time the sky turned to black beyond the portholes, the vibration of the thrusters composed a lonely chorus by themselves.

"Engine shutdown in three . . . two . . . one . . . shutdown."

Weightlessness.

Annika's eyes grew wide. Strands of hair face floated in front of her restraints.

"Pretty cool, huh?" Wyatt asked.

She turned to him and smiled.

He had not seen her do that before. She looked happy. How long since she last felt a bit of joy? The poor girl had been through so much. Her family dead. Her mother consumed by a disease they didn't understand. She had nothing left—nothing except Calista, Finn, Chris . . . and now Wyatt.

He turned to Annika. "Do you want to float around?"

An enthusiastic nod was his answer. Wyatt released his harness buckle and then did the same for her. Annika slid gracefully out from her chair and held on to the buckle as her momentum sent her feet up to the ceiling. She stood upside down, pure joy on her face.

As if in response to her delight, Wyatt's prosthetic leg decided to reduce the agony from the spaceport terminal to a slow, smoldering itch that now barely registered on the pain threshold.

Chris finally turned to watch. His face softened.

"I think we have a future RESIT cadet here," Wyatt said.

The Marine allowed himself a nod. "It seems so."

Annika flashed the biggest grin yet. She went to raise her hand in a thumbs up but the orientation of her body shifted unexpectedly in the microgravity. She scrambled to clutch the restraint harness.

Wyatt laughed. "Don't worry. First time's a little weird. You'll get it down."

"What's the plan now?" Chris asked.

"Teo has us on a trajectory to Gateway. We don't have a flight plan logged, so they'll challenge us when we try to dock. Things might get dicey."

"Finn and I are good in a fight."

"I know you are." Wyatt glanced at his arm. "You're injured. Finn's got his little girl. You two hang back this time."

"I don't really do 'hanging back.'"

"Chris. You kept us alive on Juliet. We're grateful. But we're in space now and this is my backyard. Let us do our job."

It was clear Chris wanted to argue, but after a moment he simply shrugged his acknowledgment. "Okay. Your show."

"Thanks."

"Wyatt."

"Yeah?"

Chris turned to Annika. "Why don't you go check on Calista, make sure she's okay?"

Annika frowned—she seemed to know she was being dismissed so grown-ups could talk. But the whimsy of freefall quickly took over as she climbed across the passenger seats to her longtime friend in the back.

Chris took a deep breath. "I'm glad you made it through the concourse. I've been in that position. With constricted staring at you. I've felt them before."

The hairs on Wyatt's neck stood on end. That's exactly what it was. *Feeling* them. "They called to us. I couldn't think. I didn't want to run. I couldn't understand why all I wanted to do was stop and go to them. It was like sliding down a slope, and I was struggling to do anything about it."

"It's hard to not give in. A lot of people do, obviously."

Wyatt felt uneasy at the narrow margin of error afforded him by years of training and discipline. "I guess my old drill instructor earned his money."

Chris glanced in Laramie's direction. She was farther aft, tending to Carlos.

"Laramie wanted to go into the concourse and get you."

"No. I ordered everyone to stay on the shuttle."

"I watched her flip her safety off, Wyatt. Your man Gavin held her back. Pretty sure she was going."

Wyatt frowned, a protest forming on his lips. Laramie had great instincts. But would she have disobeyed a direct order? He didn't think so—at least, not if Wyatt was the one giving it.

Chris raised his hand to cut him off. "Look. It didn't happen, so no harm, no foul. The loyalty's great." He glanced at Laramie again. "But if you're going to join this fight, Wyatt, you need to rein your people in."

"My troopers work in space, Chris. They're disciplined and they follow orders."

The Marine regarded him coolly. "Sure. But they're human beings, too."

Wyatt couldn't help but think of the terror on Maya's face as he dragged her through the barricade in the terminal.

"Noted."

Chris frowned. "I'm not . . . reprimanding you, Lieutenant. I'm just sharing wisdom. One constricted is dangerous. When there's a bunch together? They will feast on you."

"With a thousand gold sparks."

"Yeah." Chris nodded. "Or, if any of you had shot them, they'd have burned you to a crisp."

A deep quiet hung between them.

"I can understand the fear that brought in martial law."

"Sure. I *understand* it," Chris said. "But that doesn't make it okay. These aren't caricatures of some dehumanized enemy. They're real people, Wyatt. They're *our* people. A few days ago they were probably having dinner together, tickling their kids before tucking them in. Now they're, I dunno, sick. They elected government officials to protect them. Not to kill them."

"But having seen it up close, how do you fight something like that, Chris? How do you do it without ending up like them yourself?"

Chris swiveled his head aft. Dr. Bell floated in midair, crouched into a ball while he entertained Annika and Calista.

"That's what we need him for, isn't it?"

33

**On Approach, Gateway Station
Juliet Orbit, Alpha Centauri A
3 March 2272**

Chris floated just outside the cockpit and saw a magnificent view through the forward windows. It had been a long time since he had been in space. He watched in fascination as they glided toward the massive space station. Long, tubular pressure vessels comingled with structural lattices to form the scaffold of a central harbor area. At the ends, habitation rings rotated in opposite directions to provide artificial gravity.

The pilot was listening to something in his headset and turned to Wyatt hovering just behind him. "Flight Ops is pissed. They're demanding to know why we're making an unscheduled run."

"Where to start?" Wyatt snorted.

"NAV transferred to Station Control," Teo said, adjusting some controls. "Docking in ninety seconds."

Chris felt the vibration of the maneuvering jets as the shuttle made course corrections. They floated toward an empty docking boom ahead of them. Just beyond, a single freighter sat latched on to an adjacent lattice, inert and lonely.

"I wonder where all the other shipping is," Wyatt said. He tapped Teo on the shoulder and pointed out the window. "Do you recognize that spacecraft?"

"Not something that came through with us, but that might end up being our ride. I don't see any alternatives."

Wyatt turned and caught Chris's eye. "Any idea where all your interplanetary assets are kept, Master Sergeant?"

Chris peered out the cockpit for a narrow view of the long freighter. "Sorry, Wyatt. I just shoot things."

"Stand by," Teo said. "On final approach. We're about to dock."

"Okay. Excuse me," Wyatt said, pushing himself around Chris as he exited the flight deck. When he spoke to his troopers in the passenger bay, it was with the voice of command. "Listen up, RESIT Team. We are engaging in a hostile boarding exercise. Laramie and Kenny, you take point. Maya in the back, Gavin and I in the middle. Clear a path to Flight Ops. Got it?"

Multiple aye, ayes sounded as hands checked weapons. Chris felt compelled to check his Viper too, but the handling was difficult with one arm. He handed it to Finn and decided to stick to his sidearm.

The clack of a docking ring reverberated through the fuselage.

Kenny hovered near the ceiling hatch and watched an atmospheric monitor. "Pressure's matched."

Before Chris could blink, Wyatt was giving orders. "Go."

Kenny pulled a recessed lever and broke the seal with a hiss of gas. The metal door swung open and he pushed himself through without hesitation, followed quickly by Laramie.

A voice thundered from inside the docking boom. "What the hell do you think—"

Silence.

Laramie's voice came over the comm. "Clear."

Wyatt and Gavin headed up next, Vectors ready.

Maya floated near the hatch and organized the rest of them into pairs. She made maneuvering in microgravity seem effortless. Chris, on the other hand, found it incredibly difficult and struggled to remain oriented correctly. His zero-gee training had been years ago. And this time, he had a broken arm.

A tug on his sleeve caught his attention. Annika was looking at him, ready to move.

"Let's go, girl," he said. "Stay close to me."

Chris grabbed the edge of the circular hatch with his good arm and jerked his body through. The docking boom was clearly designed for small spacecraft. Rectangular sections of white insulation covered a narrow interior that stretched perhaps ten meters long. Chris floated his way up a series of orange handholds until he passed through another hatch into a large cubical compartment. Each wall was filled with a sliding pressure door bifurcated in the middle. All of them remained sealed except for the one leading to their shuttle.

Kenny and Laramie hovered next to two people wearing utility vests and maroon coveralls. One of them was trying unsuccessfully to keep a bloody gash under his eye from dribbling into the air. Chris floated closer to them to make room for the others coming up the docking boom.

Wyatt was fishing through the vest pockets of the uninjured man. A pat on the side produced a thick plastic access card. Wyatt called to Gavin and flung it across the compartment.

"The security doors don't use biometrics?" Chris asked.

"No. Wouldn't work if you're wearing space suits."

Of course. Chris felt immensely stupid. This was far out of his element. If only he were back on Juliet.

Wyatt faced the station personnel. "How many people in Flight Ops?"

The uninjured worker, a short, older man with a closely-trimmed mustache, stared straight ahead in silence.

"Do you want to do this the hard way?" Wyatt repeated loudly. "How many people?"

The worker stole a furtive glance at the RESIT patch on Wyatt's vest. "I'm not talking to you."

"Fine," Wyatt said. "Laramie, Kenny—stack up with Gav." He turned to Chris. "Cover these guys for me, will you?"

"Sure. Just a moment, though." He felt the grin forming as he moved closer to the station worker. "Hey, tough guy."

Defiant eyes flicked over to him.

In one motion, Chris grabbed the front of the man's uniform and head-butted him across the bridge of his nose.

Blood spurted into the air as he cried out in pain.

Chris yanked him close. "Listen, pal. I'm in kind of a pissy mood right now. So, tell my friend how many guys are in that room before I start breaking things on you."

"Four," the man said immediately. His hands clutched Chris's tattooed forearm, waging a losing battle at getting free. "There's four—"

"Armed?"

The man hesitated.

Chris looked over his shoulder. "Weapons free, Lieutenant."

"Wait," the man said quickly. "They don't have weapons. Only security does."

"Good boy." Chris twisted his arm free. "By the way, if you're lying, you're dead."

The space station worker glowered. "I'm telling the truth."

The whoosh of a breaking pressure seal filled the compartment. Chris watched as Wyatt and three other troopers moved up into the station.

The rest of their entourage continued to enter the compartment. The space was getting crowded now, and Chris made sure to stay close to their prisoners. They didn't look very tough, although the older man was clearly hostile. Chris didn't mind. He was happy to beat the crap out of him if he had to. Just another plug against the establishment that was killing people on the planet below.

"Make a hole," came a voice from the docking boom. Teo appeared, switching back to talking on the comm. "That's all we've got? Where's *William Tell* and the others . . . no, I'm sure I can fly it . . . okay, we'll make it happen."

"Everything all right?" the copilot asked.

Teo's face telegraphed his displeasure across the entire compartment. "Wyatt's got control of Flight Ops. There's only that one spacecraft docked. It's an antique."

"How antique?"

"Fission reactor, dual inline radiators."

The copilot frowned. "That's . . . wow."

"Wow, what?" Chris asked, intrigued and worried at the same time.

Teo shrugged it off. "That design is a good eighty years old. But it's what we've got. It'll be fine."

"*Eighty*? You're kidding." Chris grabbed the older station manager. "Where's all the top-shelf stuff, eh?"

Before the worker could answer, one of the great circular hatches on the far side of the compartment hissed and slid open. The corridor beyond was empty.

"Wyatt's opening the hatches to the freighter," Teo said. "Let's move."

Finn and Maya sandwiched their group and led the way. Chris drew his pistol and waved it at the prisoners. "You, too, tough guy."

They floated into another cylindrical pressure vessel that extended fifty meters away from the junction compartment. Cargo nets and storage lockers lined the walls except for a thin line of small windows on the right. Chris peeked outside and saw the curve of Juliet's sunrise form a brilliant crescent against the darkness behind it.

Up ahead, the windows revealed a large vessel connected to the station via another docking boom. It was the same freighter he had glimpsed from the orbital shuttle.

Space wasn't in Chris's wheelhouse, but he knew his way around heavy equipment. The freighter stretched a maybe a hundred meters in length, with two large, conical EmDrive cones mounted inline at one end. Instead of a modern design where modular containers latched onto a central spine, this spacecraft had large cargo bays integrated directly into the superstructure.

It looked like something out of a history book. The most contemporary piece of equipment visible was the docking mechanism.

Chris turned to the mustached station manager, who by this point had finally managed to slow the blood gushing from his nose. Their eyes met and the older man winced.

He jerked his chin toward the window. "What's the story?"

"It's getting ready to be decommissioned."

"Where are all the other freighters?"

The station manager just shook his head.

They reached the docking boom. Chris waited while Finn and Maya directed everyone through the hatch. He stole a last glance through a porthole. Floodlights shone brightly on the name painted on the hull. *Kumano Lily*. Hopefully that was a lucky name for a spacecraft to last so long in its service life.

He pointed his sidearm at the station manager. "Okay, guys, down you go."

"Wait. We're not going with you?!"

"Well, I'm not leaving you here."

"But—"

"Go."

Reluctance spilled over the man's face. But his eyes traveled from the pistol to the hatch, and he pushed himself down the boom with his coworker.

Chris followed until he crossed the threshold onto the freighter. Right away he felt discomfort. The crowded airlock reeked of mildew and burned plastic and spoke volumes to the spacecraft's environmental systems. Jack Bell, Finn, Elton, and the girls floated in confusion about where to go in the unfamiliar layout. Even the space station crew seemed disgusted.

A yellow ship ladder stuck out from the opposite hull wall. Maya waved her arm in a circular motion. "Everyone up to the crew deck!"

Finn helped the wounded RESIT troopers through a round hatch in the ceiling. Dr. Bell took the girls up next. Teo and Dave pulled themselves through a different hatch into a very small flight deck, where they started flipping the switches that would bring the freighter to life. Chris remained in the entry. He was having a stare-down with his head-butt partner when Wyatt appeared through the main hatch.

"Any problems?" Chris asked.

Wyatt shook his head. "Nothing a punch in the face didn't fix."

"Oh, good. I've taught you something."

The lieutenant flashed a grin before he ducked into the cockpit. "How long will preflight take?"

"Ninety minutes, but the more the better," Teo said.

"You have ten. Make it happen."

Teo and the copilot traded glances. Chris thought he heard one of them mutter something like *sure, what could go wrong* and felt his stomach do a little jump.

Wyatt withdrew from the cockpit and switched on his comm. "Laramie, are the prisoners secure?"

"Ran out of duct tape, LT, but yes."

"Copy that. Get yourselves and the provisions to the freighter ASAP."

"Roger."

Chris waved his pistol toward the two men in front of him. "What do you want to do with these bozos?"

"We'll shove 'em into the boom when we leave. No point taking them with us."

The station workers' expressions filled with relief.

Chris stole a glance out the airlock window at the growing sunrise over Juliet. He wished he were staying behind as well.

34

Kumano Lily
Juliet Orbit, Alpha Centauri A
3 March 2272

Wyatt glanced at the chronometer on his wrist. They were taking too long.

Taking control of Flight Ops hadn't been the problem. The four station workers surrendered immediately and never had a chance to call Security. But the airspace board that tracked every asset from groundside to orbit and beyond also showed a Fast Attack on patrol. Wyatt struggled to do the math in his head, but something told him *Razor* would be coming uncomfortably close to their flight path.

"How much longer?" he asked.

Teo remained all business, his voice seemingly without worry. "Almost there. Can't cut out any more."

Wyatt looked around the entry deck. Portable ration crates from the station's emergency lockers sat hastily secured against the bulkhead. By the airlock hatch, Chris supervised two tense prisoners. Everyone else had buckled in on the crew deck.

Laramie emerged from the threshold that led to the cargo bays. The metal hatch swung on hinges instead of retracting into the bulkhead, another testimony to the age of their newly acquired vessel.

"Cargo bay is secure, LT," Laramie said. "There's nothing back there. Just rusty shipping containers and leaky pipes."

Wyatt smirked. "Leaky pipes are a good thing."

"Why's that?"

"Out of leaks and you're out of fluids."

Laramie shook her head. "I can't believe we're even joking about this."

"Did you check the reactor room?"

"Gavin's on it. We'll see if he's glowing when he gets back up here."

Wyatt checked his wrist again, and tried to think of what they might have missed.

Teo's voice rang loudly from the flight deck. "Time to button up."

Wyatt pointed at the two prisoners and motioned toward the airlock. "It's your lucky day, gentlemen. Get out."

The man with the broken nose eyed Chris before floating himself through the hatch. The other prisoner didn't hesitate. He didn't even bother to look over his shoulder.

Chris swung the hatch closed and pulled the locking latch. Behind the tiny porthole, the opposite airlock door slid shut. Wyatt watched as the Marine waved his fingers at the glass and said, "Bye, bye, tough guy."

"Hatch is closed," Wyatt relayed to the flight deck.

"Copy." Teo's verbal checklist transformed into something purely functional. "Switching to onboard power . . . check. Retracting umbilical. Docking ring is unlocked. We are clear of the docking boom."

Wyatt grabbed the cargo net that held the ration crates. He motioned for Chris to secure himself. "Teo—max accel. Go!"

Over the next sixty seconds, Wyatt felt his weight increase a hundredfold. The sense of freefall evaporated as his boots slipped into the empty air. Moments later he found new footing against the rubberized deck that had previously acted as compartment walls. A ration crate shifted behind the cargo net, threatening to smash his fingers before it held fast against its neighbor.

"We're maxed, Wyatt," Teo said shortly after. "One point four gee."

"That's all she can make?"

"Affirmative."

Wyatt tried to do the math to put them at the quantum gate. Everything he came up with fell short. "If we do a midpoint turnaround, that puts us seven and a half days out. We've got less than six."

"I've got the control rods all the way out. These reactors don't have it."

"Then work it from the radiator side."

"Already trying."

He saw Chris trying to follow the conversation. The Marine stood on a bulkhead that now became the floor under acceleration. He was gingerly testing his broken arm.

"We aren't done, are we?" he asked.

"No. No, we're not."

"What's up?"

Space travel at the distances involved was anything but quick. Wyatt decided he had the time. "Most commercial spacecraft are rated for three gees. We're pushing half that. We're not going to get to the gate in time for the transit window."

"You said something about a midpoint turnaround?"

"I know what you're thinking. Just delay when you start your deceleration, right?"

"Yeah." He shrugged. "Marine logic."

Wyatt shook his head. "You want to know what one of RESIT's most important jobs is?"

"What?"

"'To destroy any inbound spacecraft operating with excessive velocity or in an unsafe manner toward a quantum gate.' Basically, protect trillion-dollar hardware from kinetic weapons and stupid pilots."

Chris gave him a skeptical look. "So, you're not going to do it?"

"No, we'll do it," Wyatt confessed. "We won't have any choice. But that brings up the second problem."

"Which is?"

"There's a RESIT Fast Attack that's on an intercept course. If we do a midpoint turn, they'll catch up to us."

"Oh." Chris frowned. "I don't like that. Do you have a plan?"

Wyatt glanced at the dinginess of the entry compartment. "In this?" He didn't bother coming up with an answer he didn't have.

"Well, if you're going to break regs, at least we won't live long enough for the court- martial."

***

The next several days of spaceflight proved to be unremarkable. Shipping lanes normally full of vessels queuing up for a transit window were empty and deserted. Communication channels across the radio spectrum delivered only the static of empty space. Teo had managed to squeeze a sustainable one point six gee out of the ancient reactor system, and they'd delayed their midpoint turnaround an entire twenty-four hours to close the gap with Thermopylae.

Wyatt was stowing his lunch trash when Teo's voice crackled over the comm.

"Lieutenant? New contact, bearing two-twelve by thirty-three, twenty-eight thousand klicks. On an intercept course with negative closure. I think our bogey found us."

The message had to come sooner or later. Wyatt sat up from his little corner in Cargo Bay C and finished chewing zero-gee rations, basically a chunky milkshake squeezed through a wide-mouthed cap. Eating under gravity seemed to make it marginally better. The flavor, not so much.

"Any hails?"

"No, sir."

"Think they've seen us?"

"It's a Fast Attack, Lieutenant. Of course they have."

Wyatt nodded to himself. Their pursuer's mission would be about elimination, not interdiction, then. Now it was just a matter of targeting accuracy. "How long until they're in weapons range?"

"Maybe eighteen hours. They must be pushing close to four gees."

"Jesus. ETA to Thermopylae?"

"Twenty hours, forty-three minutes. And that's with us coming in blazing fast."

Whoever ordered *Razor* after them wanted them shut down, bad.

Wyatt squeezed the meal tube one last time and a blob of noodles popped through all at once. A moment later, his nose was running from the heat.

"Discontinue decel, Teo. Turn us around. Shave as much off our flight time as you can."

"Sir? That velocity . . . I have to advise against—"

"I know it's screaming fast. They're going to blow us to smithereens if we don't." A dark smile crept over his face. "At least there's no commercial traffic in the way."

"Aye, aye, Lieutenant."

With no other options, Wyatt felt strangely at peace with such an audacious command. He climbed up the crew ladder to Cargo Bay B. Laramie was asleep on a makeshift cot of insulation. She held her battered ARC vest between her head and her elbow like a pillow.

"Staff Sergeant," he said.

Her green eyes popped open and stared blankly at him for a second.

"LT. What's up?"

"Fast Attack closing on us." He took her through the situation. Laramie's face remained neutral throughout it all. After he finished, she just shrugged.

"So, RESIT Dagger is coming to finish us off?"

"Don't call them RESIT," Wyatt said. "I won't believe that's who's piloting that ship."

"Doesn't matter, I guess."

"We're not dead yet."

"No. But our number's probably due." She sat up and yawned. "Shot down from orbit. Hijacked a moving train. Had a firefight with police. Ran from telepathic zombies." A sarcastic laugh escaped her lips. "These last few weeks are the definition of nuts."

"So what's one more thing? Threading the needle on a quantum gate?"

Laramie leaned her head against the bulkhead and watched him through heavy eyes.

"Wyatt. What do you think's going to happen to Juliet?"

She never called him Wyatt. It caught him off guard. He wasn't even sure how to tackle the magnitude of such a question.

"How many people did you say live there?" he asked. "Twenty million?"

"Yeah, give or take."

After a heavy silence, he opted for the hopeful. "That's a lot of brain power to figure out a problem, Laramie. Whether it's resistance groups like Chris's, or researchers like Dr. Bell. Maybe there are others we didn't see. Have faith. Someone will tackle what's worth fighting for."

"What if the someone was supposed to be us?"

Their eyes met. An incredible sadness filled Laramie's face, a sister unable to save her family as the house burned down around them. He reached out and squeezed her arm. He knew there was no way to answer that question. All they could do was focus on what was immediately in front of them.

The clock ticked away as Teo put them back under acceleration.

At twelve hours to intercept, Dave finally got the freighter's antiquated optical sensor arrays to positively ID their pursuer. It was indeed *Razor*. Wyatt frowned at the spacecraft that had butchered the crew of the *Mozambique*.

At ten hours, Thermopylae came to life. A halo of radiation filled their sensors as the quantum gates sidestepped the constraints of three dimensions, revealing a holographic universe where the concept of distance was a derived and optional attribute of space-time.

At six hours, Teo practically begged Wyatt to let him resume deceleration, before the tiniest error in their course flung them past the quantum gate instead of through it.

And that's when things started to get interesting.

35

On Approach, Thermopylae Gate
Alpha Centauri A
9 March 2272

Teo called Wyatt to the bridge and pointed to the flat panel that predated holographic visualization by thirty years. "Multiple new contacts on station near Thermopylae."

"Who are they? Our missing freighters?"

"Unknown," Dave answered. "The sensors on this hulk are absolute crap. But I see three vessels, just sitting there."

"Have they seen us?"

"Our drives are pointed at them now for decel, so we might as well be shining a floodlight in their faces."

Wyatt stroked the stubble on his chin and thought.

"Any downside to hailing them?" he finally asked.

"I guess not, but what are you going to tell them? Get out of the way?"

"I was thinking more along the lines of sending them our intel. If we're going to get waxed, at least our effort doesn't have to die with us."

"That's depressing."

"True."

Teo mulled it over for a moment. "What have we got to lose?"

"Not much." Wyatt stared at the flat-panel monitor, wondering if the newly arrived vessels would even believe him. He made his decision. "Hook me up on broad-beam. Let's put our message in its bottle before it's too late."

Teo adjusted some switches. "Mike's hot."

Wyatt didn't mince words. "Attention all spacecraft, this is *Kumano Lily* outbound from Juliet. We are being pursued by a hostile vessel and require assistance. Please respond."

Silence stretched across the radio. Wyatt felt his body sag against the continued effort of the engines to slow their approach.

"Guess I'll try again," he said. "Attention all spacecraft—"

A businesslike voice crackled over the comm. "*Kumano Lily, this is RESIT D-18 Sawtooth. Your approach vector toward Thermopylae exceeds allowed parameters. Change course immediately to three seven by ten and commence maximum deceleration burn. Acknowledge.*"

Everyone's heads swiveled in recognition. *Sawtooth.*

Wyatt fought to keep his own emotion in check as his heart leaped in his chest. These vessels were part of Caustic Team. Proxima's Team.

His Team.

He didn't know why they were here already—his recon mission was meant to prepare for such a task force, and obviously they hadn't made it back yet. But he wasn't going to question it. "*Sawtooth*, this is RESIT call sign Savage Echo aboard Kumano Lily. I say again, we are being pursued by RESIT FA-476 *Razor* which is a hostile vessel. I repeat, *Razor* is a hostile vessel. Request immediate intercept, over."

Clunking boots on the ladder announced Laramie's abrupt entry into the Flight Deck. "Caustic came through the gate?" she asked with excitement.

"Three vessels," Teo said. He pointed at the blob on the left of the radar. "I think *Sawtooth* is this one."

Laramie's eyebrows went up. "They brought the destroyer? Holy hell. Is *Vigorous* here?"

"I can't tell. This one is too small," he said, pointing to another blob. "This one could be, though it's a bit blurry—"

"*Kumano Lily, your approach vector exceeds allowed parameters. Change course immediately to three seven by ten or you will be fired upon. Acknowledge.*"

Teo sighed. "They're going to shoot us."

Laramie let loose a string of profanity. "What's the deal? Are they not receiving us?"

Wyatt keyed the ancient microphone and spoke again, slowly, with emphasis on each word. "*Sawtooth*, I say again, this is RESIT call sign Savage Echo. My name is Lieutenant Wyatt Wills, serial number 0-6-5-8-2-2-6-7, Havoc Troop, Caustic Team. I am aboard *Kumano Lily*. I am operating under orders from Major Beck. We have a RESIT recon team aboard and are being pursued by a hostile vessel with intent to destroy. Are you reading me, *Sawtooth*? Over."

Laramie hit Teo on the arm. "Hey, pilot. How do we let them know we are who we say we are? Can't you waggle your wings or something?"

Teo turned around in his seat and threw her an incredulous look. "This is an interstellar spacecraft. You might as well make a walrus tap dance."

"What's a walrus?"

"Quiet, you two," Wyatt said. He cleared his throat to try again. "*Sawtooth*, this is RESIT Lieutenant Wills aboard *Kumano Lily*. Do you copy?"

A familiar voice filled the audio channel. "*This is* Vigorous *Actual. Wyatt, what in the hell is going on?*"

A flood of relief crashed through him. Major Beck. One of the other spacecraft *was* the troop carrier.

"Major, it's a long story. I would love to tell it to you, but we're not going to live long enough. There's a Fast Attack in pursuit that has illegally fired upon us as well as other spacecraft. They'll be in weapons range any time now."

"*Say again, you're being pursued by a RESIT Fast Attack?*"

"Yes, sir. Though I do not believe it's a RESIT crew aboard her."

A few seconds of silence. "*Wait one,*" Beck said.

"I wonder what that means," Teo muttered.

The original monotone voice returned to the comm. "*FA-476* Razor, *this is RESIT D-18* Sawtooth. *You are ordered to discontinue pursuit of* Kumano Lily. *Change course to one eight zero by zero, commence immediate deceleration burn, and await further instructions. Failure to comply will result in offensive action. Acknowledge.*"

"Yeah!" Laramie shouted. "That's what I'm talking about!"

"We're not out of this yet," Wyatt cautioned. "*Sawtooth* is a long way off. *Razor* isn't."

"Yeah, but if *Razor* doesn't comply, Beck will hunt them down and they'll know that. A Fast Attack is no match for a Destroyer. They aren't going to sign their own death warrants."

"After everything we saw groundside, are you sure about that?"

Doubt crept into Laramie's face.

The copilot turned from the telemetry on the control board and patted Teo on the arm. "Aspect change in target. *Razor* is changing course."

Laramie exhaled loudly.

"They're complying?" Wyatt asked. He wanted confirmation.

"It looks like they . . ." His words died off as he scrolled through more telemetry.

"Dave?"

"No. They're turning perpendicular."

"What does that mean?" Laramie said.

"They're changing course, but not to the one *Sawtooth* ordered." Teo pantomimed moving the spacecraft with his hands. "They're going to accelerate sideways so they'll pass Beck's position at too steep of a vector to be intercepted."

"But they're giving up on us, right?"

The copilot gave the answer no one wanted to hear.

"Weapons launch. Vampire, Vampire. Inbound boarding drone, ETA eight minutes." He fiddled with the controls for a few moments before slapping his hand on the console in frustration. "Maybe less. I can't get a good vector using this equipment."

Wyatt closed his eyes. His stomach felt like he'd just been punched. Memories of *Mozambique* filled his mind, a crew that had died in minutes.

"*Vigorous*, did you copy that?" he said finally.

"*Affirmative. Standby,*" Major Beck said. The broadband went momentarily silent. "*Wyatt, Sawtooth can't target that drone—too much interference from the quantum tunnel. You'd better prepare counterboarding measures.*"

"Copy."

"*We'll keep trying, Wyatt. Good luck.* Vigorous *out.*"

36

Chris's eyes snapped open to see Laramie hunched over him, shaking his shoulders.

"Wake up. There's a Maximillian inbound."

He instinctively reached for his weapon. "I don't know what that is, but I'm sure you're about to tell me."

"A boarding drone with an offensive loadout. It punctures the hull and tries to take control of the bridge. I need your help—everyone who can pull a trigger."

Chris stood up and looked at the others in their acceleration couches. Kenny and Maya had overheard and were each pulling out some kind of form-fitting pressure suit. Finn and Dr. Bell listened intently. But what mostly caught his attention were Annika and Calista, blissfully asleep and unaware of the apparent danger. They looked so small and innocent. It didn't seem fair that they couldn't get a break.

"What do you want me to do?"

"I need everyone who's armed to assemble on the entry deck in three minutes. Wyatt will go through the plan then." She gave him a funny look. "You don't have a pressure sleeve, do you?"

"Is that a spacer thing?"

"Never mind. You'll have to take the rear."

Chris grabbed her elbow as she moved to leave. "I don't understand. If *Razor* wants to stop us, why not just shoot us? They have laser weapons, right?"

"Yeah, but range is limited by accuracy. We're in space. Space is big."

"And a drone package has a better chance of hitting us?"

"It can course-correct on the way."

Chris nodded. "Okay. Well, at least that gives us something to shoot back at."

"Believe me, that sucker's going to come in ready to wipe out everybody. Although it will do its best to not damage this jalopy of a freighter. Space assets are expensive."

"And not passengers and crew?"

A funny look flashed across Laramie's face before she finally just waggled her hand. "Meh."

Minutes later, seven weapon-carrying troopers and Marines crowded together in a compartment clearly not designed for that many personnel. Wyatt went through what sounded like a standard play for RESIT people in this sort of situation.

"Teo will angle the freighter to make the penetration as far aft as possible. He'll kill the engines and put us in microgravity right before the drone strike. It will make it easier for us to maneuver. We have four cargo bays. Each squad will defend the airlocks between C, B, and A. Aim for weak points—joints, weapon mounts. No point wasting fire on ceramic plates and recessed sensors. Put as much fire as you can on the drone until it reaches your position, then take cover. Let it pass and put more fire on it from behind—try to overwhelm its target-tracking system. It will have a high-powered laser weapon, so don't get caught in the open.

"Remember, the drone strike will vent the atmosphere where it makes contact. The drone itself will breach the other compartments as it moves on the bridge. Since we don't have any working CORE helmets, we'll wear the emergency breathers we took from the space station."

The lieutenant looked around the room and made eye contact with every trooper there. "RESIT. Most of you haven't defended against a boarding drone except maybe in training. Keep your heads. Stay in cover. Don't get shot. Any questions?"

Chris smirked. This sounded like they were going to die.

They divided into pairs and entered Cargo Bay A, essentially a large container divided into smaller sections by bulkheads and nets. The RESIT troops kept on moving aft while Finn inspected the thickness of the bulkhead dividers.

"How's that going to be for cover?" Chris asked.

Finn shook his head.

A throat cleared behind him. Wyatt appeared, holding a breathing mask. He nodded at Chris's injured arm. "You want help putting this on?"

"Don't need it. My CORE helmet still has juice."

"How? All of ours are dead."

"It may be older than dirt, Lieutenant, but it'll charge off anything."

"They don't make 'em like they used to—something like that?"

"Something like that."

Wyatt nodded. He surveyed the empty cargo bay. "Have you ever seen a drone up close?"

"Ground versions."

"Then you know what we're up against. Ever take one out?"

"With heavy weapons."

The lieutenant's eyes searched Chris's face. Then he reached out and clasped Chris's shoulders. "I'm sorry you didn't get to stay home. But I'd be lying if I didn't say I'm glad you're here."

"That makes one of us."

Wyatt smiled. But Chris could tell it was shallow, a thin veneer of spirit to cover up what the lieutenant really believed was going to happen.

***

Annika wondered if she would like life in space. The crew deck wasn't very big. The front of the compartment had a bathroom with lockers and a funny-looking shower. The rear had some kind of lounge area, where Jack, Elton, and Calista were sitting at the little table hunched over an old-fashioned flat monitor. Calista said something about watching a fight through the security cameras, but Annika couldn't think of anything more boring, so she stayed snuggled up in one of the acceleration couches that lined the walls. Across from her sat the two space troopers who were hurt. The burly one named Carlos was asleep from all the painkillers. But the other one, Izzy, stared off into nothing. He seemed out of it. Annika figured that was why he was up there with her, and not getting ready for the fight.

Jack said a bad word at the monitor, then apologized about how Calista wasn't supposed to hear things like that. Annika turned her head and watched them. They all had their backs to her and she couldn't see what was on the display. Holo monitors were much better—they made big, colorful projections that everyone could see. Why didn't this ship have one? If she saw her daddy again, she would ask if he would buy them one. They were just so much better. She turned back to the space troopers to see if Carlos was awake, she was sure he would be frustrated too at not being able to see...

Her eyes met Izzy's.

She didn't notice the tingling at first. But when her stomach seized like she was going to throw up, she knew what was happening. The little fireflies sizzled around the edges of her vision and her eyes widened, locked on Izzy in an involuntary stare from which neither of them had any power to break away. The trooper sat still in his couch and let her eyes bore into him.

No, please, she whimpered. *I don't want to do this.*

You must. He isn't finished.

The fireflies flooded across the compartment. Annika's body went rigid. She tried to will herself to turn away, to break eye contact and shut off the points of light, but her body was not her own. An invisible grip held her head like a vise. She watched in despair as Izzy leaned into the fireflies and took them in.

I'm sorry, she tried to say, but her lips wouldn't move. She began to cry.

Izzy shuddered. She knew that was bad. It usually meant they were never coming back. Summoning all her strength, Annika tried to close her eyes and break the contact.

It was no use. She couldn't even move her eyelids. Instead, Annika watched in horror as Izzy's body relaxed and his pupils shrank. She tried to scream, to cry for help, to do anything to get the attention of the others. But her body would not obey her thoughts, leaving the sounds to echo only in her mind.

37

Laramie tuned out the random banter of troopers distracting themselves on the comm. Instead, she tried to remember the one time she had fought a drone in an advanced training course. It had wiped out three squads, hers included. The instructors went over the engagement and suggested a myriad of alternative tactics in the after-action review. Laramie struggled to recall what they said, and whether any of it would translate from classroom to reality.

The comm came to life with Teo's voice. "Ninety seconds to impact. Standby for evasive."

Kenny floated next to her near a bulkhead reinforced with scrap and insulation. "How do you do evasive maneuvers in a freighter?"

"He'll go from zero to full acceleration and try to mess up the drone's final targeting snapshot."

Kenny thought on this for a moment. "Any chance it'll miss?"

"I wish."

"Well, here's to hoping anyway."

Laramie shot him a glance. He looked so much like a kid. If not for the stubble, he might have belonged in a junior high yearbook. But he had been solid in Venice—Sid dead, Carlos hurt, keeping cool during a full-on evasion while police hunted for them. Kenny hadn't missed a beat.

She wondered if this would be the last time she saw him alive.

"Hey, Kenny."

"Yeah, Staff Sergeant?"

She gave him a nod. "We can do this."

"Hell, yeah, we can."

Laramie made a fist and jerked her thumb toward her shoulder, the Julietan gesture for *be strong*. She remembered as a kid when she first saw it used downrange on the ranch. Jessamy showed her the right way to do it, like pulling on the strap to a heavy backpack. She supposed that was what it meant to pantomime.

Kenny didn't miss a beat and returned the gesture perfectly.

She couldn't help but smile. Right now, there might not be anything she could do to protect her biological family. But she would do everything she could to protect the military one.

"Time for rebreathers," she said.

They pulled on the masks. Laramie instantly missed her long-gone CORE helmet.

The comm crackled. "Evasive in five, everyone hold on! Three . . . two . . . one . . . mark!"

The cargo bay leaped away from them. Laramie let the weight of sudden acceleration push her body into the bulkhead, a last feeling of sensation before who knew what. Belatedly, she threaded her arm into the cargo netting for what was coming next.

The vibration pulsed through the hull, a harbinger of enemy contact.

"We're hit, Cargo C. Hull breach. Shutting down engines."

Gavin and Rahsaan had set up a position at the C-D airlock. Laramie and Kenny were at B-C. The drone was sandwiched between their two squads.

"Move, on me!" she ordered.

With weightlessness returning to the freighter, they floated into the cargo-sized airlock. Kenny hit the cycling button and sent the forward door gliding silently closed with the whir of electric motors. A rush of air signaled a change in pressure between the two compartments. The drone impact would be venting some of the atmosphere from the cargo bay into space. Laramie's pressure sleeve popped at the joints as the shape-memory coils compressed against her body.

The hatch to C started to swing open. The air sizzled as strokes of laser fire immediately punched pieces of metal from the door.

"Taking fire at B-C airlock!" Laramie said. She squeezed against the narrow edge of metal that lined the hatch opening, trying to take cover

"Copy," Wyatt said over the comm. "Gavin, do you have visual?"

"Affirmative. Drone keyed on the hatch movement—it's shooting the door."

"*I confirm it's shooting the door!*" Laramie yelled. A fleck of red-hot metal splashed her sleeve, making her jump.

More laser fire exploded the heavy glass in the middle of the airlock hatch. The drone fired in bursts of six without any regard for spacecraft integrity. The bastards on *Razor* hadn't held back. They had set the drone for maximum lethality.

"All squads, weapons free," Wyatt said.

***

Gavin floated against the deck, his L-6 Viper just a few centimeters from his eye. In the middle of his scope was death itself: a spheroid-shaped body, heavy appendages, gliding through microgravity like some unholy apparition. It wasn't huge—drones needed to navigate corridors designed for humans—but the stout construction was packed with weapons and boarding tools. Nearby, a round metal shroud jutted into the bay from where the delivery vehicle had punctured the hull.

The drone faced away from him and let loose another barrage at the airlock.

Gavin exhaled, a tiny echo against the hiss of atmosphere slowly escaping from the compartment.

Snap.

The exhaust of the chemical reaction jiggled his scope as invisible light burned across the bay. Gavin saw a mist of metal spring from one of the joints that connected an appendage to the drone body.

He yanked himself behind a storage bulkhead just as the top half of the drone whirred around. A split-second later a rake of laser fire ripped gashes in the deck. Gavin winced as particles of metal sizzled into the thinning air next to his head.

Snaps of gunfire echoed across the cargo bay. Gavin heard the *bzzt* of multiple shots connecting with the ceramic armor. It reminded him of a bug zapper snuffing out insects.

"Gavin—drone is advancing on your position!"

Gavin desperately looked for alternate cover, but he was cornered between the bulkheads that formed the storage corral.

"I can't displace. Draw its fire. I'll get one last shot off." He was surprised at how calm his voice sounded.

Like a circus performer of old, he rotated his body in the microgravity for a better firing position. Beyond the edge of the bulkhead, servos and rotation wheels whirred as the drone approached.

Gavin always knew how dangerous space operations could be. For close to seven years, he had gladly taken the extra pay and worn his assignment with pride. He never figured he'd be wiped out by RESIT's own equipment. But as he steadied his breathing for one last shot, he couldn't imagine spending his life any other way.

***

Wyatt's skin prickled underneath the pressure sleeve as he moved through the damaged airlock between B and C. He ignored it and peered down the sight of his Vector. One of the drone's armatures wasn't turning properly. Gavin's shot. Maybe they could disable it further and reduce its ability to orient, setting up more damaging shots.

"All squads, put fire on that damaged joint. Now!"

A flurry of snaps filled the bay. Maya and Kenny had advanced to a bulkhead just ahead of him and were laying down fire side-by-side at the assault drone. Wyatt squeezed his own trigger as fast as he could. Most of the shots snuffed out against the armor plating. But the bot, programmed to eliminate the most severe threat first, turned around to bring its weapon pods to bear.

"Take cover—"

The hatch door literally vibrated on its hinge as the bot's cannon again perforated the metal. But instead of just a quick burst, the laser blasts walked across the width of the airlock. Toward Maya on the other side . . .

"Get back!" Wyatt shouted.

Maya wiggled behind the narrow rim that surrounded the hatch, but it wasn't enough. Wyatt watched in horror as a series of bursts shredded everything. Multiple pops indicated contact with the resin in her ARC vest. The splatter of red against the airlock wall meant the vest wasn't enough.

His stomach twisted into a knot.

Laramie was talking on the comm. "Wyatt, drone is advancing on you."

"Maya's down! Get me covering fire."

More snaps. Some distant place in Wyatt's brain thought they were getting harder to hear. Less atmosphere to transmit sound. That made the sudden *crack* from back in the bay that much more jarring.

"Good hit on the joint," Gavin said in a cold voice.

The firing at the hatch stopped. Wyatt peeked around the edge to confirm the drone's attention had shifted yet again. It faced aft, the connection to its leg smoking. Wyatt immediately pushed himself across the airlock and covered Maya's limp body with his.

"Teo, I need equalized pressure in Bay B," he ordered.

"Already done."

Bless you, Wyatt thought.

He hit the Emergency Release button and overrode the airlock safety controls. A barely audible *clack* withdrew the locking mechanism from the hatch. Wyatt pulled the cycling lever and the hatch swung upward. He grabbed Maya's collar and hauled her into the momentary safety of the next cargo bay.

Laramie's voice was directing the team on the comm. "Displace to port, port! It's advancing on B. Aim at the joints, your Vectors won't scratch that armor!"

Wyatt tried to settle his breathing and turned his attention to Maya. He looked at the shredded pockets of her vest where the ablative had vaporized and tried to peel it off. Fabric and plastic stuck fast to her skin. He couldn't tell where her pressure sleeve ended and the charred remains of her lungs began. It was all melted together.

She was gone.

"Gavin's hit!" Rahsaan said on the comm.

Grabbing his Vector, Wyatt allowed himself a lingering look at the young woman floating next to him. In Parrell, Maya had led them to safety when the constricted attacked. She had fought bravely at the Health building. The two of them, together, had managed to get through the spaceport alive and in one piece.

He wondered if he would be joining her momentarily.

38

Chris watched the airlock light turn green on the A side of the A-B connection. He clicked off the safety of his Berretta. A pistol was a pathetic attempt at firepower against a drone. Even Finn's Vector wasn't likely to get the job done. But a pair of Marines weren't about to let their allies go down without bringing a monster of a fight.

"Top!"

He already had one arm in the airlock. Time was wasting. "What?"

"Over here!"

He turned toward the direction of Finn's voice. It took a moment to realize what his fellow Marine held in his hands—a small pack, folded in half, with multiple runs of plastic explosive lining the edges. A breaching charge.

"How much of that stuff do you *have*?"

"This is it!"

The Beretta suddenly felt like a toy. Chris pitched it to the side, sending it tumbling through the weightlessness. "Give it here."

He shook his head. "You have a broken arm."

"And you have a daughter!"

After a moment of hesitation, Finn threw the pack into the air. Chris caught it with his good hand. He examined the fuses, the wiring, the detonator in its own pouch. Everything still looked in good order. No doubt Finn had meant to recycle the explosives into a different form factor more suitable for demolition. Thank goodness he hadn't.

"Do you think you can distract it? Without getting killed?" Chris yelled.

"Haven't been killed yet!"

"Then let's not start today. Let's go!"

They hustled the rest of the way into the airlock and waited impatiently as the A-side door closed. Chris peeked through the thick glass window into Cargo Bay B. An overwhelming sense of vertigo struck him, like he was looking down a deep tunnel where people leapt from ledge to ledge. No wonder Wyatt wanted to fight in zero gee. If they had been under acceleration, the freighter's orientation would have been vertical, not horizontal. The only way the RESIT troopers could have moved would have been with ladders.

A whoosh of air surrounded them. Chris felt suddenly bloated as the atmospheric pressure dropped.

"Remember to exhale," Finn said. He tapped the control panel readout. "They're down to a quarter atmosphere."

Chris blew out to ease the stress on his lungs. He understood now why Laramie had been going on about pressure sleeves. He might have oxygen from the rebreather, but that didn't mean his body would be happy with the pressure differential. On cue, a prickling sensation rippled across his forearms. He glanced down to see burst capillaries mixed in with the lines of his tattoos.

The B-side door swung open. Bright flashes signaled the exchange of laser fire.

"Keep to cover," Chris ordered. "Don't draw fire until I'm in position."

"Roger," Finn said. He flattened himself inside the airlock and readied his Vector.

Chris pushed himself into the cargo bay. He saw very little cover beyond the bulkheads that divided up the area. Most of those looked like Swiss cheese. Far below him, an eviscerated airlock hatch that would never close again twisted away from Cargo Bay C. The smoke of countless chemical laser reactions swirled through the compartment and obscured the positions of the RESIT troopers pulling their triggers.

The assault drone emerged from the smoke, full of malice.

It didn't look that different from the ground units Chris had seen before—vaguely humanoid, with a wide, egg-shaped sphere that housed sensor equipment for a body. Instead of arms and legs, thruster pods replaced the sections of its armatures below the joint. Metal claws capped the ends of the pods to allow the drone to grab things. Around its waist, a metal belt rotated two laser weapons that released continuous volleys through the smoky haze. The ceramic armor had hundreds of black scorch marks across its pitted surface.

Chris's insides felt like they were going to explode in the low pressure. He struggled to pass gas and relieve the bloating in his gut. His lungs ached, daring him to breathe too deeply and cause them to rupture.

A barrage of laser fire came from the right. The drone's belt glided silently around and snapped off multi-shot bursts at a bulkhead. Terse orders flew over the comm as another RESIT trooper fired from a different location, distracting the AI with multiple threats that kept it from closing on any one position.

Through it all, the drone pushed ever forward through the cargo bay.

Despite the effort, the RESIT team didn't seem to be accomplishing much. It would only be a matter of time before they ran out of ammo. Then the drone would lock on them one by one, close, and kill. It glided with such ease through the zero-gee environment that it would be impossible to evade. It was like a shark swimming circles around a bunch of hapless swimmers.

Chris thought his ability to move through zero gee was challenged on a good day. With only one good arm to orient himself, he'd never live long enough to get anywhere close to the drone. The bay was too big, and the drone too fast, for him to have any chance to set the explosives. If there had been gravity, at least he could have run toward it.

Gravity, he thought.

He didn't know if Wyatt was even still alive. It was time to find out.

"Lieutenant, tell your pilot to hit the engines," he said into the comm.

No reply. A ripple of static followed the flash of a laser blast.

"Wyatt!"

Seconds passed. Then a confused voice, tense, distracted. "Chris?"

"Yes! Tell your pilot to accelerate the freighter. Now!"

"What are you talking about—I can't—"

Chris felt his eyes narrow as he focused on the drone. It was moving toward him, but the weapons were facing away toward the side.

"Do it now, dammit! *Trust me!*"

***

"Last mag!" Laramie shouted.

She tossed the empty chem mag into the air. It twirled end over end while she slapped the last of her ammo into her weapon.

One last magazine to score a lucky shot. One last lucky shot before death.

Wyatt's voice came over the comm. "All squads, brace for acceleration!"

What?

Horror filled Laramie's mind as she scrambled for something to grab. Her position behind the bulkhead had shielded her from the drone—sort of—but if the freighter started to accelerate, she'd essentially fall to the opposite bulkhead on the other side of the cargo partition. She'd be exposed, vulnerable, and shot.

A blast hole about the size of her fist caught her attention. She reached out, but the bulkhead suddenly jumped away from her.

A thousand thoughts flew through her mind as she started to fall. Why had Wyatt given an order that he must have known would cost lives? How many times could she shoot the drone before it erased her? Was there any better definition of "moving the goalposts" than this? Would the phrase even fit on her tombstone?

Things happened too fast for words. Instead, Laramie contorted her body to aim her Vector one last time. She pulled the red dot sight up to her eye. And then she froze.

Chris.

The Marine had taken the sling off his broken arm and was spread-eagle, flying toward the drone like a skydiver. He smacked into the armored torso with a bounce. The drone swiveled in a reflexive move and brushed him off with one of its armatures. As Chris began to plunge the length of the cargo bay, Laramie caught a fleeting glimpse of a black, oval shape seemingly stuck to the drone's body.

Her back hit the lower bulkhead, jarring her body and ruining her aim. Only her eyes remained on the drone.

And it exploded.

***

A ring of debris followed by an orange flare erupted from the drone's armored torso. Chunky fragments billowed outward in near silence. Laramie's skin felt a vague warmth that seemed incongruous with the brightness of the flash, but with the atmosphere nearly gone, there was no air left to transfer any heat. The smoke cleared to reveal an oval chunk of the ceramic armor missing, the ruined insides of the drone's AI core exposed inside.

The drone slouched and scraped the deck with one of its magnetic foot-claws. It started to tumble after Chris, its electromechanical guts raining down the compartment.

"Cut acceleration! Cut acceleration!" Wyatt yelled in the comm.

The sudden weight left Laramie's body and she floated upward into a sitting position. She jerked her head toward the bot. It looked anything but operational, and if it somehow still was, she didn't want to wait around to see it.

"What just happened?" someone asked.

Wyatt answered—loudly. "Get the wounded and fall back to Cargo A! *On the double!*"

"Aye, aye," said the first voice. Kenny.

Laramie looked past the edge of her bulkhead. Chris lay crumpled in a heap near the ruined B-C airlock. She still couldn't believe she had witnessed such a foolhardy act.

She swung herself around and pushed off in his direction.

"Chris?" she called. "You okay?"

She made contact with his body and pulled him close. She couldn't see his face because of his CORE helmet.

"Chris. Can you hear me?"

No answer. She noticed charred, black soot on his chest.

"Answer me, you stupid jarhead!" She thumped his visor with her fist.

Laramie felt a tickle on her arm. She glanced down and saw a weak hand clutching her elbow.

She peered again at his mask. His head turned as if he was looking back at her.

"That was the craziest thing I've seen in a long time, Marine."

"Me too," he croaked.

Laramie eyed the splotching on his swollen forearms. "We've got to get out of vacuum."

"I think I crapped my pants."

She knew the internal pressure of Chris's body was having a field day in the near vacuum of the cargo bay. But she couldn't resist.

"See, I was right. I told Wyatt you were full of shit."

A moment later, the Marine coughed out a groan. By the time they were floating toward Bay A, they were both somehow laughing.

39

USIC *Vigorous*
Thermopylae Gate, Alpha Centauri A
12 March 2272

"Lieutenant," Doctor Kenta said. She tapped her bare wrist. "You asked me to remind you of the time."

"Thanks, Captain. Just wrapping up."

Wyatt turned back to the hospital bunk. Carlos was watching him with two pillows under his head. The sergeant waited until the doctor walked out of earshot before flashing a grin. "Is it weird addressing a doc as captain?"

"Hey, I have no problem paying smart people to fix broken people."

Carlos started to laugh but quickly winced. "Ow. Still hurts."

"You'll be okay."

"How's Gav doing?"

Wyatt scratched his forehead. "Good. He's a lucky bastard. His Viper took most of the blast when he got shot. Splintered into a hundred pieces, but it kept him from getting it in the gut."

Carlos's face darkened. "Like Maya."

"Yeah. Like Maya."

"That's a shame. She knew what she was doing. I liked her."

"Me too."

A moment of silence hung between them. It was still hard to cope with the idea of losing troopers under his command. But after the last few weeks, he had a feeling things would get worse.

He wondered for a moment if he'd made the right choice to come back to active duty. He could have taken the medical discharge, gone back to Earth. Been with his family. Sought out Sara for a life that might have been. RESIT would have found another squad leader to do his job.

The words of Father Bradley crept into his mind. *God doesn't provide what's wanted. He provides what's needed.*

Maybe God needed Wyatt here.

He knew he had to go. Wyatt tried to put on a brave face that didn't quite feel genuine and patted Carlos on the arm. "Think about the ones we didn't lose. Izzy seems to be getting better after that coma. Gavin's recovering. You're recovering. Kenny's solid. Laramie's . . . Laramie." He smiled. "We'll be good."

"Even you managed to just limp away with one fake leg, huh, LT?"

"I'd go for a matching set except for those calibration issues."

"Did Doc get it figured out?"

"Yeah, maybe. She reconfigured a bunch of stuff. That heavy gravity gave me a lot of phantom pain. It was hard to shut out."

"At least *your* pain was phantom." The sergeant snickered, then contorted as his body protested the strain against his broken ribs.

Wyatt showed him a grin. "You really should stop that. I need you back, and every joke costs me another day of waiting for your insides to heal."

Carlos managed to draw some slow, easy breaths. After a moment, he looked up at Wyatt with complete seriousness. "I know we're short or manpower, sir. I'll heal up as fast as I can. You won't need to wrangle the replacements without me."

"I know you will." Wyatt stood up. Replacements was actually what his next meeting was about. "Get some rest, trooper."

"Aye, aye, sir."

Wyatt left the hospital behind and headed toward Major Beck's quarters. His heart sped up when he realized he'd have to hurry. Beck was a stickler for punctuality, something he preached along with attention to detail as a set of critical spaceborne survival characteristics. Wyatt ducked around any number of troopers and crew on his way to the bridge section. Even though *Vigorous* maintained a manageable half gee under constant acceleration, Wyatt really didn't want to climb multiple decks and show up panting and sweaty. He prayed he wouldn't have to wait in a queue for the elevator.

He made it with twenty seconds to spare. The adjutant raised a disapproving eyebrow but didn't say a word as he poked his head around the open hatch, fighting to slow his breathing.

"Sir, Lieutenant Wills reporting as ordered."

"Come in."

Wyatt stepped across the threshold to find that Beck wasn't alone. A man wearing captain's bars stood up from one of the small chairs and unfolded his arms. Yancey Chappelle. Wyatt's boss.

"Captain. I didn't realize you'd be here as well."

"I am. Sorry we missed each other before your last mission. We were tied up downrange."

"Yes, sir. I expected my squad to rejoin the team when I got back. It was quite a surprise when we didn't."

Chappelle and Beck glanced at each other, their eyes exchanging some silent message. "For me as well."

"Have a seat, Lieutenant," Beck said. He gestured at the chair next to the captain. "I think we still have a couple minutes before our guest arrives. I want to make sure that *you're* sure about what you're asking for."

As Wyatt sat, his eyes fell on the peninsula desk extending from the far bulkhead. Every command officer's quarters had one. But Wyatt found that the similarities ended there, with each work area reflecting the owner's personality. He thought back to Acevedo's desk on the *Cromwell*. Sparse, simple, big picture. Beck's, on the other hand, provided a platform for a number of meticulously arranged trophies and knick-knacks.

"I'm positive, Major," Wyatt said. "He's an extremely capable individual. Even if we had a room full of senior noncoms, I'd take him in a heartbeat."

Beck looked over at Chappelle.

"He's not trained for RESIT," the captain said. "I'm sure he's a good fighter. But you know it takes more than that for a typical RESIT mission."

"Sir, you've read my after-action report. We'll have to go back down to Juliet. If our missions end up being more ground-pound, there's no doubt in my mind he'd be a huge asset."

Chappelle sighed. "There is in mine, Lieutenant. But let's see what happens."

"Sir?" the adjutant said outside the hatch. "Master Sergeant Thompson is here to see you."

Wyatt and Captain Chappelle stood again as Chris entered. He barely recognized the Marine without his scraggly beard and the usual coating of dirt. Chris was clean-shaven, his hair trimmed, and he wore a borrowed set of RESIT utilities that clearly made him uncomfortable. Or maybe it was because of the brass in front of him.

Chris's eyes scanned the people in the room and lingered on Wyatt for an extra beat before returning to Beck. "Major. Master Sergeant Christopher Thompson, U.S. Marines."

Beck nodded. "Master Sergeant. Please, sit down. I've heard a lot about you."

Chris's eyes flitted to Wyatt and back. He remained silent.

"Lieutenant Wills here seems to think very highly of your abilities. Your actions onboard the freighter likely saved the lives of everyone onboard."

"Thank you, sir."

The major watched him carefully. "Chris, we have a manpower problem. Getting individuals who know their way around a fight is of paramount importance right now. The fact that I had a shortage of trained personnel back at Proxima was hard enough. It's worse now that I've committed my battle group to Alpha A."

Chris stiffened. His eyes darted to Wyatt before he looked down and adjusted his sling.

Beck continued. "How long were you—"

"With respect, Major, I appreciate where I think you're going. But you've got the keys to the puzzle already. Jack Bell. If there's anyone that's going to help you plan a successful operation, he's the guy. I'm committed to a different path. My place is back with my people."

Beck narrowed his eyes. "It sounds to me like your people were getting slowly killed off, Master Sergeant. Don't you think the best chance to keep them safe would be to work with us?"

"You don't want me, sir," Chris said. He shook his head. "If you knew about my past, you'd be glad I left the service."

"If I knew about your past?"

"Yes, sir. You don't know me. Lots of baggage."

Beck leaned back, his eyes drifting to the ceiling. His voice took on a rhetorical quality. "Master Sergeant Christopher Larson Thompson. Born 23 November 2236, Phoenix, Arizona. Enlisted in the US Marine Corps at age eighteen. Eleven combat deployments on Earth, including Mongolia, South China Sea, East Africa. Two combat deployments on Mars. Two Silver Stars. Navy Cross for your actions during the Tharsis Push." He cocked his head. "I think I understand your baggage very well."

Wyatt watched Chris turn several shades paler.

Beck leaned forward. "You *are* that Chris Thompson, correct?"

"Yes, sir, I am." Chris stiffened in his chair. "And if you know my record, you know my reputation. Multiple disciplinary reviews. Demoted twice. 'Reckless, with a difficulty in following orders,' according to my last commanding officer."

Beck and Chappelle traded glances.

"Yes. We're aware," Chappelle said. He gave Beck an *I told you so* look. "And why is it you have a problem with authority, Master Sergeant?"

"It's not that, Captain. I'm just not onboard with stupid officers."

Chappelle raised an eyebrow. "Rangamati, Bangladesh. December 2259. While in a forward area, you were tried and convicted of dueling another noncommissioned officer. So, instead of fighting the enemy, you sat in the brig. Quite a disservice to your unit, wouldn't you say?"

"If you're talking about Sergeant Rangel, that guy was an abusive bastard who unnecessarily put his men in harm's way. Again and again. The brass wouldn't listen. The rest of us noncoms decided to teach him a lesson before he got more guys killed. I just drew the lucky number."

"So, you're saying your justification was that he deserved it?"

"Yeah. He was an idiot."

"August 2261," Chappelle continued, glancing at Beck, "while sweeping the Boma region of South Sudan, you disobeyed a direct order to break contact with multiple hostile elements and pull back. Your actions resulted in six KIAs and four wounded."

Chris was bristling now. "We had line of sight to the enemy observation post they were using to call in rocket strikes. We took 'em out before they could fire. If we had pulled back, our entire unit would have been wiped out."

"You ignored your lieutenant's orders."

"It was an unlawful order that would have gotten us all killed. The court-martial exonerated me."

Chappelle turned more forceful. "You want some examples from back home? How about California, United States, 2264. During a wargames exercise, while playing the role of the opposition, you acted as a forward observer and called in a simulated artillery strike of white phosphorous against soft targets—a complete violation of both the Geneva Convention and the Oslo Accord."

Chris tilted his head and glared at Captain Chappelle like he was crazy. "I was playing the role of the *enemy*. I can do *whatever the hell I want.*"

Wyatt sat and watched the whole thing in silence. He could tell Chappelle was getting a little hot. But a quick glance at Beck told him all he needed to know.

"I think that will do," the major said. He picked up his tablet keyboard. "Master Sergeant Thompson, I'm reinstating you to active duty, effective immediately—"

Chris blinked. "What?"

"—and attaching you to Caustic Team, RESIT Command, per the authority of the Maritime and Spaceborne Emergency Powers Act—"

"You can't do that!"

"You will be assigned to First Platoon, Captain Yancey Chappelle commanding." He placed the tablet back down on the desk next to the little figurines in their orderly rows. "Lieutenant Wills can help with equipment and orientation."

Chris's jaw hung open as his head jerked back and forth. His eyes finally settled on Wyatt. "I helped you guys, Wyatt. Help me out! I'm not even supposed to be up here. I need to get back down to the surface—like, ASAP!"

"I'll get you there, buddy," Wyatt said. "It's just going to have to be as part of RESIT."

Wyatt's sympathy was genuine, and he desperately hoped Chris could feel it. Sure, the master sergeant was in shock right now. But Wyatt had seen constriction firsthand. He had experienced the fear of those running from infection. His team had fought a paramilitary organization—one that exterminated with equal indiscretion.

Yes, they would be going back. In force.

Epilogue

Chris heard the footsteps hurrying in the corridor behind him before the voice betrayed their owner. "Wait up!"

He stopped abruptly. The burly trooper next to him grabbed his arm.

"Keep moving, Master Sergeant."

"A minute. Just . . . a minute."

Chris gave the trooper next to him a pleading look. Reluctantly, he nodded and stood aside.

A panting Finn rushed toward them. "How did it go? Your meeting?"

"It was the weirdest job interview I've ever had."

"Huh?"

"Called back to active duty, Finn. Only somehow, they say I'm assigned to RESIT now."

Finn gave him a blank look. "I hear these words coming out of your mouth, but they're full of crazy talk."

"I'm serious. Apparently, press gangs aren't just a thing of the past. Major Beck said they have a manpower shortage. Same thing is happening to you, too."

"Me t—he can't do that. Can he?"

"That's what I said. He seems to think he can."

Alarm grew in Finn's eyes. "No way. What did you tell him?"

"I expressed my displeasure."

Finn waited expectantly.

A big sigh. "Beck's desk was full of all these little knick-knacks. I guess he's some kind of neat freak. I got really pissed and swept them all onto the deck."

"That couldn't have gone over well."

"It could have been better, yeah."

Finn shook his head. "Jeez. I gotta get my head around this. Want to hit the mess hall, talk it out?"

Chris felt a frown tightening on his face. "Later. I'm going to be a bit indisposed for a while."

"Why?" Finn let out a laugh. "It's not like Beck's throwing you in the brig or something."

Chris glanced at the trooper escorting him. It took a moment before Finn picked up that "something" was exactly right.

***

Annika stifled a yawn and tried to stay awake. The view through the porthole next to her hospital bed surpassed anything she could have imagined. Juliet hung like royalty against the dark sky, a wide crescent of blue and green, wisps of white looming in front of distant, twinkling jewels. To the left, a smaller crescent betrayed the presence of Romeo. Annika smiled. Two star-crossed lovers forever entangled in each other's grasp, just like the stories her mother had told her. The chance to see them with her own eyes was something that she never wanted to end.

A noise drew her attention away from the outside. She saw Mister Jack rub his nose with a groggy hand before he returned to his slumber in the visitor's chair. Annika wished she could talk. She wanted to thank him for staying with her. But it had been forever since she had made words, as if the knowledge of how to form the sounds had been cut out of her mind.

Where was Chris? She wanted to know where he'd gone, the one constant in her life since they had fled home. She hadn't seen him since they boarded the big spaceship.

Wasn't that the last time she saw him?

Why can't I remember?

Her eyes wandered over to a burly man asleep in the next hospital bed. Big bandages covered his hands, smaller ones on his face. Annika thought she should remember him, too. But all she felt was guilt, like she had forgotten a birthday or something else important. Her mother would have been mortified at her poor manners. Where was her mother? Annika couldn't picture her face, but she was certain she knew what her mom would have been thinking.

I should be able to remember my parents' faces, shouldn't I?

She looked down at her arm, at the plastic tube that led to a tiny bandage against her skin. When had that happened?

Perplexing, for sure. But she could figure it out later. Another yawn and Annika shifted in her bed.

She stared out the porthole. Beautiful, sparkling Juliet. Home. All she wanted was to be able to go back.

***

The trooper barracks pulsed with activity, but to Laramie McCoy, the compartment felt empty.

Carlos would recover. It would take some time, but she felt good about that. Gavin, she wasn't so sure. His Viper had exploded in his hands when the drone shot it. Maybe he'd be back if he didn't lose his fingers. The docs were fifty-fifty on whether the nerve therapy had been started in time.

At least Gav had a chance. Laramie closed the drawer under Maya's bunk and cinched the drawstring on the duffel bag full of her belongings.

What a waste. An experienced trooper. Someone who went out of her way to help her teammates. Earnest. Laramie hardly knew anything about Maya's family—parents, siblings, friends. Their time in the same squad had been too short. But Laramie knew she had liked her. And now, like so often happened in RESIT, a good person was lost to the hazards of the job. Only this time it was due to circumstances that never should have happened.

Fighting an assault drone. Absurd.

Laramie had never seen one in action. Drones were a measure of last resort, a desperate option to eliminate an enemy crew before opening fire with laser cannons.

Now, in the span of a month, she had witnessed two illegal deployments.

She didn't believe the crew driving *Razor* was RESIT. Something bad had happened. Beck would surely get to the bottom of it. But even then, *Vigorous* was just one troop carrier. Dagger Team had a lot of assets that could be thrown into the fight.

And with so many replacements, more RESIT troopers would surely die.

Laramie stood up and threw Maya's duffel over her shoulder. This was the worst part of being a squad sergeant, and she wanted to get it done. Tomorrow, she'd sit down with each of her people and make sure they were processing everything okay. Depression and detachment were common symptoms of losing a brother or sister. She turned to exit the barracks when she spied that very thing over by the viewport.

"Izzy."

Corporal Isi Watanabe turned away from a brilliant view of the sunrise creeping over Juliet. His eyes seemed distant and unfocused. Haunted.

A staff sergeant knew well the face of post-traumatic stress. Laramie walked over to the young trooper and put her hand on his shoulder.

"You okay?"

Izzy furrowed his eyebrows. He seemed to be thinking about the question, uncertain around how to answer. A few moments went by before he simply nodded.

"Get some rest," Laramie told him. "We've all been through a lot. I'll be around to talk when you're ready. Okay?"

Another delay, another nod. Izzy's absent eyes returned to the window.

Laramie wheeled around and marched toward the exit. She wanted to get some rest herself—plus a shower, and most importantly, food. Lots of hot food to replace the seven kilos she'd dropped since the start of their mission. While she felt powerful in the lower gees of *Vigorous*, she knew as soon as she put boots back downrange that the heavy gravity would quickly dispel that notion if she didn't build herself back up.

As she stepped through the hatch, she looked back at Izzy one last time. His hand pressed against the glass, as if he too wanted nothing more than to return to Juliet.

ABOUT THE AUTHOR

Jonathan Isaacs never thought he'd be a writer.

In college, he studied to be an engineer. But after years of his wife telling the screaming children to "use their words" (which comes naturally to neither toddlers nor engineers), he too decided to give it a go. Now what he says even occasionally makes sense.

Isaacs now works as a technology executive in Texas, where his hobbies include poking fun at other technology executives.

Check him out on his website at http://jpisaacsauthor.com/ for the latest noise he's making around writing the next book.

You can find him on Facebook at: http://www.facebook.com/jpisaacsauthor.

Follow him on Twitter at @jpisaacsauthor.

Or if you want a late-night conversation, drop him a line at jpisaacsauthor@gmail.com because he works in the technology industry, doesn't sleep, and is actually a robot.

ALSO BY JONATHAN PAUL ISAACS

Armchair Safari
The Hazards of War
The House the Jack Built

Printed in Great Britain
by Amazon